The Land Beyond
the Waste

The Land Beyond the Waste

B. F. Peterson

ROUNDFIRE
BOOKS

London, UK
Washington, DC, USA

CollectiveInk

First published by Roundfire Books, 2025
Roundfire Books is an imprint of Collective Ink Ltd.,
Unit 11, Shepperton House, 89 Shepperton Road, London, N1 3DF
office@collectiveink.com
www.collectiveink.com
www.roundfire-books.com

For distributor details and how to order please visit the 'Ordering' section on our website.

Text copyright: B. F. Peterson 2023

ISBN: 978 1 80341 645 8
978 1 80341 691 5 (ebook)
Library of Congress Control Number: 2023947139

A CIP catalogue record for this book is available from the British Library.

Design: Lapiz Digital Services

UK: Printed and bound by CPI Group (UK) Ltd, Croydon, CR0 4YY
Printed in North America by CPI GPS partners

We operate a distinctive and ethical publishing philosophy in
all areas of our business, from our global network of authors to
production and worldwide distribution.

Contents

Dedication   vii
Map   viii
Preface   ix

Chapter 1: The Alterran Queen   1
Chapter 2: Tessex   12
Chapter 3: Fallout   24
Chapter 4: If the Mighty Ones Return   41
Chapter 5: The Waste   57
Chapter 6: Dragon Rider   71
Chapter 7: A Strange Land   85
Chapter 8: Neremyn   99
Chapter 9: The Shards of Edriendor   116
Chapter 10: The Chase   132
Chapter 11: A Clash of Sorcerers   146
Chapter 12: The *Tirisslythra*   161
Chapter 13: Rydara's Petition   173
Chapter 14: The Elves' Decision   190
Chapter 15: Lost Hopes   203
Chapter 16: Leaving Edriendor   214
Chapter 17: Flight   225
Chapter 18: The Alliance   239
Chapter 19: Hope   253
Chapter 20: The Battle for Helos   265
Chapter 21: Sacrifice   288

Epilogue   296
Acknowledgments   301
About the Author   303

For my father
Who knows how to keep a plot moving.

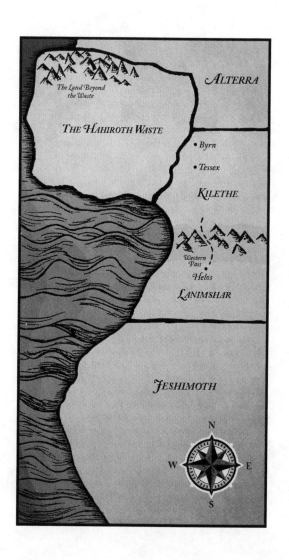

Preface

Three and three and three they came
The Mighty Ones, disgraced
With powers three and three aflame
The earth they soon defaced.

But powers three and three their foes
The Loyal Ones, embraced
The ancient evil, they exposed
The Mighty were unbraced.

The Loyal won great victory
But praise was soon replaced
By hate and fear, so they did flee
To the Land Beyond the Waste.

In their secret paradise
They stay where they were chased
Their forgotten sacrifice
From hist'ry near erased—

But if the Mighty Ones return
My child, make haste, make haste:
The meek may yet our rescue earn
In the Land Beyond the Waste.

—"If the Mighty Ones Return," from the Rishara oral tradition

Chapter 1

The Alterran Queen

"You brought an *ishra* into our camp?" the Alterran in front of Rydara demanded, rounding on her brother when he noticed her face.

Rydara sank deeper into the hood of her winter cloak. *Ishra* was the Alterran word for her mother's people. Her resemblance to them earned her no favor.

"She is as loyal to the Six as you or I," her brother Aander told the soldier, his face darkening. Of the Six deities recognized by Alterra and the tribes, the Red Goddess was the most hostile to heretics, and she presided over war. Bringing an *ishra* into a war camp would have invited a divine curse—but Rydara was not technically *ishra*, having never worshiped the god of her mother's people. She had never even met anyone who did.

If the Alterran soldier assumed heresy ran in her blood regardless, he would not be the first.

"She is a king's daughter," Aander added, and Rydara winced. "Mind your manners."

"We were not informed of this," the soldier said brusquely. "She cannot be taken to the queen without permission."

"We will wait." Aander's tone was final.

Rydara rubbed her forehead while the Alterrans sent a runner to their queen. The fact that she worshiped the Six was enough. Aander had not needed to broadcast her parentage, and she had counseled him not to, because it would do nothing to raise the tribes in the Alterrans' esteem.

But Aander just lifted his chin as if he did not notice Rydara's discomfort or the resentful glances cast her way by the rest of their own retinue. As if his word and their blood connection could give her as much a right to be there as anyone.

Aander was everything Rydara was not. Male. Fair-skinned. His hair was raven black like hers, but his was soft and wavy where hers was coarse and unmanageable. Well-known, well-loved, and beautiful, Aander was the pride of the Noraani kingdom and the envy of other tribes. Men loved to follow Aander, and his word did count for something. When the runner returned, Rydara was allowed into the Alterran camp with the rest of their party.

A pavilion had been erected in the center of the war camp. It was nearly as large as her father's audience chamber, and its white canvas roof rippled in the breeze.

The Alterran queen sat on a cushioned seat in the back of the tent. She was dressed in high-necked violet silks, and her face was shrouded in a black veil according to the Alterran custom. Only the Alterran king could view her beauty.

Four armed guards stood behind her, and a woman in black velvet stood at her right hand. She was a handsome woman with tightly-braided blonde hair, and her face was uncovered. She was the queen's Voice.

The eight soldiers of their Alterran escort split to take up positions against the sides of the pavilion while their party approached the queen. Aander stopped six paces from her, representatives from other tribes on his right and left. Rydara and two retainers from their own tribe stood behind them.

All six of them bowed low.

"You may rise," the Voice bid them. "Her Majesty understands you have traveled here from the Noraani ... kingdom, and that you wish to present a petition. You may speak."

"Your Majesty." Aander bowed his head again, briefly. He gave the queen a rueful smile. "All the tribes of Kilethe are mere fleas beside the might of Alterra, and it may seem odd to you that we of Noraan style ourselves a kingdom. We have done so ever since my ancestor Tulaan united the tribes, though we do not hold sway over as many of them as we once did.

2

Nevertheless, now that Rinton and Ferlore have rejoined us, we speak for half the people of the Kilethi marches, and our alliance may still grow to encompass the rest.

"I am Aander tu'Noraan, son and heir to King Cressidin tul'Noraan, who presides over this alliance, and I have been empowered to seek peace with Alterra on its behalf."

It was a good opening. Disarming, humble—as befitted them, considering their weak position—but still a reminder to the queen of their legitimacy and the number of people they spoke for. Rydara could not have scripted the lines better herself, and Aander delivered them with the charisma and personality that only he could.

"You seek peace with Alterra?" The Voice smiled. She did not even glance at the queen, who remained motionless and inscrutable behind her veil. "Consider yourselves fortunate, then, little prince, for Alterra makes no war with you. You have traveled some way for little cause, but you may return to your father with assurance of our goodwill."

"Yes, we understand you have no grievance with us." Aander inclined his head, and Rydara was proud of him for keeping his attention on the queen. He had known very little of Alterra or its customs before this trip, but Rydara had been studying Alterra since she was eight. She had coached him well. "Nor with any Kilethi tribe. You are merely passing through to make war on your real enemy, Jeshimoth, which lies beyond Lanimshar, many leagues to the south.

"Noraan does not begrudge you the passage, though we have claim to the land through which you pass. Nor do we seek reparations for the crops and game you have taken or the farmland you have destroyed. Consider it our gift. We are content to go on supplying your army as long as we must.

"However," Aander paused, glancing at the Ferlore representative beside him. The man kept his gaze lowered in deference to the queen, but his jaw was tight with anger. The

Alterrans had not been kind to Ferlore in their passage. "We have heard reports of violence and destruction that far exceed the standard of necessity." Aander returned his gaze to the queen, and his voice grew more passionate as he sought to connect with her. "Homes ransacked. Women raped. Entire villages put to the sword.

"And so, we have come to sue for peace. We entreat you to speak to your general. Rein in your army. You have no quarrel with the tribes of Kilethe, and we have no wish to quarrel with you. We are, as I have said, mere fleas beside your might, and we could not hope to expel you from our lands by force of arms, even should we wish it. But surely even fleas are better made your servants than your foes. Fleas can bite, and harry, and annoy, and though we have no wish to quarrel with you, we will do what we must to protect our people.

"So please," Aander sank to one knee, holding the queen's gaze as best he could through her veil, "let us supply your army. If you lack anything, you have merely to ask, and we will be most pleased to negotiate. But leave our people unharmed as you pass. We beg of you."

Aander bowed his head, and Rydara and the rest of the retinue knelt around him, also bowing their heads.

They had no standing here, and nothing to bargain with. Rydara was not even sure if the queen had the power to enact the change they sought. She was respected in Alterra, but only the king ruled, and his general was the one who commanded his army.

When Aander and Rydara had found out that the general led from this very camp and that Alterra's queen was currently his guest, they had been lucky to secure a meeting with her. Aander hoped to win the queen with the justice of their cause and that her advocacy would be enough to sway the general. It was a better hope than if the camp had been run by a low-ranking officer with no reason to listen to them, but it was still far from a sure thing.

It did not matter. This was their only play.

The Voice took a few steps forward, stopping in front of Aander. "We take what we must. The men may, on occasion, have been carried away where we encountered resistance. But entire villages put to the sword? In a land with which we have no quarrel? Such a thing would be beneath our honor. Perhaps someone has slandered us to you."

The Voice returned to the queen's side. "You may rise." They stood, and the Voice glanced at the queen. "We will speak with General Dameires on your behalf," she continued, though the queen had given her no signal that Rydara could see. "The king does not wish your lands destroyed or his army taxed by frivolous skirmishes with a people who are not our enemy. We will ensure the general knows this."

The words sounded hollow in Rydara's ears, and she could feel the Voice's lack of conviction. It was a talent Rydara had, and the reason her father had had her trained in diplomacy and sent her with Aander on missions like these. The tribes called it the Knowing magic.

She considered whispering her insight to Aander, but her brother was not foolish enough to take the concession at face value. Nor had he forgotten the reports that brought them here.

"Thank you, Your Majesty." Aander bowed again to the queen. "If our petition has found favor in your sight, may we carry the news at once to the people of Tessex? It is a village of Ferlore, only two miles north of here, behind your lines. A woman reached us from there with word of the villagers' suffering. We wish to assure them that Alterra has heard our plea, and to escort any who wish to resettle away from your lines."

"That would be most improper," the Voice said curtly. "The villagers have no need to resettle. They are safe where they are."

This time Rydara could sense a thread of anxiety beneath the words. The Voice, Rydara was sure, did not know that the villagers were safe, and she did not want Aander to pry.

5

"That may be," Aander said, his gaze flicking to the Voice. "And yet, this report has reached us." He returned his attention to the queen. "Your Majesty, since Ferlore has joined our kingdom, I am now prince to these people. As such, it is no less than my sovereign duty to respond to a call for aid such as this. Even if the report we received was exaggerated, I wish to make known to the people of Tessex that Noraan will not ignore them."

"That is quite impossible," said the Voice, shaking her head. "We cannot allow a potential—"

The queen lifted a finger, and the Voice fell silent.

"Voice." The queen's voice filled the pavilion, and it washed over Rydara with the gentle musicality of a wind chime, flooding her with a superficial assurance that everything would soon be put right.

Rydara could feel the lie of it. Something was wrong.

"You have much to learn," the queen continued, chiding. "Can you not see the young prince's dilemma?"

The queen stood, and all the Alterrans in the room—the Voice included—dropped to their knees. The Noraani followed suit.

"Don't trust them," Rydara whispered to Aander, kneeling behind him. "This is an act."

Rydara did not know if he heard her. His gaze was fixed on the queen.

She walked toward him. "His people have called for a savior, and where would he have them turn, if not to himself? He cannot take our word that they are well when they have called upon him to act, and even if he could—how could they appreciate his rescue if he does not appear before them, bearing word of the favor he won from us?"

The queen stood close enough that Rydara could see through the semi-transparent portion of veil that covered her eyes. They were big and green and beautiful, and they danced as they considered Aander, kneeling before her. He was transfixed.

The queen was not merely staging an act. Somehow, she was controlling the room with her voice. Rydara could feel it, and she could see it on the faces of the men who knelt beside her, staring at the queen in awe and self-abasement.

Rydara started to sweat. She did not know what kind of power this was, but it seemed she was the only one immune.

The queen glanced back at the Voice. "See how he humbles himself before me, to beg only a brief show of heroism for his people? Can you not see how much it would mean to him? And you would have us turn down such an innocent request? No. No indeed, we shall grant it.

"Rise, Prince of Noraan," the queen said, and Aander stood. He was a full head taller than the queen, but instead of lending him gravity, his height made him gangly and awkward in front of her. "If our word is insufficient," the queen continued, lifting her chin to look up at him, "and you wish to see for yourself that the villagers are well, such a thing can be arranged."

"Forgive me, Your Majesty." Aander paused, discomfited. "I did not mean to question the sufficiency of your word. If you say the villagers are well, we have no reason to doubt you. It is just—"

The queen reached up to cup Aander's cheek in her gloved right hand, and a chill shot through Rydara. It was unlawful to touch the Alterran queen.

"You wish them to see how you rode to their rescue." The queen nodded as she looked up at Aander, her voice soft and intimate, her hand still resting against his face. "We understand. The people should see that you came and worked the deliverance they requested." The back of Aander's neck flushed red, and Rydara could sense the queen's spell at work, making Aander look vain and foolish in his own eyes.

She did not know how to stop it.

"Yes, the villagers must see you." The queen withdrew her hand from Aander's face. She walked back to her chair. As she seated herself, the Alterrans in the room rose to their feet, and Rydara and the rest of the retinue copied them.

The Voice took a step forward. "But you must understand," she said, resuming her role as the queen fell silent, "we cannot escort a foreign party behind our lines without the general's awareness. A runner will be sent. You may remain with us while we wait."

"We beg your pardon, Majesty," Aander said, chagrined. "We do not need to cross behind your lines ourselves. If you could only let it be known to the villagers—"

Rydara tugged at Aander's cloak as unobtrusively as she could. "We need to see them," she whispered.

Aander cleared his throat and put a hand behind his back, covertly waving her off. "Let it be known to the villagers that you intend them no harm, and that they are free to come and go as they please. That is all we ask."

The Voice nodded. "Very well. We shall go ourselves."

"Aander," Rydara whispered as the Voice spoke. The queen was distorting her brother's judgment, and she needed to warn him. They had to see the village.

The queen lifted a finger, and the room fell still once again.

"It seems your *ishra* seeks your attention, Prince of Noraan." The queen spoke, and Rydara went hot with shame at attracting her notice. "Do you often permit her to interrupt her betters?"

"Your pardon, Your Majesty," Aander said, bowing his head. "She is my sister."

He acknowledged her so simply. As if Rydara had never advised him to leave the connection unspoken, or he had never really considered it.

She loved him for it, frustrating as he was.

"Ah yes, the king's daughter." The queen waved her forward. "Step closer, *ishra* princess, and tell us what is on your mind."

Rydara looked to Aander, who stepped aside for her. Her father would have been furious with her interruption, but if

Aander felt anger or shame on Rydara's behalf, he gave no sign of it.

That did not stop Rydara from trembling as she moved past him, feeling sick to have drawn so much attention. Every eye was on her, and the queen was waiting. Rydara sank to her knees and pressed her head to the floor in the posture of a slave. "Please forgive me, Your Majesty, but I am neither *ishra* nor princess. I am just an adviser. I meant only to offer a brief word of counsel to my prince."

"So then, the king's *illegitimate* daughter. And still, the prince calls you sister. Curious. Stand, girl." Rydara rose to her feet and found the queen was leaning her head against a hand, her elbow resting on the chair's arm as she considered Rydara. "Since you've interrupted us already, why not go ahead and share your counsel out loud with all of us? If, of course, the prince feels he needs any input regarding the issues at hand."

Rydara felt the coiled power in the queen's words before she saw their impact on Aander. His jaw tightened as he stepped up next to Rydara, his eyes cast downward. He was about to silence her and end the audience.

"We need to see the village," Rydara said quickly, before she could lose her nerve. Technically, the queen had invited her to speak, and it was her only chance to deflect the magic at work in the room. "Forgive me, Your Majesty." She curtsied deeply to the queen. "We are very grateful for your ruling, and we don't mean to question your word. But since the people of Tessex have called on us for help, it is the prince's duty to go to them himself and provide a safe escort for any who wish to leave. If you are still willing to inform the general and take us there, we would owe you our eternal thanks."

"She not only speaks, she gives decisions!" The queen laughed, and the sound tinkled merrily through the pavilion. "You wish to see your brother recognized as a hero, little *ishra*?"

"N—no, Majesty," Rydara stammered, feeling her cheeks flush. She narrowed her eyes, realizing that some of what she felt was the work of the queen's voice. She was not fully immune, then. "But—"

"But what, then?" The queen's voice hardened, soft and dangerous, and Rydara flinched. "You don't mean to question my word, but still you must see for yourself? You trust the villagers are safe, but you insist on providing their escape? Which is it, little *ishra*?"

Rydara sank to her knees, overcome with remorse as the queen's words rained down on her. She gritted her teeth, fighting it. "Beg pardon, Your Majesty, but everywhere your army goes, our people cry for help. The village of Caana is gone. A refugee from Byrn said the women of his city were raped, and every night another villager goes missing, never to return. A woman escaped from Tessex reports the same and begs our aid. And you would have us turn back two miles short of the village, without even a glimpse of how they—"

"Enough." The word fell from the queen's lips with the finality of a death knell, and Rydara choked on the end of her sentence. "Your *ishra* admits she is not a princess, and yet she dares to address me in this manner? Does she speak for Noraan when she brings these accusations against my army?"

The queen's voice was thunderous in its displeasure, and Aander sank to one knee beside Rydara. "Forgive us, Your Majesty. She speaks out of turn, and I am to blame. Noraan makes no accusation."

Rydara looked at Aander, trying to warn him of the queen's power with her eyes. She could not speak.

It might not have mattered if she could. Rydara had the Knowing magic, and the queen's voice was enough to command her silence. Aander was defenseless against it.

"She bears the blame herself, then. Though it puzzles me that you permit her to remain in my presence," the queen said, her voice now a gentle purr. "You may rise, Prince of Noraan."

Aander cleared his throat as he stood, and Rydara knew he was going to dismiss her. He would not ask to see the village. The queen might make him forget his mission to protect the tribes altogether—if she had not already convinced him there had been no need for it in the first place.

The queen spoke again, now studying Rydara. "Indeed, it puzzles me that she retains a place in your kingdom at all."

Her voice was ice, and it chilled Rydara to the core. Eyes wide, she looked in panic to her brother, trying to speak.

Aander was the only soul in the world who loved her. Could the queen turn him against her, too?

Aander looked down at her, his expression stony and compassionless. "Leave us, Rydara."

Rydara scrambled to her feet, her voice finally unlocking. "Aander—"

"Leave us now!" The prince commanded. He turned back to the queen. "Please forgive us, Your Majesty. Rest assured, we will reconsider her position, and you will not see her again."

Rydara choked back tears as she left the pavilion, powerless against the queen's sorcery.

She had never felt so alone.

Chapter 2

Tessex

Rydara fled as far as the horses, left picketed at the Alterran outpost. None of the soldiers seemed to care.

She threw her arms around her horse, a beautiful bay mare, and pressed her forehead against its mane. The horse snuffed gently and turned its head toward her.

"What am I going to do, Astral?" she whispered. Fingers of ice clawed at her stomach, and she shivered as she remembered Aander's words.

We will reconsider her position, and you will not see her again.

What had she been thinking, speaking to the queen like that? Speaking at all, in an audience of royals? She had given Aander ample reason to revoke her position, even without the influence of the queen's magic.

And yet, what could she have done differently? What good was Rydara's own magic if she did not speak up to defend her brother from threats like the power in the queen's voice?

Hearing the crunch of footsteps in the snow, Rydara turned. Her eyes found her brother's as he returned with the others.

"Aander, I'm sorry—" she began, but he held up a hand.

"We will speak about your position later." He gave her a cold glance as he mounted his horse, and Rydara's heart twisted inside her.

At least he was not sending her away.

Not yet.

She kept an anxious silence as they started back toward their own army, such as it was. They had left them a two-days' ride from the Alterran lines, overseeing the evacuation of Ferlore villages ahead of the Alterran advance.

It was too late for Tessex, but Aander and her father would save all they could.

Unless the queen convinced them to stop.

Rydara looked at Aander. He was letting her ride next to him, but he kept his eyes straight ahead. His posture was rigid and aloof.

But then, as she watched, his shoulders loosened. He checked his horse and glanced at her, his brow furrowing as the party came to a stop behind him.

"I'm sorry—I shouldn't have said that," he said. "We don't need to discuss your position. Our approach to the Alterrans, maybe. But that's all."

Rydara closed her eyes in relief, feeling tension drain from her whole body. "It was the queen. She has magic, a kind we don't have in the tribes." She opened her eyes and looked around at the other riders. It was a little unorthodox for her to address them, but her point depended on their impressions. "Do you remember? When she talked about how Aander should be recognized as a hero in Tessex, did you feel ashamed, like our mission was only ever about his vanity?" She met the eyes of Kell, the man from Ferlore. "Do you still, or has the effect worn off?"

The men traded glances. They had never liked Rydara much, but everyone loved Aander.

"I felt that," one of the Noraani retainers admitted, his ears flushing red in embarrassment. "I thought our work here was done, and that we were no better than foolish children, bringing accusations against the queen. But what did we actually accomplish? We haven't done anything for Tessex, have we?"

"And when has our prince cared for anything beyond the welfare of the tribes?" the second retainer added.

The others nodded along, but Kell wore a worried frown. "What kind of magic could change our thoughts?" he asked Rydara.

"The Speaking magic," Aander surmised, glancing at Rydara. "Rydara's mother told us stories about it, though I've never seen it among the tribes."

Rydara nodded slowly.

Aander remembered her mother better than she did. He had been nine when she died, and Rydara only six. He had repeated her mother's bedtime stories for Rydara for years after her passing, and Rydara had never known where they ended and Aander's own fancies began.

But she remembered the Speaking magic. Among the tribes, there were only three forms of magic—Knowing, Showing, and Perceiving—and no individual ever developed more than one form. In her mother's stories, though, the ancient demons had wielded six, and they had each had access to all of them. Their Speaking magic could burst eardrums and twist the hearts of men, forcing them into patterns of thought and behavior that were not their own.

The description fit close enough.

"What do we do now?" asked Kell, looking to Aander. He was a few years older than the prince—they all were, besides Rydara—and his father had been the Ferlore chief, which made Kell something like a prince himself. But their desperation to save Ferlore had driven them into this alliance whole-heartedly, and Kell followed Aander without question.

"We need to find out what happened in Tessex," Rydara said to Aander. "It may be too late to help, but we need to know what we're facing."

Aander nodded. "Best not to risk talking to the queen again. We'll sneak past their lines. Kell, how many of us could you hide?"

Kell had the Showing magic, which meant he could Show things that were not as though they were. Its most common application was in hiding.

He shook his head. "I'm sorry, Prince Aander, but even you and me would be pushing it. Certainly no horses."

"What if we waited for nightfall? We should take Rydara, since her Knowing may tell us where to look."

"Night would make it easier." Kell nodded, glancing at Rydara. He had always been a little softer toward her than the others, and now she saw some respect in his gaze. Ferlore cared less about the stipulations of the priests than Noraan, and their magic users were regarded highly. "I think I could hide the three of us in the dark. As long as they don't have strong Perceivers."

"Good. We'll wait for night, then," Aander said. "The rest of you, continue on. Father should know about the queen's magic and the threat it poses as soon as possible."

The men agreed, and Aander led Rydara and Kell a little farther from the Alterran lines to picket their horses and wait for night.

"You scared me," Rydara told Aander softly while he unsaddled his horse. She traded Astral's bridle for a halter and looped the lead rope around a tree next to Aander. Kell was seeing to his own animal, a bit farther away.

"Rydara," Aander turned to look at her. "I'm sorry. I should never have said those things—I would never actually send you away. You know that, right?"

Rydara bit her lip as she unsaddled Astral and took out a brush, avoiding his gaze. "I know it was just the queen." She started brushing Astral, a familiar, soothing motion. "But if her magic had worked on you—or if you ever changed your mind—"

I would have no one. Rydara's eyes burned, and she left the thought unspoken. She knew full well that it was only Aander's love for his little "sister" that had convinced their father to let her continue as part of their household after her mother died. Her talent with the Knowing magic helped justify her place, but she was an embarrassment to the king, and he did not care for the gossip she inspired among the tribes or the ill will the priests bore him on her account.

The king had loved her mother. He must have, to have kept her despite the priests' disapproval and to have let her play mother to his heir. Aander's mother, the king's legal wife, had died in childbirth, so Rydara's mother raised them both until a sickness took her, too.

The king may have loved Rydara's mother, but that affection had never extended to Rydara herself. Were it not for Aander's determination, the king would have sent her off to her mother's people long ago, though they were strangers to her.

"Rydara." Aander laid a hand over Rydara's, stopping her brush. "Do you remember what I told you, when Father sent you to apprentice with the shaman in Kale?"

Rydara closed her eyes. She had been ten years old. Old enough to understand her father's ambivalence, but too young to understand what getting trained in the Knowing magic would mean for her. She had thought her father was sending her away forever.

"You said—" Rydara's voice broke, and she wiped moisture from her eyes, frustrated. It was not proper for the prince's adviser to cry.

"I said as long as I have a place in the Noraani court and our father's household, so will you," Aander said, squeezing her hand. "I swore it to you, Rydara, and that's an oath I mean to keep. No matter how many queens with Speaking magic try to stop me."

Aander pulled her into a hug, and Rydara pressed her forehead against his chest.

"Thank you," she whispered.

He mussed her hair and grinned as she ducked away, indignant. "What's a brother for?" he asked, winking at her as she went back to brushing her horse.

He could always make Rydara smile.

After the animals were seen to, Aander had Kell practice hiding himself and Rydara. Rydara could see a slight distortion to the air while Kell worked his magic, as if she were looking at the world through water or curved glass. She had no idea how invisible they were, though. It was a one-way illusion.

Showing was a far more complicated magic than Knowing. Knowing attuned Rydara to others' emotions, enabling her to discern more about them than they let on. There was not much skill involved, and little that Rydara had to do to activate her magic. Lies just sounded different than the truth to her, and if she paid attention, she could feel the emotions that lay beneath people's words and sense how they shaped the speaker's intentions.

The Knowers among the tribes varied considerably in the strength and consistency of their Knowing. Rydara ranked among the most reliable, but as far as she knew, the talent was completely innate. After basic training in how to distinguish between Knowing and guessing, there was not much a Knower could do to grow in strength.

Showing was different. From what Rydara understood, it was an exercise in memorization, visualization, and concentration. A Shower had to imagine the thing they wanted to Show before they could make it appear, and it would be only as detailed as the image they held in their mind. If their concentration broke, the image would disappear.

Hiding a small, stationary thing was relatively simple. To disguise a footprint in the snow, the Shower could simply imagine the snow unbroken and anchor that image over the footprint. To hide three people while they moved, though, was a far more ambitious endeavor. Kell had to imagine how the landscape would appear without them in it from an onlooker's perspective at every angle and hold those images in a full circle around them, updating each one with every step.

Kell was a skilled Shower, and Rydara knew he practiced visualizations daily, but it still seemed an impossible task. Aander waited until full dark before deciding they were ready.

The illusion did not have to be perfect in the dark.

Aander let Kell take a break from his magic as they started back toward the Alterran lines. They did not risk bringing a torch. The sudden appearance of a light source would be far too conspicuous in the darkness, should Kell's illusion fail for even a moment where a soldier might see them.

It was slow going, with each of them watching their feet and trying to make as little noise as possible. Rydara could not judge their position well in the dark, but Kell had memorized the terrain. He led them back toward the Alterran outpost, and when they could make out the soldiers' fire up ahead, the three of them paused, and Kell raised his illusion.

They crept forward even more slowly. Kell set the pace, and he gave the outpost a wide berth. Aander and Rydara each walked with a hand on his shoulder, helping him maintain awareness of their positions in the dark.

They had to pass through the main camp to reach Tessex. The snow was trampled and melted enough that Kell did not have to worry about their footprints giving them away. Most of the soldiers were sleeping, and the camp was quiet, but lookouts were posted at regular intervals. They passed within thirty feet of one, not far outside the flickering light cast by his fire.

A twig snapped under Aander's foot, and Rydara's heart stopped. The lookout looked directly at them.

The three of them froze. Rydara tried to still her breathing. She made direct eye contact with the lookout, and though she could see that funny distortion in the air between them, she was convinced he could see her.

But his gaze moved on. The three of them resumed creeping forward, and soon they were through the camp.

Rydara relaxed slightly when the camp was behind them. There were many more Alterran camps—they might well stretch all the way back to Alterra—but as far as they knew, this had been the only one lying between them and Tessex.

Making their way through the forest was challenging by moonlight. Rydara kept a hand on Kell's shoulder, impressed by his sense of direction. All the forest looked the same to her, even in daylight. But Kell had grown up in these woods, and he led them straight as an arrow.

Tessex was a minor village—no more than a collection of huts in a clearing where a handful of Ferlore families had made their residence. The place did not even have a proper road. A web of little dirt footpaths connected the buildings, dusted with snow, and a stream ran through the middle.

Rydara felt a sense of foreboding as they approached. The place was quiet. Too quiet, even for a village asleep.

"It hasn't been torn down," Aander whispered, optimistic.

Rydara shook her head. "There's no one here," she said softly. If there had been people inside those huts, she would have registered something of their emotions in her Knowing, faint and uninterpretable though it would have been.

But there was nothing.

"Surely you can't be certain," Kell whispered, glancing at Rydara. "Not from here."

"We'll check," Aander agreed, leading them forward.

Rydara was certain, but she did not have the heart to say so. They had not come so far to turn back now. Enough moonlight reached the clearing that they did not need to rely so heavily on Kell's guidance, though they stayed close together. He was still hiding them.

Aander slowly opened the door of the first building they came to—a single family dwelling, by the looks of it. A quick scan revealed three empty beds and a deserted kitchen area.

It was the same with the next hut and the next.

Rydara's sense of foreboding grew, and it started to feel somehow *centered*. Its locus was somewhere in the woods on the far side of the village.

"There's no one here," Rydara repeated. The foreboding, she realized, came from her Knowing, but the source did not feel like another person—nor a poison or weapon, as she had sometimes experienced. No person or commonplace object could be the source of such dread, and Rydara wasn't sure she wanted to see what was. "Something is happening out there, though." Rydara stared in the direction the dread was pulling her. Her Knowing registered a much fainter emotional presence in the same direction.

She glanced at Kell. "People are there. We'll have to be careful."

Kell's face was expressionless in the moonlight, but his anguish was loud in Rydara's Knowing. It was a sharper and more desperate thing than Aander's sorrow or her own fear. He had known these people.

"Let's go," Aander said, and Kell nodded.

They stole across the village and into the woods, nearly as noiseless as they were invisible. Kell picked a path for them through the trees, following Rydara's sense of direction through her silent cues. Her apprehension grew with every step.

When the trees parted in another clearing, it was hard to see what they revealed. The moonlight glistened on snow, but the ground was lumpy and uneven. It was not grass underneath.

As they drew closer, Rydara could make out the edge of a hole dug in the clearing. A large hole, filled with...

"Oh, no," Kell breathed, sinking to his knees. The lump nearest them, partly covered in snow, extended unmistakably into a human hand.

Someone had dug a pit here, and the pit was filled with bodies. Rydara could make out the features, now. Limbs. Torsos. Faces. Dozens of them. Some of them far too small.

"I'm so sorry," Aander whispered. He began a prayer for the departed under his breath.

Rydara squeezed Kell's shoulder and looked at Aander, pressing a finger against her lips. There were living people close by, she Knew—and as horrible as the pit was, it was not the source of her dread. She pointed across the clearing.

Kell took a moment to compose himself before leading them across.

They saw the light of a lantern through the trees. The sound of a female voice reached them as they drew closer. She was chanting in a foreign tongue.

Rydara had thought the pit would prepare her for whatever came next, but this was somehow worse. In the light of the woman's lantern, she saw a body tied to a tree. The rope was secured across the man's chest and under his arms, which were stretched back behind him. His head slumped forward, lifeless, and a dagger was driven through his chest. Blood still ran from the wound.

A man stood next to the body, stooping to hold a black crystal against the dead man's chest, getting the crystal wet with his blood.

The man straightened as the woman ceased her chant, studying the crystal in his hands. Through the faint distortion of Kell's Showing, Rydara recognized the blue and white uniform of an Alterran soldier. The two pairs of crossed swords in his insignia marked him as their highest-ranking officer.

This was General Dameires.

"You are behind my lines, and that pathetic thing you call a Showing does nothing to hide you." The general's voice carried the same coiled power as the queen's, and he lifted his eyes to look right at them.

Rydara panicked, checking the distortion. It was still there, but it did not matter. He must have had Perceiving magic—but he also had the Speaking magic. That was impossible.

No one had more than one magic.

"So we meet again, little *ishra*," the woman spoke, her voice deceptively gentle, and Rydara recognized the queen. Her face was uncovered—a violation of Alterran law, here in the presence of a man who was not her husband—but it was the same green eyes, the same violet dress, the same imperious voice.

She could see them, too.

"Kneel," the general commanded, and the three of them fell to their knees. "Enough of that." He waved a hand impatiently, and Kell's Showing disappeared.

"What have you done?" Kell demanded, his voice thick with horror. "All of them? The children! Why?"

"Hush, you." The queen flicked her wrist, and her attention turned to Rydara. "You perceived my deception and convinced these men to follow you here. Impressive, for one in your situation. But you could be so much more."

"We don't have time for this," the general said, moving toward them, but the queen held up a hand.

"These are the king's children," she said, and the general narrowed his eyes. "Indispensable, if we want the tribes to stay quiet while we fill the crystal." The queen turned back to Rydara. "This could go one of two ways, *ishra*, considering the strength of your talent. Would you consider working for me?"

Rydara's brow furrowed in confusion. She stared at the dead man, still drooping against the rope that held him to the tree, and then she glanced at the bloody crystal in the general's hands.

She wanted nothing to do with this evil, but Aander and Kell's lives might depend on her. "Would you let them live?" she asked, her eyes meeting the queen's.

"I could offer you power beyond your wildest dreams," the queen said instead. "And immortality. All it will cost is your lingering ties to the White—the All-Color, you call him—but that shouldn't matter if you worship the Six, should it?" The queen smiled, but the expression faded, and her mouth twisted in annoyance. "The spell requires you to agree to terms you understand, so here's the gist: you'll lose your conscience. Your soul, so to speak. But we'll let your brother live, at least for now."

"Rydara—" Aander began, giving her a look full of warning.

"Nothing from you, either," the queen silenced him. "Only Rydara can make this deal."

The silence stretched as Rydara tried to consider. The All-Color was the god of her mother's people, and the whole situation seemed to have come straight from her tales of the ancient demons. Stories made up to amuse children. Rydara sensed no deception in the queen. But if making this deal was a real option, how was Rydara supposed to price some abstract notion about her "soul" against their real and present danger?

"She won't do it," the general said. Rydara sensed absolute certainty in his claim, which puzzled her. "Can't you tell? She's been fed too many lies about good and evil."

"Perhaps." The queen's mouth twisted in disapproval as she studied Rydara. "You imagine your people will love you one day if you're good enough, don't you?"

Rydara's cheeks burned. The queen posed the question with such mockery, as if Rydara's dearest, most secret wish were a child's delusional fantasy.

"We'll just have to discredit her." The general crouched in front of Kell, brandishing a dagger as they stared into each other's eyes. "Cooperate."

The command was not directed at Rydara, but she felt its power like a physical blow. The general seized Kell's collar and pulled him to his feet. Then he shoved him up against a tree.

Kell did not struggle, and Aander and Rydara were powerless to move or even speak as the general plunged the dagger through Kell's chest.

Chapter 3

Fallout

The general twisted the dagger and withdrew it, still holding Kell against the tree with his left hand. Kell moaned softly, and his body sagged as the light left his eyes. The general wiped the dagger on Kell's shoulder before letting him crumple to the ground.

Rydara felt Aander's rage in her Knowing, and she sensed he was straining against the power that kept him kneeling beside her.

"Well, she won't do it now," the queen complained.

"Recruit on your own time, Lux." The general shot the queen a look that bordered on contempt. "Altering memory is complicated, and we need this dealt with."

Rydara barely registered the exchange. She stared as Kell's blood spread across his shirt and soaked the snow around him, dark red in the light of the lantern.

The general sheathed his dagger. "Come with me," he said, pulling them to their feet.

The words settled around Rydara like a vise, propelling her forward. She did not try to fight them. Aander's efforts were futile, anyway.

The general marched them back to the camp, pulling each by an arm. The queen followed, lighting their way with her lantern. A distant part of Rydara noted that she had replaced her veil.

A pair of lookouts intercepted them as they approached the camp, and they bowed to the queen. The general issued a string of orders in Alterran that Rydara did not try to understand. Her mind was frozen on the image of his dagger in Kell's chest.

The general pushed Aander and Rydara toward the lookouts. Aander swung a fist at the nearest one, and Rydara noticed belatedly that the general's command no longer bound them.

The soldier blocked Aander's punch with a swipe of his arm, but Aander's kick to his groin connected, and the soldier doubled over in pain as Aander spun back toward the general.

Too slow. The general was taller, stronger, and more experienced, and his fist connected hard with Aander's temple. The prince fell to the snow. The soldier he had kicked knelt on top of him and roughly pulled Aander's hands behind his back, tying them together with a short length of rope.

Rydara just watched, letting the other soldier tie her hands without so much as a murmur. She was not a fighter, and fighting was useless when the enemy could freeze them with a word. But her mind—the part of it that had not frozen in shock—worked to trace the edges of this new threat.

Did the general and the queen have Knowing magic, in addition to Speaking and Perceiving? Is that how the queen had discerned so much about her?

If they both had multiple magics, could that mean they had all six, like the ancient demons?

Were they the ancient demons, returned?

The soldier finished tying her hands and started to pull her away. Rydara's eyes met the general's, and she wondered what he would do to Aander. *Altering memory is complicated...*

Could the general make them forget the horror of this night?

He smiled a wicked grin.

The soldier tugged her again, and Rydara stumbled after him.

He took her to a wagon, where he had a brief conversation with another lookout. Then he loaded Rydara inside.

"Our horses," Rydara said, remembering Astral as she knelt in the bed of the wagon, her hands still tied behind her back. "We left them picketed in the woods south of your outpost. Will you send someone for them?"

The soldier did not answer. Rydara tried again in broken Alterran. The soldier just drew his knife, keeping it ready in his hands while they waited.

As if she posed any threat.

I'm sorry, Astral, Rydara thought, closing her eyes in despair. She always tied the lead loosely. Maybe the mare could break free. *I'll come back for you if I can. If I remember.*

A long time later, two more soldiers came, carrying an unconscious Aander between them. They laid him in the wagon next to Rydara. One of them climbed in with him and sat, becoming their second guard. The wagon started to move.

The soldiers conferred briefly in Alterran, and then one of them leaned back against the side of the wagon and went to sleep.

Rydara stared at Aander, nervous, but his temple had not even bruised — as far as she could see in the dark — and his breathing was deep and regular. But something was not right.

Rydara remembered, then, that the general had said they would discredit her. They did not mean to alter her memories, then. Only Aander's.

Rydara did not know of any magic that could alter memories, and she did not remember any mention of such a thing from her mother's stories. But if Aander woke with no memory of what had happened, she would have to convince him that uniting the tribes was more important now than ever. That the Alterran queen and General Dameires had strange and horrible powers that could compel obedience and change people's memories to accord with their lies.

"Aander," Rydara whispered, shaking him gently.

"Quiet." The word from the Alterran soldier watching her was filled with power, and Rydara looked up at him, stunned. "Let your brother sleep."

Rydara tried to touch her brother again and found she could not. She tried to speak. Tried to scream.

Nothing.

"Please," the Alterran scoffed. "Your Knowing may have impressed Lux, but it's not enough to resist me. Don't bother. Lucky for you, I'm just taking you home."

Rydara stared at him, her eyes wide with terror, but he said nothing else.

How many Alterrans have the Speaking magic?

They drove through the night. Rydara did not think she would sleep after the horror she had witnessed, not while sitting next to a man who shared the magic of the Alterran queen and general. She almost envied her brother. He appeared to be sleeping peacefully, albeit uncomfortably, lying on his side with his hands still bound behind his back. When he woke up, he would not carry the weight that she did.

Not unless she could convince him to.

Rydara did sleep, despite everything. When she woke, it was daylight, and the wagon stopped so the guards and driver could rotate positions. Aander was awake, and the Alterrans let the two of them out of the wagon to stretch their legs.

"Are you all right?" Aander asked her as they stumbled out of the wagon, the transition awkward with both their hands still tied behind their backs. There was a faint worried crease in his forehead—concern on her behalf—but he seemed in otherwise fair spirits.

"Quiet." It was a different guard who gave the order than the one who had spoken to her the night before, and Rydara did not think his words carried any power.

But the one who had the Speaking magic was standing next to him, and he smiled at Rydara.

She looked at her brother and tried to speak. She could not.

"You could untie us, you know," Aander said to the guard, oblivious to her predicament. "You're taking us back to our own army, aren't you? We have no reason to run."

"I said, quiet!" The guard took a step forward, brandishing his knife.

Aander stepped back, raising his hands. "All right, all right," he said. "It's fine. We'll be quiet." He looked at Rydara and then nodded to the guards, illustrating their ability to be quiet.

"Good," the guard grunted. "Back in the wagon."

Aander did not speak to her again.

The sun was setting when they reached the Noraani camp. The Alterrans unloaded Aander and Rydara from the wagon, and the Alterran with the Speaking magic explained to the Noraani soldiers who stopped them that they bore a gift and a message from the Alterran queen.

Aander and Rydara were the gift, and the Alterrans pushed them toward the Noraani soldiers.

"Behave, now," the one with magic commanded her as they changed hands, and Rydara shuddered as the words settled around her.

"Prince Aander, are you all right? Did they hurt you?" one of their men asked, hastily cutting them loose. The drab gray uniforms of the Noraani contrasted with the sharp blue and white of the Alterrans, and the tribesmen seemed almost servile as two of them escorted the three foreigners into camp.

Rydara opened her mouth to tell them to stop, to warn them about the Speaking magic, only to find she was still choking on air. She wanted to scream.

Beside her, Aander just smiled sheepishly. "No, we're fine. Just a diplomatic misunderstanding. Our fault, really."

Rydara stared at him, shocked by his nonchalance. *Can't he see the panic in my eyes?* She tried to grab his shoulders and found she could not.

"Where are they taking the Alterrans?" Aander asked the soldier.

"To see the king," he said. "He arrived this morning, and he—um. The rest of your party got back shortly before you did, and he wasn't ... happy ... with their report. He said he wanted to see the two of you as soon as you returned, though the queen's message will take priority."

"Father is here, is he? I don't suppose we could take some time to clean up before we see him." Aander wrinkled his nose. "It's been a long couple of days." The Noraani exchanged glances, conflicted, and Aander smiled, clapping one on the shoulder. "Never mind. Now it is. Are you ready, Rydara?"

Rydara felt sick, but she found herself nodding. The magic was controlling her still.

"Rydara?" Aander stopped walking, finally perceiving something was off. He put a hand on her shoulder. "Are you all right?"

Rydara shook her head and tried to speak. "I…" The magic was starting to fail. She was breaking free.

"I know Father is hard on you," Aander said. "But I'll be right there with you. We'll face him together."

"It's not that!" Rydara was finally able to say. "It's—" Rydara stopped, staring after the Alterrans. They had gone into the king's tent to speak with him.

The one with Speaking magic was in an audience with her father. *Planning to discredit me,* she realized. If she screamed for the Noraani to stop him, what good would it do? Even if they wanted to listen to her, the Alterran could just command them not to. He could do whatever he wanted, and there was nothing Rydara could say that would stop him.

That was why she was free from the magic.

Rydara's heart sank. She turned to her brother. "Aander, the Alterran queen and general have powers we do not understand. They said they would change your memory, and they must have—you really don't remember what they did?"

"What are you talking about?"

Rydara bit her lip, not knowing how much to tell him or where to begin. If the king did not believe her account or wish to act on it, it might only hurt her cause if Aander sided with her too quickly.

The king called them inside before she could say anything more.

"I'll explain inside," Rydara told Aander, shaking her head.

Sorovan, the king's brother and right-hand man, escorted the Alterrans out of the tent. He paused to squeeze Rydara's shoulder on his way out, giving her a sympathetic nod.

Aander frowned and stared after him. Sorovan was not an affectionate man, and he seldom noticed Rydara, but Rydara understood the gesture entirely. It filled her with dread.

Aander held open the flap of the tent's entrance, and she followed him inside.

King Cressidin tul'Noraan was in his middle forties, and his hair was fully gray. His stature was average and his clothes, though thicker and more finely woven than the average soldier's, were gray and brown. The fur stole draped around his shoulders was his only ornament, and the command tent was empty of furniture, so he stood.

But he stood like a king.

When they were little, Aander and Rydara used to practice standing like him. They would pace around the kennels with dinner plates balanced on their heads and command the dogs to heel, sit, and fetch as though they were battlefield commanders.

The first time the king had let Rydara attend an important meeting, he pulled her aside afterward and told her that her haughty posture drew too much attention. She had given up the practice after that.

The king's back was to them when they entered, and he let out a deep sigh before turning around. "What were you thinking?" he asked, his eyes settling on Aander. "We spent the last six months strategizing about how to protect ourselves from Alterra, running across all Kilethe to try to bolster our alliance and stay one step ahead of their advance, all the while hoping and preparing for a meeting with someone influential like the one you had the good fortune to stumble into—and what did you do? You made a deal with them only to *immediately* turn around and violate their terms. By the Six, Aander. You couldn't even wait one day? What if they had taken your little reconnaissance mission as an act of war?"

"Father, you heard the woman from Tessex," Aander lifted his hands in a kind of shrug. "And you weren't in the meeting with the queen. We all agreed something seemed off and we needed to see Tessex for ourselves ... right?" He turned to Rydara, not knowing what to make of what she had said.

"Yes, I heard from our retainers that Rydara was quite insistent on that point," the king said, frowning at Rydara. "I see the years of diplomatic training were wasted on you. Daughter." The word sounded like a curse in the king's mouth, and Rydara winced.

"The decision was mine," Aander said, lifting his chin. He gave the king a hard stare. "I won't pass off the blame to an adviser."

"Blame must go where blame is due," the king returned, eyeing his son. "As it turns out, all is well in Tessex, is it not? And you used Kell's Showing to sneak you there after explicitly agreeing not to go. They wonder if the whole parley was a charade to get you close enough to spy out their camp unsupervised, perhaps to assassinate their queen or general—how could they not? And that *after* Rydara managed to offend the queen. We *will* make reparations."

"Reparations?" Aander repeated, frowning. "What do you mean, reparations? We're nothing to them. No harm was done. What could we even offer?"

Rydara pulled her cloak tighter as the king started to answer. The king beat around the bush for a while, mentioning de-escalation and gestures, but she could guess where he was headed. There was one sure way to discredit her among the tribes, and that was to remove her voice entirely. The Alterrans would not have asked for the execution of a king's daughter.

But they could demand her exile.

"Everything is not all right in Tessex," she whispered.

"What?" Aander asked her, interrupting the king.

Rydara raised her eyes to meet her father's, begging him to listen before he sent her away. "Everything is not all right in Tessex. All the people that were living there are dead."

The king's expression darkened. "What?"

Rydara dropped her eyes, wishing she could shrink away under his glare. "Your Majesty, I don't know what the Alterrans told you, but it's not the whole story. I don't want to overstep my position here, but since you had me trained as a Knower and a diplomatic adviser, I think it would reflect poorly on both your charity and my education if I didn't at least give you my account."

Rydara took a deep breath and glanced at Aander. He returned her gaze with concern.

"Have a care how you frame it, Rydara." Her father tightened his lips, not quite forbidding her to speak. "You are already on thin ice."

"Father—" Aander started to chasten him, but Rydara interrupted.

"I understand." Rydara swallowed and considered her words. Making any direct accusations against Alterra would put the king in a difficult position, and he would not thank her for it. But if he had already agreed to make reparations by sending her away, she had to persuade him the Alterrans could not be trusted. He needed to know the danger, anyway. He and Aander both did.

If only Aander remembered what had happened. Her father would have trusted Aander, but whether he would believe Rydara over the Alterran queen's messenger was anyone's guess.

"When I saw Tessex last, it was empty. There was a mass grave in the woods just outside of it. Kell is dead, too," Rydara said. She glanced at Aander, wishing she did not have to bear such terrible news. "I saw him die. A man in an Alterran uniform stabbed him through the heart."

"You are telling me the Alterrans murdered Kell?" the king challenged, a clear warning in his tone. He glanced at Aander. "What do you know of this?"

"Not the Alterrans, necessarily," Rydara hastened to say, stammering. "I have reason to believe the Alterran army has been infiltrated by powerful sorcerers—sorcerers with powers like the ancient demons from Rishara lore. The Speaking magic, along with an ability to manipulate memory, and other magics—perhaps all six. I heard the man who killed Kell say they would discredit me and that they could alter memory. Aander was with me when I saw the grave and Kell's murder, but we were powerless to fight back. They used the Speaking magic to control us. And now, Aander remembers none of it, so they must have succeeded in changing his memory."

Aander stared at her, his blue eyes wide in astonishment.

"What an outlandish tale," the king murmured, considering. He glanced between them. "Almost too absurd for fiction. Aander, what do you say happened?"

"Well..." Aander scratched his head. "Rydara's right, I don't remember it that way at all. I remember getting caught while spying out Tessex, but the people seemed fine, and Kell asked my leave to stay behind. But if that's not right and Kell was murdered—if Tessex is gone—we ... we have to do something..."

"Warn the Alterrans, perhaps, of this possible infiltration?" The king arched an eyebrow at Rydara, and Rydara could tell he was suspicious.

Suspicious that she had a more direct accusation to make.

"I don't think that would help," Rydara said softly, biting her lip. *Don't offer problems, Rydara. Offer solutions,* her training echoed in her mind.

The only solution she could think of came from her mother's stories. She doubted the king would prove receptive to chasing Rishara myths, especially given the danger—but what other choice did they have?

Rydara took a deep breath. "If the sorcerers I met are somehow related to the Rishara histories of demons," she said, "then we have to hope that the stories about their enemies are also true. Allegedly, the demons were once defeated by the Loyal Ones—elves, who later fled to the Land Beyond the Waste. I would recommend that we send a delegation across the Hahiroth Waste to search for this land and beg the elves who live there to help us fight back against the Alterran sorcerers."

"A delegation? Across the Waste? To seek a land from fairytales?" The king's questions were each more incredulous than the last. "On what grounds, exactly?"

"I believe the sorcerers mean to continue slaughtering people from the tribes, as they did at Tessex, as part of the rituals they perform that enhance their power," Rydara said, closing her eyes and seeing the dark crystal in the general's bloody hands, remembering the queen's foreign chanting. What else could it be but a ritual? *Indispensable,* the queen had said of her and Aander, *if we want the tribes to stay quiet while we fill the crystal...* "We cannot hope to defend ourselves against them without great help, help that exceeds anything our own magic users have to offer."

"You'll have to do better than that, Rydara," the king said flatly. "The Alterrans brought me a message from the queen herself, reiterating that Alterra has no quarrel with any but Jeshimoth and that she intends to speak to the general about restraining the army. She assures me that the people of Tessex are safe and claims you and Aander saw as much with your own eyes. But if Aander's memories are forged and she is mistaken, as you claim, why would I not send a delegation to her, or to General Dameires, rather than to some mythical realm across the Waste, considering the danger and the vast improbability of success?"

"Because," Rydara paused to wet her lips, "I have reason to believe these sorcerers have infiltrated the Alterran army at the highest level."

"Who killed Kell, Rydara?" Aander asked the question she had been trying to avoid. He believed her—of course he did, despite whatever the Alterrans had done to his memory—and he wanted to understand what had happened to his friend. He was sensitive enough to pick up on the fact that Rydara knew more than she was saying.

He just wasn't sensitive enough to understand what was at stake in this conversation, or that the king would take any excuse to dismiss accusations from his bastard daughter against a nation they could never hope to defeat.

"Answer the question," the king ordered, his tone hard. He had warned her that she was on thin ice, but now he was practically goading her to break it. To say something that could not be unsaid. To force him to address an act of open aggression against the tribes—or to dismiss the accusation as falsehood.

Rydara pressed her hands together. "A man in the uniform of an Alterran officer. There were two pairs of crossed swords in his insignia."

"General Dameires." The king spoke the name that Rydara would not, and she closed her eyes in agony. She had wanted to leave open the possibility that someone had stolen his uniform and impersonated him—but she Knew it really had been the general, and she could not gainsay the king.

His jaw grew tight with anger. "And I suppose the queen knows of this already?"

"She was there," Rydara admitted, feeling her credibility crumbling around her. It was no use trying to maintain the delicacy appropriate to a diplomat, trying to leave the Alterran leaders deniability. The king wanted to force this issue.

"Their general killed Kell and the queen lied to us about it?" Aander said, horrified. "And the whole village of Tessex was slaughtered? They did it themselves, didn't they? Are they the sorcerers?" Rydara didn't answer, and Aander took her silence

35

as confirmation. "Father, we have to act on this," he said, turning to the king.

It was the worst thing he could have said.

The king held up a hand. "One more question, Rydara," he said, his tone heavy with scorn. "A simple, direct answer will do. You know the queen took issue with your insistence on seeing Tessex and with what you said about her army. The fact that you spoke at all in an audience between royals is bad enough, especially knowing their views on *ishra* as you do, and it is little wonder that she objected to what you said. So tell me, Rydara: did you Know the Alterrans who brought you here carried a message from her and General Dameires asking for your banishment from the Noraani kingdom?"

Rydara bit her lip. She did not think it would help her case to mention that one of those Alterrans had had the Speaking magic as well, or that he may have used it on her father. "I suspected."

"And you bring me this absurd slander against them, to what end? To persuade me they deserve no token of friendship? You're a smart girl, Rydara—do you not realize your accusations could incite an all-out war?"

"I just thought you should know," Rydara whispered. Through her Knowing, she could sense her father's anger and fear, and she did not believe it mattered whether the Alterran had used the Speaking magic on him or not. The effects of the Speaking magic should have started to fade, now that the Alterrans had left.

This reaction from her father was not going to fade. It was who he was.

"Seven years, I was married to Alanca before she carried Aander to term," her father said, studying her with a critical eye. "Seven years, five miscarriages. One child.

"Then I met Landri, with whom I never intended to have any children, and she was pregnant inside a month. The priests wanted me to send her away, but I kept her, and when you were born, I kept you, too. Out of consideration for Landri, I let you be known as my daughter, though it went against all tradition and advice. Then she died, and *still* I kept you.

"All these years, I have clothed you and cared for you. I gave you an education that would lead to a position of prominence and respect in the tribe, though I was counseled against it. When the Knowing magic was found in you, I made sure you were trained in that, too.

"And this is how you repay me. You offend a foreign power that could crush us like a bug, which we have escaped so far only by avoiding their full attention. And then you fill my son's ears with slander against them? Tell me, Rydara, do you wish to see us destroyed?"

"No," Rydara whispered, her eyes on the floor.

"Are you sure? Perhaps my kindness was not enough for you, your position not enough. Perhaps you believe that you should have been a princess, that the tribes should treat you with respect instead of viewing you askance for your heritage."

"No." Rydara raised her eyes to meet her father's. "I know my place."

"No, Rydara, you do not know your place. An adviser who knew her place would not seek to incite a war that would surely mean our end!"

"I would not advise war," Rydara stammered. "We need—"

"Help from beyond the Waste?" the king challenged. "And how do you suppose the Ferlore chief would react to news of his son's murder? Of a massacre at Tessex? You know exactly what you're doing, Rydara. You know Alterra wants you gone, and you seek to undercut any diplomatic solution—to cut off all negotiations. No matter the price to the tribes."

"No—" Rydara objected.

"Father, how could you think Rydara might do anything like that?" Aander came to her defense, his brow furrowing in anger. "You sound like you've never met your own daughter. She's never given us bad counsel before, has she? So what if she Knew the Alterrans wished her gone? They would, if she knew what they were, wouldn't they?"

"Convenient, isn't it?" the king snapped back. "They killed Kell and changed *your* memories, but did nothing to her? How do you account for that, Rydara?"

"I don't know," she said. "Maybe because of my Knowing..."

"Your Knowing made you too powerful for ancient demons to tamper with your memory?" the king mocked. "I suppose it made you impervious to murder, too?"

Rydara had no answer for that. Aander's disappearance would have been ill-received by the tribes, even if the Alterrans pretended not to know what had happened. But who would have missed her, if the general had killed her and erased it from Aander's memory? Why had the queen called her indispensable?

Only Aander would have missed her. But surely two sorcerers with the power to manipulate memory could have convinced one man—who was under their direct influence—that her death had been an accident. *Couldn't they?*

Rydara knew too little about their powers. She shook her head. "I don't know why they let me live."

"I see." The silence stretched, heavy with her father's displeasure. "I won't have this slander in my kingdom. You are hereby banished."

The words were so simple. After the power of the queen's voice, the general's, and the Alterran soldier's, her father's short speech felt flat and impotent. His words lacked the magic to compel obedience.

And yet, they sealed her fate more firmly than the Alterrans ever could.

"Father," Aander's hands clenched into fists at his sides. "You can't."

"I can and I have."

"What if she's telling the truth?" Aander demanded. "If Kell is dead and the people of Tessex have been massacred, you're going to banish *her* and say nothing to Alterra?"

"Was Kell dead when you saw him last?" the king retorted. "Were the villagers of Tessex buried in a mass grave?"

"We can't just assume that my memory is right. She's a Knower," Aander returned.

"If you send for Kell and he answers, then I'll be proven wrong," Rydara offered, pleading.

"Your position has been abolished, girl!" Her father growled, and Rydara recoiled. "Do not presume to advise me."

"Father!" Aander objected.

"You will not move me in this, Aander. Not this time."

"Forget me. How could you do this to *her*? Your only daughter?"

"I have no daughter." King Cressidin looked at Rydara as he spoke, and his face was wholly impassive.

Rydara felt numb. Banishment was cruel enough, but the Alterrans had demanded it. To be disavowed entirely ... Somewhere inside, a little girl screamed and cried as the man whose acceptance she had sought her whole life finally broke her heart.

But Rydara just bowed her head.

"I have instructed Sorovan to make provision for you, Rydara," the king said. "You may take your pick of the horses, and you will be outfitted for a three days' journey and paid a handsome wage besides. You will no longer be known as a king's daughter, but you are seventeen, not a child, and there is no reason you cannot make your own way in the world. Where you go is up to you, so long as it is outside the Noraani kingdom. But understand, if you go to another tribe, and that tribe later joins our alliance, you will not be welcomed back along with them. I recommend you rejoin your mother's people instead."

"I understand." Rydara's voice seemed to come from someone else. It was strangely steady. "Your Majesty." She bowed and turned to go.

"No—I won't stand for this!" Aander moved to stop her. "What if Landri could see you now?" he demanded of the king. "This is how you treat her daughter? You *disown* her? As if Landri's love and the years of her life she wasted on us didn't matter? Didn't make us a family? Aren't you the one who taught me blood was everything, Father?"

"Landri understood our situation," the king returned. "She would agree I've been more than generous, considering."

Rydara clasped Aander's arm. "You are not the king, brother," she whispered, smiling faintly through the tears gathering in her eyes. This was not over for him—not by a long shot—but she knew whatever he said would not matter. He could not protect her anymore.

But there was one last thing she could do for him.

"I release you from your oath to me," she said. As long as he was not the king, Aander did not have the power to ensure she had a position in the Noraani court, let alone in their father's household. It had been a foolish oath for him to make.

Feeling caught in some strange, cruel echo, Rydara left the tent in disgrace, dismissed from her brother's side once again by the word of a sovereign.

This time, she knew the decree would last.

Chapter 4

If the Mighty Ones Return

It did not take long for Rydara to gather her things. The Noraani army had been on the road for six weeks, and this was only a temporary camp, so she was practically living out of saddlebags already.

But she had never taken so much as a single day's journey alone. The prospect overwhelmed her.

Rydara tried to keep her mind on the task at hand as she retrieved a lantern, packed her clothes, and sought out Sorovan to collect her stipend. She found him going over ledgers in the camp's logistical headquarters, not far from the command tent where Aander was still arguing with the king.

Her uncle glanced at her saddlebags and counted out a sum of coins for her.

"Will you tell Aander I'll wait for him in the stables?" Rydara asked.

Sorovan folded his hands and looked up. His expression was critical, though not without pity. "Why would you do that, Rydara?"

"To say goodbye," Rydara said, furrowing her brow. Surely her uncle did not think she should leave Aander forever without even saying goodbye.

"Do you mean for him to go with you?"

"Of course not. I've been banished. He hasn't."

"And how do you think the prince will react, once he figures out you're really leaving?"

Rydara knew Aander would hate it, but the idea that he might try to go with her had not crossed her mind. She stared at her uncle in confusion.

"What good could come from drawing out your goodbye?" Sorovan pressed. He shook his head. "You and I both know the prince's place is here, but his judgment has always been clouded when it comes to you. If you want what's best for him, you should leave before he thinks of doing anything we'll all regret."

"But he'd never forgive me," Rydara stammered. "I have to say goodbye."

He watched her fight back tears, and his tone was gentle but firm when he said, "I'll give him your regards."

Rydara turned away and rushed to the stables, angry with this final cruelty. But Sorovan was right. It would be kinder not to give Aander time to think of going with her.

She picked out a nondescript gray mare from the stables, figuring the animal would be little missed. The king had said she could have her pick, but she knew he would think less of her if she chose one of his prize animals.

It hardly mattered. She would never see him again. But she did not want to give him the satisfaction of believing she had reached above her station when she left.

She intended to get Astral back before she did anything else, anyway. She knew the king would not send anyone for the horses, with relations with Alterra as fragile as they were. But as an exile, she could go where she pleased.

She would get Astral, and then she would make for the Land Beyond the Waste. If the king ever heard of her journey, maybe then he would realize how wrong he had been to banish her. The king, Sorovan—all of them.

They would realize she had been loyal to the bitter end.

Rydara rode for hours by the light of her lantern. She was exhausted, and it was hard to tell which way she was going in the dark, but she wanted to put some distance between herself and Aander before she could change her mind about saying goodbye.

When fatigue overcame her, she stopped and made a fire. She tied the horse nearby, and her gaze fell on a pale blue flower in the branches of an evergreen shrub. It was a rydar flower. Rydara's mother had named her after the plant, which was native to both cold and desert climates. *You, too, are a child of two worlds,* her mother had told her once. *And like the rydar, you will thrive and add color wherever you grow.*

Rydara laughed aloud, her tired brain finding something hysterical about the irony. She had only ever known her father's world, and she had never fully belonged to it. Now she was native to nowhere.

It was well after dawn when she woke. Her fire was dying, and the smoke from its embers curled lazily in the breeze.

Aander was asleep nearby. He had laid his cloak next to the fire, where most of the snow had melted, and curled up on top of it. He could not have been warm or comfortable, but even in sleep, he looked determined. He must have walked through the night.

The sight of him filled Rydara with joy. She hurried to get bread and water for him.

He groaned when she shook his shoulder, but he accepted the water and drank deeply. "You thought you could leave me without even saying goodbye?" he grumbled, wiping his mouth before tearing into the bread. "That was cold, Rydara."

"I'm sorry," she said, and she meant it. She sat next to him and caught him in a hug. "Sorovan convinced me it would be better for you. I wasn't thinking."

"Clearly." Aander patted her arm before she released him. He frowned at her horse. "Didn't Father say you could have your pick of the horses?"

"I'm going to get Astral back."

"Excellent." Aander nodded and took another drink. "We'll have four horses, then. Good thinking."

"What? No." Rydara scooted around to face him. "I shouldn't have left without saying goodbye. But you can't come with me."

"Just how do you plan to stop me?" Aander lifted an eyebrow and continued eating.

Rydara leaned back on her hands. "Well, my first attempt was riding away in the night. But I'm sure I can get more creative."

"If you keep going in this direction, you'll miss the entire Alterran camp by over a mile. You need me."

"I'll do better by daylight."

"You'll do better with me navigating."

Rydara frowned, frustrated. She might have been able to find the horses on her own, eventually, but Aander had a better sense of direction—and the longer it took, the greater the chances that predators or the Alterrans would find the horses first. "Fine. If I let you help me get the horses, will you promise to go home after?"

"I don't have a home."

"What does that mean?"

"I mean, I've renounced it," Aander explained, finishing off the loaf she had given him. "I'm no longer the prince or father's son or even a Noraani. I've renounced everything, and I'm going to join the Rishara with you."

"But why?"

"I meant my oath to you, Rydara, and you can't just unilaterally release me. I won't allow it. And I won't be part of a family that doesn't include you."

"No." Rydara shook her head, disturbed that Sorovan had been right to tell her not to say goodbye. She knew her brother was stubborn, but this was a more serious rebellion than she had expected. "No, this can be undone. Father will take you back. I'm sure of it."

Aander nodded, eyes narrowed. "Yes, and the smug bastard is sure I'll give him the chance after a day or two of hard living. But I'm not going to, Rydara. Not if I can't bring you with me."

"It's Alterra that wants me gone, Aander." Rydara met his gaze, trying to make him see reason. "Father won't cross them. He'll just sacrifice you, too, if you make him."

"So be it." Aander looked past her at the fading embers, entirely unmoved.

"What about your mission to unite the tribes?" Rydara tried again. "What about Jemine? You have obligations."

Jinn was the biggest tribe in Kilethe that had not yet joined the Noraani alliance. Their chieftain had no sons—only one daughter, Jemine. She and Aander were promised to one another—an arrangement that King Cressidin and Aander had both worked hard to secure. Jinn had agreed to enter the alliance formally on the day of their marriage, set for six weeks from now, when Jemine came of age. None of that would happen if Aander renounced his heritage.

Rydara had never met Jemine, and Aander had met her only once, when he and King Cressidin had visited the Jinn tribe and agreed to the engagement. But Rydara knew Jemine was beautiful, and Aander had been excited about marrying her. Most of his friends were married already, and a few had little ones. Aander had been waiting for a match that would benefit the tribes for a long time.

But he merely shrugged. "I hardly know Jemine, and my honor is more important than my role in this alliance. Family is more important. *You* are more important. Besides," he added, "if the Alterrans are as powerful as you say, the alliance is pointless." His brow furrowed, and when he spoke again, his tone was somber. "If everything is as you say, I couldn't protect Kell, and I don't even remember it. I'm useless to the tribes against this threat."

"You really believe me, then? Over your own memory?"

Aander glanced at her, nodding slowly. "The truth is, I remember *that* we saw Tessex and that Kell asked if he could stay there, but I don't remember going, and I don't remember the conversation I had with Kell. I just have this image of the Alterran queen and general confronting us in the middle of a town of healthy tribespeople, and I remember feeling very sheepish while Kell waved goodbye. But before and after that, there's nothing until our ride in the wagon. And when I think about Kell, I think he's safe in Tessex ... but I don't *feel* like he's safe in Tessex. I feel ... loss."

"Loss" was the word he settled on, but Rydara could feel an echo of the emotion that clouded him in her Knowing, and it had many layers. Grief, helplessness. Rage.

It was similar to what she had sensed in him at the moment of Kell's death, though fainter.

"They're not all-powerful, then." Rydara had begun to think of the Alterran sorcerers as if they were, so the gaps in their work on Aander's memory encouraged her. "They created a false memory for you, but it's flawed."

"I would never have noticed if you hadn't drawn my attention to it. But yes. Besides the fact that I'd never believe you would lie about something like this, the way I remember it makes no sense."

Rydara nodded. "I'm not going to the Rishara," she announced. "I'm going to cross the Waste."

Aander cocked his head. "You're really convinced that these sorcerers are the ancient demons from Landri's stories, then? The Mighty Ones?"

"They used at least two magics each—maybe three—besides what they did to your memory, and the queen offered me immortality in exchange for my soul. But it doesn't matter if they are exactly the same thing as the ancient demons or not. They have powers we can't fight, and if there's even a chance that there's a land out there somewhere where more powerful sorcerers live, I have to look for it. We need help."

"If the Mighty Ones return..." Aander quoted a line from an old Rishara rhyme. Rydara remembered repeating it line by line after her mother, and then after Aander. Aander had told her all Rishara mothers ensured their children learned it by heart.

"My child, make haste, make haste," Rydara continued the poem. "The meek may yet our ransom earn in the Land Beyond the Waste."

The message was clear enough, though Rydara had never suspected the Mighty Ones were real or that they might actually return. Even now, it seemed like a stretch.

But Rydara was unwilling to do nothing, and the last thing she wanted was to ride off and join the Rishara. The people of the tribes may have seen a Rishara girl when they looked at her, but that had never been what she was.

Her loyalty had always been to the tribes.

"What about the White Plague?" Aander asked.

No one knew what caused the White Plague, but the wasting sickness claimed one in three from the tribes who passed through the Hahiroth Waste. They had long since learned to avoid it. "The White Plague isn't as common among the Rishara," Rydara said. "Having mother's blood may finally be good for something. But that's why you can't come with me."

Aander shook his head, a deep sadness in his eyes. "You would risk your life to save a people who reject you. It's a good thing I followed you. Now we might actually have a chance."

"Aander, you can't come. You're not Rishara, and you have too much to live for." Rydara glared at him. "You can't just throw it all away on a fool's errand."

"But you can?" Aander challenged.

"I have nothing to throw away."

"What about your life?"

"Go home, Aander," Rydara said. She stood up, determined to make him obey. "When you get there, tell Father..." She gazed off into the distance while she considered what final message she would give to the man who had raised her. The man she had never quite been able to please.

I'm sorry the priests didn't let you marry my mother. I'm sorry my skin always broadcast your shame.

I'm sorry Aander hates you because of me. I never asked for that.
She shook her head. "I guess I have no father. Never mind. Goodbye, Aander."

She walked to the horse, but Aander hurried after her and grabbed the reins. "Don't be stubborn, Rydara. I'm not going to let you ride into the Waste alone. It may be a fool's errand, but you're right, it's also our best hope. And you need me."

"No, you are not coming!" Rydara shoved him away from the horse, and his eyes widened in surprise. "I only told you where I was going so you would realize you have to let me go alone."

Rydara tried to mount the horse, but Aander pulled her back down. "Rydara." She pushed him again, hard, but he grabbed her arm and pulled her closer, wrapping his arms around her while she struggled. "Rydara, stop it! This is ridiculous."

Rydara stilled, breathing heavily. Her efforts were futile; Aander was too strong. He released her, and she rubbed her arm, glaring at him.

"Just how are you planning to survive a trip through the Waste by yourself?" Aander demanded.

Rydara tightened her fists in frustration. She had no answer. She had only enough food with her for three days, and it would take longer than that to cross the Hahiroth. Aander knew how to live off the land. She did not.

Maybe a part of her had been planning to die in the wasteland, unwanted and alone.

"If sending a delegation across the Waste is the best hope for the tribes, don't you think we should at least give it a *chance* of success?" Aander pressed. "The White Plague is worth considering, but with only the two of us going, odds are neither of us will get it."

"The odds for you aren't much better than a coinflip, Aander," she protested.

"It's a coin worth tossing." Aander grinned. "Besides, you know me. I never get sick."

Rydara shook her head. He was being too flippant—but what else could she say? He had no right to risk his life because everyone loved him?

It sounded childish, and maybe it was. "Do you really want to cross the Hahiroth with me?" she asked, defeated. "You're not going to try to talk me out of it?"

Aander smiled. "Actually, I'm glad that's where you're going. I would have gone with you to the Rishara, but I'd have been useless there. In the Hahiroth I might actually be able to help—you *and* the tribes."

"You would have joined the Rishara with me? Why?"

"I have promises to keep." Aander lifted an admonishing finger when Rydara opened her mouth. "And not just to you. I promised Landri I'd look out for you. No one can release me from that oath, now—even if I wished it, which I don't."

"Landri understood our situation," Rydara repeated her father's words grimly. He had known the woman far better than she, and it fit with what Rydara did remember. Her mother had never argued with the king. She had modeled nothing but deference and gratitude toward him and taught Rydara the same, though it had always been harder for Rydara. "And I'm not a child anymore. She couldn't have meant for that promise to bind you forever."

"That's what Father would say," Aander said, dismissive. "Sometimes it feels as though he and I remember two completely different women." He met Rydara's eyes. "Landri would have given her life for you or for me. She would have expected us to do no less for each other—no matter how old we get."

He held her gaze a moment longer, and Rydara sensed how earnestly he believed that, and how important he felt it was for her to accept his truth about the woman she had known so little.

All Rydara knew for sure about her mother was that she had left Rydara all alone with a people that would always view her as an outsider.

"Come on," Aander said. He mounted the horse. "Let's go get some more horses."

Rydara sighed and pulled herself up behind him. She had not wanted this for Aander, but it seemed he was giving her no choice.

The more selfish part of her was glad he had come.

The day was cold but cloudless, and the trees were far enough apart to let sunlight reach the ground, where the snow glittered with diamonds of reflected light. Rydara was still banished, but her father's rejection was easier to bear with Aander for company.

They made good time that day and the next. Aander led them straight as an arrow to where they had left the horses, and Rydara heard Astral's distinctive whinny when they drew near. The mare trotted to her, the lead dangling from her halter, and Rydara grinned in delight. She had been able to break free after all.

Then Rydara noticed a folded parchment secured under the animal's halter. She unfolded it slowly.

Rydara,
Know that your father offered to banish you before my associate Numbran even raised the topic. None of his magic was required. When you tire of wasting your loyalty on a people who care nothing for you, reconsider my offer. I know your value, and my soldiers have instructions to bring you directly to me if you approach any of our camps.
Accept the return of these horses as a gesture of my goodwill.
—Lux Lucisa, Queen of Alterra

The other horses were still tied up, but they had been cared for. The packs that Aander, Rydara, and Kell had left nearby were undisturbed.

"What's wrong?" Aander asked, noticing Rydara's trepidation. She showed him the note. "I guess we should be grateful," he said. "They don't mean to capture us."

"I guess," Rydara said, but the note filled her with dread. The Alterran queen still wanted her soul. For a moment there in Tessex, Rydara had thought about letting her have it, and though she still did not understand what that would have meant, she suspected it would have been a terrible mistake.

The Hahiroth Waste lay thirty miles to the west. On the way, Aander and Rydara crossed paths with the Kerim tribe, which was heading south to escape the Alterrans. They traded their extra horses for more food and a few weapons and snares.

The Kerim had heard of Aander and the growing Noraani alliance, and they were shocked that he was abandoning it to strike out through the Waste. They tried to persuade him and Rydara not to go, sharing stories of the White Plague and its devastation. At Aander's prompting, Rydara told them what she had seen in Tessex. The dreadful power of the Alterran queen and general. Kell's murder. The mass grave.

Aander explained that they had to seek the Land Beyond the Waste in case there was power there that could help. The Kerim had heard of the place from their dealings with the Rishara, but they assured Aander that no one had ever gone there and returned to tell the tale. They did not believe it was a real place, and Rydara could tell they had their doubts about her story, too.

Still, it was plain they feared the Alterrans. Aander encouraged them to seek refuge with the Noraani alliance, and Rydara could tell his words found traction with some. Watching him establish such effortless influence over people they had just met reminded Rydara how lucky she was that he had come with her. If they did find any elves in the wasteland, Aander would have a much better chance of persuading them to help.

Rydara could plan talking points as well as him—if not better—but she had next to no practice delivering them. Aander seemed to come alive in front of an audience, but for Rydara, being the center of attention never ended well. The feeling of too many eyes on her made her want to run away and hide.

They spent one night with the Kerim and set out early the next morning. When they approached the river that bordered the wasteland, Aander checked his horse, and Rydara drew Astral to a stop beside him.

The river was shallow and narrow here. Rydara might have taken it for a stream, except she knew it ran all the way from Alterra to the sea. Green grass poked through the snow on their side of it, running all the way up to the river's bank.

The far side of the river was brown and barren. As far as the eye could reach, there was not a single blade of grass or even a snowflake—just hard-packed soil, close to sand or gravel in its consistency. A few rock formations reared up in the distance.

According to the tribes who ventured as far as the river, whenever it rained or snowed, not a drop fell on the far bank. Sheets of rain cut off abruptly over the river, eerily following the same meandering line.

The tribes, the Alterrans, and the Rishara all had their own accounts of what had happened here, but everyone agreed on one thing. The Waste was cursed.

"The Hahiroth Waste," Aander pronounced, gazing across the river. He was smiling. "They are going to sing songs about us, Rydara. The disinherited children of Noraan, braving the dangers of the desert wasteland to save all the people of Kilethe. And Lanimshar," he added. Lanimshar was the name of the territory south of the mountains, which, like Kilethe, lay between the armies of Alterra and Jeshimoth. News from there told of the Jeshim army advancing to meet Alterra, committing many of the same atrocities.

Rydara shook her head, amazed at her brother's smile. "Who will sing for us if we die in the Waste? We may never find what we're looking for."

"The Kerim will sing for us." Aander shrugged, still smiling. "I didn't say it would be a happy song."

"And if Alterra kills all the Kerim, and everyone else?"

"Then we'll sing with them in the Realm of Porphyreus." Aander gazed somberly at the wasteland before turning to look at Rydara. "But let's do our best to make sure it doesn't come to that. You ready to find some of these mythical Loyal Ones? Remind General Dameires and any other ancient demons that might be prowling about why they lost the Celestial Rebellion?"

Rydara managed half a smile as she looked back at him. "Who better for the task than the Self-Exiled Prince and his kid sister?"

"You mean the Unbuyable Knower and her brother?"

The title chilled Rydara. If she never had to contemplate giving up her soul again, it would be too soon. "Race you to the Waste!" she challenged, kicking Astral into a gallop. Aander cursed and urged his horse after her.

Rydara laughed as she loosened the reins and rose in the stirrups to prepare for the jump. Astral sailed over the river, and Rydara brought her to a stop on the far side, turning to watch as Aander and his horse splashed inelegantly through the water to join them.

"I win," she announced.

"Yes, you won the race of ten spans in which you had a five-span head start," Aander grumbled as they rode into the wasteland. "Very impressive. Nightmare and I will be happy to take the two of you on in a fair steeplechase any time."

"Nightmare?"

Aander patted the mane of his black mare. It was not a warhorse, and therefore not Aander's favorite mount. Though he often rode it on longer journeys, he had not previously given it a name. According to tribal breeding standards, it was as fine an animal as Astral, though Rydara would never believe any horse quite as fine as her bay. "Any animal braving the Hahiroth Waste with us deserves a name. Besides, they'll need something to call her in the songs."

Rydara studied the landscape as they rode on. It was all harsh grays and browns. She glanced behind her at the snowy grassland they were leaving behind and wondered briefly if they would ever see it again.

It was easy to imagine dying in this cursed place.

"What did Mother tell you about the elves?" Rydara asked, determined to focus on something less morose. "I remember your stories about them and the flying beasts they rode. But I never knew how much you made up just for fun."

"The dragons, yes," Aander smiled. "I didn't make those up. They came straight from the Rishara histories, according to Landri."

"Could the elves really communicate with them?"

"That's what she said. They could speak to many animals, and even some plants. They valued life and all living things— even the ancient demons. They didn't kill them at the end of the Celestial Rebellion, you know. They found another solution."

"What was it?"

"I don't know, but maybe they knew it was only temporary, and that's why all the Rishara teach their children that poem. If Queen Lux and General Dameires really are two of the ancient demons returned, I'm going to have a few words with the elves about their foreign policy. Sounds like their stance on rampaging demons could use sharper teeth."

Rydara smiled and pressed Aander for more information. By the end of the day, he had her half-convinced this was a grand adventure, after all—not just the last-ditch attempt of a reckless exile to find meaning for her existence. Aander talked of returning at the head of an army of flying sorcerers who would quickly subdue both the Jeshim and Alterran armies and teach everyone a more peaceful way of life. Rydara had not thought so far ahead when she decided to come here, but now that she had Aander, it almost felt possible.

If anyone could defy the dangers of the Waste and return triumphant with the power to save the tribes, it was her brother.

He showed her how to set up snares before they made camp. Rydara was half-convinced they were the only living things in the entire Waste, but by the morning of the third day they had caught a jackrabbit. Aander taught her how to skin it. It was a gruesome process, but the taste was tolerable once the animal had been cooked. Their stores of food were already nearly gone, despite their careful rationing. They had to take what they could get.

As the days went by, they rode steadily northwest, using the sun to guide them. If the Land Beyond the Waste existed where the stories placed it, it would be nestled at the foot of the cliffs on the far side of the wasteland—the impassable cliffs that no one had been able to travel through when approaching from Alterra or the sea.

They drank as little water as they could. They tried sucking on pebbles to assuage their thirst, as the people in Landri's stories had done while crossing the Waste. Rydara could not tell if the pebbles made a difference. The thirst was relentless.

Aander did his best to keep their morale up with his stories, but Rydara could tell he was worried by how little they caught in their snares. On the sixth day he pointed out the tracks of a curled-horn sheep and told her they must not be far from an oasis. By the next morning, their waterskins were completely dry. They did not talk at all that day.

They nearly fainted with relief when they saw the oasis up ahead: a large pool with dense green trees and bushes growing all around its edges, tucked between the gently sloping dunes. They crossed the last hundred spans with renewed energy, and after they quenched their thirst, Aander taught Rydara a song about an elf named Eldaerenth and his duel with the demon Os Noxcint. They refilled all their waterskins before riding out the next day.

Without her brother, Rydara knew she would have died in the desert. If hunger had not killed her, the loneliness would have. She was so glad of his company, her attempts to leave him behind seemed laughable.

Until the tenth day, when he got sick.

Chapter 5

The Waste

It started with a light cough.

"Breathed in wrong," Aander said after the first fit—just four coughs in a row, as though he needed to clear his throat. Rydara almost believed him.

It was hours before he coughed again. Still only a few coughs, and Aander took a small sip of water. He said that perhaps he had been rationing it too harshly.

But they both knew.

By the end of the day, the cough had developed a hacking sound, and it left Aander breathless. He helped Rydara set up camp and care for the horses, but he worked more slowly than usual, and she did much of it by herself.

Nights in the Hahiroth felt cold—mostly due to the contrast with the heat of the days—but their blankets had been sufficient until then. That night, Aander got up to move his bedroll closer to the fire three times.

Rydara got up and moved next to him, combining their blankets.

"Sorry," he said as she lay down. As if it were somehow his fault that he was sick. "And thanks. I couldn't quite get warm enough."

Rydara stared up at the stars, cold and distant points of light in a sky as black as her existence. She wished she had never told him where she was going. Then she could have given him the slip after he caught up with her, and he would have looked for her among the Rishara. He would have been safe there.

"I should never have let you come," she said.

Aander shifted, and Rydara felt him shiver. "Don't think that," he said. "I didn't give you a choice. And I don't regret it. You would have died out here without me."

"Better me than you," Rydara whispered.

"Stop that," Aander rebuked her. He started coughing, and his body shook with the force of it. He rolled onto his side, facing the fire, and Rydara regretted speaking.

He should not be wasting his energy trying to console her.

His breathing was heavy after the coughing ceased, but when it slowed, he spoke again. "I gave Landri my word. And the tribes need us to find help. It is my right and my duty to spend my life on this mission—if it comes to that. But I'm not dead yet. You don't need to talk like it's already over."

"Nobody survives the White Plague, Aander."

"Maybe it's not the White Plague."

Rydara did not answer. Aander had not had a cold in years, and the White Plague always began with a cough.

She could hear the lie in her Knowing, anyway. Aander knew what he had.

"Or maybe," he tried again, "the elves know how to cure it. Nobody has gone far enough to ask them. First time for everything."

"Maybe," Rydara murmured. Far above, the stars blurred and swam. A tear leaked from Rydara's left eye, tracing a warm and salty track toward her ear.

Every drop of moisture was precious out here, and she could ill afford the waste.

Please, Virens, she prayed to the Green Goddess, the goddess of life. *Please, let the elves have a cure. Let us find them before it is too late.*

She got up before dawn the next day. Their snares were empty, but it hardly mattered. The White Plague would kill Aander before starvation did.

Water, though, would still present a problem. The White Plague killed in seven days—eight at most. Their water would last for six.

What Rydara did not know was how long Aander would be able to travel. He was already weak from the fever. When Rydara woke him in the pre-dawn dark with both horses saddled and ready to go, he did not complain. He was tired, but he was able to ride his horse, even when he coughed so hard Rydara was sure he would fall off.

Rydara wanted to ride through the night. They had traveled a long way across the Waste, and the terrain was changing, rising up in plateaus and rock formations that made the horses' footing uncertain and forced them miles out of their way. But the night sky was clear, cold, and cloudless, and they could see well enough to travel. Rydara did not know how much farther they would have to go. They should cover as much ground as possible while they could.

Less than an hour after sunset, though, Aander mumbled that he needed to stop. He slid off his horse without waiting for a reply and sat down. He was shivering, and when Rydara wrapped him with a blanket, he apologized for being too weak to help her set up camp.

Rydara shushed him and built a fire. With some coaxing, she got Astral to lie down next to Aander to help keep him warm. He mumbled his thanks and was asleep within minutes.

That was the second day.

The third day passed in much the same manner, but Aander practically fell off his horse at sunset and was asleep before Rydara brought blankets to him. After she set up camp and made Astral lie down next to him, Rydara took Nightmare and rode to the nearest bluff.

It was a hard climb, made worse by the fact that Rydara had left their water behind. She was weak and dizzy when she reached the top, but she had a clear view over the Waste.

She thought she could see the cliffs that made up its border. They were taller and stacked closer together than the bluffs, plateaus, and boulders that broke up the intervening landscape. They were not so very far. Perhaps three days away, if she could find a route for them through the jagged landscape.

But she saw no sign of elves, nor of any civilization.

Maybe it's on the other side of those cliffs, she told herself. *Just out of sight.*

Rydara wanted to believe it. She wanted to hold onto hope.

She could get them as far as those cliffs—or, at the very least, she could try. But she knew in her bones that it would make no difference.

They were alone out here.

Rydara stared at the landscape for hours, trying to memorize it. It was hard to guess what might lie in the shadows between the towering rock formations, but Rydara did her best to plan a passable route to the cliffs. Then she planned another, and another, just in case. She guessed at three places where she might find an oasis, based on pockets of heavy plant life and, in one case, the glint of moonlight on water in the shadows of the surrounding bluffs. That one was close—a two-days' ride at most.

Only then did she take Nightmare back to camp. She drank deeply, confident she could soon renew their water supply. When Aander stirred in another coughing fit, she made him drink, too.

The fourth day of Aander's illness, Rydara had to help him get onto his horse, and after an hour of riding, it became clear he could not keep going by himself. Rydara mounted behind him, and they rode double on Nightmare for half the day with Rydara helping to support him, feeling his body shake when he coughed. Then they rode Astral until sunset.

That evening, Aander coughed up blood.

There was nothing to give him to ease the pain, no way to relieve the fever. Nothing Rydara could do except build a fire and try to keep him warm. Every few hours, he woke up coughing, and Rydara woke, too, exhausted and desperate and helpless.

"Here," she said after the third or fourth time he woke, crouching in front of him to offer the waterskin.

He had become uncharacteristically biddable in his illness, but this time he refused. "I'm not thirsty," he said, the words coming out in a dry rasp.

"Drink anyway," Rydara insisted. "You need it."

"We'll run out."

"There's an oasis close by. We'll get there tomorrow."

Aander did not answer, and he made no move to take the waterskin. Rydara wrapped her arm around his shoulders, trying to prop him up so he could drink the water. Astral, lying beside Aander, opened her eyes and whuffed at Rydara, but the horse stayed where she was.

Aander was already easier to move, his body wasting away with the fever. He did not fight Rydara, but he turned his head away when she brought the waterskin to his mouth.

"I don't—" he started to say. Then he coughed again, a deep, wracking cough that sounded like it would tear his throat apart. Rydara held him through it, squeezing her eyes shut and hating herself for bringing him here.

How she wished she could be sick in his place.

"I don't think," Aander continued when the cough subsided, still gasping to catch his breath, "I can ride again tomorrow."

"You will," Rydara said, bringing the waterskin back to his mouth. "I'll help you. Drink, and then sleep."

Rydara tilted the waterskin, and Aander choked down a few drops, knowing better than to let them spill. But he was still trying to pull away, so Rydara lowered the waterskin. She eased him back down onto his side. She stood.

"Rydara," Aander rasped, his eyes finding hers in the moonlight.

That was all he said, but she could see the rest on his face. The water could not save him. Neither could the oasis. He was dying, and he knew it.

He was giving up.

"You will make it to the oasis," Rydara said, her voice firm.

Aander took a ragged breath and let it out in a deep sigh. His eyes fluttered closed, and his breathing settled back into the rhythm of sleep. Rydara went back to her own blankets and tried to get some rest before morning.

But the argument was not over. Aander's fever was higher when the sun rose on the fifth day, and his body shook with shivers. Between coughing fits, he mumbled incoherently.

The delirium was setting in.

Rydara tried not to think about it as she loaded the horses. Today, she put all their baggage on Nightmare.

Despite how rapidly his body was wasting away, Aander was still too heavy for Rydara to lift, and today, he was too far gone to help her move him. Rydara coaxed Astral to lie down next to him again, and then she pushed and pulled him over the horse's body until he was lying facedown in the horse's mane, his legs draped across the saddle. Rydara turned his head sideways so the mane wouldn't suffocate him. Then she sat behind him and leaned forward, so she was practically lying on top of him, and buried her hands in Astral's mane, holding her brother in place.

"All right, Astral," she said. "Let's try this."

She made a clicking sound, and Astral stood. Aander shifted dangerously. Rydara nearly fell off with him, but she clung tightly to Astral with her legs and her hands, and they made it.

Riding that day was slow and difficult. Rydara spent all of it worrying about the oasis. Perhaps she had not really seen the moon glinting on water, or perhaps she had chosen the wrong path through the rocky landscape. Maybe it was farther away than it had seemed.

Her worries persisted even as she began to hear what sounded like running water, but the oasis was just where she had guessed. As evening fell, they rode up to a large pool nestled in the rocks between three bluffs. A little waterfall tumbled into it from a depression halfway up one of the cliffs, and a smattering of plant life grew around the pool's edges. A few rydar flowers peeked out from among the shrubs.

Rydara's face split into a grin.

"Aander, we made it!" she exulted, squeezing her brother in a kind of hug. "Another oasis! And you thought I couldn't navigate without you."

Aander coughed violently, wiping the smile from Rydara's face.

The horses were happy to see the water. Nightmare splashed into the pool and drank, and Rydara spoke a harsh word to keep Astral from following suit. Aander was shivering enough already without getting wet.

The dismount was inelegant. It ended with Aander falling on top of Rydara in a heap on the rocks while Astral splashed off to join Nightmare.

Rydara called Nightmare back and unpacked the animal. She settled Aander in his blankets before unsaddling both horses and brushing them. Then she made a fire, set a few snares, and used their new water supply to make a soup for Aander out of the plants that grew around the pool. It tasted terrible, and she did not blame Aander for coughing it up. He had no appetite anyway, but she made him drink water, and she used a wet cloth to clean his face and hands.

After all of that had been done, Rydara took a turn in the water. Her body was caked in sweat and grit from the desert. The heat of the day had been oppressive, especially with Aander's burning body in her arms for so many hours, and it was only after the pain began to subside that Rydara realized how her head had been pounding.

Aander was sleeping soundly when Rydara changed into dry clothes and laid what she had been wearing out by the fire. She was glad for it. He had not exactly been awake during their ride, but the constant jostling had done him no favors.

What does it matter? the darker part of Rydara whispered. *He's just going to die anyway, sleep or no sleep.*

The thought filled her with an anguish too deep to process, and Rydara shoved it away as she lay down to sleep. She watched Aander as he slept on the other side of the fire, huddled next to Astral under his blankets. He was pale and wan, and his body shook with the occasional shiver—but he looked almost peaceful. Rydara could almost pretend he wasn't dying.

Her eyes snapped open hours later to the sound of his deep, wracking cough.

Wearily, she got up and brought him some water. He was still feverish, but the delirium seemed to have subsided. For now.

Aander accepted the water, looking across the fire at the oasis Rydara had been so excited to find. He managed half a smile after he drank.

"You learn fast," he rasped, and Rydara's heart wrenched.

"There are cliffs to the north, maybe two days from here," Rydara said, sitting cross-legged in front of him. "If there's an elven homeland out here, it must be behind them. We can still get there. There's time."

Aander just looked at her. His blue eyes, normally so optimistic and full of life, carried the weight of unspeakable weariness, and worse. An unacceptable truth.

"It has to be there." Rydara's voice broke. "You have time. We have to see."

"You'll see." Aander was hoarse, and Rydara could hear how the words scraped and pained him physically even as they tore at her soul.

"No," Rydara whispered. Her eyes stung, but they didn't fill. They had access to water, now, but her body was still too dry for crying.

"It only..." Aander breathed heavily, his lungs working hard to force the words, "gets worse, Rydara. You know."

Aander's illness was following the trajectory he had once described to her in his stories. Baolan the Slayer and eleven of his troublemakers had pursued the elves into the Waste when humanity had turned against them after their triumph over the demons, chasing the secret of their powers. Four of them, including Baolan, had fallen sick in their second week of travel. First, cough. Then fever, weakness, and chills, all steadily worsening over four or five days. Delirium set in around the same time that they started coughing up blood.

On the fifth or sixth day, when their companions thought them as good as dead, the delirium turned violent. It came in waves, and when it came, men who had been too weak to hold up their heads were infused with a hellish vigor. They screamed and thrashed. Their bodies were emaciated, and they burned with fever, but in the grips of their hallucinations, they could stand. They could fight. They could grab weapons and slash at those around them, and though they had little of their former skill, they were impervious to pain.

The first two to fall sick reached the delirium near the same hour, and they killed each other before their companions could pull them apart. The third attacked a healthy man days later and was killed by him in the scuffle. But Baolan the Slayer, the fourth and last man to reach delirium, killed seven of his healthy companions, and no one could bring him down. The last man of the company fled and hid until Baolan's delirium passed.

He found Baolan dead in the camp when he returned, finally claimed by his wounds.

The stories the Kerim had told them were similar, though those foolish enough to risk the Waste in their stories had known to tie up their companions who fell ill. But that wasn't always enough. At the height of the delirium, the sick were sometimes strong enough to break their bonds. But regardless of their strength, their violence, or their companions' ability to keep them from injuring themselves, everyone died within eight days of their first cough.

It was considered merciful to kill them before the delirium worsened.

Aander kept holding Rydara's gaze, lying helpless and shivering in his blankets, and Rydara knew what he wanted to ask even without the benefit of her Knowing, which she was doing her best to ignore.

She couldn't do it. She *wouldn't* do it. He was her *brother*.

"You have to..." Aander started, and Rydara stared back at him in dismay, twitching her head in an almost imperceptible "no."

Could I really refuse him? she asked herself.

"... leave me," Aander finished, closing his eyes in resignation. Even in dying, he considered her.

"Tell Jemine..." he went on, the words rasping and slow, "that I'm sorry. I wanted to marry her. I think ... I would have loved her ... well..."

"I know you would have, Aander," Rydara said, kneeling beside him and clasping his hand. "You would have been the best husband in all the tribes."

"But there will be ... another man for her. Only one brother ... for you." Aander squeezed her hand weakly, and Rydara leaned over and pressed her forehead against his, clasping his hand to her chest.

"Don't leave me, Aander," she begged. "How could I possibly go on without you?"

"I'd stay if I could..." Aander mumbled. Rydara pulled back, still holding his hand, and found the ghost of a smile on his lips.

She couldn't smile back. Not this time.

"You'll find a way," Aander rasped, his smile fading. "You have to. Do it ... for me?"

Rydara was shaking her head no, but she couldn't say no. Not to her dying brother. "I'll try, but I can't leave you. Not yet. You still have time before ... before..."

"Tomorrow," Aander said, the word as stern as he could make it. "I'd never forgive you if you let me hurt ... the horses. After I named one and all."

Rydara choked out a laugh that was more of a dry sob, and Aander managed a small smile. Rydara slept next to him in Astral's place, even though his coughing woke her every few hours and the heat from his burning body left her sweaty and hot.

Rydara rose early on the sixth day of his illness and tied his hands together in front of him while he moaned and mumbled through another wave of delirium. He was so wasted away that the prospect of his becoming violent seemed laughable, but she tied his feet together, too. Then she dragged him into the shade of a bordering bluff.

What are you doing, Rydara? she asked herself. Keeping him from hurting himself would only prolong the inevitable. She could not bring him with her any farther—certainly not as far as the cliffs—so he was as good as dead already. If she were a smarter person, she would say her goodbyes and ride away as fast as she could, not looking back.

If she were a better person, she would end his suffering before she left.

After checking her snares and finding a jackrabbit, Rydara packed the horses and took them a mile back the way they had come, where a gentle slope let her lead them up one of the bluffs that overlooked the oasis. Aander had asked her to leave him today, and in a way, she was leaving him. She and the horses were far enough away to be safe up here.

But she couldn't just ride away. Not while he was still breathing.

She tied the horses to a tall cactus, made a fire, and cleaned and cooked her rabbit. She tried making stew again, and it tasted a little less horrible than before. She could hear Aander moaning and thrashing below as the delirium grew worse.

He quieted down around noon, falling into a heavy sleep, and Rydara took him some stew and water. His breathing was shallow and ragged, and his face and body were bruised and scratched where he had thrashed against the rocks. He did not wake up when Rydara tried to prop him up and spoon-feed him. Half of it ran down his face, and Rydara soon gave up, settling for cleaning his scrapes with a wet rag.

She was torturing herself. If Aander had been aware enough to speak, he would have forced her to ride away before he grew dangerous.

There was little shade in the oasis when she left, but Rydara moved Aander where the shadows would lengthen as the day wore on. Another meaningless kindness.

Aander broke his bonds during the next wave of delirium and attacked a small tree near the water. Rydara, having retreated to her perch atop the bluff, turned her back when it became too hard to watch. He screamed while he fought the plants, his voice hoarse and enraged, and Rydara buried her head between her knees to try to keep out the sound.

She had thought she wanted to be here, to stay with her brother to the bitter end. She had not realized the end would feel so pointless.

He grew quiet again near sunset. Rydara waited until full dark, making sure the wave of delirium had passed, before making her way down the bluff.

His scrapes were deeper and more numerous, and his ankle was swollen. He must have twisted it during his mad attack against the plants. He'd torn up all three of the trees growing on this side of the pool. Branches, leaves, and pale blue rydar petals lay broken and scattered on the ground around him.

Rydara washed Aander's scrapes and bound his ankle. Then she kissed his forehead — still burning hot with fever.

"You were the best brother I could have asked for, Aander," she told him softly. "Far better than I deserved. I'm sorry I wasn't a better sister to you. I should have found a way to make you go home." Rydara's voice caught, and her eyes stung. She sniffed and looked up at the stars, so clear and bright in the cloudless sky, as they always were in the Waste.

So indifferent to her suffering. So indifferent to this whole cursed land.

"I will try to keep going like you wanted. I'll try. But I don't know if I can." Rydara kissed his forehead again, and she gave his hand one final squeeze. "Goodbye, Aander."

Then she turned and walked away.

She didn't go back to the horses. She didn't know why, or where she was going instead—just that she wanted to be far away when Aander woke again and started screaming. She couldn't watch anymore.

She wandered aimlessly through the night. Bluffs reared up in her path, forcing her to circle around them, and in the end, she lost all sense of direction. She was not far enough away when the screaming started.

Rydara fell to her knees on the desert floor. A keening sound tore from her chest. Prostrating herself on the ground, she cried, aloud, to the Six, begging them to have mercy on her and save her brother. She promised she would journey to the holy city of Lystra and become a thrice-ordained priestess to Virens, Ignescens, and Coelestens, the three goddesses. She promised she would give all the wealth she earned in life to Xanthinus, the god of fortune, and dedicate one son each to the orders of Aurantiacus and Porphyreus.

Then, since she figured a half-Rishara priestess might prove unacceptable to the Red Goddess, she promised to sacrifice her beloved Astral on Ignescens' altar—if only any of the Six would appear and grant her one boon.

No one answered. Rydara fell silent, her breath sounding heavily in her ears. Aander still screamed in the distance. Her eyes, which had been dry for days, finally filled with moisture, and tears ran down her cheeks.

Then Rydara prayed to the god of her mother's people, the All-Color, offering to forswear the Six and dedicate her life to the Rishara way.

Aander's screaming continued.

Rydara rose to her feet, cursing herself for a fool. What god would speak to a half-breed outcast? *One just as quick to forsake her gods and her people as her licentious mother?*

Rydara stumbled forward in the dark, her vision swimming with tears. She had to get away from this place, away from Aander's screams.

But then she paused, a strange sensation in her gut. It pulled her toward her left.

It took her a moment to recognize her Knowing as the source.

Rydara turned, following the draw as it led her around another bluff and then upward. This was unlike any other Knowing she had experienced. She had no sense of what awaited or whether it was good or bad. She did not even feel where the source was located, only the path she was meant to take. The climb became difficult, but Rydara hurried to follow the prompting, leaving herself sweating and breathless as she finally pulled herself to the top of a plateau.

An enormous creature stood before her, silhouetted by moon and stars. It was easily ten times the size of her father's largest stallion—as large as the Alterran queen's pavilion. It had four legs, but it was covered in scales, and two enormous wings, clawed and almost bat-like, sprouted from its spiny back. Its neck was nearly as long as its body, and its head was rimmed in spikes. A long and snake-like tail curled behind it.

The creature folded its wings and lowered its head toward Rydara, bringing her face-to-face with its slitted, yellow eyes. Rydara started to step backward, nearly falling off the plateau, but the creature's tail wrapped around her, steadying her, and she was flooded with a sense of welcome and comfort.

This creature was one of the elves' mythical dragons, Rydara suddenly Knew—and it had invited her up here.

Chapter 6

Dragon Rider

"Ciri somno?"

The strange syllables flowed over Rydara with a graceful tenor music. A figure emerged from behind the dragon's shoulder. He was human in form, but taller than any man from the tribes, and he moved with a fluid grace that made him seem one with the sky behind him and the ground he walked upon. It was a grace that no human could achieve, and his ears tapered into delicate points at the top—another feature attributed to his race.

His skin was black. Darker than Rydara's, or even her mother's. As black as the night sky. No one had mentioned this feature to Rydara.

She dropped to her knees. "Please, my lord elf, my brother is dying. Do you know any cure for the desert sickness?"

The man—the *elf*—walked toward her, though the movement seemed to have more in common with the gentle flow of a river than discrete and clumsy human steps. He stopped in front of Rydara, and she could not help but stare. He was dressed in a fitted shirt and breeches beneath a flowing cloak of a color Rydara could not determine in the dark, and a bow and quiver peeked from over his shoulder. His face, smooth and expressionless as he returned Rydara's gaze, seemed to have been etched with an artistry that far exceeded what the gods wasted on human faces. The cheekbones were high and symmetrical, the jaw angled with grace and power, and the eyes large and deep with the secrets of untold years.

He was the most beautiful creature Rydara had ever seen.

"Please?" she repeated, pleading, even as she realized that, of course, he could not understand a word of her strange speech.

Aander's screaming still echoed across the Waste, though, and Rydara pointed toward the sound and then clasped her hands together, hoping the supplicant posture could transcend language. "Can you save him?"

The dragon exhaled next to Rydara—a mannerism that reminded her of Astral's whuff. At the same time, Rydara felt an affirmation through her Knowing, a sense that surely, the elf could do as she asked.

But the affirmation came from the dragon, and Rydara got the distinct sense that it meant the elf *could* help her, rather than that he *would*. The dragon's eyes were fixed on the elf. The elf gave no indication of understanding, and Rydara focused all her attention on him, trying to glean something, anything, with her Knowing.

The elf did understand her. Not her speech, perhaps, but it was obvious what she wanted, and after a moment she felt something stir in him. Something like doubt. Not a "yes"—but not a "no," either.

"Please," she begged, catching a handful of his cloak in her hand. "If there's anything, anything you can try..." Rydara released his cloak, belatedly realizing she had no idea what such a gesture might mean to his culture. Her touch might be an insult, or an unthinkable presumption. "Please." She dropped her eyes.

The strange and graceful creature sank to one knee, folding his hands atop the other, so that he faced her eye to eye. *"Thall ailtaro salorara,"* he said intently, the syllables holding a warning, or perhaps a refusal. *"Dreth somnuria nimthall. Gormail. Nimmaran, varré."* The elf glanced past her at the dragon, and Rydara thought she sensed a rebuke.

The dragon whuffed again, whipping Rydara's hair back in a sudden wind, and she felt scorn radiate from the creature. There was a thread of friendship underlying the reaction, but it was a scathing judgment nonetheless: a judgment directed at the elf.

The elf glanced at Rydara sharply, and she felt as though she had been caught eavesdropping.

"Please," she whispered, clasping her hands again and closing her eyes against the sting of tears. A few escaped anyway. They ran down her face.

The adviser in Rydara noted that this was a dismal beginning to diplomatic relations with a foreign race. This abject plea to save Aander could only hurt her position when the time came to entreat the elves to fight the Alterran demons. But in that moment, Rydara did not care.

She would have given anything to save her brother.

"*Farr*," the elf said to the dragon, reluctant. The dragon lowered its right wing, and the elf grabbed the bony claw extending from the wing's middle ridge and gracefully leapt onto the ridge. He turned and held out a hand toward Rydara. "*Tarest.*"

Under any other circumstances, Rydara would have been too overcome with awe to believe that this mythical being was inviting her to join him on a dragon. But Aander screamed in the distance, and Rydara took the elf's hand.

He closed his hand around hers, his grip strong. Rydara's clumsy feet bore little of her weight as he pulled her onto the midline ridge and led her up the rest of the wing. He settled into a kneeling position between the creature's neck and left shoulder, still holding Rydara's hand, and she slowly knelt beside him. With her free hand, she grasped the spike that protruded from the dragon's spine before her, though the elf held nothing but her hand, and Rydara guessed that was solely for her benefit. The elf spoke another strange word, and the dragon shifted beneath them, spreading its wings. Rydara caught her breath.

The wings beat against the air, and Rydara's stomach lurched in terror as they rose off the plateau. The sensation was dizzying, and Rydara clenched so tightly to the dragon's spike that she would have cut her hand if it had been any sharper.

They sailed through the night sky, staying low over the bluffs. Every time the wings rose and fell to adjust their course, Rydara swayed dangerously, but the elf beside her adjusted for the dragon's motion as if the two were a single entity. It was not until the dragon spiraled down into the rocks, landing thirty spans from the oasis, that Rydara realized she had a death-grip on the elf's hand.

Her embarrassment was drowned out by Aander's screams.

Her brother had crossed the pool and completed his campaign against the plant life. The handful of trees on the far side had all been pulled down and torn to pieces, pieces even smaller than those left strewn on the near bank. Now Aander, soaking wet and bleeding from a dozen places, smashed his fists into the rocks of the far cliffside and scrabbled madly at its crevices, as if seeking to pull it down.

Rydara covered her mouth with her hands.

"*Trydest khyr.*" The elf touched her shoulder, and Rydara Knew that he was telling her to stay. He leapt to the ground, took off the bow and quiver he carried, and moved quickly across the rocks that bordered the pool.

Aander turned and bellowed in rage. He sprinted to meet the elf, and Rydara clutched the dragon's spike in concern.

The elf hardly slowed as he reached Aander, effortlessly evading Aander's attacks as he slipped inside her brother's reach. Then the elf was behind him with both hands on Aander's neck. Aander kicked and swung at empty air, but his efforts soon died away.

Aander collapsed and the elf ducked, pulling Aander across his shoulders in a singular, fluid motion. He walked back toward Rydara, no more encumbered by her brother's weight than he had been by his bow and quiver.

Rydara, breathless with anxiety, looked for a way down from the dragon, and the beast lowered one of its wings. She stumbled across its scales toward the wing and half-slid, half-fell down along it, catching herself on hands and feet on the ground.

She hurried to meet the elf, who was laying her brother on the ground.

"Is he all right?" Rydara asked, sinking to her knees next to Aander. His knuckles were shredded and bloody, his ankle swollen to twice its size, and his left arm bent at an unnatural angle. His breathing seemed shallow, and he still burned with fever. He was not all right. He was dying. "Can you save him?"

The elf made no response, and Rydara sensed doubt with her Knowing. He produced a waterskin from his belt and uncorked it. Reaching inside a pocket of his robe, he then withdrew a small pouch. He opened it and dumped the contents in the water.

The elf knelt next to Aander, across from Rydara, and dribbled some of the water into his mouth.

"Is that a cure?" Rydara asked, excited. The tribes knew of no treatment for the White Plague. "Is that enough? Does he need to swallow it?"

Rydara bit her lip, realizing belatedly that her questions could only be a distraction.

The elf studied her brother, his gaze tracing Aander's many wounds. He looked at Rydara. Then he turned and pointed to the top of the neighboring bluff.

"*Corrom faelest,*" he said. Rydara had left the horses up there, and she understood he wanted her to get them.

She hated to leave Aander, but he was in better hands than hers.

By the time she returned with Astral and Nightmare, both fully loaded and ready to go, the elf had reset Aander's arm, bound his ankle, and bandaged both his hands. Aander was still unconscious.

"Will he wake up?" Rydara asked.

"*Farr. Saeleth.*"

Rydara could not guess what the words meant, or even whether the elf had understood her. She continued to sense only doubt from him with her Knowing. Doubt, and perhaps reluctance.

The dragon snorted. Rydara felt a wave of confidence from the creature. She turned to look at it, and the creature lowered and raised its head.

Was that a nod? Rydara wondered.

The creature bobbed its head again. Nightmare reared, balking at the movement from the massive reptile. The elf moved to take the horse's lead and spoke soothingly to her in his strange tongue. After calming Nightmare, he turned to Astral and spoke to her as well. Astral whuffed in response, and Rydara wondered if the two of them could understand each other, as Aander's stories had suggested.

Finally, the elf looked at Rydara. *"Athulash pyrral,"* he said, nodding to the dragon. *"Lifendavòn corrom,"* he added with a glance at the horses.

Rydara nodded mutely. They would take the dragon. What the elf had said about the horses, Rydara could not guess, but it did not matter. She would agree to whatever he decided.

The elf walked back to Aander and lifted him again. The dragon lowered a wing, and the elf climbed up to the middle ridge, making it look easy to walk the ramped, uneven surface with a fully-grown man lying across his shoulders. He turned and held out a hand for Rydara.

"Tarest." It was the same invitation he had used before. Perhaps it meant "come."

Rydara took his hand and climbed up the dragon's wing, kneeling behind the spike near its neck as she had done before. There was more than enough room for the three of them. The elf laid Aander near the dragon's shoulder and crouched next to him, steadying him with a hand. Then he spoke to the dragon, and they lifted off the ground.

Rydara kept a tight grip on the dragon's spike. Her eyes were anxiously glued to her brother, but he did not fall. He did not even sway, held in place by the elf's steady hand.

They flew higher and faster than before. The Waste stretched beneath them, its bluffs and rock formations shrinking to resemble representations of themselves on a map. The desert seemed endless, dark and foreboding under the night sky, and Rydara wondered where the elf was taking them. Could there be a large settlement of his people tucked behind the northern cliffs, as she had hoped? Or was he one of only a few? Perhaps he lived alone with his family and dragon in some nearby cave, eking out a living from the desert rocks.

Would there be enough of them to challenge the Alterrans?

The northern cliffs were still up ahead in the distance when everything changed. One minute, they were flying over the barren wasteland, and then suddenly there was a forest beneath them. The trees were thin and as tall as the bluffs, packed together and bursting with foliage, and they stretched out over rolling hills. A river looped through the forest, broad and resplendent with reflected moonlight.

"What—" Rydara, gripping the dragon's spike even more tightly, slowly turned her head to look back.

The desert was receding behind them, the demarcation between Waste and forest even more abrupt and logic-defying than its border with the Kilethi marches.

"How—?" Rydara looked ahead, shocked by the change. There had been nothing but barren wasteland only moments ago. Now they were following the course of the river through the forest, a river that seemed to shine—or, rather, *glow*—through the darkness. It was not just reflected light. Where moonlight caught the ripples, the river sparkled white and silver, but there was also a faint aqua light emanating from the water itself.

It was wondrous and surely magical.

"Quimo dain i ruvneï," the elf said. Rydara did not understand the words, but she doubted they would have answered her question if she had.

Perhaps she need not have been so amazed. She was sitting beside an elf on a flying dragon, after all. Why shouldn't their homeland be invisible?

The forest gave way to meadow, and the land rose in a gradual hill. Gardens, paths, and elegant stonework structures sprang up along the river, sometimes lit with little beacons of the same strange aqua glow. Rydara marveled at the massive structure that sat on top of the hill—some form of palace, she guessed. She could make out little detail in the dark, but it had obviously been built for beauty rather than defense, all graceful arches and sweeping curves. It stood over the source of the river.

The dragon lowered as the hill rose to meet them, and they followed the river up through an open gate and landed in the palace grounds. The air was fragrant with the scent of flowers.

The elf lifted Aander over his shoulders, and Rydara's wonder at her surroundings faded, replaced by worry for him. They were strangers here. Even if the elves could cure the desert sickness, they may not wish to. She sensed a grim mood in the elf as he gracefully descended the dragon's wing. It did not bode well for what lay before them.

He turned and held out a hand. *"Tarest."*

Rydara took his hand and scrambled down to the ground. He led her to a marble walkway that lined the river, and Rydara was able to get a closer look at the water. The aqua glow was bright here, lighting up the lower ends of white pillars that lined the walk and casting shadows on the palace walls. Rydara wondered how she had even briefly mistaken it for reflected moonlight.

The palace entrance was wide and open, allowing the river to flow through it. Its upper reaches were lost in shadow, but as they entered, the marble walkway expanded into a marble floor, and the distant roof blocked the moon and stars. Light came from the river and from evenly spaced fixtures on both sides of the hall that contained the same soft aqua glow. The sound of running water filled the space—a gentle sound, for such a broad river.

"*Sundamar,*" a male voice spoke quietly, and Rydara started.

The speaker glided toward them from behind one of the pillars up ahead. He was taller than Rydara's guide but no less graceful, and his features bore the same black and chiseled beauty. He was dressed in a flowing robe and bore no weapons.

His gaze took in Aander, unconscious and hanging from the first elf's shoulders, and came to rest on Rydara. "*Mizäelera nim najiravòn.*"

Rydara could discern nothing from his expression, but her Knowing registered a faint disapproval.

The elf who carried Aander nodded. Resigned. "*Ciri laïslor somno Nuilyr?*"

"*Ferzasho.*" The second elf stepped aside and swept his arm out in invitation, bowing his head slightly. Rydara's companion nodded to him and continued forward, and Rydara hurried after, pressed to keep up with his long strides.

"Sundamar." Rydara tried out the strange syllables, embarrassed by how much grace they lost on her tongue. Her elf guide glanced at her. "You are Sundamar?" Rydara guessed. The elf nodded, but his mind was focused elsewhere, and Rydara spoke no further.

They had to be on their way to meet whoever lived in this palace. If Sundamar's manner was any indication, they were unlikely to receive a warm welcome, and Rydara began to worry about what she would say.

Surely Sundamar would not have brought her brother here if there was no chance he could be healed, but would Rydara be permitted to stay while he recovered?

And what about their mission to save the tribes? If the elves were displeased by her presence here, it seemed unlikely they would be eager to help.

The corridor opened into a vast inner chamber open to the night sky. A glowing fountain, the source of the river, was centered in a pool on a marble dais, and a small waterfall flowed from the dais into the river that ran through the middle of the chamber. Two dozen elves lined the walkways, half on each side of the river. They were all dressed in flowing robes, standing tall with their hands clasped behind them.

Rydara stood a bit straighter as she followed Sundamar toward the dais, feeling short, clumsy, and deeply out of place.

Behind the fountain, twelve elves sat in elegant silver chairs arrayed in a semi-circle. Rydara's eyes were drawn toward the chair on her far left, which had a taller back than the rest. A large, diamond-shaped crystal filled with the same aqua glow as the river decorated its crest. The elf who sat there rose to her feet as Sundamar and Rydara climbed the steps to the dais.

Rydara had thought the males of this race beyond compare. The elf queen took her breath away.

As with the male elves, her skin was dark and her features etched with an otherworldly grace. She was tall and slender, dressed in a flowing gown of pale blue—or perhaps it only appeared so in the glowing aqua light—and her hair was unlike anything Rydara had ever seen. Tightly-wound coils were pulled back at even intervals around her face, framing a lustrous, coal-black volume that rose above her head like a crown before extending behind it, reaching as low as her middle back. A silver half-circlet adorned her head, and a small glowing crystal hung against her forehead.

Her face was smooth, ageless, and expressionless, reminding Rydara of the distant stars in its cold, indifferent beauty. Sundamar laid Aander on the dais before her and sank to his knees.

Rydara knelt beside Sundamar. She had not bathed or re-braided her hair since evening the day before, and her clothes were worn and dirty from the desert. Furthermore, they were men's clothes, a brown wool jerkin and trousers that permitted her to ride. She was not fit to be seen in any court—let alone to represent all the tribes of Kilethe and Lanimshar before this devastatingly beautiful race.

"*Sundamar,*" the elf queen spoke, and Rydara heard the same power in her voice as that of the Alterran queen and general. Sundamar lifted his head, and the queen spoke a few more sentences.

The Alterrans had wielded the magic of their voices with the brute force of weapons, forcing their listeners into the thoughts and behaviors they willed. Rydara sensed a gentler power in the music of the elf queen's voice. Though the words were unintelligible to her, she sensed the quiet disappointment that permeated them, a disappointment that invited Sundamar to be persuaded that he had done wrong.

Sundamar gave a short reply, and at another word from the queen, he rose to his feet, bowed his head, and stepped to the side, turning his gaze on Rydara.

The queen also looked at Rydara. Her forehead drew together in a near frown—an expression which failed to diminish the perfection of her face.

Rydara remained kneeling, afraid of the elf queen's displeasure.

The queen's features smoothed back into serene neutrality, and when she spoke again, her voice was gentle. Her words were no more intelligible than before, but Rydara discerned through her Knowing that she was being asked to account for herself.

"My name is Rydara," Rydara said, keeping her eyes on the floor of the dais. She knew so little about this culture, but the words of the ancient rhyme that had inspired her to come here had suggested "the meek" might win favor from them. The elves might not be able to understand her words, but Sundamar had knelt before the queen. They understood the body language of submission.

Rydara did not need to work to portray it. She felt as low as a worm before this magnificent being, and it took all her courage to speak. "My brother, Aander, was dying of the desert sickness when I came across this elf, who took mercy on us and brought us to you. Please, I seek asylum from the desert for us both and beg you to save my brother's life if you can."

"*Rydara*," the elf queen repeated, giving the syllables a grace and beauty they had never held in the Common tongue. Somehow, the queen had understood Rydara's speech in full. She asked another question, and Rydara Knew that her account had been deemed insufficient. The queen wanted to know why Aander and Rydara had wandered so far into the Waste in the first place.

If the queen was suspicious of them because they were human, Rydara discerned no hint of it through her Knowing, but it would fit with the Rishara stories. Humans had driven the elves into hiding after they had defeated the ancient demons together.

"Please, we mean no harm to your land or your people." Rydara bit her lip as she studied the floor of the dais, picturing herself coming right out and asking for the elves to go to war to save the Kilethi tribes. Desperation had made her bold in pleading for Aander, but saving the tribes was a much bigger favor to ask. If there was a way to get the elves to agree to it, Rydara could not guess what it might be. It seemed impossible they would do so at her mere request, given their cold reception.

Aander was the one with the charisma to win others to their cause. If he were conscious, he would have had the courage to plunge ahead through this uncharted territory, to communicate the suffering of the tribes and the evil of the demons who led

Alterra. He would have appealed to the fellow feeling one might expect of all sentient races, to the strength and courage the elves had displayed in their last alliance with humanity so long ago. He would have made a case for their cause, with all his passion, by every reason and entreaty he could supply or imagine.

But Aander was not conscious, and everyone was waiting on Rydara.

"We came to the Waste to seek out your people, to present a request on behalf of our race," Rydara said slowly, her eyes still on the ground. She could not possibly make that request now. She was not Aander, and even if she had all his charisma, it would be better to delay, to give herself time to learn something about what motivated this foreign race. "If it please the queen, I ask that we might appear before her again in ten days' time to present our petition?"

Rydara risked looking up at the elf queen, hoping she had not overstepped—and hoping against hope that the elves would save Aander and that in ten days, he would be well enough to present their petition himself.

The queen lifted her chin and studied Rydara with eyes as dark and beautiful as the night sea. She turned to look at the elves sitting in the semi-circle behind them, her gaze scanning each of them from right to left, and Rydara wondered if she had been wrong to address the queen exclusively. Perhaps she shared power with these other elves seated on the dais, though none of them wore jewels against their foreheads and not even the females among them had their hair styled so elaborately. Perhaps the elf standing before Rydara was not even a queen.

But none of the seated elves spoke before the jeweled one returned her gaze to Rydara and nodded, and Rydara sensed that the chamber deferred to her authority.

When the jeweled elf spoke again, it was for the assembled audience. Rydara understood nothing of her meaning or her emotions, but as the speech drew to a close, her eyes returned to where Rydara knelt on the dais, and Rydara received an impression of the time that would pass before they met again.

Rydara had asked for ten days. The elf queen was giving her forty.

Chapter 7

A Strange Land

That's too long. Rydara's gut twisted at the thought of what forty days would mean for the Kilethi tribes. How many more villages would meet the fate of Tessex? How many had already been destroyed while Rydara and Aander traveled through the Waste?

She bit her lip as she looked up at the elf queen, and she Knew that the elf sensed her distress. Her face remained serene, beautiful, and indifferent.

It would be useless to argue. She had made her decree.

A pair of elves carried a stretcher up onto the dais while the assembled audience broke apart, and they helped Sundamar lift Aander onto it. Rydara followed as they carried him down the steps.

Another elf—one of the males who had been sitting on the dais—laid a hand on Rydara's shoulder and gestured toward a side corridor. Rydara panicked as the stretcher bearers continued forward, afraid of being separated from her brother.

"Please!" Rydara looked frantically between the new elf and Sundamar. "Where are you taking him?"

"*Llew somno,*" Sundamar said, and Rydara sensed a reassurance that Aander would be well.

"*Ferkalynest,*" the other elf told her, and Rydara felt that he found her concern—though understandable—quite impractical in her current state. "*Saar ferrylly yar ferlory. Salorara linual moiravèn ail demaur. Tarest.*"

That last word meant "come." Rydara's Knowing also received a vague reassurance that she interpreted to mean she would be permitted to see Aander later, so she let him lead her away. She was exhausted. Perhaps it was best to let the elves take care of Aander without her.

The elf took her to a corridor that was partly open to the night, with evenly spaced pillars on the left-hand side of the walk supporting the awning that stretched overhead. On the right-hand side, the wall of the palace was lined with windows. Rydara's guide flowed through the shadows as though he might have been one of them. He opened a small wooden door between two windows, and Rydara followed him into a spacious room lit by another aqua-glowing light fixture. Inside, there was a wooden wardrobe, a small table with two chairs, and a canopied bed that looked more comfortable than anything Rydara had ever seen. The elf opened the wardrobe, showing Rydara an assortment of clothing.

Everything was spotless and beautiful, and Rydara was reminded of how dirty she was. She was afraid to touch anything, though the elf spoke a few cursory words that suggested Rydara was meant to sleep here and change into some of these clothes.

The elf continued to the far side of the room and opened another small door, leading Rydara into a large, high-ceilinged chamber that held four pools, one of which contained a small fountain. At first Rydara thought the water held the same glow as the river, but as she walked farther out on the stone floor, she realized aqua light fixtures had been built into the sides of each pool, under the water.

The elf spoke again, drawing Rydara's attention to a shelf set in the near wall. Several neatly folded linen towels sat next to five glass jars, each of which contained a different colored ointment. Rydara understood that she was welcome to use them.

The elf studied her for a moment longer, and Rydara felt a spike of alarm, thinking perhaps he meant for her to bathe in front of him. But a corner of his mouth curved upward, and Rydara sensed his amusement at her discomfort. He bowed his head. *"Latha ail kellor, nimlyr,"* he said. *"Rydara,"* he added. Then he left her alone in the chamber, closing the door behind him.

Rydara looked around, taken aback by the size of the space. She wondered if it was a public bathing area, or if it was meant only for residents of the palace. Surely it couldn't be for her use exclusively.

The aqua glow from the pools was the only light, leaving the chamber laced in shadow. Rydara could make out a few other shelves supplied similarly to the one near her door. But she was alone—at least for now—and in the end, the thought of going back to her spotless guest quarters dirty became a bigger concern than modesty, so Rydara collected the jars and a towel, undressed, and slipped into the nearest pool.

The water was hot and soothing. If she had not been so exhausted—and unnerved by the light in the water and the possibility of being disturbed—she would have stayed there a long time. The ointments in the jars smelled like flowers and perfume. Rydara did not know what they were or how she was supposed to use them, but under the assumption they might be something like soap, she tried putting some on her skin. It softened noticeably. She tried some in her hair next and found an even greater softening effect. She used only a little ointment from two of the jars before carefully closing them. They were surely expensive.

Rydara went back to the bedchamber wrapped in the towel and set her dirty clothes on top of the table, unsure what to do with them. She dressed herself in a clean garment from the wardrobe that looked like it would serve well as a nightgown, towel-dried her hair, and crawled into bed, feeling cleaner and smelling better than she ever had in her life.

So much remained uncertain. Aander, the fate of the tribes, how she would use the forty days she had been given ... but sleep took Rydara as soon as her head hit the pillow.

***

When she woke, sunlight streamed into the room from the windows near the door, replacing the aqua glow from the night before. Rydara rose right away, anxious to find out what was happening with her brother.

Her first challenge was getting dressed, but this was simplified when she went to the wardrobe. Her options were all similar. The gown she had slept in was cream-colored, soft, and sleeveless, and there were several more like it along with floor-length colored robes with bell-shaped sleeves and open fronts. These had lines of fabric loops running the length of the chest on both sides, and cords were strung through the loops to hold the robes loosely closed. Based on the design, Rydara gathered that the robes were a kind of overlay, meant to be worn over a gown and laced together in the front. She dressed accordingly, choosing an overlay of dark red.

As she worked her hair into the familiar single braid she had worn for most of her life, Rydara wondered if her hair could be coaxed into a style such as the elf queen wore. The women of the tribes had hair that was soft, flat, and easy to twist, braid, or curl, and Rydara had always considered the extra volume and springy texture of her own hair a hindrance. But there was no denying the beauty of the elf queen's style, and it required far more volume than any woman from the tribes could match.

I probably couldn't do it either, Rydara told herself. The queen was not even human, after all, and though Rydara did wonder at the similarities between the elves and the Rishara, she doubted they were more than surface deep. Her mother, while comely enough to catch the eye of the Noraani king, had been no paragon of perfection such as these creatures.

Rydara finished her braid and opened the door to the outside, intent on finding her brother.

Between the white pillars that lined the far side of the walkway, Rydara could see the sun rising over the palace gardens. It was a sight to behold. A few marble steps ran the whole width of the walkway, leading to a grassy lawn on a downward slope that stretched a few dozen spans, ending in a wall of birch trees growing so close together they seemed to make up a fence. Shorter, flowering trees and bushes were sprinkled across the lawn, each one standing alone in a spacious pocket of grass and bursting with color: pale pink, magenta, deep red, violet, white, and light blue. The blossoms ranged from pea-sized to as large as Rydara's head, some clustered together to form conical shapes and others spread evenly across the whole tree. Impossibly, every plant appeared to be in full bloom at the same time, the petals all open and perfect. The sun peeked between the trees lining the far side of the garden, casting the sky into shades of pink and orange.

A dragon was sitting out there, a stone's throw distant from Rydara in an expanse of treeless lawn large enough to accommodate its bulk. In daylight, Rydara could see that its scales were sleek and dark in color, with a faint pattern of mottled greens and black swirled across its surface. An elf stood beside the dragon in a cloak of forest green with a bow and quiver slung across his back. He turned toward Rydara as she emerged from her room, and she recognized Sundamar.

He smiled at her, and she was startled by the change in his demeanor. Yesterday he had seemed so somber and distant. Rydara had not seen any elf smile yesterday, and she had assumed the race was as aloof as it was beautiful. But Sundamar's smile was open and genuine.

It was also brief, fading back into serene neutrality almost as quickly as it had appeared.

Rydara held her skirts as she descended from the walkway and went out to meet him, glad to have found someone to speak to so quickly.

"*Cith morgäelé, Rydara,*" he said as she approached, and Rydara was taken by the music his tongue gave to her name.

She curtsied, lowering her eyes. "Cith ... morgäelé, Sundamar," she attempted, taking the phrase for some form of greeting. His mouth curved upward again—briefly—and Rydara understood that she had guessed right. "Do you know where I can find my brother?"

"Fur fer librywethirïa cir kelly," he said.

The phrase did not sound like a question, but Rydara sensed an offer that required a response. She furrowed her brow. "Please. I would like to see him."

"Tarest." Sundamar leapt onto the dragon's wing and offered a hand to Rydara.

Her eyebrows shot up in surprise. The dragon snorted, and a sense of its amusement flooded Rydara's Knowing. It turned its head to look at her, and Rydara felt an attitude when she met its yellow eyes that translated itself into words with little effort. *How did you think we were going to get there, silly human?*

"Pardon me," Rydara said aloud, startled by the creature's personality. *Or is my Knowing playing tricks on me?* she wondered. "I, uh," she started, glancing between the elf and the dragon. She had flown with them once already, of course, but that had been a flight of desperate circumstance in the dead of night. Now that she was properly attired and safe—in the full light of day—it seemed impossible that she was being invited to take the elf's hand and fly with them once again. "Is it—do you wish me to—"

This time Rydara sensed amusement from the elf as well as the dragon, though Sundamar's face remained neutral.

Just get on, the dragon seemed to suggest, twitching its tail and moving its extended wing.

Rydara bit her lip and took Sundamar's hand, and he led her up onto the dragon's back just as gracefully as before. This time, though, Rydara was mindful to release his hand after she settled down behind the dragon's spike, as his touch made her flustered and self-conscious. She clung only to the dragon as they took off.

Thank you for letting me fly with you, Rydara thought toward the dragon. If the creature had magic like hers, perhaps it could understand the attitude of her thoughts, if not the linguistic content.

Rydara's Knowing filled with a sense of the dragon's pleasure and satisfaction as they soared into the air—a response that could only indicate, *You are welcome.*

Rydara caught her breath, watching the palace garden grow smaller beneath them. They flew over the palace. Rydara could see the river—glowing only faintly now in the light of the sun—and the elven city of stone, white marble, and structured gardens spreading to the south. They flew west, over the birches and down the hill toward another, more secluded building set in the woods.

Can Sundamar read my thoughts, too? Rydara tried asking the dragon. It was a significantly more complicated idea, and she doubted the creature would understand.

But she received the distinct impression that it was laughing at her. And then—*No more than you can his.*

That was a more nuanced impression than Rydara had ever discerned with her Knowing, and she wondered what magic the dragon had. She glanced up at Sundamar, who crouched beside her with a hand on the dragon's neck, and wondered what magic *he* might have, and if he could tell how overwhelmed she was by all the beauty and wonder of his strange world.

He glanced back at her, and Rydara broke eye contact. But her Knowing picked up a gentle reassurance. He did not need magic to perceive her shock, awe, and timidity. Rydara was broadcasting it with her wide eyes and nervous body language.

"*Cith somnol corrom,*" he said. "*Moire forlinual, cyn saar somno kastana.*"

Corrom—Rydara thought he had used that word about her horses. *What did he say?* she tried asking the dragon.

By way of response, her Knowing received an impression of Nightmare and Astral galloping in an open field somewhere under the care of the elves. It seemed as though she could visit them if she wished, but they were not nearby.

Rydara smiled at Sundamar. She had nearly forgotten the horses in her concern about Aander, but she was glad to know Astral was well. "Thank you," she said. The elf nodded.

The building they flew toward was tall and rectangular, and it enclosed a large stretch of garden in its center. They landed outside of it, where a broad stone path led to the building's main entrance: a large, round wooden door with an iron knocker.

Thank you, Rydara thought toward the dragon again. *What is your name?*

An impression of playfulness, dancing flames, and fierce resolve filled Rydara's Knowing. And then a word: *Lëanor.*

Thank you, Lëanor.

Sundamar offered Rydara a hand again for the dismount, and soon they were on the ground. Sundamar strode up to the building, and after a few heavy knocks, another elf opened the door. This one was female, and her hair was secured atop her head in a voluminous poof.

Every elf seemed to stand and move with impossible, inhuman grace. Sundamar's was the grace of a hunter, where Rydara's guide from the night before had the more unassuming grace of a shadow. This elf, though, reminded Rydara of the queen, commanding attention with all the grace and immutable majesty of a mountain, though she wore no ornaments and her garb—a blue smock dress with white sleeves—appeared simpler than Rydara's.

She spoke with Sundamar briefly, and Rydara could hear power in her voice. Then she turned to Rydara and took Rydara's hands in her own. She leaned closer and kissed Rydara's forehead—stunning Rydara. "*Cith morgäelé, nimkeïass.*"

Rydara sensed the term carried an intimacy that matched the gesture, but she could not guess what it meant. She curtsied. "Cith morgäelé... ?" She looked up at the elf in question.

"*Chaenath,*" the elf supplied.

"Cith morgäelé, Chaenath," Rydara repeated, doing her best with the strange syllables. Her efforts were a paltry imitation of the elves' flowing speech. "Is my brother here?"

Chaenath nodded. Then Sundamar spoke again, and Rydara understood he was telling her she could follow the path back to the palace whenever she wished to leave. She nodded.

"*Nuväest cith,*" he said, nodding back to her before leaping onto the dragon's wing.

"Nuväest cith," Rydara repeated. Something to say when leaving.

The dragon took off, and Rydara turned back to Chaenath. "Can I see him?"

A somber attitude settled over Chaenath. She gestured for Rydara to follow her inside.

Rydara started to worry. She had been so sure the elves could save Aander. Had something gone wrong?

Chaenath led her down a long, low-ceilinged corridor to the left. Large windows lined the left-hand side, flooding the building with sunlight. Doors were spaced at even intervals along the other wall. Eventually, Chaenath stopped and opened one.

Aander lay under a wool blanket on a bed low to the floor, curled on his side with a compress resting across his forehead. He was mumbling to himself, and his body shook with shivers.

Rydara rushed to his side and knelt, clasping his hand. It was clammy and feverish. "He is still sick?" she asked in shock, turning to Chaenath. The White Plague always killed in eight days. This was the seventh since Aander's first cough. If he was still sick...

Rydara shook her head, trying not to panic. Aander was no longer violent, as he had been in the oasis. That had to mean he was improving.

That had to mean he wasn't going to die.

"Farr." Chaenath said simply. Yes, Aander was still sick. Chaenath did not seem surprised. She studied Rydara in pity, and then she began speaking again. Rydara could not parse all the words, but Chaenath seemed to be telling her that Aander would be sick for a long time.

"But he *will* get better?" Rydara asked. He had to get better. She could not do this without him.

Chaenath paused before replying. *"Nimthall ailtaravòn."* It was not a direct answer.

"He will improve?" Rydara tried again. Tears welled in her eyes.

Chaenath nodded slowly.

"How long will it take? How long will he be like this?"

"Quitris aur," Chaenath said. Rydara's Knowing suggested the time was longer than a week, or even two, but she could not tell how long. Not as she had when the queen spoke.

"How many days?"

Chaenath lifted all ten fingers. She closed her fists and opened them three more times. *"Roi."*

Forty days. At least.

No. Rydara looked down at her brother, dismayed. It was too long. Far too long. He would only begin to recover by the time of their second audience with the queen. He would not be able to help Rydara prepare. He might not even be strong enough to come with her, let alone take the lead in presenting their petition.

Tears welled in her eyes. He would improve, but why hadn't Chaenath agreed that he would get better? What kind of damage would remain?

Aander's mumbling turned to moans, and they grew louder.

"Saar lathy," Chaenath said sharply, gesturing for Rydara to move back. *"Ail naur."*

Aander thrashed, throwing his arm across the bed, and Rydara jerked backward. Chaenath pulled her to her feet, and

Rydara let herself be led across the room. Chaenath drew aside a curtain, revealing a second door made of glass. It led into the garden the building was built around.

"Arbeth rissest," Chaenath told her, gently pushing Rydara into the garden. Chaenath closed the door and let the curtain fall shut behind her.

Rydara looked around, dazed. This garden had rows of flowers in orderly beds of soil separated by lengths of grass. The rows led toward the center of the yard, where a fountain spurted high into the air from the mouth of a stone dragon, falling into a pool around its base. The rows of flowers stretched out in lines in that direction and then curved around it, forming concentric circles before running on to the other side of the yard. Every color of the rainbow seemed to be represented. The outermost row held a range from pale pink to deep red, the middle row oranges, yellows, and white, and the innermost was all shades of blue and purple.

To call it beautiful would have been an understatement, but Rydara just wanted to weep. There were a few benches near the dragon fountain, and she walked that way, trying not to sob aloud as she crossed the yard.

Rydara sank onto the bench and buried her face in her hands, crying softly. When she had seen Sundamar's dragon on top of that bluff, she had dared to hope. With all the magic and beauty of this strange race, she had been sure that they could heal Aander if they wished to. The queen had let them stay, and she had been sure Aander was out of danger. She had assumed he would recover quickly. She had thought they would figure out this strange new world together, that he would help her build a case and then be the one to present it before the elf queen.

But the White Plague was always fatal.

Why did I think recovery would be easy, or even complete?

Perhaps that had been what Sundamar had tried to communicate, when she had begged him to save her brother. That it would take a long time.

That the elves could only do so much.

"Cith morgäelé, nimlyr. Ciri laere?"

Rydara looked up, startled to find an elf sinking to a crouch before her, bringing them eye to eye. He produced a small square of cloth from his pocket and offered it to her. Rydara accepted it, hesitantly, and he gestured to her face.

Rydara looked down at the cloth. It was a fine fabric, as soft as silk, and it was embroidered with the most perfect stitches she had ever seen, forming the picture of a flower. She could not imagine soiling such a thing.

The elf took it back from her and folded it once, so the image of the flower was inside-out. It was only marginally less fine, but he pressed it back into Rydara's hands and gestured to her face again.

She wiped her eyes with a small smile at his kindness. "Thank you," she said, sniffing as she tried to compose herself. "I'm sorry, I didn't see you. Are you one of the healers here?"

The elf shook his head and spoke a few short sentences. Rydara understood he was more like a patient. Then his tone rose in a question, and Rydara thought he was asking about Aander—if he was the reason she was crying.

"Yes. I thought the elves would be able to heal him, but he is still sick. He may never fully recover—" Rydara's voice broke.

The elf sat on the bench beside her. Then he spoke again, and Rydara understood his attitude more clearly than she had with some of the other elves. He was offering comfort, telling her there was reason to be optimistic about Aander. Even suggesting that the other elves may have painted too pessimistic a picture.

Rydara's brow furrowed. "Really? You think Aander will get better, after all?"

The elf nodded, smiling again, and said something that made Rydara think Aander was unlikely to notice long-term changes.

Rydara started crying again.

"Ciri laere, nimlyr?" the elf asked her again, a faint crease of concern marking his forehead. Then he asked another question, and Rydara thought it had to do with her parents.

It seemed a strange question. Rydara was an adult by tribal standards, and there was no reason she should have been traveling with her parents. But, glancing at the elf again, Rydara got the impression that he had seen many, many more years than his beauty might suggest. She must have seemed quite young to him.

"My mother died when I was young," Rydara began, "and my father—" she choked on another sob, feeling very young and abandoned after all.

This elf had no less grace or beauty than any of the others, but he smiled more and felt approachable. Perhaps it was the handkerchief, or the fact that he had asked after her parents. Maybe it was the faint touch of silver in his hair that reminded Rydara of a grandfather—though his face had not the slightest trace of a wrinkle—but whatever the reason, she soon found herself pouring her heart out to this stranger. She told him about how her father had banished her for her accusations against the Alterrans. How the Alterrans wielded strange and terrible magic like nothing known to the tribes. How her mother used to tell her stories about elves and ancient demons and had taught her and Aander the poem about the Land Beyond the Waste. How she and Aander had dared to cross it. How afraid she had been when he had fallen sick.

And now, even though she believed he would recover, it wouldn't be in time to help her learn about the elves or what might convince them to save the tribes. They had an audience with the queen in forty days—forty days during which the Alterrans would continue to kill and conquer. It was too long, but also, perhaps, too short for Rydara to learn all she needed to know, to build the best case she could. When it came time to present their argument to the queen, Rydara might have to do that alone, too—though she did not have a fraction of Aander's charisma or his experience.

The elf listened to all this with a sympathetic air, nodding occasionally. When she finally finished, there was a long pause, and Rydara realized she had no idea how much he understood. The elves seemed to vary in how well they understood her, as she varied in understanding them.

When the elf finally spoke, he shocked Rydara by declaring, in perfect Common, "I will help you."

Chapter 8

Neremyn

The elf's name, Rydara soon learned, was Neremyn. He explained, in Common, that he did not know her language, but he was able to pick up its words and grammatical structure by listening to her speak because of his Knowing. He told her the Elvish word for Knowing translated as "insight" and that it was not considered "magic," but just another one of the senses, which they called "sights." The Perceiving magic also fell into this category. The elves recognized Speaking, Showing, and a power called Prophecy as a different class of ability, which they called "imaging" talents.

Rydara had been able to tell instantly that the queen could Speak and that Chaenath could as well, but Neremyn told her that all elves had all the abilities, and most spoke with some level of Speaking magic in their voices most of the time. The more of the talent they used, the more the words impacted their listeners. In Rydara's case, the elves' Speaking had been acting as a complement to her Knowing, helping them transcend the language barrier to communicate with her when they wished. Dragons had the talent as well.

When Rydara asked if the Speaking magic could be used to manipulate, deceive, and control, as the Alterrans had done, Neremyn grew somber. He nodded. "It is against our code to deceive or control, except in combat exercises. Also, insight—or the Knowing magic, as you call it—provides some protection against it. Just as a strong Perceiver will see through the effects of a weak Showing, a Speaker cannot control or deceive a Knower of equal strength. At best, his Speaking will neutralize her Knowing, and she will be uncertain of the truth. Even if he is stronger, the effects of the Speaking magic wear off with time. This limits an elf's ability to violate our code and get away with it, as all are Knowers. But yes, among magicless humans, I imagine a powerful Speaker could do much damage."

"Can the Speaking magic be used to erase memories?" Rydara asked next.

"Strange you should ask. Memories cannot be erased with Speaking alone, but it is possible to change what someone remembers by using a combination of sights and imaging powers. It is rarely done. Any proposed use of the practice must be approved by our First Elf, Arcaena, and the Council of Twelve."

"First Elf?"

"You called her the elf queen before, but I believe 'First Elf' is a closer translation of our term for her." Neremyn smiled. *"Nuilyr."*

"Nuilyr Arcaena," Rydara repeated, practicing the syllables. It would be important to pronounce the title correctly when she saw the First Elf again. "The sorcerers I met. They appeared to be human, but they could see through our Showing, so they must have had Perceiving magic as well as Speaking. Among the tribes, I have only ever heard of a human displaying one magic, if any. We did not think it was possible to have more than one. Only the elves and the ancient demons in my mother's stories had all six. Do you think the Alterran sorcerers … are demons?" Rydara furrowed her brow. It was a strange idea. Her mother's stories of elves and demons had inspired her to cross the Waste, but she was holding out hope that the sorcerers were just uncommonly gifted humans, and that it would be a simple thing for elves to defeat them.

"We call them *Muirünikish*. High Wizards," Neremyn said. "There were nine in the Celestial Rebellion, five elves and four humans. Tenebrus, Atra, Os Noxcint, Numbran, Vesper, Lux Lucisa, Dameires, Ei Desidi, and Auror. Their names live in infamy."

"Lux Lucisa and Dameires—and Numbran," Rydara added, realizing that the Alterran queen had called the third Alterran sorcerer "Numbran" in the note she had left for Rydara. "Those are the sorcerers I met! They have been alive all this time? Since the Celestial Rebellion?"

"No." Neremyn frowned, shaking his head. "No, that is not possible. All but two of the High Wizards were captured or killed by the elves at the end of the Celestial Rebellion. Only Tenebrus and Atra escaped. But they must have found a way to remake the compact. We did not think it possible, after the injuries they suffered ... But yes, they must have found a way, and I suppose the new High Wizards would have taken the same names as the old ones. They would have bonded the same demons, after all."

Tenebrus and Atra? Compact? Demons? Rydara tried to sort through the rush of new questions. It seemed the sorcerers did represent the return of some ancient and devastating evil, after all. *But if the elves defeated them once before...* "Tell me about the Celestial Rebellion."

"I have no personal memory of those days, but I will tell you what I have been told." Neremyn settled back on the bench, and his voice took on the quality of a storyteller. "It began with an elf called Theodluin, whose imaging powers were beyond compare. He was one of several dozen elves at the time who had earned the distinction of 'wizard,' having achieved mastery in all the sights and imaging talents. He was also the firstborn child of the First Elf Leilatha. His favorite talent was Prophecy, a magic that allowed him to walk the space between the physical and spiritual realms, the Realm Between, and to discern many possible futures.

"It was while walking the Realm Between that he encountered the demon Tenebra, one of nine lords of hell. Tenebra convinced Theodluin that he need not wait for Leilatha to make the journey to the Realm Beyond to ascend to primacy himself, and that he deserved far more than the simple distinction of 'First.' Tenebra promised Theodluin godhood. All he needed to do was assemble nine Prophets willing to host the lords of hell in the physical realm, and they would subdue the earth under Theodluin's reign.

"Theodluin took the name Tenebrus when he and eight others became hosts to the nine lords of hell. The symbiosis enabled the human Prophets among them to access the powers of the demons, achieving instant mastery in all of the magics they had previously lacked. They all gained the knowledge and skills of the demons, becoming far more powerful than any other wizards. They became known as 'High Wizards.'

"Tenebrus murdered Leilatha and took control over elves and humans. He and the other High Wizards proclaimed themselves gods and demanded homage. Through the force of their impossibly powerful Speaking, they bent the whole world to their will, and there were none left to oppose them. They even forced the creator out of the physical realm, though he had formerly walked among elves and humans and was known to them as Nivalis.

"But Tenebrus thirsted for more. He knew that as long as Nivalis lived free in any realm, there would be one god more true and powerful than he, and that Nivalis might one day reclaim the physical realm from him. So Tenebrus abused the people, knowing Nivalis would not be able to stomach it. When Nivalis came to confront him, Tenebrus promised to return authority over the physical realm to the elves and humans he had enslaved. In return, he demanded Nivalis turn over his power and his person to the High Wizards so they could destroy him once and for all."

Rydara was not quite sure what all of that meant, but the story had started to sound familiar. Neremyn went on to say that Nivalis took the deal and was killed—as had happened to the All-Color in the Rishara stories—but the god's death had a violent backlash that crippled the powers of the High Wizards.

"Elves and humans were released from Tenebrus' mind control," Neremyn went on, "and some came to their senses. Under Arcaena's leadership, elves and humans fought together against those who remained loyal to Tenebrus. Most of the High Wizards were captured or killed."

"And then the humans turned against the elves," Rydara remembered. "And you all fled here, to the Land Beyond the Waste. Why? With all the magic elves have, you could have crushed us."

"It is not our way." Neremyn shook his head. "I told you, it is against our code to deceive or control. It is also against our code to kill. Arcaena would not hear of breaking it, not for any reason. And there was no need. We could hide from you just as easily. And there are advantages to living separately."

"But these High Wizards—they are enemies to your race?" Rydara asked hopefully. "When the rest of your people find out the High Wizards are back, will they try to stop them from taking over the world again?"

Neremyn shook his head again, his expression turning grim. "When the humans drove us from their lands, Arcaena rebuked them for how quickly they had forgotten our role in saving them from the High Wizards. She vowed that we would not return to help them if another hour of need arose. She spoke for us all."

"But didn't they kill your god?" Rydara pressed. "Don't they need to answer to your code?"

"Our code governs those within this land. As long as these new High Wizards stay far from here, they are unlikely to be seen as any of our concern."

Rydara's heart sank. It had been too much to hope for, that the elves might have their own reasons for wishing to confront the Alterran sorcerers.

Worse, they had already sworn never to help her people again.

"So the stories of the Rishara are true," Rydara mused. Neremyn had given her a lot to digest. She hardly knew what to think, let alone ask. "There was a god who allowed himself to be killed by the ancient demons. Nivalis? The Rishara called him the All-Color. Is he still dead? The demon—the High Wizard. Lux Lucisa. She offered me a deal. Immortality, in exchange for my 'lingering ties' to the All-Color—but she called him the White."

Neremyn nodded, smiling. "Our word for the color 'white' can also be translated as 'all-color,'" he said. "It is one of Nivalis' titles. Did you know that every other color is contained in white light?"

Rydara shook her head. She did not even know what Neremyn meant by saying white light "contained" other colors, but she chalked it up to a strange cultural belief of the elves. "She said my lingering ties to the White, or my conscience. My soul. As if those were all the same thing."

Neremyn made a dismissive sound, shaking his head. "The demons that joined with Prophets to become High Wizards were obsessed with godhood and Nivalis. There may be traces of Nivalis somewhere out there, in the spiritual realm or even the Realm Between. But when it comes to the physical realm, I assure you, he is quite absent. Your soul and your conscience have nothing to do with him, though the peculiar obsession of her demon may have led this Lux Lucisa to believe otherwise.

"Her deal would have enabled you to live forever at the expense of being able to create meaningfully new mental pathways. You would not have been able to change or mature, and much of life would have lost its emotional color. It would be like freezing your reflective and emotional nature in time, while allowing your physical nature to go on enjoying itself indefinitely. She was right to say you would have lost your conscience, for morality loses its meaning when connections with other living beings are lost."

"She could have done that to me?" Rydara bit her lip, remembering how narrowly she had escaped the queen's deal.

"Not without your consent." Neremyn patted her shoulder in reassurance. "There are some limitations on the blacker magics possible in this realm."

"Is that what it is like for her and the other High Wizards?" Rydara asked. "Do they lose their souls when they become hosts to the demons?"

Neremyn shook his head. "The demons become their companions, not their masters. If the High Wizards surrendered their souls in the way that the Knights do, they'd have little capacity for planning or self-control. They would become vulnerable to manipulation—and if there's anything a High Wizard hates, it's vulnerability.

"Demons, on the other hand, are creatures of instinct, and their instincts are darkness and hate. They hate even the High Wizards who host them, though they thrill to have partners in carrying out their desires and appreciate that their hosts will help them establish a broader, longer-lasting reign of darkness and terror than what they would accomplish alone."

"The High Wizards become hosts to creatures that hate them?" Rydara's brow furrowed, unable to comprehend why anyone would agree to such an arrangement. "Why?"

"The promise of unrivaled power is worth the discomfort to some."

Rydara tightened her lips as she considered what to ask next. She hoped she would eventually have the time to press this elf for everything he knew or guessed about demons, the High Wizards, magic, the All-Color, the elven race, and the Rishara, and whether the latter two had anything to do with one another. And what the Six had been up to during all of this.

But she had only forty days to prepare for her audience with the First Elf. She had to stay focused.

"Tell me more about this code you live by. What is life like among the elves?"

Rydara kept Neremyn talking for hours. In the early afternoon, he suggested they move indoors to break their fast, and Rydara realized both that she was famished and that the elves did not take a morning meal. That would take some time to get used to.

Neremyn had a suite of rooms for his personal use, and one of them was a dining room with large glass windows facing the garden. Chaenath was laying out a meal when they came inside. The table was large enough for six but set for only one. When Chaenath saw Rydara, she laid out a second place and doubled the portions on the table, but she did not join them herself.

She gave Rydara a cool glance as she left. Rydara thought her Knowing registered disapproval, but it was too brief to be sure. Rydara might have thought she disapproved of her eating alone with a male, but Neremyn's attitude betrayed no indication that it should be strange, and surely Chaenath could tell there was nothing romantic between them. Rydara was unwilling to give up Neremyn's counsel in any case.

She soon forgot about Chaenath, as the food absorbed her attention. There were strange vegetables in a creamy sauce with spices she had never tasted served over some starchy plant she had no word for. It was strange but appetizing, and it took Rydara a few minutes to realize the meal contained no meat.

That would also take getting used to.

Neremyn continued instructing her on the peculiarities of elven culture while they ate. She learned all about the First Elf and the Council of Twelve. Rydara's Knowing had suggested quite clearly that Arcaena ruled the elven realm, but the station of First Elf was not sovereign like "king" or "chieftain." Rather, the First Elf was considered first among equals, and her decisions were not considered law, but merely advice.

Nonetheless, it was highly unusual—and deeply frowned upon—for anyone to defy her. Allegedly, Nivalis himself had been close friends with her mother Leilatha, and the elves had made Leilatha First among them because of her great wisdom and righteousness. Since the fall of Theodluin, Arcaena was considered Leilatha's rightful heir, and the elves treated her with just as much respect and deference. More, in some cases, because she was the one who defeated Tenebrus and led them to "Edriendor" — the name of their homeland, which the Rishara called "the Land Beyond the Waste."

Rydara stopped to visit Aander before heading back to the palace that evening. He was still unconscious, but seemed to be sleeping more peacefully.

"I made a new friend today, Aander," she told him, kneeling by his bedside. "He's helping me prepare for the audience. And he thinks you'll recover your full strength. It will just take longer than we thought, is all." Rydara brushed hair back from his forehead, where it had matted in sweat. Chaenath had taken the cold compress away. "We might be able to do this after all. You just focus on getting better." She kissed his forehead before she left.

The next several days passed in a similar manner. Rydara made the short walk to the infirmary each morning. She took all her meals with Neremyn — on days when the elves ate, as it turned out there was a country-wide fast every seventh day — and he began teaching her the Elvish language and their written script. Rydara thought it impossible that she would learn enough in forty days to give her petition in Elvish, but Neremyn insisted that she try. The more she learned, the more the Council would respect her. She would have a better chance of connecting with them during her audience.

Rydara could not have done it without her Knowing. As her lessons with Neremyn continued, it seemed as though she became able to use it to greater advantage, guessing more precisely what novel words meant before Neremyn interpreted them, even when he used no magic to aid her. Though Rydara spent the first fast day convinced she would starve to death in this bizarre culture, food was plentiful when it was available, and Rydara slowly learned it was possible to survive on the elves' strange diet.

On the twelfth day of their lessons—which coincided with Rydara's second fast day in the country—Neremyn announced that she was ready to visit the library. Rydara had no idea what a library was, and when Neremyn explained, in Common, that it was a place where books were stored, Rydara still didn't understand.

"Like scrolls or ledgers," Neremyn said, somehow discerning that she was familiar with those concepts. "But in a different format, with pages and pages stacked together, with written information on all kinds of subjects."

The concept of a library, when Rydara finally understood it, stunned her. *All the knowledge of this culture, written down? Gathered in one place?*

And I could just look through it?

"Ciri dale cir shryn somni?" Rydara asked, her tongue tripping over syllables that asked, *Do you think I'm ready?* Rydara had only recently become comfortable mapping Elvish letters to the corresponding syllables. There were still so many words she did not know.

"Elven books are made with magic," Neremyn answered in Elvish, smiling. "They will aid your understanding."

Rydara thought Neremyn would come with her, but he said he could not leave the infirmary because of his health. This seemed odd to Rydara, since he seemed perfectly healthy, and she realized she had never asked him why he was a patient here. He said it was complicated but nothing to be concerned about, and he would be happy to discuss it with her at greater length when she returned from the library.

He sent her to Chaenath to ask for directions, which also seemed odd to Rydara. She had hardly spoken to Chaenath since her first visit, except on days when Chaenath forbade her to visit Aander or hurried her out of his room when his delirium started to return. But when Rydara asked about the library, Chaenath nodded, and Rydara sensed something like approval through her Knowing. Then Chaenath patiently explained how to get there and what the building would look like. Instead of going straight along the path back to the palace, Rydara took the branch that led to the rest of the elven city and followed Chaenath's landmarks to the river.

The library was a domed building several stories high, and it sat on the bank of the river. Rydara stopped by the water and scooped some into her hands. She brought her cupped hands close to her eye, covering the water from the sunlight to see if it still had that aqua glow.

It did.

Another thing I need to ask Neremyn about, Rydara thought. Or maybe she could find something about it in the library. *Not today,* Rydara told herself sternly. There were still so many things she needed to learn.

Today, she needed to find out more about something Neremyn had called "the shards of the Scepter of the Covenant." Yesterday, she had told him about the strange black crystal that Queen Lux and General Dameires had been using in their ritual at Tessex. Neremyn had gone silent for a time, deep in thought. Then he told her that when Nivalis had surrendered to the High Wizards, he had given them a crystal scepter filled with power—the power that had enabled them to kill him. When he died, it had shattered, along with the wizards' mind control and the sanity of their demons. The elves had collected three shards from the staff and learned they still had power to augment magic. Neremyn speculated that there may originally have been more shards, and Tenebrus and Atra might have taken some when they fled. The shards the elves had were translucent and closer to white in color, but he thought if the High Wizards had been using their shards in death rituals, the process might have changed the color.

Rydara hoped the library had more answers. If she could understand more about the shards and what the High Wizards were up to, she would be better able to explain it to the First Elf. Hopefully, the library would also tell her enough about elven laws and customs to guide Rydara in presenting her petition.

Rydara let the water fall back into the river, shook her hands dry, and entered the library.

When Neremyn had said "a collection of books," Rydara had imagined there might be as many as ten. There were thousands. Shelves of them stretched from the floor all the way up to the domed ceiling. Staircases led to balconies, making the higher volumes accessible though the space was not divided into separate floors. The ceiling, high above, was made of glass, and sunlight filled the building. There were several long tables in the middle of the floor, and a few elves were seated at one of them, talking quietly. Each of the balconies had one cushioned chair, and some of these were occupied by solitary elves holding books in their hands.

Reading.

Rydara's mind reeled. She did not know a number for how many pages of script must be contained in all these volumes. Even if they had been written in Common, she would be able to read only a fraction of a fraction of them in forty days. She might not have been able to read them all if she had forty lifetimes.

Rydara drew closer to where the shelves began. It seemed unbelievable that she would be allowed to explore this place and touch these remarkable "books" — let alone to read them. But no one stopped Rydara as she reached out a hand to touch the first volume.

An elegant script was carved on its spine. The Elvish language looked as beautiful as it sounded. When Rydara's fingers brushed against the letters, their sounds seemed to echo in her mind, and when she finished the first word the idea of a beautiful forested land with a river running through it presented itself to her consciousness. In this case, she did not need the extra help, because she had recognized the Elvish word already. *Edriendor*. The other words told her the book was a description of the features of this land, its plant life, and climate. Rydara had no doubt that it could have engrossed her for hours, but it was only the first book of thousands. It was not what she was looking for.

While browsing the shelves, Rydara discovered periodic signs that explained the subject matter of the different sections. She eventually made her way to a section about sights and imaging powers and found a title referencing the shards of the Scepter of the Covenant. Rydara pulled it off the shelf and opened the volume.

Rydara was a slow reader at first, as she paid attention not only to the meaning of the text but also the sounds the syllables formed in Elvish. It was as good as listening to Neremyn speak and then interpret for her, but she could go at her own pace. It was exhilarating, and it got easier as Rydara progressed deeper into the volume, learning incredible things about the magical properties of the crystals and the history that surrounded them.

She stood there for hours, utterly entranced by the trove of knowledge in her hands. She did not notice when an elf came up behind her.

"Rydara."

Rydara jumped at the sound of her name in the elven accent, hurriedly turning to apologize to the elf behind her for whatever it was she had done wrong.

But the elf smiled. It was not an open or even a friendly smile, as Neremyn's were, but it was a smile nonetheless. Her alarm had amused him.

He spoke again, and though he spoke in Elvish, Rydara had learned enough of it by now to understand him. "You've been standing here for hours," he said—although the corresponding elven unit of time translated more directly as "counts," and was a little shorter than the tribal "hour." "Perhaps you would like to sit down?"

"I'm sorry," Rydara answered in Elvish. She was still flustered from her surprise, and her lack of fluidity with the strange syllables flustered her further. She recognized this elf. He had been the one to lead her to her room after her audience with the First Elf. "You know my name. I never heard yours."

"You have learned some Elvish!" he chuckled, and Rydara was taken aback. Chaenath was always so silent and serious—similar to what little she had seen of Sundamar and the First Elf. Neremyn was more friendly, but she had never heard him laugh, and if he did laugh, Rydara imagined it would be a joyful laugh, sharing mirth with whoever was with him.

This elf's laugh seemed private—as though it might have come at her expense.

"Not bad, for a mortal," he continued. "My name is Faedastan."

"Well met, Faedastan," Rydara said, using the customary Elvish greeting. She curtsied. "Are you one of the Councilors?"

"Consuls," he corrected. Her attempt at transforming the Elvish word for "council" had not been quite right. "Indeed I am. You continue to impress."

"I have had some instruction from a patient at your infirmary," Rydara explained. "I go there daily to check on my brother."

"He was your brother? The pale-skinned man with hell plague? I had not considered he might be your sibling."

"The son of my father, though not of my mother. His mother died giving birth to him," Rydara explained, flushing. The elves did not have the same concept of marriage, as far as Rydara could tell—they did not live together in pairs with their children, as was the case in the tribes—but Neremyn had told her elves did not change mates after taking one. Rydara did not know if they had a concept for "bastard" or if it would matter to them that she was one. But she felt shame whenever the topic arose.

"Do you know if the First Elf..." Rydara trailed off as she tried to remember how to conjugate in the Elvish subjunctive.

"Speak your own tongue, if you like," Faedastan told her, still in Elvish. "Your spoken words make the feelings in your mind take more specific form to my sight, even if I do not understand them. You must experience something of the same, with your ability."

Rydara nodded slowly. She understood Faedastan's words, and she recognized the process he described, though she had never thought about it in exactly those terms.

"Do you know if the First Elf might be open to hearing my petition sooner than the forty days she set?" she asked in Common. It was a relief to use her own language, in which she was better able to achieve exactly the shade of meaning she intended. But she had to keep practicing, so she switched back to Elvish after getting that sentence out of the way. "The request I have to present to your people is urgent, though I was not in a state to make it while my brother was dying, as a total stranger to your land and culture."

"And now that you have learned a little Elvish, you understand all you need to know about us? Is that it?" The corner of Faedastan's mouth twitched upward.

She shook her head. "No, of course, I am still a stranger," she said, dropping her eyes in embarrassment.

"Arcaena is seldom known to change her mind. Forty days is not so long a time, and you may be grateful for the preparation when you stand before her again. If your request is on behalf of your father's people, it will take a great deal to persuade her to sympathy."

"My father's people?" Rydara caught the qualification, and it made her curious. "Do you think she would be more willing to sympathize with my mother?"

"If your father is pale of skin, then your mother must have been a lost daughter." The Elvish word was *nimkeïass*, and when Faedastan spoke it, Rydara remembered Chaenath had used it to greet her the first time she had visited the infirmary. "If her people sought refuge from the persecution of other humans, Arcaena might have been stirred to help. We were so persecuted, once."

"Lost daughter?" Rydara echoed the Elvish term. "Are we ... descended from elves? My mother's people?"

"You are fully human, child," Faedastan assured her. "When we left the lands of men, there were some among us who did not agree with Arcaena's decision. Dasyra, Aravae, Itylara, Nithenoel, Lyeneru, Thaciona, and Myantha. The seven lost daughters of Edriendor. They stayed behind to teach the humans our way of life and history. Away from this land and the power of the shards, they eventually grew old and died after the manner of mortals, and their children, born to human fathers, were human. Limited to one magic, if any, and far shorter-lived than their mothers. But you have inherited something of our coloring."

Rydara hardly knew what to think, let alone say. The idea that the Rishara could have descended from a race as powerful and beautiful as this, and that the elves would cherish them as lost children, when they were so distrusted and despised by all the tribes ... but then, the tribes had come to hate the elves, too, if the stories were true.

And it seemed they were.

"Did not Neremyn explain this to you?" Faedastan asked, noting her surprise.

Rydara shook her head. "I have had so many questions. There is so much to learn. We had not covered that yet." She paused, then glanced up at him. "You know Neremyn?"

"We are all very old here, Rydara, by your short human standards, and we seldom procreate. Most of us know everyone in Edriendor to some extent. And Neremyn, well—he is quite famous."

Rydara's brow furrowed. Neremyn had taught her the Elvish word for "famous," but her Knowing registered a heavy negative connotation when Faedastan used it. Perhaps "infamous" or "notorious" was closer to what he meant.

"Everyone knows he is the sole 'patient' at the 'infirmary,'" Faedastan continued, giving the terms a light touch of irony, "where he has been kept for many hundreds of years."

"He told me he could not leave because of his health," Rydara said, confused.

"He cannot leave the infirmary because it is his prison. Leaving would present no risk to his health, or even interfere with Chaenath's 'treatment' of him. Not unless he stayed away for decades. Or even centuries."

"What does Chaenath do to him?" Rydara asked, dread pooling in her stomach.

"You haven't been told anything about this?" Faedastan seemed as surprised as he was amused by the extent of her ignorance. "We have a code we live by, and most of us keep it well enough. But when crimes are committed, if the criminal is deemed unrepentant and a continued threat to our way of life in his current state of mind, the Council of Twelve approves the final intervention: treatment of the mind and personality. The criminal's memories are erased, and a new way of life and thought are introduced to him. Chaenath checks and refreshes her interventions in Neremyn's mind every day. Though the frequency is quite excessive, as I said. Her blocks could endure for centuries."

Rydara did not want to ask the next question, but she had to. "What did he do?"

He was the only patient in the infirmary ... and he had been for centuries.

Faedastan smiled a mocking smile. "My dear little mortal, haven't you guessed? Neremyn was one of the High Wizards."

Chapter 9

The Shards of Edriendor

"You are familiar with the High Wizards and what they did?" Faedastan continued casually, as if the subject were of little consequence. As if he had not just shattered the fragile new framework Rydara had been using to help her make sense of the world.

Rydara's breath sounded loud in her ears. She tried to focus on what Faedastan was saying.

"Yes, I see you are." He frowned. "Why such distress? What the High Wizards did was terrible, true, but it was hundreds of years ago, and nothing to do with you. Neremyn is quite removed from..." He paused and tilted his head. "But it *does* have something to do with you, doesn't it? Interesting. How is that possible? And why is it that you're reading about shards?"

Rydara was quite unused to having her emotions read by other Knowers, and Faedastan's perspicacity unsettled her. "The High Wizards..." she swallowed, unsure whether confiding in Faedastan now was a good idea. As a member of the Council of Twelve, he would be present at her audience with the First Elf and play a role in their consideration of her petition. If she told him what it was about beforehand, he would have more time to develop arguments to sway others to his view. *Would he be for me or against me?*

"*Zìlnesh nyll liwynathìmo,*" Faedastan muttered, eyes growing wide. Rydara had not noticed when he began using the Speaking magic to aid her understanding, but it was obvious when he stopped. The phrase meant nothing to her. "That's why you're here," Faedastan continued, and this time she noted the light touch of magic he added. "They have a shard, and they're using it against your father's people."

Rydara nodded slowly. He could read the answer in her emotions anyway, so she would just have to hope telling him was not a mistake.

Faedastan was silent for a long moment, and though the only change in his expression was a slight narrowing of his eyes, Rydara felt him flicker through half a dozen emotions. Surprise. Envy. Intense interest. Malice. Resolve. And then—so brief she almost missed it—excitement.

His eyes flicked back to her then, and it was as though a wall suddenly dropped between them. Her Knowing sensed no more of his emotions.

He had cut her off, somehow, with his Speaking magic, but too late. Whatever decision he had just arrived at signaled danger to Rydara's Knowing, and Rydara's pulse quickened as she returned his gaze, her own eyes wide. She summoned to mind a memory of the glowing aqua fountain in the First Elf's audience chamber, pushing awareness of her Knowing to the edge of her consciousness. She focused on the image of the fountain, remembering the water's sound and motion, forcing her breaths to stay slow and deep.

Calm, flowing, glowing water. There are any number of perfectly innocent reasons he might be interested in the High Wizards. Calm, flowing, glowing water. Nothing to see, nothing to worry about. Calm, flowing, glowing water...

Faedastan was watching her closely, his eyes narrowed. She could only hope the meditation might soften whatever reaction he was reading from her.

"Yes," she said aloud, thinking to distract him from his study. *Calm, flowing, glowing water.* It would be rude to let on how uncomfortable she was, Rydara told herself. She had no wish to be rude. "I believe they are murdering my people and using their deaths to corrupt the shard they have, to change its purpose in some way ... I do not know how, or if that is even possible, but I saw them kill a friend of my brother's and let the blood flow over a shard..." Rydara closed her eyes, reliving the horror of that moment. It was a safe emotion to let Faedastan see, and Rydara did not have to work to slip into it.

Her eyes snapped open. She did not like the memory. "Now you understand my urgency. We cannot fight these High Wizards. My people have no magic to defend themselves. They do not even understand the threat. But if the First Elf—" Rydara frowned and switched back to Common. She would have to figure out the subjunctive later. "If she would agree to see me sooner than the forty days—I know she was able to stop the High Wizards once before..."

Faedastan's eyes narrowed further, and Rydara's voice faltered, thinking he might have seen through her paltry facade. Her Knowing still sensed nothing from him.

Perhaps it had been a mistake to fall back on Common. He must know she was nervous.

But his posture relaxed. "Arcaena has set the time," he said. "She will not move it, and if she had known the nature of your petition, she might not have agreed to hear you at all." His face was drawn, and there was something in his eyes that looked like sorrow. "Your father's people turned on us, long ago, despite our role in defeating the High Wizards. Arcaena will have no compunction about leaving them to their fate."

Faedastan's tone suggested that despite whatever sympathy he might have for her people, he believed Arcaena's position was reasonable. Rydara had not won an ally. "But they conquered the whole world once before," she argued in Elvish, hoping to reverse any damage she might have done to her cause. *Yes, I am concerned about my upcoming audience. I must persuade him not to argue against me. That is all.* "Don't you think they will come here, too, after they subdue Alterra, Jeshimoth, and the tribes? Surely, it must be better to take the fight to them before they grow too powerful—don't you agree?" Rydara stumbled through her last question, unsure if she had used the correct grammar.

"You have some reading yet to do." Faedastan nodded to the book in her hands. "This land is protected by the power of the shards. No demon can cross its boundaries. If a High Wizard attempted it, they would leave their demon behind and cease to be a High Wizard."

Rydara nodded slowly and let her gaze drift to the book in her hands, aware that Faedastan was still studying her. There were more implications to be drawn from his words, but Rydara tried not to think about them. *Calm, flowing, glowing water.* "I have so much to learn," she said. "Perhaps I will need the forty days after all. Thank you for your wisdom."

Rydara focused her mind on the enormity of the task before her. The First Elf was biased against her people, and all Rydara had learned about her and the rest of the elven people so far had come from a source she no longer trusted.

There was much to worry about, and every reason to feel that time was short.

Faedastan nodded. "I shall leave you to it. Best of luck, Rydara." There was a small smile on his lips as he turned and glided down the balcony stairs.

Rydara moved to an empty chair and sat gingerly, finding her place in her book. She did her best to focus on the reading for a full two pages. Then she stood, moved to the balcony railing, and surveyed the library carefully.

Faedastan had gone.

Rydara exhaled heavily and let herself focus on her Knowing, turning over the sense of vast and imminent danger Faedastan's decision had filled it with. His malice had not been for her, and neither was the threat he posed — at least, not directly. It was bigger.

Malice for Edriendor, perhaps, or for the whole world. He was excited by the High Wizards' return and whatever decision the news had inspired him to make.

Rydara had to warn someone.

***

Two hours later, Rydara was exhausted and dizzy from trekking through the woods. She had decided to tell Sundamar about her fears, not knowing whom else to trust. Neremyn had told her Sundamar was part of the Edren Guard, and a map in the library had shown her the way to their practice grounds, but she had not realized how long it would take to walk there. Not for the first time, she wondered if her physiology was incompatible with the elven diet. Fast days were difficult enough without taking long treks through the forest.

But she was afraid of Faedastan. She was afraid of what she had set in motion and the danger it might pose to this beautiful land. She had to continue.

Eventually the trees thinned, and Rydara came to an open field. Two dragons flew overhead, and five more dotted the field. There were elves with them.

The dragons in the air were locked on a collision course. Rydara watched breathlessly as they zoomed toward each other. Fire bloomed in the air between them, two massive balls of it spreading from each dragon toward the other, and Rydara, shocked, thought the beasts would collide in a giant conflagration.

But their riders shouted, and though the yells were wordless, they thundered with power that rocked Rydara back on her heels. The dragons both turned at the last second, narrowly missing each other, and though they cut straight through the fire, each was surrounded by a pocket of air that divided the fire around them. Nothing burned. Flaming sparks fell toward the meadow and were quickly extinguished.

"*Licilirest! Taro likeerad!*" one of the riders cried. *Look, we have a visitor.*

The speaker's dragon peeled off in a backward somersault that should have thrown the rider. The beast dove toward

Rydara, waiting until the last second to open its wings and come to a graceful stop, whipping Rydara's hair back from her face in the process.

She tried not to cower.

The rider jumped lightly from the dragon's back. She had widely-spaced eyes, a small nose, and full lips, and she wore her hair in dozens of tightly-plaited braids. Her lips curved upward—not quite a smile, but close—as she walked toward Rydara.

Rydara would never get used to the beauty of this strange race.

Musical syllables flowed from the elf's tongue. They meant, "You are Rydara. Well met," but as usual, the translation hardly did them justice. "I am Ildylintra. What brings you here?" Rydara could hear the gentle hum of Ildylintra's Speaking, helping to impress the meaning on her mind, but she already knew the words.

"I am looking for Sundamar," she replied in Elvish. "Is he here?"

The second dragon landed next to them in another gust of wind, and Rydara recognized Lëanor. Sundamar leapt to the ground. "You speak Elvish," he said, and though he did not smile either, there was a faint twinkle in his eyes, and Rydara sensed a flash of genuine pleasure.

"Only a little." Rydara smiled briefly. *Well met, Lëanor,* she thought, glancing at the dragon. *It is good to see you again.* A gentle warmth let her know the dragon was pleased to see her, but Rydara's pleasure was tempered by the news she carried.

Sundamar's brow creased. "You wanted to see me?"

"I didn't know who to speak to," Rydara said. "Something has happened. I'm afraid I've put your people in danger..." Rydara looked at Ildylintra, considering whether she should speak in front of her. Sundamar seemed to expect her to, and Rydara was hesitant to demand a private word. She did not even know if he would take her claims seriously, and if he did not, she would need to find someone else to warn anyway.

It might as well be Ildylintra.

"Will you understand me if I speak my own language?" Rydara asked in Common. The elves both nodded, so Rydara plunged ahead, briefly recounting her conversation with Faedastan and everything she had sensed from him. "I think he means to harm Edriendor, or worse. Something must be done to stop him."

"You believe there are High Wizards in the world again," Sundamar repeated in Elvish. Rydara nodded, knowing he was using his magic to assess her claim. Sundamar exchanged a long look with Ildylintra, and then they seemed to accept it. "You brought news of this to Faedastan, and you think it inspired him to harm us?"

"Faedastan, the Consul?" Ildylintra's brow furrowed. "You are sure it was him?"

"He was there when Sundamar brought me before the First Elf," Rydara answered, switching back to Elvish. "The one who showed me to my room. He said his name was Faedastan."

Sundamar nodded, but his expression remained doubtful. "Then it was Consul Faedastan, but you must be mistaken. He has served hundreds of years on the Council of Twelve and is above reproach."

"Besides," Ildylintra added, glancing at Sundamar, "the Consul is a masterful seer and imager. What we call a wizard. If he had something to hide from you, he would have done so. I mean no insult to you or your insight, which must be truly remarkable for you to have learned our tongue so quickly. But you are, after all, only human, and your talent is no match for his."

Rydara pursed her lips. She would have liked to accept their reassurance, and if all this had happened on her first day in their country, she might have. But her Knowing had been growing stronger since then—likely due to the influence of the shards—and her ability to interpret it had also improved.

One of the first things a Knower learned to do was to refuse to let leaders or other advisers talk them out of what they Knew to be true. No matter how powerful the king or chieftain, how well-informed his other advisers might be, or how strong their opinions were, only a Knower had the Knowing magic. It was the Knower's responsibility to make their Knowing known and not to second-guess or back down from it because others found it unlikely or inconvenient. If a Knower doubted herself, her magic was useless, and she might as well forfeit her post.

The shaman in Kale had made sure Rydara learned that lesson. The first time he had tried to poison her, Rydara had ignored her uneasiness and drank the cup of offered tea. She had been sick for days. She had never failed his tests again, even when she had had to knock a glass of poisoned wine out of her father's hand in the middle of a banquet that the shaman had attended.

It was different with these elves because they also were Knowers. But they had not been in the library with Faedastan. They had not glimpsed his envy of the High Wizards or his malice. The threat he posed now was not as easy for Rydara to point to as a glass of wine, but she Knew it would be a mistake to do nothing to stop him.

If only Aander were well, she wished, uselessly. *Aander would make them understand.* Rydara was fortunate to serve as Knower to someone who trusted her talent so completely. When her powers of persuasion failed, she could always count on Aander to make sure her Knowing was not waved aside.

"You said he is a wizard," Rydara said. "Are his imaging talents stronger than your sights? Would it be simple for him to deceive you about his character?" It felt rude to impugn these elves' insight, but Rydara could think of no other argument.

"Yes," Ildylintra said. She did not add, *and it would be even simpler for him to deceive you,* but Rydara knew she was thinking it.

"You said he is above reproach," Rydara said slowly, "but what if—" she frowned, unsure how to construct her next thought in Elvish. She switched to Common. "What if that is only the impression he wished to give you?" She glanced between the two of them and went back to speaking Elvish. "He knows I am 'only human,' as you say. He may not have given much thought to hiding his nature from me. And as I said, I sensed nothing from him at all after his initial emotions. He must have underestimated my insight, not realizing he had already given himself away."

The other elves in the meadow, likely waiting on the conversation to resume their exercises, walked closer to hear what it was about. Some of their dragons came with them, flying leisurely and low to the ground.

Rydara tried to think of them as more potential allies, instead of more potential witnesses to her wild accusations against their Consul.

"You thought he had given himself away," Sundamar said as a few dragons landed. "That you saw his malice and the threat he posed. And you think he did not perceive this? That his own insight failed?"

Rydara twisted her hands in frustration. She was not getting through to them. "Or perhaps he did know and did not care, because he knew no one would listen to me. What do you think, Lëanor?" Rydara turned and addressed Sundamar's dragon, a little startled by her own boldness.

The creature twisted its neck, turning its spike-rimmed face to one side in an oddly human gesture.

I have met Faedastan on several occasions. I would not consider him above reproach.

"He serves on the Council of Twelve," Ildylintra objected to the dragon's comment, confirming that she and the other elves also heard it. "And though he is a wizard, his powers are no match for Arcaena's. If there were anything objectionable in his character, she would not allow him to serve."

Rydara tightened her lips. "Perhaps. But still, I must speak to the First Elf and warn her." Without anyone to advocate for her, Arcaena seemed even less likely to take Rydara seriously than her current audience, but taking the time to come here appeared to have been a mistake.

I will take you, Lëanor volunteered. *If Sundamar will excuse me.*

The gathered elves turned their gazes on Sundamar, and Rydara wondered that none of them asked what was going on. Perhaps their insight had brought them up to speed already. In Neremyn's brief overview of elven culture, he had mentioned the Edren Guard was made up of promising magic users chosen from among the elves' youth, none of them more than a century old. All of them were likely to become wizards in later development, which meant their powers of both imaging and sight were among the strongest in the country.

"We will both go," Sundamar decided. "Regardless of Faedastan's intentions, the First Elf must be informed of the High Wizards' return without delay. She may not be willing to receive you to hear your account of it and your warning, but I will endeavor to persuade her."

"Is that wise?" Another elf spoke up. All the females of this group wore their hair in many-plaited braids like Ildylintra, but there was something in this one's face that reminded Rydara strongly of Arcaena. The delicate lines were similar, and so were the big brown eyes. "You have not returned to favor. Perhaps another of us should take her."

"It is my responsibility, Sarya, and she cannot ignore me. I will go. Ildylintra can lead the exercises." Sundamar leapt onto Lëanor's wing and extended a hand toward Rydara. "Come."

Rydara climbed aboard, her stomach fluttering at the prospect of another flight. When Lëanor took off, it was a little less disorienting than before. "You are the leader of the Edren Guard?" she asked Sundamar, still speaking Elvish. She was glad it was Sundamar and Lëanor taking her. They were a touch of familiarity.

Rydara had precious little of that, and it hurt that she could no longer trust Neremyn.

"A minor station, but I perform the duties as well as I can," Sundamar agreed.

Rydara frowned, puzzled that leading the Edren Guard would be considered "minor." They were the elves' only point of contact with the world beyond Edriendor and the land's first line of defense. Perhaps he was being modest.

"It's because of me that you are out of favor, isn't it?" Rydara asked. "Because you rescued me and my brother."

"Arcaena believes I broke our code," Sundamar replied, keeping his eyes on the horizon. "But she admits it is open to interpretation. And she did not see how you suffered."

"Thank you," Rydara said. The words were wholly inadequate, but Rydara could offer nothing else. "I am sorry you lost her favor."

"I would do it again." Sundamar turned his gaze to meet hers. He had no regrets.

The moment stretched, and Rydara felt something more in his gaze. Something like what came into Aander's eyes when he spoke of Jemine. It was a gaze no man of the tribes had ever turned on Rydara, nor had she ever thought one might.

Rydara blushed and looked away. Nothing in the world was as beautiful as an elf. It was impossible that she could hold any quality to attract Sundamar.

Rydara began another meditation on the fountain, worried the elf would sense her embarrassing mistake. But he gazed at her a moment longer, and despite her best efforts to ignore it, Rydara's Knowing suggested there had been no mistake.

The sun was setting when they landed in the palace grounds. Rydara was forced to take Sundamar's hand for the dismount. She planned to break the contact quickly, but he kept holding her hand when she reached the ground, his grip firm and inescapable. He met her eyes, and Rydara caught her breath, afraid he would see everything she thought and felt.

"I think you are wrong about Faedastan," Sundamar said in the beautiful music of his tongue. "But you have nothing to be embarrassed about, much less to apologize for. It is my people who were wrong, to think I should have left you to die in the Waste."

Rydara returned his gaze, abruptly forgetting the urgency of their errand and her own awkwardness. For a moment it was just the two of them.

Then Sundamar released her hand. He strode toward the palace, and Rydara returned to her senses. She hurried after him.

An elf intercepted them as they approached the audience chamber, and Sundamar exchanged a few words with him to convey their purpose. The other elf brought them into the hall with the fountain and the chairs for the Council of Twelve. Today they were empty. Sundamar told Rydara he would convey her concerns to Arcaena and try to persuade her to see Rydara. Then he and the other elf disappeared down one of the corridors, and Rydara was left alone at the foot of the dais.

She waited uneasily, thinking back to her conversation with Faedastan and that brief series of emotions she had sensed from him. He envied the High Wizards, and he meant to do something terrible.

But what? Now that Rydara had done what she could to stop him, her mind turned to the question of what kind of threat he posed. If the High Wizards had reforged the compact, then, presumably, there were already nine of them, and they had already become hosts for the nine lords of hell. She did not think Faedastan could become one of them.

Perhaps he did not envy them for the demons they hosted. The High Wizards controlled Alterra and probably Jeshimoth, and the tribes could not resist them. They had their shards, and immeasurably more power than the human race. Perhaps Faedastan wished to share in that dominance.

Or replicate it. *But how could he?* Rydara did not think he could seize power here in Edriendor. The elves were married to their code, and their magic was too strong for Faedastan to topple their hierarchy and deceive them about how he did it.

And this land is beyond the High Wizards' reach, Rydara remembered. Faedastan had said Edriendor was protected by the shards, so he could not think to invite them here and use their dark magic to aid his bid for power.

The shards. Of course. The shards contained the power of a god. If Faedastan stole them, they would augment his power. Rydara did not know by how much, or if it would be enough to let him seize control.

But he wouldn't have to. If he wanted to harm Edriendor, all he had to do was take the shards, and the land would be vulnerable to the High Wizards. If Faedastan brought the shards to the High Wizards, he might earn himself a respected place among them, even if he could not become one himself.

The shards could be in danger. Rydara fretted that Sundamar had not yet returned with Arcaena. The prospect of speaking to the First Elf made her stomach tighten with worry of a different kind, but someone had to warn them, and soon.

Rydara looked around, but the chamber was still empty. Her gaze settled on the fountain—or perhaps it was a spring, forced to shoot higher by the structure that had been built around it. The water fell into a white marble circle before cascading into a larger pool and then tumbling over the edge of the dais into the river. It was beautiful, and the sound was calming.

Decorations lined the upper tier of the fountain. White gems. At least two were built into the marble circle. The water flowed around them as it fell to the lower pool.

Rydara's brow furrowed as she thought back to the black crystal General Dameires had held while he murdered Kell. The gems in the fountain were similar in shape and size. *Could they be...*

Rydara took the steps up to the dais and approached the fountain. There were three gems fixed at even intervals around the circle. Little sconces in the marble held them in place. They were nearly white in color, but translucent.

No. All three of them, here? Rydara looked around, incredulous. The chamber was still empty. *Would the elves really leave them unguarded?*

Would they leave me *alone with them, unguarded?*

Perhaps they were magically bound to the fountain and impossible to remove. Rydara reached out and took hold of one.

It came away in her hand.

Rydara stared at it in dismay, thinking — *wishing* — these could not possibly be the three shards that protected all of Edriendor.

But she knew they were. The elves had their code, and nobody ever broke it. Nobody but Neremyn and the other High Wizards, hundreds of years ago. The elves trusted each other, and they were not afraid of one human girl with the Knowing magic. How far could she get if she tried to steal one? The shards should have been safe here.

Rydara could feel power in her hand. The crystal pulsed with an energy she had come to associate with the Speaking magic. She wondered if the shards gave the water its aqua glow, and if it was a natural effect of their magic or if the elves had designed it on purpose.

"Very clever, Rydara. But altogether too slow. Did you think I didn't know you were on to me?"

The Elvish words chilled Rydara to the core. Her eyes darted up to see Faedastan entering from one of the corridors on the far side of the dais, the fountain partly obstructing her view.

Rydara leapt down from the dais and started to run.

"Stop," he Spoke, and Rydara froze. She opened her mouth to scream.

"Quiet."

She was choking on air. One of the shards of Edriendor was still in her hands.

But the magic was not like before, with the Alterran queen and general. She was not completely immobilized, and a quiet moan escaped her throat. She might have been able to force out a little more volume.

Instead, Rydara reached a hand toward the river and dropped the shard beneath the current. Faedastan was circling the dais, coming closer. He may not have seen it yet.

She stopped thinking about it.

"Arcaena wouldn't have believed you, of course," Faedastan said, taking the steps up the dais. He was not looking at her. He might not have noticed. "She would not have taken action against me. But she's not a fool. If you had come straight here after our chat, she might have arranged better protection for these before I could secure my escape." He plucked the shards from the fountain. Then he frowned. "Two?" he muttered to himself. "Where…" he turned and glared at Rydara. "You've taken it. Where did you put it?"

Rydara stared at the fountain, forcing everything but its image out of her mind. *Calm, flowing, glowing water. Calm, flowing, glowing water.* Nothing else existed. Nothing else mattered. There was nothing else for Faedastan to read from her.

He strode toward Rydara, placing the two shards in pockets within his robes. "Where is it?" he demanded, the words laced heavily with magic. "Answer me!"

Rydara clung stubbornly to the image of the fountain, fighting down the urge to speak. She refused to let the answer form, even in her mind. The fountain was her entire world. *Calm, flowing, glowing water.* There was nothing else.

Faedastan roughly frisked her whole body, but there was nothing to find. "Foolish mortal," he cursed. "Where did you put it?" he whispered fiercely, pushing her up against the dais.

Her mental image of the fountain broke. "The river," Rydara gasped, the words rushing out against her will. She bit her tongue, hard, but too late.

"There, that wasn't so hard." Faedastan smirked, releasing her, and Rydara clapped a hand to her mouth as she staggered away from him, appalled at what she had done. "Stay." She sank down to the floor, unable to retreat farther.

Faedastan turned and studied the river for a moment. Then he jumped in, and when he resurfaced, Rydara knew he had all three shards. "Don't be so hard on yourself, Rydara," he said as he pulled himself out on the other side. "One wouldn't have been enough to keep Tenebrus from coming here anyway. Now nothing will stop his return." Faedastan whirled away and retreated down one of the corridors, his footfalls soon fading in the empty chamber.

Tears pooled in Rydara's eyes as she fought to move and failed, fought to scream and failed at that, too. Precious moments went by. Rydara was still crouched by the pillar, powerless, when shouts finally rang through the palace.

Chapter 10

The Chase

A half-dozen elves soon rushed into the chamber. One of them was a Consul, Rydara guessed, based on her style of loose-fitting robes. Another was Sundamar.

They ran toward the dais. Sundamar reached it first and searched the fountain. "They are gone," he told the others. Then his gaze fell on Rydara, and he hurried to her. "Are you all right?" he asked, taking her hand. Faedastan's magic had already started to fade, but the last of it dissipated with Sundamar's touch as he helped her gain her feet. "Was it Faedastan?"

"Yes, he went that way," Rydara pointed down the corridor he had taken, still marked by the water that had run off him after his dip in the river. "Five minutes ago, maybe less."

"Go," the Consul ordered Sundamar. Sundamar ran down the corridor, whistling. Rydara could hear magic in the notes, and she guessed it was a signal for Lëanor.

The Consul strode up to the fountain, and the other elves eyed Rydara while they waited for further instruction. Rydara could feel their fear, and some of it was directed at her.

She had brought this disaster upon them.

"All three of them," the Consul muttered, inspecting the empty places where the shards belonged. She bowed her head, and Rydara sensed great sorrow.

"I'm sorry," Rydara stammered. "I tried to save one, but—I couldn't."

"What happened?" the Consul asked, turning to look at her.

Rydara explained as best she could. The elves questioned her for a long time, but they were not disrespectful. The Consul even asked for her consent before using magic to order her to speak the truth while repeating her story.

In the end, the elves were persuaded Rydara had not been involved. She supposed she had their magic to thank for that. She could not have faked the depth of shame she felt at her failure, and she had no doubt they all sensed it.

The Consul startled her by laying a hand on her shoulder. "You are not to blame, Rydara. He is a wizard, after all—too strong for you to resist his commands. You did what you could to warn us."

Rydara stared back at the elf, speechless. Among the tribes, leaders usually took all the credit for any right moves while letting the blame for mistakes rest squarely on those beneath them—yet here, this Consul was recognizing Rydara's effort and pardoning her mistake. Even though the consequences for the country would be devastating.

Even though Rydara was obviously at fault.

Perhaps it was foolish to imagine she should have been stronger, but Rydara could not help but remember that Faedastan's magic had not been as strong as the High Wizards'. She had not been completely powerless. She had held back the shard's location for a time, and her concentration had broken before the words escaped her. Perhaps if she had been more skillful at setting her entire mind on her meditation and holding it there, Faedastan's magic would not have been enough to prize the information from her, and he would have left with only two shards.

"It is in Arcaena's hands now," the Consul spoke again, "and in the hands of the Edren Guard. Thank you, lost daughter. You may go."

"Thank you," Rydara stammered, taken aback by the term. "And I—I'm sorry." Rydara nodded so deeply it was almost a bow and then hurried away before the Consul could refuse her apology.

Not knowing what else to do, Rydara went back to her room and paced, wondering what the elves would do to stop Faedastan. Whether they would be successful.

Why this strange race, to whom she had already done a great disservice, kept calling her "daughter" when her real father, whom she had faithfully served her entire life, had stripped her of that title and sent her away.

She slept little. No one came to bring her news. When the sun finally rose, the waiting became unbearable, and Rydara decided to visit Aander. She was still nervous about seeing Neremyn again, but when she got to the infirmary, she slipped inside and managed to get as far as her brother's room without crossing paths with him.

Aander was sitting up in bed.

Rydara's face broke into a smile. "Aander!" she rushed to him and knelt by his bedside, taking his hand. "You're awake! How are you?"

Aander managed a smile, too, though his was smaller. He squeezed her hand. "Weak." He coughed a few times, and his voice was scratchy. But the horrible wrack had subsided. "Could you be a little quieter?"

"Of course, of course," Rydara said softly, squeezing his hand back. Her eyes filled with sudden moisture, and she wiped her nose on her sleeve.

"Hey." Aander turned his face toward her, brow furrowing. "Who died?"

"You didn't." Rydara choked out a laugh, resting her forehead against Aander's shoulder. "By the Six, Aander, I thought you were going to."

Aander patted her hair weakly. "Just like you, always panicking prematurely."

Rydara laughed again, raising her head to look at him. "I have so much to tell you."

"Let me guess." Aander cleared his throat. "We found the elves, and we're set to present our petition to their leaders in … twenty-seven days? An amiable elf came to see me last time I woke up and shared a few details. Said he was a friend of yours, and that you'd gone to see some ... ledger collection?"

"Neremyn? Aander, we can't trust Neremyn. He used to be a High Wizard. Like the sorcerers who murdered Kell..."

It was a long story, and Rydara had to explain all the new terms. But eventually she brought Aander up to speed on High Wizards and the current crisis with Faedastan.

Aander was quiet for a long moment. "Perhaps you are being too hard on him."

Rydara's brow creased. "What?"

"Neremyn. You've spent a lot of time with him since we've been here, haven't you?"

"Yes."

"And then you had one conversation with Faedastan, and you Knew he was up to no good."

"And?"

"And, has your Knowing ever suggested anything like that about Neremyn?"

Rydara tightened her lips as she thought back over the last twelve days. She had been in Neremyn's company almost constantly. She had sensed nothing but friendship and eagerness to help.

Except, perhaps, when she had asked why he could not leave the infirmary. He had been reluctant to speak of it. Not secretive or duplicitous—just reluctant. She had not pressed him.

"I'm only just beginning to wrap my head around all this," Aander said. He sounded tired. "And I don't want to minimize the evil of the High Wizards. But Neremyn isn't one of them anymore. He hasn't hosted a demon in hundreds of years, isn't that right? He doesn't even remember any of that."

Rydara nodded slowly.

"I remember Tessex now." Aander's gaze was distant, but Rydara felt a shadow of grief through his exhaustion. "I remember the mass grave. Kell's death. How helpless we were. I don't know why I remember it now or how they ever made me forget ... I think I understand why you wouldn't want to trust a High Wizard." Aander's lips tightened.

Then he met Rydara's gaze. "But Neremyn didn't kill Kell. Or the villagers from Tessex. And I think that if he were a threat, you would have sensed something." He coughed a few times, and Rydara was sad to see it was still a struggle for him to catch his breath. "Just saying. He seems like he wants to help us, and it sounds like we need all the help we can get."

It was just like Aander, to hope to find an ally in an old enemy. To offer someone a second chance. To believe people could change.

Rydara had seen his hope work magic on Kell's father and the Rinton chieftain, but this felt different to her. Perhaps the horror she remembered from Tessex was partly to blame, but Neremyn had willingly partnered with a lord of hell and helped kill the god of the elves and the Rishara. He must have participated in scenes like Tessex along the way, and the idea of accepting his help now disturbed her.

Rydara?

Rydara rose to her feet, startled by the impression in her Knowing. *Lëanor?*

Through the glass door of Aander's room that led into the garden, Rydara saw a sudden shadow fall across the plants. Wind stirred them, and Rydara watched in fascination as the leaves and petals of every flower folded tightly inward. The wind intensified as Lëanor and Sundamar landed, blowing the garden almost flat, but when the wind died, they eased back into position. Petals reopened in every row, quickly returning the garden to its former vibrancy.

Rydara looked back at Aander.

"Go." He managed a faint smile, a slight crease to his brow the only sign of his disappointment that he could not follow. "Find out what happened. I could use some rest."

Rydara kissed his forehead. She hurried outside.

Sundamar wore a grim expression, and his head and shoulders were slightly bowed. "Faedastan has escaped with two shards."

"Two?" Rydara asked in Elvish, stepping toward him. "You got one back?"

"He let it fall as he approached the border. Its power augmented the Showing he cast to distract us, and he was able to slip across."

"Why are you back? Are you hurt?" Rydara closed the rest of the distance between them, moving to touch his arm in concern—but she caught herself before she did. They did not have that level of intimacy.

"Arcaena recalled us after we failed at the border. I am sorry." Sundamar knelt and took Rydara's hand, bowing his forehead against it and leaving her utterly stupefied. "I should have heeded your warning with much more urgency."

"I ... uh..." Rydara's cheeks flushed as a tremor shot through her body. Sundamar had no reason to be kneeling in front of her, and if she let him hold her hand any longer it was going to sweat. She tried to pull it back, but the effort was feeble and he seemed not to notice. "You could not have known," she protested.

"I could have listened." Sundamar raised his head, and then his eyes trapped hers as firmly as he held her hand. "You saw what we failed to, and if you had not, we might have lost all three shards instead of responding fast enough to save one. You have done us a great service."

Rydara gave no answer, mute and frozen in his grasp. Then he nodded to her, stood, and released her hand, and she breathed again.

She shook her head, dropping her gaze. He was giving her far too much credit. "I told Faedastan the High Wizards were back before I told you or the Council. If he hadn't known, he wouldn't have tried to steal the shards. It's my fault they were ever in danger."

"No." Sundamar shook his head. "Faedastan would have learned of the High Wizards eventually, and without you, we would have been ignorant of his intentions."

"Maybe." Rydara glanced up at Sundamar. He was no longer staring at her. Instead, the elf paced back and forth on the walkway, the action doing nothing to dispel the restless energy she sensed inside him.

The elves had recovered one shard, and that was something— but they had still lost two. Faedastan had shamed them and endangered their country, and Sundamar obviously did not want to be doing nothing.

Yet here he was. He seemed to have no intention of leaving.

Rydara's brow furrowed. "I don't understand why Arcaena recalled you," she said. "Does she mean not to pursue Faedastan any farther? Is she giving up the other two shards for lost?"

"Yes." Sundamar stopped pacing and turned to face her. "He has crossed the border. Beyond it, we lack the powers of this land. And he has fled to the High Wizards. Together their powers will be very great."

"Won't their powers be greater by far if they gain two more shards?" Rydara pressed. "Don't your people need to stop Faedastan before he gets to them?"

"Our best chance was at the border. Arcaena is not willing to commit our lives. It would take many of us to ensure victory. The High Wizards have no designs on this land that we know of. And we still have one shard."

Rydara closed her eyes tightly and clenched her jaw, working to contain her alarm. "Sundamar, Faedastan let you have one shard because it won't be enough to protect your people from Tenebrus."

"We cannot know that."

"Faedastan told me so, and I felt his conviction. But isn't it obvious? Your land was built on the power of three shards, not one. One can't be enough."

"One shard may not be enough to protect our borders, but it will be enough to ensure quick access to the Realm Between for even the weakest imager among us. We will be able to escape, at least, if it comes to that, and Arcaena believes this is the better choice than risking lives. And neither we nor Faedastan can know for sure whether the High Wizards even mean to come here."

Rydara opened her mouth to argue, but she did not know what to say. She did not understand what he meant about escaping to the Realm Between, but she was sure he was wrong to think the High Wizards posed no threat to his people. Even if he was right, two more shards in the hands of the High Wizards could mean only greater disaster for her own people.

Her spirits sank as she stared back at Sundamar. Despite his eloquent apology for not listening to her before, he still would not take her side.

"No!"

Rydara whirled at the voice behind her, startled to see Chaenath striding toward them. The elf had taken her hair down from its customary poof and wore tightly-plaited braids like the elves of the Edren Guard. She was dressed like them, too, in a fitted shirt, forest-green cloak, and trousers, and she wore boots better suited for the Waste than the halls of the infirmary. A bow and quiver were strung across her back.

Rydara had not heard any footsteps, but now that her attention was focused on Chaenath, she could sense the elf's quiet fury.

Chaenath stepped closer to Sundamar, and Rydara retreated a few steps, intimidated.

"Arcaena is a coward or a fool. Or both." Chaenath's words were touched with scorn and Speaking magic. "This mortal child can see better than our First. We should all be ashamed."

Rydara saw that Neremyn had entered the garden, and he came closer to hear what they were saying. Her gut twisted at the sight of him.

"What has happened?" Neremyn asked, looking between Rydara and the elves.

Rydara's eyes dropped to the ground. It was Chaenath who answered.

"Consul Faedastan has stolen two of our shards and crossed the border, and Arcaena has given them up as lost to the new High Wizards. Sundamar and the Edren Guard have followed her lead and are doing nothing."

Sundamar's jaw tightened. "It is not my choice. Arcaena is First, and I must defer to her wisdom in discerning what the code requires."

"It is always your choice, Sundamar. You know the code well enough to know Arcaena's judgment has its flaws." Chaenath glanced at Rydara.

"This is different," Sundamar objected. "I am not convinced Arcaena's decision is wrong."

Chaenath looked past him to the dragon. "What of you, Lëanor? Will you stand party to this cowardice?"

Rydara did not register any words from the dragon, but Lëanor lifted her head in a proud gesture, and Rydara Knew she had agreed to carry Chaenath.

"I cannot allow it," Sundamar spoke, glancing between Chaenath and the dragon.

"We did not ask your permission, child," Chaenath returned.

"Can I come with you?" Rydara asked. She did not know if she would prove an asset in a contest with Faedastan or High Wizards, but his betrayal was her fault. She had to do something. "Please."

"I, too, would fight beside you, Chaenath," Neremyn said, glancing at Rydara. There was some uncertainty in his manner, and Rydara guessed he could sense the new distance between them. But there was no uncertainty in his offer. "For this land, and for the sake of Rydara's people. If you believe I can."

Chaenath gave him a long look, and Rydara knew she was weighing him with her insight. Then she nodded. She glanced at Rydara. "We will all go."

Chaenath turned to Sundamar. "We do not ask your permission, but we do invite you to join us. The Edren Guard will follow your decision, and we could use their help."

Rydara could feel Sundamar's distress. "I cannot."

"We are all free here, Sundamar." Chaenath's voice was cold. "Do not hide behind Arcaena."

"I will not. I will not defy the First." Sundamar glanced at Neremyn and Rydara. "If you must go, Chaenath, please do not take them with you. It is not safe."

"We have little chance of success as it is." Chaenath approached Lëanor, who extended a wing to let her board. "Less without Neremyn and Rydara."

Rydara was as surprised as anyone that Chaenath was allowing her to go. She would have liked to say goodbye to Aander first, but she did not want to give the elf time to reconsider. And she knew her brother would only try to convince her to stay. Rydara followed Chaenath and Neremyn up onto Lëanor's back, hoping they would return before Aander had time to worry about where they had gone.

Sitting next to Neremyn made Rydara uncomfortable, but she tried to remember her brother's advice. She sensed nothing but sincerity from him. Perhaps he had changed. Rydara hoped Chaenath knew what she was doing, bringing him along.

Bringing them both along.

Sundamar moved in front of Lëanor. "I cannot stand by and let this happen."

"What do you intend to do, child?" Chaenath's voice was tinged with scorn. "Will you break our code and try to keep me here by force?"

Sundamar's jaw worked, but he had no response.

"You have wasted enough time already," Chaenath told him. "I will fill your station now, and you will watch over Aander until we return."

Lëanor leapt into the air. They left Sundamar watching helplessly from the ground, and Rydara was torn between frustration and regret.

She wished he had chosen to come.

What do you think, Lëanor? she thought toward the dragon. *Do we have any chance with only the four of us?*

Faedastan would be no match for Chaenath or Neremyn, either one, alone, the dragon told her. *And the shards he took will not obey him over Chaenath. If she can reach them, we might prevail against two or three High Wizards. But if they have shards of their own, or if all nine are together...*

Rydara sensed certain doom. *Do you think we can catch him first?*

He is flying with Dosta, the fledgling of one of my roost-mates. With the words came the sense of something like a snort, and Rydara's Knowing was flooded with the dragon's scorn. *I am faster. But he is proving difficult for Chaenath and I to track.*

Rydara stopped asking questions. She did not know what went into the dragon's tracking process, but she did not want to be a distraction.

She glanced over at Neremyn. He was kneeling close to her, while Chaenath crouched farther up the dragon's shoulder.

"They told you about me, didn't they?" he said softly, turning to meet her gaze. "About what I did. Why I am kept in the infirmary."

Rydara tightened her lips and did not answer.

"I meant to tell you. Chaenath restricts my memory because I broke the code long ago. They told me that much, and I was going to tell you. But you didn't ask until yesterday, and then..." Neremyn's gaze drifted into the distance, and Rydara sensed a vast loneliness.

It made her feel stupid. She had spent nearly all her time with this elf since arriving in Edriendor, and she had asked him nothing about himself. He had been in that infirmary for hundreds of years, and he had probably been all alone. Rydara had not seen anyone else on the premises but Chaenath and Aander during her visits.

That mountain of loneliness must have been there, just beneath the surface—pushed back, perhaps, by Rydara's presence. She had been a purpose and a friend for him, however briefly.

Rydara had been so consumed with the plight of her people and her own insecurities that she had failed to notice. *And I call myself a Knower.*

"I thought you might look at me differently, once you knew," Neremyn glanced at her again, a sad smile on his lips.

Rydara could understand why he had not wanted to tell her. She could almost forgive him, except for what he was.

What he used to be, she reminded herself.

The silence stretched, and Rydara could feel Neremyn's acute desire for her to say something.

"Do you know the rest? How you broke the code?" The question pained Neremyn, as Rydara had thought it might, but it was all she could think to say.

"I have a guess." Neremyn turned his gaze forward, and Rydara let the topic die.

Aander may have been right about Neremyn, but Rydara could not bring herself to trust him.

They flew for hours. Soon the lush forests of Edriendor were replaced by the barren bluffs of the Waste. The day wore on, and still they flew.

Near evening, Lëanor swooped into a dive. Rydara's breath caught as the dragon breathed out fire. She saw the family of curled-horn sheep just before they were consumed.

"We eat and continue," Chaenath said as Lëanor landed beside the remains.

Rydara followed Chaenath and Neremyn down Lëanor's wing. Chaenath drew a dagger and began skinning the first sheep. Lëanor unceremoniously tore into another.

Chaenath took a mouthful as she worked, then cut out a piece and tossed it to Neremyn. She did the same for Rydara.

Rydara watched uncertainly as Neremyn ate.

"I thought elves did not eat animals," she said.

"Not if there is no need," Neremyn agreed. "But time is of the essence, and we need the sustenance."

Rydara nodded and took a bite. It was charred and unflavored, but she had tasted worse.

They returned to the air as dusk fell, and before the moon had fully risen, they left the Waste behind them. Rydara did not know whether they emerged in Alterra or Kilethe, but the snowy grassland looked much as it had where she and Aander had parted with the Kerim, weeks ago.

Lëanor must have covered hundreds of miles.

They flew through the night. Sleep eventually took Rydara. She startled awake when Neremyn touched her arm, and consciousness brought a light sense of nausea. The sun was rising. They were high in the sky—so high the clouds seemed close.

Rydara blinked the sleep away, thinking she might be getting sick. There was a hazy quality to the air. Far below, the ground was dotted with tiny blue and white tents, but Rydara's view of them was distorted.

She slowly pieced together that they were inside a Showing. One of them must have created it to hide them from the people below.

Neremyn touched her arm again and gestured toward the horizon. Rydara squinted in the sunlight. She could make out a dark blur far ahead.

"We are not far from a corrupted shard," Neremyn said grimly. "And likely, the High Wizard who carries it."

She was not sick, then. Her "nausea" was a lighter version of the dread she had experienced at Tessex, the last time she had been close to a corrupted shard.

"We will take them in the air," Chaenath said, looking back at Neremyn and Rydara over her shoulder. "And pray we can escape with the shards before our enemies multiply. Take this." She pulled a dagger out of her boot and passed it to Neremyn. "Hold onto Lëanor, Rydara." Chaenath took out her bow and nocked an arrow. They were rapidly gaining on the blur, and Rydara could soon tell it was another dragon. "Or me or Neremyn. But do not trust your eyes."

Chaenath let her arrow fly. Something deflected its course, but Lëanor was still closing on their target. Fast.

Rydara's breaths came quick and shallow as she realized they were about to collide with an enemy a thousand feet above the ground.

"Breathe," Neremyn told her, tightening his grip on the dagger. "We are stronger than they are, alone."

"*Faedastan!*" Chaenath Spoke, and her magic deafened Rydara's Knowing.

The air exploded with fire, and they crashed into the other dragon.

Chapter 11

A Clash of Sorcerers

It was a tangle of wings and claws and fire. Rydara felt searing heat, but the flames exploded around them, catching nothing but sky. Faedastan shouted back at Chaenath, and their voices boomed with a force that pressed Rydara first one way and then the other.

Lëanor twisted in the air, and everything inverted. Rydara was upside-down, and her death-grip on the dragon's spike lasted only a moment before her hands ripped free.

She was falling.

She crashed into the dragon's wings. They had folded backward to catch her. Rydara scrambled to grab hold of something, anything, but Lëanor was still rolling, and she fell back into the dragon's body. The collision knocked the wind out of her, and Rydara stared at the spikes she had narrowly missed in a daze.

The dragon's body thrashed, sending Rydara sliding, and she grabbed at one of the spikes.

She was going to fall. It was just a matter of time.

Lëanor was locked in a struggle with the other dragon, her claws sunk into its shoulder. Chaenath and Neremyn were nowhere to be seen, but Rydara could hear them shouting.

Then Neremyn appeared, nimbly running across Lëanor's foreleg toward Rydara. He had been on the other dragon. He grabbed Rydara's arm and pulled her to her feet, yelling, "Trust me!" in Common. Then he leapt off Lëanor entirely, pulling Rydara with him.

They fell through open sky. Alterran tents and soldiers were rising to meet them, growing larger from their miniature versions by the second.

Rydara felt strangely calm, her arm held fast in Neremyn's grip as her skirts whipped up around them. He had used the Speaking magic on her, and Rydara Knew the calm was a lie. But she did not fight it, seeing no reason to spend her last moments in panic.

She watched the ground with casual interest as they plummeted toward it. There was a figure falling below them and well to the right. The streaming green cloak identified Chaenath. Another shape fell farther below her.

Rydara felt another wave of power as Faedastan shouted something. His figure slowed and started growing bigger as Rydara kept falling. Chaenath's voice thundered, and the whirl of green fabric overtook Faedastan. He tumbled down toward an Alterran tent while Chaenath slowed.

Neremyn Spoke again, and Rydara felt herself slowing as the two of them drew even with Chaenath's elevation.

Another shockwave rippled through the air as Faedastan crashed into the tent, and he froze in place, the roof partially caved in beneath him. Soldiers fled the vicinity, shouting and pointing at the dragons battling far above.

"Identify yourselves!"

The words slammed into Rydara as she and Neremyn drifted lightly to the ground, and she collapsed to her knees. "I am Rydara il'Noraan—no, exiled from Noraan—a tribeless orphan and Knower," she babbled, unable to stop the words though she did not know who had given the command or whether they could hear her.

"Faedastan of the elves! I come bearing—"

Faedastan's words cut off as Chaenath launched herself into Faedastan's tent. It came down around them in a cascade of poles and fabric.

"Stay here," Neremyn said to Rydara. His eyes were fixed on a distant soldier, who was striding toward the collapsed tent with a haughty assurance at odds with the disarray around him.

General Dameires. The soldiers near him left off their shouting and fell in behind him. Neremyn ran toward them, but Rydara was frozen by the same helplessness she had felt at Tessex, when she had watched him murder Kell.

No, Rydara told herself. *It's not the same.* The general had not noticed her, and there was no magic holding her down. *What can I do?*

"Stop." General Dameires held out a hand toward Neremyn. The air concussed between them, and Neremyn faltered, missing a stride. But then he was running again, brandishing the dagger Chaenath had given him.

"Stop them," General Dameires commanded. Then he vanished—into thin air—and the group of soldiers charged Neremyn.

"Stay out of this," Neremyn hissed in Elvish, disappearing himself. The air between him and where Dameires had been burst into flames, and the soldiers ran to get out of the fire.

But none of them were burning. The flames were an illusion.

A whistle split the air, and Rydara's gaze darted toward Chaenath, who had emerged from the mess of a tent and had her eyes on the sky. Faedastan was scrambling out the far side, running away from her.

Time was short, but Rydara suddenly knew what Aander would do if he were here. There was one small way she might be able to help.

She whirled around to look for a soldier. One stood nearby, his wide eyes fixed on the spot where his general had disappeared.

"Listen to me," Rydara hurried toward him, grabbing his arm to secure his attention. He startled backward, and she raised her hands to show she carried no weapon. "Your king no longer rules Alterra. General Dameires and Queen Lux Lucisa are controlling his decisions. The two of them are sorcerers allied with the ancient demons."

Power cracked in the air around them, and fire rained down from the sky. One of the dragons was wounded badly, careening off course as the other pulled away.

The soldier stared at Rydara, stupefied. "What?"

"The entire war with Jeshimoth is a ruse meant to weaken us. To justify our slaughter. You have to tell your companions. Your officers. Your king. Free him from their magic."

"Who are you?"

Rydara was not getting through to him. The wounded dragon was falling fast, and Rydara watched in alarm as it struggled to spread its wings. One was broken and spurting blood, and the other flapped uselessly before the dragon crashed hard into the ground.

It was still where it lay. Dead. Blood gushed over scales that glinted gold and brown in the sunlight.

Not Lëanor's black and green.

The other dragon—Lëanor—looped in the sky, victorious. Rydara exhaled in relief, and Lëanor dove toward Chaenath.

"A Knower," Rydara told the soldier, hoping it would mean more to him than it had to her father. "A witness to the massacre at Tessex and the black magic in the corrupted shard your general carries. My brother Aander tu'Noraan and I found elves in the Land Beyond the Waste, and we will bring them back to save us all if we can."

Rydara turned to run and join Chaenath, but the soldier grabbed her from behind. "I have to go!" she insisted.

He pulled her closer. "I must take you to the general."

"No!" Rydara yelled, struggling to pull away. He turned her easily and wrapped an arm around her, bringing a dagger to her throat as he dragged her forward.

"Let her go! Rydara, jump!" Chaenath Spoke, and as the soldier released her, Rydara sprang into the air with more power than she would have believed possible. Lëanor was there, sweeping a wing beneath Rydara's lifted feet. Chaenath grabbed Rydara's arm as she landed on the dragon's wing, pulling her toward the dragon's body as they hurtled through the air at a dizzying speed.

Chaenath's eyes searched the ground as they gained altitude, and Rydara, kneeling near Lëanor's spikes, realized they were leaving the Alterran camp behind.

"What about Neremyn?" Rydara asked in Elvish. "Where is he?"

Chaenath did not answer, and Rydara's Knowing could not interpret her silence.

The sky went dark. Lëanor pulled up abruptly, nearly throwing Rydara. Chaenath's arm steadied her, and they hovered in place.

"White have mercy," Chaenath muttered in the pitch black. Rydara heard the rustling of her clothes, and then there was dazzling light. Twin orbs of it, one in each of Chaenath's uplifted hands.

The shards. She had taken them from Faedastan.

"Mortals, flee this place!" Chaenath bellowed. Her words were still Elvish, but as had happened with the soldier, her magic transcended language. The Alterran soldiers took to their heels, running from Chaenath in every direction.

Female laughter rolled through the forest, musical and sourceless. It chilled Rydara to the core.

The image of a woman appeared in the sky, five times larger than life. Her dress was lowcut and scarlet, her hair waves of amber that cascaded past her shoulders. Rydara would have known those green eyes anywhere.

"Chaenath." Lux Lucisa's voice reverberated from every direction, and her image smiled coyly in the sky. "How kind of you to bring me two more shards. I shall enjoy filling them with the blood of elves."

"Close your eyes, Rydara." Chaenath said quietly. No magic, this time—just the words. "Tell me where her magic originates, if you can."

In a louder voice, she called out, "You waste your strength on theater, Lux. Just like the Prophet who bonded your demon before you. Come out and face me." Rydara could feel how the taunt pulled and demanded. It did not seem to matter that the two of them spoke in different languages. Rydara closed her eyes.

Lux laughed again, and Rydara attuned her Knowing. The echoes were loud and disorienting, bombarding her from every direction.

Some were fainter than others.

"Just you and Lëanor?" Lux drawled. "And that little *ishra* mortal? Please. Put the shards down and join my service instead. Why keep fighting for a land that doesn't care to defend itself?"

Rydara turned her head slowly, tracing the echoes. She lifted her arm and pointed. "There," she whispered to Chaenath.

The lights in the elf's hands went out. Lëanor turned in the darkness and swept silently in the indicated direction.

"Are you hiding from us, Chaenath?" An image of General Dameires appeared next to Lux in the sky, twice as large. "Surrender, and work for me instead of Lux. No need to humiliate yourself in service to an old rival."

His magic originated somewhere different. Rydara worked to trace him as they closed on Lux, her stomach turning as dread grew in her Knowing. The corrupted shard was closer now, somewhere past Lux—and not with Dameires.

Lëanor released a stream of flame, illuminating the Alterran queen on horseback before Rydara could speak. The fire parted around horse and rider, and the animal reared in panic. Chaenath, two dazzling lights in her left hand and a dagger in her right, dove through the bubble that protected Lux from the flames and tackled her to the ground. The horse bolted.

The darkness and the images of the High Wizards disappeared, revealing blue sky again. A wave of magic concussed the air, throwing Chaenath off Lux and rocking Lëanor backward. Rydara clung tightly to the dragon's spikes.

Lifting her eyes, she saw a man on horseback several dozen yards beyond Lux, at the edge of the now-deserted Alterran camp. Rydara recognized him—he was the High Wizard Numbran, the one who had taken her and Aander back to their father after Tessex. His hands were raised toward Chaenath.

One of them held a black crystal.

Chaenath stood and turned to Rydara, fear in her eyes. She threw one of the recovered shards to her, and Rydara caught it, bewildered. "Go!"

Rydara felt the force of her command, and she clung to Lëanor's spikes as the dragon turned.

"Stop!" Numbran yelled, and Lëanor paused. Rydara looked back in time to see the High Wizard thrown from his horse.

Darkness fell again, chilling and absolute. "There will be no escape." Dameires' voice filled the forest. A wall of fire sprang up in front of them.

Rydara could sense the dragon's uncertainty. There were at least three High Wizards now, and Chaenath had commanded them to flee. They could fly through the flames, which were probably illusions, and hope Chaenath could do enough with the remaining shard to distract the enemy.

But hadn't Lëanor said they might be able to prevail against three High Wizards? *But where is Neremyn?*

"Rydara, here!" Neremyn called out in Common from behind them.

We have to help, Rydara thought toward the dragon, and she sensed Lëanor's agreement as they looped around toward Neremyn's call. Straight into the nauseating dread that still emanated from the corrupted shard.

Can you illuminate my shard for Neremyn? Rydara asked, fighting back the urge to flee. *Command me to make a good throw to him?*

Lëanor agreed, and Rydara felt the dragon Speak. The sound was wordless but powerful, and she threw the shard in the direction she Knew she must.

The shard lit up like a beacon when Neremyn caught it, shining light toward the third High Wizard. The light died before it reached him, leaving him wreathed in shadows. The darkness deepened in layers around him, culminating in a fist-sized source of unnatural blackness hungry to devour more light.

Rydara did not know if she could truly see the blackness of the corrupted shard in the shadows, or if she only thought so because of how the horror rolling off it sickened her Knowing.

Then Neremyn seemed to split into twenty versions of himself, all of them holding beacons of light shining at the blackness from different directions, making the shadows retreat closer to the High Wizard's form. Rydara heard the snick of a sword leaving a scabbard, and the shadowy point of a blade emerged from the shadows. Then the High Wizard divided himself to match Neremyn's move, and soon there were a dozen pools of shadow eating away the light. Neremyn's form danced around them all, using his dagger to catch and turn the High Wizard's shadowy blade. The light in his hand vied with the darkness in the hand of the High Wizard, pulsing first brighter and then dimmer. The dark shard deepened in blackness as the lights held by Neremyn's copies dimmed, and Rydara caught her breath, afraid he was losing.

Then a scream split the air, and all the figures disappeared at once. Daylight returned.

Neremyn crouched over the body of the third High Wizard. The shard of Edriendor protruded from the man's bloody chest. Neremyn snatched the dark shard from the High Wizard's lifeless hand and pulled the other out of his chest, whirling to face the other High Wizards with a shard in each hand.

"LEAVE US!" he shouted, and the ground began to rumble and quake. A wind tore through the forest, somehow whipping away from him in every direction, harassing the High Wizards. Lux staggered to her feet away from Chaenath, a transparent shard in one hand and a bloody dagger in the other. "LEAVE THE SHARD!" Neremyn's shout was followed by a clap of thunder, and lightning split the cloudless sky, striking the shard in Lux's hand. She dropped it. "GO!"

Balls of fire splayed from Neremyn's hands, pursuing Lux, Dameires, and Faedastan. Lëanor flew as far as Chaenath, breathing her own fire after Lux for good measure. Lux turned and ran, and so did the others.

Rydara caught her breath as Lëanor landed next to Chaenath. The elf was breathing and alert, but she bled heavily from her abdomen. Viscera protruded from the ugly wound, and her rich black skin seemed somehow duller. Rydara scrambled down from Lëanor's back, though she did not know how to help the fallen elf.

"I can heal her."

Rydara turned to Neremyn, hearing something new in his voice. It was as laden with power as any word Rydara had heard from the High Wizards, Chaenath, or the First Elf, but that was not the only difference. It was deeper, graver, haughtier. More insidious.

The shard that Rydara had thrown him was different, too. Between the spatters of blood, tendrils of black swirled in the formerly transparent crystal. It had become a second source of dread to Rydara's Knowing, though a much dimmer one than the first.

Rydara tensed as Neremyn strode toward Chaenath, both sources of evil moving with him. Lëanor started to uncoil her wings, but Neremyn glanced at her, and the dragon stilled. Rydara sensed Lëanor's uncertainty.

Chaenath tried to lift her head as Neremyn approached, her breaths shallow and ragged. "What have you done," she gasped in Elvish. Rydara could feel the elf's horror, and it had nothing to do with the fact that she was dying. Neremyn knelt next to Chaenath and tucked the black shard in a pocket, laying his now-free hand on her stomach.

With a mighty effort, Chaenath wrenched herself upward and spat in his face. The air concussed with magic, knocking Neremyn backward.

Then Chaenath collapsed, and her chest went still. Neremyn rose to his knees and touched her stomach, his brow furrowed in frustration. Chaenath's skin knit itself back together under his touch, closing her viscera inside her.

But it was too late. Rydara's Knowing was attuned to Neremyn, and his shock was a mirror of her own as they realized that Chaenath's act of defiance had finished her. Rydara felt bitterness and rage surge in Neremyn, swirling around a profound sense of helplessness. Then he took a deep breath, and the storm passed.

Rydara was slower to process what had happened, and as grief began to well inside her, all she could sense from Neremyn was a quiet scorn.

"Neremyn?" Rydara asked, her sorrow turning to dread. She did not understand how or why it had happened, but somehow Neremyn had changed.

Or perhaps he had not changed, after all. He had become what he once was, long ago.

"I am the High Wizard Numbran," Neremyn replied, drawing himself up to his full height as he turned to Rydara.

"What—how..." Rydara's question trailed off as she looked at him. His gaze was regal and aloof. Haughty. Distant.

Her throat tightened.

"That human imposter carried my old companion, Lord Umbra of the second circle of hell. Now I have reunited with him, and with memories long forgotten." Neremyn's gaze drifted to Chaenath, and his jaw tightened. "She recognized his presence in that wizard. It is why she commanded you to flee."

There was bitterness there, but Rydara felt a flicker of sadness, too. She sensed that the elf that had volunteered to fight beside Chaenath on behalf of Edriendor and Rydara's people was not gone entirely.

"You didn't kill her," Rydara said, trying to reach him. Trying to let him know that there was more to him than only evil, and that she could see it. "You don't have to do this."

"What would you have me do instead? Return to a life of isolation and oblivion?"

"You don't have to be what you were." Rydara was not sure if her words were true. She could feel Neremyn's sense of inevitability, and she understood it. There was nothing for him in Edriendor but captivity, and taking up this mantle had been his only way out. Perhaps his only chance to prevail against the other High Wizards.

"I will let you take a shard back to Edriendor, if you wish." Neremyn scooped up the shard Lux had dropped and turned back to Rydara. "But realize, if Arcaena has two shards, she'll have double the excuses to sit idly by and hope Tenebrus leaves her alone."

Rydara swallowed, all too aware that he spoke the truth. "I'll take it." Taking the shard might not be the best move for her people, but Chaenath had died to recover it. Rydara could not betray her now.

Neremyn handed it to her, and Rydara clutched it tightly. "What about the other one?" she asked, looking at the shard he still held in his left hand. A tendril of black still curled inside it, and it showed no signs of fading.

"It's useless to Edriendor now, so I'll keep it."

"How can it be useless?" Rydara could see the tendril of darkness in it clearly enough, but she had just seen Neremyn use it to wield tremendous power. Surely that power wasn't gone.

Neremyn sighed, looking at the shard in his hand. "It was the Scepter of Nivalis once. The locus of his power. Nivalis was light and love and life, and his power cannot be used for darkness. But I used it to kill. Not the power in the shard—that would have been impossible—but I drove the physical shard through the wizard's heart, and it killed him. Now the shard is polluted."

"I don't understand."

Neremyn rolled his shoulders and scoffed, and the sound drove a shiver through Rydara's body. There was venom in that scoff.

"I wouldn't expect you to." Neremyn tucked the polluted shard in his pocket. "But don't worry. I won't take it to your enemies. I'll disappear from this struggle."

Rydara pressed her lips together. Neremyn had changed, and he frightened her, but in some measure, he was still on her side—or at least, it sounded as if he wanted to be.

"We could use your help," she said.

"I am an abomination, Rydara, and no elf would fight beside me even if I wished it. They would die first. Like Chaenath."

"Fight with me, then, and the tribes." Rydara closed her eyes, and tears ran down her cheeks. She grieved for Chaenath, but she was also angry at a decision she did not understand. *What purpose did her death serve, other than pushing Neremyn further into darkness?* "The elves won't listen to me anyway."

"You must convince the elves to join you, if you hope to stop Tenebrus." Neremyn took a handkerchief out of his pocket. It was embroidered, like the one he had handed her on her first day in Edriendor. He folded it once so it was inside-out and handed it to Rydara.

The gesture inspired more tears, and Rydara pressed it against her eyes. When she looked up again, there was a glimmer of hope in Neremyn's gaze.

"But why do you care, Rydara?" he asked. "Your people never cared for you. They didn't ask you to fight for them. The only person who ever loved you was your brother, and he is safe in Edriendor. Why not go back and get him, and then come and join me? I can't stop Tenebrus, but I can keep the two of you safe from him."

Rydara's grip tightened on the shard she carried, afraid he would change his mind about letting her go and transform her into something terrible. Something without a soul.

He shook his head sadly. "I wouldn't ask you to become a Knight. Not if you didn't wish it. You and your brother would be safe with me."

He gazed at her, and for a moment Rydara could almost see it: the three of them a strange little family, with Neremyn taking the role of a father who actually wanted them. A father who would listen to them and keep them safe.

Lëanor shifted beside Rydara, perhaps nervous that she would consider his offer. But it was just an idle dream. "Aander would never desert our people," Rydara said.

"*You* could never desert your people," Neremyn corrected gently.

It was easier to blame Aander than sort through her own emotions, but Neremyn was right. Rydara took in a breath and tried to explain. "They always saw me as an outsider." Her throat constricted, and she waited until she could speak again without crying. "If I desert them—especially now, in their hour of greatest need—well then, that's exactly what I'll be, isn't it?"

"Do you think what you do will change what they see?"

The question stung, the more so because Neremyn asked it honestly. Nothing he had done in the years of his imprisonment had changed what the elves saw when they looked at him.

He wanted to know if she thought her people were different.

Rydara shook her head. She had imagined she could change their minds about her, once, but now… "I doubt I'll get the chance to find out, so—it doesn't really matter how they see me. It matters how I see myself." Rydara seldom disclosed so much about herself, and the words felt raw and inadequate. Neremyn's mouth twitched in a small, bitter smile as he looked back at her. He nodded.

He seemed to understand.

Rydara wrapped his handkerchief around the shard in her hands. "I'm sorry you never had an Aander," she said, and she meant it. Her life would have been so different without him. "I wish you'd had someone to believe in you, to fight for you. To see something in you that no one else did. I wish..." *I wish I'd been that person.* The words caught in Rydara's throat, and she left them unspoken.

Instead, she had been horrified when she found out about his past. Just like Chaenath, and all the other elves in Edriendor.

"I wish that, too," Neremyn agreed, but Rydara sensed no blame in him. Certainly none for her.

Stooping down, Neremyn picked up Chaenath's body and carried her toward Lëanor. "Her body must be returned to Edriendor." Lëanor lowered a wing, and Neremyn carried the elf's body up to the dragon's back, laying her gently on Lëanor's shoulder.

When he climbed down, Rydara wrapped her arms around him in a sudden embrace.

She Knew his surprise. There were threads of distaste and disdain in it, and evil lay so heavily around him that Rydara had to fight the impulse to recoil. Not all the darkness was sourced in the shards he carried. But after a moment, Neremyn hugged her back, and Rydara understood the disdain she sensed came from the demon he now hosted. The elf was grateful for this embrace, and Rydara was glad to have given it.

She pulled away, wiping tears from her eyes, and Lëanor extended a wing to let her board.

"I guess we can only be who we are," he said. "Good luck to you, Rydara."

Rydara climbed the wing and settled herself next to Lëanor's spikes. It was hard to be so close to Chaenath's body, but Rydara knew it was right to take her back to Edriendor.

She glanced at Neremyn, troubled by his words and by the evil she sensed in him. "I don't believe hosting a demon defines who you are," she said. "You still have your own soul. You don't have to do what it wants."

"Umbra doesn't much care for you," Neremyn noted, a distant look in his eyes. "Though that's hardly surprising. Good luck, Rydara. I'll convince some of the others to desert with me if I can. Perhaps it will make your fight easier."

Rydara nodded. She sensed a conflict within him, and she did not know if he would be able to make good on his resolution—but words were cheap, and hers had come too late. His course was set now, whether for good or ill. "Good luck to you, too."

Let's go, Lëanor, she instructed the dragon, and the creature smoothly rose into the air. Rydara's stomach dropped. There was no elf to steady her this time.

Instead, she was responsible for steadying Chaenath's body. She laid a hand on the elf's shoulder. It was already growing cold, and more tears welled in Rydara's eyes.

She was alone again, and she understood this beautiful and obstinate people less than ever.

Chapter 12

The *Tirisslythra*

Lëanor stopped to kill a deer and drink from a river before they crossed into the Waste. Rydara drank little and ate less, distracted by the burden Lëanor bore. The dragon's movements were fluid and careful, even as she devoured the deer, and Chaenath's body stayed balanced on her back.

"Why did she do it, Lëanor?" Rydara asked, cupping her hands under the flow of the icy river. Her knees were wet with snow—there was no way to avoid it—and Rydara shivered as she brought the water to her mouth. Her hands burned from the cold, and when she drank, the chill spread to her stomach. "Why didn't she just let Neremyn heal her?"

Lëanor tore another piece of meat from the deer, gulped it down, and exhaled a small puff of smoke. Rydara sensed weariness from the animal. *The elves are a stubborn race.*

"I do not understand." Rydara wiped her hands dry on the sleeves of her dress. She was shivering.

Neither do I. Lëanor lowered her head and ripped into the animal again, spraying a little of its blood across her snout. Rydara averted her eyes. *But you are wrong to keep calling him Neremyn.* Lëanor moved closer to Rydara and plunged her head in the water, drinking deeply before raising it again and shaking it off. Droplets ran down her spike-rimmed face as she turned yellow eyes toward Rydara.

He is the High Wizard Numbran now, enemy of the White, the elves, my race and yours. The elf who flew with us from Edriendor no longer exists.

"Why did he help us, then?" Rydara asked. "Why give us the shard?"

He is partner in mind and flesh with a thing from hell that lusts for power and enjoys inflicting pain, Lëanor tried again, and Rydara sensed impatience from the creature. The matter was quite settled in the dragon's mind. *Numbran may not plan to join our other enemies, and that makes him a lesser enemy for now, but if we meet him again, it will not be as allies.*

Come. It will not be cold in the Waste.

Lëanor extended a wing, and Rydara climbed aboard, her whole body shaking now. She sank to her knees and pressed her head against the scales of Lëanor's neck as they took off. The dragon was warm to the touch.

Rydara tried not to look at Chaenath. The elf's face was peaceful in death, but dried blood congealed on her clothes where her wound had been. Her eyes were empty.

The flight back to Edriendor was long and somber. Rydara's clothes dried out as they left the snowy forest behind, and the chill of Kilethe was replaced by the relentless heat of the Waste.

The day dragged on, but Lëanor did not stop again. Toward evening their solitude was broken by the appearance of another dragon. Rydara recognized the dragon's rider from the brief meeting she had had with the Edren Guard. It was Sarya—the elf whose facial features reminded her so strongly of Arcaena.

Sarya and her dragon did not hail Rydara as they approached. Instead, they made a graceful arc in the sky and fell in behind Lëanor, taking a position near her right flank.

Their escort grew as they continued through the Waste, with other members of the Edren Guard joining as the night deepened. There were six of them by the time they crossed the magical barrier into Edriendor, and they fanned into a V-formation with Lëanor at their head.

The view of tall, closely-packed pine trees around a glowing river reminded Rydara of her first flight to Edriendor. She had been desperate then, but the elven land had seemed full of hope and wonder. She had thought she had found the key to saving Aander and the tribes, if only she could learn to use it.

The river's aqua glow was fainter tonight. It was because of the lost shards, and though Rydara was bringing one of them back, she was also returning the body of the only elf in Edriendor who had been willing to fight to keep them.

As the trees gave way to the elegant buildings and garden networks that made up the city, Rydara saw that many elves had come out of their homes to watch the dragons fly past. In the moonlight and the glow from the river and their aqua lamps, they all seemed to be wearing clothes of the same light color, contrasting with their dark skin.

Lëanor flew to the palace. They landed in the gardens near the entrance the river flowed through. Sarya and the rest of the Edren Guard stayed in the air, hovering over the grounds.

A dozen elves had come out of the palace to greet them. By the light of the moon and stars, Rydara could see that Arcaena herself was among them, wearing white robes like the others and the diadem that marked her station. The jewel hanging against her forehead glowed dimmer than at their first meeting.

Rydara tensed at the sight of her. Arcaena carried herself with the same majestic poise as at their first meeting. Her hair was tightly braided across the top of her head, from which point it cascaded into springy curls that poured down her back.

There was a deep irony in how Rydara had been denied the opportunity to see the First Elf before forty days had elapsed, only to be ambushed by her now. Rydara's dress was still caked with mud where she had knelt in the snow, and she had not had a proper meal, night's rest, or chance to change her clothes in over two days. She was exhausted, and hungry, and angry. The First Elf had given up on the shards, forbidding support for Chaenath's mission, and yet she was the one coming to receive the fallen elf's body.

Rydara clenched her jaw as she climbed down Lëanor's wing to meet the First Elf. She had to hold herself together and show respect. She could not afford to offend this race.

Arcaena stopped a few feet from Rydara, raising a fist to her lips at the sight of Chaenath's body. She bowed her head, and the elves with her did the same. Three of them approached Lëanor, who extended a wing, and they climbed up in silent procession. They lifted Chaenath and carried her toward the palace, their movements as silent and sobering as the grief Rydara sensed from them. The Edren Guard stopped circling above them when Chaenath's body was taken inside, dispersing into the night.

It was all very formal and might have been touching, but if they had truly cared about Chaenath, they might have flown out to fight with her. Even one or two more sorcerers could have made all the difference, and the hypocrisy in this show of respect was not lost on Rydara.

Arcaena turned first to Lëanor. Her expression was serene, and Rydara could sense very little with her Knowing.

Lëanor was more expressive. As the silence stretched, the dragon's resentment grew, and her body coiled inward. She pawed the ground and her nostrils flared. Then the dragon unfurled her wings and took off into the night.

Rydara bit her lip to keep her questions and opinions to herself. When Arcaena turned to her, she held out the shard.

"*Wran firbrywethe,*" Arcaena said softly, taking it. The words meant, *You return one to us,* but the word Arcaena had chosen for "one" may have been meant to emphasize "only one." Rydara did not know if she was being thanked for bringing the shard back or rebuked for having failed to retrieve both of them.

Her Knowing registered nothing, but Rydara guessed the ambiguity was intentional. The First Elf could make herself understood when she wished.

She bowed her head. "Chaenath gave everything to save it," she said in Elvish, trying not to let resentment color her tone.

Arcaena let the silence stretch, and Rydara cursed inwardly as she remembered all elves were Knowers. She had to do more than control her behavior around them. She needed to control her feelings.

Rydara took a deep breath and tried to meditate on the fountain, hoping her resentment would fade from the First Elf's Knowing.

"You believe I am in your debt." Arcaena narrowed her eyes, still speaking Elvish, and Rydara could not suppress a flare of frustration. This confrontation was completely unfair, and it could sabotage Rydara's chances of winning rescue for her people.

"No." Rydara made another effort to calm herself. Lying to a Knower was pointless, so she would have to work her way out of this with the truth. "I have brought back one shard, but I am the one who brought the news to Faedastan that inspired him to steal them. The shards belong to Edriendor, and I have done no more than the duty I owe to this place. And to Chaenath."

"Yet you want something."

Rydara opened her mouth to object, but stopped herself. She could not lie, but she had to tread carefully. She took a deep breath, trying to calm herself. "You know I wish to present a petition on behalf of my people," she said instead, choosing the most formal of the three Elvish forms for "you." "It is urgent."

Arcaena glanced at the elves who accompanied her. Rydara saw no change in their expressions, but she wondered if they communicated silently with one another, as they could with the dragons.

"Tonight we walk the *Tirisslythra* for our sister," Arcaena said. Rydara could not guess the translation of *Tirisslythra,* but her Knowing received the impression of a great ceremony that all Edriendor would attend. Rydara included. "Edriendor must mourn for seven days. Then we will hear your petition."

"Edriendor must mourn." Rydara's mouth twitched at the irony. How better to honor an elf who died fighting the High

Wizards than to spend seven days continuing to ignore the threat they posed to the whole world? "Of course."

Arcaena stiffened, and Rydara cursed inwardly, realizing her mistake. The First Elf drew herself up to stand even taller, fixing Rydara with a gaze cold enough to freeze glass. She turned and left without another word. The other elves followed her, some with glances nearly as cold and more incredulous.

What have I done? Rydara's throat constricted as they left her alone in the gardens. *Sarcasm, with the First Elf? What is wrong with me?* She was frustrated and exhausted, but that was no excuse. *I need their help!*

Rydara brought a palm to her forehead and tried not to cry. She had no idea how much damage had been done and no choice but to move forward. Arcaena expected her at this great ceremony for Chaenath, so she could not even afford time for moping. When the ceremony was over, she would be able to sleep. She would visit Aander after that and tell him everything, including this offense she had given the First Elf, and he would know what to do. He could fix it.

By the time Rydara washed and changed and made her way to the city, there were more elves out than before. They were all walking along the riverbank. Rydara followed them to where the river branched. The main river continued toward the forest and Edriendor's border with the Hahiroth. The smaller branch turned west, and a white marble footbridge connected its two banks.

Over a hundred elves—or perhaps two hundred, Rydara could only guess—had gathered, along with four dragons. Rydara recognized Lëanor's mottled greens and black on the far bank, and she crossed the footbridge to go to her.

Rydara was surprised and delighted to find her brother sitting with his back against the dragon. Aander was bundled in a thick white coat with a white blanket wrapped around his shoulders, and Sundamar stood next to him.

"Aander!" Rydara hurried to him and crouched to pull him into a hug, eager to tell him everything.

"Rydara," Aander murmured, returning the embrace. He was weak, but Rydara guessed he was holding her as tightly as he could. His emotions were a mix of exhaustion, frustration, and relief. "A dragon chase is no place for a diplomat."

She pulled back and smiled, but when she looked at him, she saw his face was drawn and pale. His whole body seemed to have shrunk into itself, leaving his bones oddly prominent and fragile-looking, as though he might snap if she hugged him too tight. He leaned back against Lëanor, obviously tired by the exertion.

Rydara's smile faltered, and her eagerness to seek his counsel dried up. Her brother was still so weak. Her problems could wait.

She stood and turned to Sundamar. "Thank you," she said in Elvish, grateful that he had taken the trouble to bring Aander. She bowed her head to him, and then she bit her lip, not sure what to say next. She could sense something of his grief for Chaenath, and it ran deeper than she would have expected.

Yet he still hadn't fought with them. It was a disappointment that stung worse now.

"I am not Chaenath, but I try best to help patient," Sundamar said in Common, his accent halting and uncertain.

Rydara returned his gaze, noting that this was the first time she had seen an elf attempt something that stretched their natural capabilities. Sundamar had gone out of his way to be kind to her and Aander ever since their arrival. His failure to pursue Faedastan was her only mark against him.

And for that, Rydara reminded herself, he was not truly the one to blame. Arcaena had ordered him to stand down. Loyalty and obedience were virtues that Rydara could respect, even if she did not believe Arcaena deserved them.

"Sundamar hasn't left my side since you went away," Aander told her. "He's learned a lot more Common than I have Elvish. It's embarrassing, frankly."

Sundamar looked past Rydara, taking one step toward the river. Rydara turned to look.

A small white fleet sailed down the river from the direction of the palace. The lead vessel was long and narrow with tall sides and a hollowed-out center, just big enough for the four white-robed elves who sat single file within, all bowing their heads. Two identical vessels carrying seven more elves flanked the lead boat, trailing it by no more than a span, and between them was a white raft. Rydara did not have a good view, near the outskirts of the gathering as they were, but she knew the white raft carried Chaenath. The body that lay there was now dressed in white, and in the light of the moon, Rydara could just make out a sprinkling of what seemed to be flower petals covering it.

The gathered elves and dragons had not been making much noise, but a deeper silence fell as the white fleet drifted closer. Somewhere, a rich male tenor hummed the first, lovely notes of a melody, and the magic in his voice filled the night. Then he began to sing.

It was hard for Rydara to parse the Elvish words in the unfamiliar rhythm, but she did not need to. The music created the impression of a hopeful beginning. A soaring soprano joined the tenor, followed by an alto, and then a bass, weaving together in a harmonious, joyful theme.

Then the music turned thrumming, insistent. More voices joined, carrying a warning of something ominous. The music turned confused and discordant, the voices splitting into dozens of parts with vying rhythms and strains that spoke of crisis and terror.

The parts faded back into four-part harmony, with the earlier theme now echoed in a minor key. The song finished with a single tenor repeating the opening notes.

The last note drifted into silence, and Rydara found her eyes had misted. She had never heard music so intricate, with such tragic beauty, nor did she expect to again. Feeling the power of so many Speakers threaded together in song was an experience she would never have words to describe, but she would remember it always.

The fleet had come as far as the footbridge, and now the four elves standing on it each took hold of a vessel as they arrived and guided them toward the left bank, where the water was shallow enough to let the vessels run aground. Rydara recognized Arcaena as she rose from the lead vessel and stepped ashore. She led the ten elves who sailed with her onto the footbridge, and they spread out behind her.

"Tonight we walk the *Tirisslythra* for Chaenath," Arcaena Spoke in Elvish, the magic in her voice carrying her words over the assembly with ease. "The first of our sisters we have lost since the Rescission." Arcaena fell silent, bowing her head and pressing her fist against her mouth.

All around Rydara, the elves repeated the gesture. She did the same.

"She did not die for nothing," Arcaena continued, lowering her hand to her side. "Tonight our river glows brighter and our land is stronger because of her sacrifice."

It was true, Rydara realized. The river was brighter now than it had been when she had first flown back. Arcaena must have returned the shard to its place.

"For seven hundred years, this land has been our home. We are protected and nurtured by the power of the shards, and our young have never known another life. They have never known want, difficulty, or persecution. The shards have been good to us. But if the choice had been mine, I would have given up all three rather than stand before you tonight to lead you in the *Tirisslythra*. The greatest gift Nivalis gave us was not the shards, nor this safe and comfortable home, nor its beauty and peace. Life is the greatest gift. I would have sooner committed us all to the fate of hunted wanderers than see one life lost irrevocably."

Somehow, Arcaena's eyes found Rydara in the crowd, and Rydara warmed with shame. Whatever her shortcomings, Arcaena did grieve for Chaenath. Rydara could feel in her Knowing that she spoke only truth when she claimed she would sooner have lost the elven homeland than Chaenath's life.

"Chaenath and I did not agree on this." Arcaena's gaze moved on. "She knew the risk when she took it upon herself to hunt down Faedastan. She knew the High Wizards had been reforged and that they might contest her in her efforts to reclaim the shards. She knew all this, yet she tried anyway. She died courageous, a warrior, as she was in life.

"The young among you did not know her as such. You knew her as the widow of Theodluin, the elf who conceived the original compact, unmade himself into the pattern of the High Wizard Tenebrus, and killed Nivalis. You knew her in her self-imposed isolation, her centuries of tending to the High Wizard we captured alive and sought to rehabilitate."

Rydara's lips parted in astonishment at the history she would never have guessed.

"Many times," Arcaena continued, "I reminded Chaenath that Theodluin was my own brother, that his betrayal besmirched us all, and that she acquitted herself with honor in the struggle that followed. Many times, I urged her to end her days of penance and look to the future, to take up the office of Consul that she deserved. But she steadfastly refused that honor, recommending her son, Faedastan, in her place.

"As your First Elf, I alone am responsible for appointing Faedastan Consul. I failed to perceive his ambitions. I failed to anticipate his betrayal. Chaenath was no more to blame than any one of us who walked beside him every day. She was less to blame than I.

"I would have told her as much, but my insight tells me it would not have mattered." Arcaena fell silent for a moment, her eyes turning to where Chaenath lay on her raft near the bank of the river, bobbing gently in the current. "My admonition to forego the chase did not matter. The Edren Guard's refusal to accompany her did not matter. Chaenath valued the shards and the chance to thwart her son's betrayal as well worth her life and more, and now she cannot be convinced otherwise.

"Now she has crossed into the Realm Beyond, where I know she stands in favor with the White. Nivalis demonstrated how he loved us in spite of our shortcomings long ago, when he let himself be killed by the High Wizards in order to win our freedom, though we had all forsaken him and succumbed to their magic and deceit.

"We asked neither penance nor sacrifice from Chaenath, but now she is gone. She will not be returned to us unless and until we, too, cross over into that Realm. All we can do is respect her decision. We offer our gratitude for the shard she recovered. And we walk the *Tirisslythra* in support of her spirit's passage."

Arcaena repeated the gesture of pressing her fist to her lips, and the assembly mirrored her. Then the First Elf walked down the footbridge and circled back to Chaenath's raft. She waded into the water and took hold of the raft, pushing it deeper into the water. She let go, and the current took it, pulling it under the bridge and slowly on down the river.

Arcaena started to sing as she walked toward shore, her robes heavy with the weight of the water. It was a gentler, simpler song than the first, but no less beautiful. It spoke to Rydara of a spirit's crossing into the Realm Beyond, where there was rest and peace.

Arcaena finished her song by the time she was out of the river. She continued walking, following Chaenath's raft, and the gathered elves began to walk with her in heavy silence.

Sundamar helped Rydara pull Aander to his feet so they could follow. He started out bravely, waving Sundamar away and leaning only lightly on Rydara, but he did not last long. When his legs gave out, Sundamar carried him up Lëanor's wing and laid him on her shoulder, where he fell asleep.

Rydara's heart hurt to see him reduced to such a shadow of his former self. It hurt for Chaenath, too, and Neremyn, and all she had never known or guessed about their tragic history. It hurt for her people, and for the elves, and for the falling out that had made them flee from humans and found this place in the aftermath of the All-Color's death.

It hurt because Arcaena, in all her cold inscrutability, cared more for the life of one elf who defied her than for the secure comfort of all the rest of her people. Life was cheap in the tribes, and so was death. The massacre at Tessex had not prompted its king to ask a single question, and here all Edriendor had turned out to walk through the night for a single elf who had been a hermit and a rulebreaker.

She had judged them too quickly. She still did not understand the First Elf's refusal to face the High Wizards, but it was not born out of cowardice or stupidity, as Chaenath had claimed. Rydara had not sensed the faintest thread of either in Arcaena's speech. There had been no self-justification. Only sincerity— which meant the First Elf had a deeper respect for each individual elven life than Rydara could fathom.

Exhaustion settled deeply over Rydara as the night went on. She nearly nodded off on her feet more than once. The walk went on until dawn.

As the sun rose, a rushing sound filled her ears, and she saw the forest ending up ahead where the ground dropped in a cliff. The river plunged over it in a waterfall, creating little rainbows in its spray.

Their walk had finally ended. Rydara watched in silence with the gathered elves as Chaenath's craft tipped over the waterfall and disappeared in a swirl of mist.

Chapter 13

Rydara's Petition

Aander's participation in the *Tirisslythra* left him exhausted and sicker. He slept for the better part of three days, waking only for brief fits of terror. Rydara sat with him through one of these, stroking his hair while he trembled and yelled, twitching away from imagined horrors. Neremyn had told her he might always suffer from nightmares, though they would lessen as his strength returned.

Sundamar stayed in the infirmary to look after him. Rydara would have dearly loved the elf's advice as she prepared her petition, but at the end of the *Tirisslythra*, Arcaena had announced that Edriendor would commence seven days of fasting and silence.

It was hard to pass Sundamar in the halls of the infirmary and say nothing. The first time it happened, Rydara paused and almost broke the silence, anxious to ask him about something she had read. He stopped, too, and looked at her, but her question died on her tongue. Grief lay heavily over him, clouding his eyes and her Knowing, and she offered a sad smile instead. She would not ask him to violate his mourning ritual. He might not even have the answers she sought.

Despite the country's fast, Sundamar still brought Aander meals, and the pantry continued to be replenished. Rydara took this as tacit permission for her to eat, too, when the hunger became too much. She did so circumspectly.

She spent most of her time in the library, poring over Elvish histories and treatises, looking for anything she could use to convince them to face the High Wizards. At night, she returned to her room and practiced speaking out loud in Elvish, trying to improve her accent and fluidity. She also practiced meditating, still haunted by her failure with Faedastan and her lapse in front of the First Elf. She might not have another opportunity to resist the Speaking magic, and even if she did, all the practice in the world could not save her if the Speaking was too strong.

But when it came time to present her petition, she could at least keep the elves from perceiving any untoward emotions if she learned how to keep herself calm. They couldn't see what wasn't there.

Rydara worried that asking Arcaena to hear her petition sooner may have been a mistake. Now she would give it on her twenty-first day in Edriendor instead of her fortieth. Every day she spent among the elves could cost more lives among the tribes, but if the elves turned down her petition because she had not given herself enough time to prepare, she could lose her chance at saving anyone.

Then again, if she had had all the time in the world, there would still be no guarantee she could convince the elves to help her. She would have thought a potential threat to their homeland would be reason enough to confront the High Wizards, but with Sundamar's intimation that the elves could just escape to another Realm, she was no longer sure. Especially given how little Arcaena had seemed to care about losing one of the shards that made up their most potent defense.

There was something promising, though, about the elves' religion. Their accounts of Nivalis were different from what Rydara had been taught about the Six. The tribes considered all the gods and goddesses worthy of fear and worship, but none was entirely without flaw. Ignescens was strength and passion, but she could also be cruel. Aurantiacus was justice and balance, but he was indifferent to suffering. Xanthinus was warmth and good humor, but his favor could turn on the flip of a coin. It was the same with the rest.

Nivalis seemed to have had all the virtues of the Six and none of their flaws. The elves who had known him wrote of his passion and his constancy, his fairness and his compassion, his wisdom and his humor. Everyone remembered his love, how each of them had felt seen and valued in every encounter with him. Rydara did not understand how so many virtues could coexist in a single entity.

She would have liked to have met him.

Admiring the elves' god made her uncomfortable. She remembered the vows she had offered the All-Color in the Waste, back when Aander was dying. She had promised to convert if he saved Aander. Even if Rydara won the elves' help and saved the tribes, forsaking her people's religion would cement her identity as an outsider. It was also something she had sworn never to do. She had promised herself she would never forsake her people, her gods, or her family in the way that her mother had done.

Rydara was not looking to escape her deal with the divine, though. Aander's life was worth it. She just was not sure which of the gods she owed his rescue to, or if any of them had been involved. She had offered the same promise to the Six, after all. She could not keep her oaths to both the Six and the All-Color.

On the fourth day of the fast, Aander was lucid enough to speak to her. Sundamar was out, so Rydara closed the door to Aander's room and broke the silence to tell him everything, including how she had left things with the First Elf.

With the way Aander's eyes kept drifting shut while she paced his room and talked, she was not sure how much he followed, and when she finished, there was a long stretch of silence.

"Three days?" Aander eventually asked. He coughed.

Rydara sat on the edge of his bed, releasing a deep sigh. Somehow, she had thought that telling Aander all her worries would make her feel better—that he would know just what to say to help her find her way forward.

But he was still so weak.

"I don't know…" he spoke again. "I think you'll have to argue for us. I don't know if I can."

"I know." Rydara stared at his door to the garden. She had given up hoping Aander might be well enough to present their petition some time ago. "It might be for the best. They do not look fondly on pale-skinned humans, but apparently the Rishara are descended from elves. Chaenath called me *nimkeïass,* and so did one of the Consuls. It means 'lost daughter.'"

"Really?" Aander took a few long breaths while he considered. "That's good. It gives you some standing with them."

"Maybe it did." Rydara shrugged her shoulders, feeling helpless. "Before I insulted the nation's grief in front of the First Elf and the entire Council."

"Rydara," Aander moved to sit up a bit, sliding back to lean against the headrest. "I don't know what it's like to read minds, or grow up in Edriendor, but they would have to be fools to hold that conversation against you. You'd just lost a friend—two friends—and you were emotional. Surely, they can understand that. What you said—'Edriendor must mourn'?—that's not even offensive."

"But what I *meant* by it was, and they don't make a distinction. I'm not sure they even experience emotion the way we do. They're all so … *steady.* All the time." Rydara studied her hands, flexing them in her lap. She looked at Aander. "They seldom change their minds or their feelings, and things like hunger and sleep deprivation seem not to affect them. I'm not sure they would even understand if I tried to explain that I was rude because of exhaustion, or that I didn't really mean it."

"Well then, maybe you did mean it."

"What?" Rydara's brow furrowed.

"You weren't wrong to feel the way you did. Chaenath died trying to save the shards, and the elves could have honored her by fighting with her or at least bringing her murderers to justice, but instead they show their respect by putting off the petition of the person who did fight with her. It's hypocritical."

"But it's not. The elves honor life above everything, and they weren't willing to risk lives to protect the shard. Chaenath made a different choice, and they respect that. But they weren't willing to risk any other lives to help her, and they certainly won't risk any to avenge her now that she's past saving."

"Well, maybe it's consistent, but it's still wrong." Aander frowned. "It's wrong for them to sit by and do nothing while the rest of the world burns. You believe that, and you're passionate in your belief, and that's why you criticized them. You need them to see your passion if you're going to change their minds."

Rydara was not sure if he was describing how she felt or how he thought she *should* feel—and how she should communicate it to the elves—but he was right about one thing. Passion mattered. The Noraani alliance had been forged almost entirely on Aander's zeal. Rydara knew how to observe and advise from the shadows. She was good at reading people and giving Aander the information he needed to avoid giving unnecessary offense. But passion was the part *he* was good at. He was the one who changed minds and hearts.

"I don't know how to do that, Aander." Rydara flexed her hands again. "I don't know how to connect with people like you do, and I'm not sure even you could convince the elves of anything they didn't already believe."

"You've learned so much about them, and that's the hard part," Aander said, finding one of her hands with his. He gave it a squeeze. "You don't have to be like me to connect with them. Just speak from your heart. That's what I do, after you tell me what matters to someone and where we can find common cause. And you still have three more days to figure that out."

Rydara was not sure if his advice was good, or if she would take it. A part of her resented that he was still sick and wished he would take this burden away from her. He was the tribes' beloved prince, after all. He was the envoy they would have chosen. He was the one her father *had* chosen, always, to represent the kingdom.

I am Edriendor's nimkeïass, Rydara reminded herself. Even if Aander had been well, she might have suggested that she take the lead in presenting their petition because of her mother's people. She could see, intellectually, that her heritage made her a better ambassador to the elves.

She just didn't feel like a better ambassador. She didn't feel like any kind of ambassador. She had no experience, and her last conversation with Arcaena had been a disaster. Moreover, she had come here as a bastard in exile, at no one's request, so the idea that she would soon be speaking on behalf of all Kilethe and Lanimshar felt like some kind of cosmic joke.

But it did not matter whether she was the right choice to represent the tribes. She was the only choice.

***

The day of the audience dawned clear and crisp. Edriendor was beginning its colder season. It was milder by far than the snowy winters of Kilethe, but Rydara shivered as she left her room and walked to the palace entrance.

Rydara had heard nothing from Arcaena—or, indeed, from any elf—since the *Tirisslythra*. They had never confirmed a time or place for the audience. But the First Elf had named today as the day to hear Rydara's petition, and Rydara felt certain Arcaena had neither forgotten nor reconsidered. Silence could only mean that no further words were needed.

Rydara walked into the audience chamber just after first light, and she was not surprised to find Arcaena and the Council already seated in their semi-circle around the fountain. One of the chairs was empty—the one Faedastan had occupied on her first night in the city. No other elves stood in the chamber today.

She was not surprised, but she was intimidated to find them all sitting there, staring at her. Waiting. As Sundamar had modeled during their first audience, Rydara made the long walk to the dais in silence, her eyes fixed firmly on the floor. She mounted the steps and knelt in front of the fountain, trying to still her trembling. The continued silence stretched long enough to make Rydara second-guess her understanding of the protocol. But Arcaena had been the one to break it on that first night, so Rydara held her tongue.

"*Rydara,*" the First Elf finally spoke. "*Tarìme zumsaidera firlifaevath.*"

There was no magic to accompany the words, but Rydara knew what they meant. *You have come to give us your petition.*

Rydara was grateful Neremyn had pressed her to learn so much of the language. The elves could make themselves understood when they wished, but the First Elf had no intention of making this easy for Rydara.

Rydara allowed another beat of silence before taking Arcaena's words as permission to speak. "By now, you must have guessed why I am here," she said in Elvish, still kneeling in front of the fountain. She had rehearsed this speech at least a dozen times, choosing only Elvish words she knew she understood, but their accent was still hard for her to emulate. She did not speak with half the music that the elves did—but at least she was trying. "High Wizards walk the world again." She raised her head to look at the elves not blocked from her view by the water.

The sight of all of them still staring at her made Rydara's breath catch. Years of experience in her father's court had taught her to be silent, to avoid drawing attention to herself, to wait until she was alone with her father or brother to say anything except in the direst of circumstances, when her magic demanded an immediate response to a threat.

Rydara's magic was quiet now, but the circumstances were no less dire. She forced herself to make eye contact with the elves in front of her.

Arcaena sat on the far left, and Rydara met her gaze last. "I have come to ask—no, to beg—for your aid in standing against them." Rydara bowed her head and waited.

"We have been made aware of their new compact." Arcaena answered, also in Elvish. Still without any Speaking magic to aid Rydara's understanding, but at least she spoke slowly enough for Rydara to parse the words. "Yet we were unwilling to chase Faedastan into their midst to retrieve our shards. We were unwilling to stand beside our sister Chaenath when she chose to do so despite our decision. You have learned little of our ways if you believe we would reverse our course now, at your mere request."

"May I have the Council's permission to stand?" Rydara asked. She had hoped Arcaena would invite her to stand unprompted. But she could not proceed with her plea while half the Consuls were blocked from her view, and she had planned to ask if Arcaena declined to offer.

Arcaena flicked her gaze to the Consul who sat on the opposite end of the semi-circle, another female. The Consul nodded, and so did the male sitting next to her. The nod circled all the way back to Arcaena, skipping Faedastan's empty chair.

Arcaena also nodded. "You may," she said.

Rydara rose to her feet. "My thanks." She nodded deeply.

Then she took the liberty of circling in front of the fountain so she could address the Consuls in the middle of the semi-circle more directly. Her hands were still trembling, and she pressed them together and tried to calm herself as she continued her speech. "I am, of course, aware of the First Elf's recent pronouncements pertaining to the stolen shards and the passing of your highly regarded sister Chaenath." Rydara bowed her head and pressed her right fist, held sideways, against her mouth, as she had seen the elves do in their mourning. The Consuls mirrored the gesture. Arcaena was last to make the salute.

Rydara kept her expression neutral, showing respect to the dead, but she was glad to see the Consuls follow her lead. She had established some rapport, and that was a victory in itself. "I am also aware of the animosity that my race once showed to yours, and that long ago the elves vowed to wash their hands of humankind for good." She stepped farther around the fountain, now addressing the Consul on the far right. The Consuls were in many senses considered equal, but the rightmost position was where the least senior, and therefore least influential, member sat.

She was the Consul who had called Rydara "lost daughter" after Faedastan stole the shards, and Rydara nodded briefly in recognition. The elf gave no acknowledgment in return, but Rydara was glad to see her. She let her gaze move on, and as she resumed her speech, she made a point of addressing each elf in turn so that the audience was not experienced as merely a conversation between herself and Arcaena.

"I am furthermore conscious that I have not endeared myself to this Council of late. When last I stood before you and addressed the First Elf, I belittled your nation's customs and its grief. In my impatience to present my case to you, I showed contempt for a way of life and a system of values that I did not understand. I have since come to appreciate my ignorance and the error I made in passing judgment upon you in the midst of my own pain and failure. I demonstrated some of the worst characteristics of my race, and I humbly beg your forgiveness."

Rydara had circled back to Arcaena, and now she knelt in front of the First Elf and took Arcaena's hand, pressing her forehead against it. Aander, she decided, had been wrong to think that she could shame the elves into helping her, or that she could proceed in this audience without admitting fault at their previous encounter. The elven histories described humanity as proud, rash, ignorant, impatient, and entitled. Rydara had to show the Council that despite their frequent failures, humans were capable of learning from their mistakes.

The First Elf's hand was cool to the touch, and Rydara's stomach clenched in anxiety over her own daring. While preparing her speech, she had gone back and forth about whether it would be a good idea to invade the First Elf's physical space in this manner. It was the posture Sundamar had shown to Rydara when he apologized for not listening to her about Faedastan. She would have loved to ask him about it before her audience, but in the end, she had decided to trust her instinct and assume the gesture was customary.

Rydara could not see the Consuls or their reactions, but her Knowing registered surprise from some. Surprise, and a little softening.

She had made the right call.

"Any personal offense you may have given us has been absolved," Arcaena spoke after a moment. "Though the other obstacles to a favorable decision remain."

Rydara stood, releasing the First Elf's hand. She nodded, surreptitiously wiping her hands on her skirt. They had started to sweat. "My thanks to the First and the Council. You are more than generous." She stepped back into the center, in front of the fountain. "My petition, then, shall proceed in three movements. First, I shall recount my understanding of the code that Edriendor was founded upon and its roots in your history with Nivalis. Next, I shall report on my experiences with the High Wizards and plead for your compassion on behalf of my people's suffering, which I will liken to the plight the elves were once delivered from by Nivalis' great mercy. My petition will conclude with an appeal to your practicality and self-interest, outlining what I believe the High Wizards plan for our world and how you may come to regret it if you take no action against them at this time."

She sensed more surprise from the Consuls. Summarizing an argument up front was a common technique among elven scholars, and every book Rydara had found in the library represented itself as consisting of three movements, regardless of its length or complexity. Rydara was not sure it was appropriate to apply the format to a petition, and the Council's mixed reactions suggested that they did not know, either. Two or three seemed impressed, their reactions registering as a light touch of approbation in Rydara's Knowing, but others gave off a more critical energy. Several glanced toward Arcaena.

Rydara tensed as she, too, looked toward Arcaena, wondering if the First Elf would rebuke her for turning what was meant to be a request for the Council's aid into a formal argument about why they should give it. It could be perceived as another example of human entitlement.

Arcaena held Rydara's gaze for a long moment. Then the First Elf nodded.

Rydara breathed a sigh of relief.

"In my first movement, I recount my understanding of the code that you live by," she began, stepping back into the center of the semi-circle. "Leilatha, your first First Elf, wrote that the highest aim of an elf's life was to honor your creator, Nivalis. Nivalis taught you that all sentient creatures are precious to him. He taught you to honor and respect one another, and that sometimes even those who are considered least among you have something to teach the rest. He taught you the value of freedom, and the importance of accountability.

"But Nivalis walked among you in better times. Times before the High Wizards, times before magic was used to seduce my race and yours away from Nivalis and his precepts. Times before the atrocities both our races suffered in the Celestial Rebellion.

"It was then that Nivalis taught us his final lesson: forgiveness and sacrifice. He surrendered himself on the altar of the High Wizards' ambition, knowing his death would cripple their power and free elves and humans from their oppressors. Your First Elf Arcaena led you in claiming that freedom." Rydara bowed her head toward the First Elf in a token of respect, and Arcaena nodded an acknowledgment.

"But when the humans turned against you," Rydara continued, taking a deep breath, "scorning the memory of both Nivalis' sacrifice and your race's courage, it became clear that an elven community dedicated to Nivalis' ways could not exist in peace or unity with humans free to trample those ways underfoot. And so, led by your First Elf, you agreed that the best way to honor Nivalis was to separate yourselves from humanity, who had chosen against his ways, and create your own society where you would be free to follow his ways in peace."

Rydara paused, scanning the Consuls to gauge their reactions. She had not been able to find the "code" the elves lived by stated explicitly anywhere, though she had come across many references to it in both books and conversation. She had eventually decided there was no explicit code; "the code" was an idea that might contain any number of largely agreed-upon principles in elven society, depending on who was referring to it. Rydara was making her best guess at the common understanding.

None of the Consuls were so generous as to confirm her suppositions with a nod, and Rydara's Knowing was unhelpfully quiet. But she had to suppose that if she had made any egregious mistakes, they would have shown more disapproval.

"Such a conclusion made sense at the time," Rydara continued. She cleared her throat. "Humans were under no threat. In fact, humans had themselves become a threat. Separation was the only solution that preserved the lives and dignity of both races.

"But that is not true today." Rydara turned her gaze to the rightmost Consul, pleading for empathy, for understanding. She hoped this Consul might be more favorably disposed toward her than the First. "In my second movement, I appeal to both your code and your compassion."

Rydara recounted what she had witnessed at Tessex: the power of the Alterran queen and general, the shard they carried, and the death ritual that had changed its color and purpose. She explained that her people had no defense against their magic, no idea even of what was going on. She told the elves that the High Wizards had intended to slaughter more tribespeople to complete the corruption of the shard they carried. "And I stood before Faedastan, your brother, when he promised to bring Tenebrus two more shards," she continued, meeting gazes with Arcaena. The elves often referred to their neighbors as "sisters and brothers"—always placing "sisters" first, Rydara had noticed—even when there was no blood relation, but in Arcaena's case, there was another tie. Faedastan was her brother's son. In Elvish, the word for "brother" and "nephew" was the same.

During her speech at the *Tirisslythra*, Arcaena had sounded like she had forgiven herself and Chaenath both for their family connections, but Chaenath had not—which meant family ties meant something in elven culture. If Arcaena felt any lingering responsibility for her nephew's betrayal, Rydara wished to appeal to it.

"You all know more of Tenebrus than I do," she continued. "You know his ambition. You know what his strength once was—enough to cow humanity and elven-kind together and bring them under his reign.

"He did all of that without a single shard. You may think him weakened from the injury he suffered upon Nivalis' death, but he was strong enough to forge a second compact with the lords of hell. I do not know how many shards the scepter broke into or how many Tenebrus has now. Faedastan did not succeed in bringing him two more, but even if the one lost to Neremyn does not make it into their hands, these High Wizards are more than powerful enough without it to reassume the control over humanity they once had. It will not be long before they have slaughtered all among us that they wish to and set themselves up as gods over those who remain. My race will know no better than to thank them for it."

Rydara paced slowly to the other side of the fountain, locking gazes with the rightmost Consul. "You may wish to wash your hands of this, to say my race can get no worse than it deserves. We rejected your offers of kinship once before. We spurned you, and your god Nivalis, and spat upon your code. We had no interest in binding ourselves by it, so how, now, could it bind you to concern yourselves with our fate?

"For one reason only. I believe it is what Nivalis would ask of you."

Somewhere during the movement, Rydara had forgotten her anxiety, conviction in her own practiced words taking over. Now she looked at each of the Consuls in turn, unafraid to meet their gazes. She had no Speaking magic, but she knew her words pulled and demanded from these Consuls all the same, aggressive in both their assumption and their confidence.

Rydara did not know much about Nivalis. She had certainly never walked with him or spoken to him directly, as some of these elves may have done in ages past. She was not even sure how accurate their histories were, or if they had misrepresented how much of the world Nivalis was responsible for creating.

But she Knew she was right about this.

It was strange, because her Knowing usually only guided her interpretation of the people around her. Right now, the elves before her were distant and inscrutable, and Rydara could read no indication of whether they agreed with what she said. But Rydara had the same gut assurance she had long ago learned to associate with her Knowing, and it was telling her that she was right about what this long-dead, perhaps partly-mythical figure would have wanted.

Nivalis would have asked these elves to save her people.

"Once, long ago," Rydara continued, "your race was as humanity is today. Lost under the sway of High Wizards. Their Speaking is powerful, but you all know that there are limits on the blacker magics possible in this realm. The High Wizards could not have forced you all to desert the ways of Nivalis and bow to them instead had it been completely against your will. Some of you were alive then. All of you fell under their sway. All elves were in some measure guilty of the devastation that followed."

Rydara had been stunned to read this in their histories, but all the elven scholars agreed on this point. The Speaking magic could only overwhelm the mind temporarily, and elves were far more resistant to its effects than humans. It could not have made the elves forget Nivalis entirely or recognize the High Wizards as their gods unless the elves had in some measure wanted, and chosen, to do so.

"But Nivalis did not hold that against you," Rydara continued. "He did not wash his hands of you and leave you to your fate. He gave himself to the darkness to free you, so that you could have a second chance. A fresh start. A chance to make a different choice.

"He did this because all sentient lives are sacred to him. Even those that reject him and choose to go their own way. Your code binds you to honor his memory. You know that human lives are precious to him, as elven lives are. You know that he sacrificed himself to save humanity along with elven-kind. You know that he would do so again, and that he would call any who follow his ways to follow him also in this example."

Rydara paused to let that point linger. The Consuls' faces remained expressionless, but subtle edges of resentment pricked at Rydara's Knowing, along with a few fainter trickles of sorrow and shame. Rydara could not distinguish which emotions belonged to which Consuls, but she hoped some of them were swayed by her argument.

"You may deny, or disagree, with what I believe Nivalis, and your code, would ask of you, and that is your freedom and your right. But in my third movement I appeal to your practicality, regardless of what you may think of Nivalis and his wishes.

"Today, the High Wizards are humanity's problem. Today, it is the humans who are deceived and dying. You have grown comfortable here in Edriendor, safely hidden from the humans who once wished you harm, untouched by difficulty. Your First Elf has said that life is the greatest gift of all, and that she would sooner commit every elf in Edriendor to the fate of hunted wanderers than to see one life lost irrevocably, and this is in part why you have been unwilling to challenge the High Wizards so far. Such a confrontation may indeed cost lives.

"But I challenge you with this. You know the ambitions of the High Wizards better than I. It knows no bounds. Once humanity has fallen, their eyes will surely turn here, to Edriendor. Your boundaries are weaker now, with one shard lost and the High Wizards in possession of who knows how many. You may be willing to forsake this place and take up the lives of hunted wanderers if your protections fail. But will the High Wizards be content to let you remain so? Will they not hunt you down—even if you flee into the Realm Between—and seek to make themselves your gods, as they once were? Will they stop short of killing any they cannot bend to their will?

"If you confront them today, some of you may lose your lives, as Chaenath did. But you may not. The power of your race is great. Chaenath did not have the power of her sisters and brothers behind her, as you could if you march forth today.

"But if you wait until humanity is destroyed, until the High Wizards have collected and corrupted all the shards they can, and until they bring the fight to your door, more of you may be lost. Attempting to travel physically through the Realm Between comes with its own dangers."

Rydara had read about these, though she had not been able to find as much information on it as she would have liked. One book in the library had suggested that the longer an elf stayed in the Realm Between, the more difficult it became to return to the physical realm. Even if the shards could ease the passage,

Rydara was willing to wager that if the elves were forced to hide from the High Wizards in the Realm Between for a long time, not all of them would be able to return.

It was considered a form of death.

"And so my argument concludes," Rydara said. "I appeal to your code, to your compassion, and to your practicality, and I entreat the Council to send aid against these High Wizards now."

Rydara knelt in front of the fountain. The Council's resentment had grown sharper in her Knowing during her last movement, and she realized she had lost the threads of sorrow. Somewhere, somehow, she had made a mistake.

The First Elf looked to the rightmost Consul, and Rydara followed her gaze, pleading silently with the elf who would begin the vote. She could not tell if the hostility she sensed was shared by the entire Council. She hoped she had not lost them all.

But the Consul shook her head, voting "no," and looked to the male seated next to her. He shook his head as well.

The gesture was repeated by each Consul in turn until the vote came to Arcaena.

"You have learned much of our tongue and our ways in the time you have been here, little mortal," the First Elf spoke, rising to her feet. "You have brought news of a danger against us, revealed a traitor in our midst, and retrieved one of our shards from Faedastan, and for that you are to be commended.

"But if you had never come, Edriendor might still have the protection of three shards instead of two. Our sister Chaenath would be alive, and Neremyn safe in his confinement, instead of yet another weapon who may soon be wielded against us. There is much you do not know and may never understand about our code, our capabilities, and our commitments." Arcaena slowly shook her head, concluding the vote. "Our answer is no."

Chapter 14

The Elves' Decision

Heat flared in Rydara's chest, and she clenched her jaw to contain her frustration. *Calm, flowing, glowing water. Calm, flowing, glowing water.* She had already offended the Council. It would not do to let them Know the extent of her outrage or just how foolish, hypocritical, and cold she thought this decision was.

The Consuls could wall away their emotions with their magic whenever they wished, but Rydara had no such luxury, so she took a deep breath and fought to calm herself. *Calm, flowing, glowing water.* Rydara had hoped to sway the Council. She had spent so long rehearsing her argument that she had even begun to believe they would see the truth of it and rule in her favor.

But she had thought of one thing she could try if they didn't.

Rydara rose to her feet, ignoring the ripple of surprise and disapproval that the movement provoked from the Council. She no longer needed to endear herself to them. All she needed was to avoid antagonizing them, so they would be able to listen and rule fairly on her last request.

She gathered herself in as firm a calm as she could. "With all due respect to the Council of Twelve," she began, nodding deeply to the First Elf and again to the rest of the Council, "it is my conviction that this matter is of too great import to your race and to the world to be decided by only a few. I call upon the full assembly."

Her declaration was greeted with silence. The elves' astonishment echoed loudly in Rydara's Knowing, and one Consul went so far as to shift in her seat. All eyes looked to Arcaena.

From the First Elf, Rydara sensed nothing at all. Arcaena was an instantiation of the tranquility Rydara had been searching for as she studied Rydara.

"You are human, and an outsider," the First Elf spoke. "Only a guest in Edriendor. You have no standing to call an assembly."

"I do not," Rydara agreed, staring back into the First Elf's gaze. Arcaena's attention usually made her feel small and insignificant, but not now. In this moment, it was the First Elf's traditions and stubbornness that were small, and Rydara had no impulse to back down. "But you know that Chaenath did not agree with your judgment on this point. Had there been time, she might have called a full assembly. She had the standing.

"And so did Dasyra, Aravae, Itylara, Nithenoel, Lyeneru, Thaciona, and Myantha," Rydara continued, casting her gaze over the rest of the Council. "Dasyra called for such an assembly when Arcaena first pledged to forsake humanity and found a separate homeland. The seven lost daughters of Edriendor dissented and stayed behind.

"I do not know from which of them I may be descended, but as blood of their blood, I plead the right to speak in their place. I plead the right to call an assembly on behalf of those whose dedication to kinship with my race cost them their immortality and the opportunity to stand before you today to make any further pleas. I plead the standing."

Rydara knelt again, fixing her eyes on the rightmost Consul, conscious when Arcaena signaled her permission to begin a vote. This time, the Consul nodded. The male next to her shook his head, and Rydara's breath caught in her throat as the vote continued.

Two more nos. Three yeses. Another no. A yes. A no.

The vote was split, five to five, and all eyes turned to Arcaena.

The First Elf nodded. "Very well, Rydara, you shall have your assembly at noon. But among all the elves, we were chosen to serve as Consuls for a reason. The others will see this as we do."

Rydara nodded to the First Elf, tightening her lips grimly. "Perhaps."

***

By the time the sun was high in the sky, every elf in Edriendor had again assembled on the banks of the river where they had begun the *Tirisslythra* eight nights ago. This time, Rydara stood on the white footbridge to address them. Arcaena stood next to her and gave a short introduction, explaining that the Council had granted her request to petition the full assembly on the basis of her descent from one of the seven lost daughters of Edriendor. Then Arcaena stepped aside, nodding to Rydara to proceed.

Rydara stepped forward. Never in her life had she spoken to so many, and the sensation of all their eyes upon her made her words catch in her throat. Her palms were sweating profusely, now, and her stomach was so knotted up with anxiety she worried she might throw up in front of everyone. She trembled in the silence.

If Rydara lived a hundred more years after today, she doubted anything she said or did would compare with the significance of this short speech she was about to give. She could not afford to fail—but she still wasn't sure what to say. She had practiced and polished her petition to the Council so many times. But it hadn't worked.

She had to adapt it—but by how much? Should she keep the first two movements the same, or was Aander right? Would it be better to scrap it entirely and just speak from the heart?

Rydara closed her eyes and took a deep breath. *Calm, flowing, glowing water.* Somehow, she found a place of stillness within herself—the place that had eluded her during her petition before the Council. Her body stilled, and she opened her eyes.

"Elves of Edriendor," she began in Elvish. Her words reverberated across the river, startling her with their loudness. With a quick glance at Arcaena, Rydara realized the First Elf was amplifying her voice for her. Rydara had not known that was possible. "Thank you for hearing me today. I am here to plead for your aid in the struggle my people now face against your ancient enemies, the High Wizards. I will present my petition in three movements."

Rydara took a deep breath. Once she named her movements, there could be no going back. "First, I will describe the character and nature of the people I am asking you to save, as I have experienced it growing up among them. Second, I will tell you what I have observed and come to admire about your race, as a guest and a stranger here whose people are so different from your own. Finally, I will explain why I wish you to save my people, despite their flaws, and I will ask you to consider your own ideals and to decide whether you will let them inspire you to come to humanity's aid."

And so, Rydara did. She told them about her mother's dark skin and how she had left her people, the descendants of the elves, to have a relationship with a tribal king that was not a marriage, and that she, Rydara, was the result. She told them that the pale-skinned people of the tribes were wary of the Rishara and their ways—as they had once been wary of the elves—and that they had never fully accepted Rydara as one of them. She explained that she had only heard of the ancient demons and the Land Beyond the Waste because of her mother's stories, and that when she had tried to tell her father of the massacre at Tessex and the High Wizards who led Alterra's army, he had banished her. She admitted that some of the evils that had driven the elves to flee from humans and found Edriendor after the Celestial Rebellion still plagued the human race. They were still petty and sometimes cruel. They were still slow to listen and quick to punish. They still feared what they did not understand.

Then Rydara described the elves. They had been generous to her and Aander, despite the longstanding precedent of not allowing humans into Edriendor. They had been merciful to Neremyn, though he had been one of those who murdered their god and enslaved them in the Celestial Rebellion. They had loved and respected Chaenath, though she had secluded herself for centuries and defied the First Elf's decision not to pursue the shards. To Rydara—who did not have the standing of even the most junior elf among them—they had given the privilege of addressing the Council of Twelve, and though they had not ruled in her favor, they had done her the further courtesy of permitting her to speak again before the full assembly. It was a courtesy that would never have been shown among the tribes. It was possible only because the elves were different—in so many ways better than humanity. Where human leaders so often clung to power and spent their followers' lives in pointless quarrels over land and insults, the Council of Twelve valued the lives and respected the judgment of each individual in Edriendor. In some ways, Rydara had felt herself more welcomed and valued here than she ever had among the tribes.

Rydara's speech was far from elegant. More than once, her Elvish failed her, and she was forced to fall back on Common. But she spoke from the heart, and she trusted the elves' magic to help them discern her meaning.

When she came to her third movement, she spoke about Aander. About his courageous act in forfeiting his title and his home in protest of her banishment. How he had kept a promise he long ago made to her mother that he would watch over her. He had risked the danger of the Waste to do it and nearly paid with his life.

As her eyes searched the gathered assembly, seeking to see and connect with each elf there, she noticed her brother near the back of the crowd. He was wrapped in a blanket, leaning against a tree with Sundamar standing next to him. She did not know if Sundamar was interpreting for him or how much he could understand. But he was there. He was listening.

Rydara's eyes moistened, and for a moment she faltered. She cleared her throat before she went on, looking away from Aander.

"I would not claim that many humans resemble Aander in their love, their honor, or their courage. I cannot say that any hold themselves to the beautiful code you have here in Edriendor, that fosters patience, wisdom, mercy, and forgiveness. But there is beauty in my race, alongside all its flaws. According to your own memories and teachings of the White, the creator loved us, as he loved you. We have the potential to love, to learn. To choose what is good. We do not always live up to this potential, but even when we fail, the potential to do better remains.

"Once, long ago, Nivalis sacrificed himself to give my race and yours a second chance. As an outsider who has only begun to learn of your ways, I cannot presume to teach you what your code requires. But as an outsider, I look at your ways, and I wonder: you aspire to mercy and forgiveness, but do not your traditions and practice still fall short of the example Nivalis set for you? He sacrificed himself to save two races that had turned against him. You may have forgiven yourselves and each other for your failures in the Celestial Rebellion, as he taught you to, but did you forgive those who turned against you? When you spared Neremyn's life and consigned him to an eternity of loneliness and penance, was that forgiveness? When you withdrew from humanity to settle here after you experienced persecution, was that forgiveness? Can you say that you here in Edriendor have always lived up to your own potential for loving, for learning, and for choosing the best good? Or was it Dasyra, Aravae, Itylara, Nithenoel, Lyeneru, Thaciona, and Myantha who chose a better good, a good more in keeping with Nivalis' example, when they declined to join your exodus and stayed behind to teach humanity of Nivalis' ways?

"I may be descended from one of those seven elves, but I cannot fairly stand before you and claim to speak for them today. I am human, a descendant also of those who persecuted you. Today the fate of my race is in your hands, and though I have come before you to plead for rescue, I know that you owe us nothing, and that my arguments and my opinion count for nothing. You are the ones who must decide what best honors your code and your memory of Nivalis. I ask only that you do what you deem is right."

Rydara knelt and prostrated herself on the bridge before them, pressing her forehead against the cold white stone.

Arcaena stepped around her. The First Elf's voice rang out across the river, calling for a vote on the question of whether the elves should leave Edriendor to face the High Wizards and save Rydara's people. There was a short silence, and then the first response called back from the southern bank.

"Kindroth son of Isarrel. My vote is no."

Rydara clenched her hands where they stretched out before her on the ground. Whenever elves voted, they spoke in order from youngest to oldest, under the theory that more influential elves were less likely to be swayed by the opinions of their juniors. She had failed to persuade Kindroth, but there were over a hundred elves left to speak, and he was the least influential among them. Surely some would side with her.

"Eriladar son of Fayeth. My vote is no."

"Mylaela daughter of Myrrh. My vote is no."

"Othorion son of Rosaniya. My vote is no."

The vote went on. When Rydara counted the twentieth no, she rose from her prostrate position, settling herself on her knees so she could see them. She could no longer address them, and there was nothing left to say, but she could look at them as they decided her people's fate. She could plead with them with her gaze.

It made no difference. The vote continued to be no.

Rydara did not need them all. She did not even need a majority. If the elves voted against her petition, any dissenters among them might act in accordance with their own opinions anyway, as the lost daughters of Edriendor had done.

Neremyn and Chaenath had bested three High Wizards, and there were only nine in total. Perhaps nine elves could prove their match. If Neremyn proved true to his word and convinced some of the High Wizards to leave the fight, perhaps they would not even need nine.

There had been seven dissenters the last time a full assembly was called. Seven might be enough to save Rydara's people.

"Phaerille daughter of Isilynor. My vote is no."

"Halanaestra daughter of Delimira. My vote is no."

"Bellas son of Naevys. My vote is no."

Each decision was another knife to Rydara's hope. With the exception of Arcaena, the elves stood too far away for her to sense much from them with her Knowing. The First Elf gave away little, as usual, but as the vote wore on, Rydara sensed a quiet hum of self-satisfaction from Arcaena. The First Elf's prediction was proving true.

Rydara watched helplessly, wishing she had made friends in the crowd of unfamiliar faces. She had not noticed when Sundamar and Aander left, but they had, and no wonder. It was a marvel that Aander had lasted as long as he had.

With Chaenath gone and Arcaena and the rest of the Council having given their opinions already, there was no one left to vote in the assembly that Rydara even recognized. She did see Ildylintra and other members from the Edren Guard, but like Sundamar, they would not be able to participate in the proceedings. They were too young.

Sundamar had declined to face High Wizards with her once already. She could not have counted on him, even if the elves had considered him old enough to vote.

Rydara's throat constricted as her hopes slowly bled out before the full assembly, her eyes growing hot with moisture. She had given this petition everything, and it was not enough. She had failed. Somehow, she had failed—again. This time there was nowhere left to turn.

The vote came to the Consuls last. Rydara knew their opinions already, and though she desperately wished that even one of their votes might be different this time, they each repeated no. Finally, it was Arcaena's turn to speak, and Rydara closed her eyes.

"You make a fine petition, Rydara of the Noraan," Arcaena said, turning to look down at her. "This one better than the last. Even the least among us may have something to teach the rest, and I think you, a mortal and an outsider, may have done this today, for some of your questions do merit further reflection." Rydara blinked her eyes open and stared up at Arcaena, wondering if, out of all the elves in Edriendor, the cold, inscrutable First could possibly have been moved by her speech.

"Did we show the same grace to Neremyn that Nivalis showed to us?" Arcaena asked, turning her gaze toward the rest of the assembly. "I think perhaps we did not. Perhaps if we had, he would not have turned against us a second time."

Arcaena looked back at Rydara, and for once Rydara's Knowing registered warmth from the First. Compassion, even — but not enough.

"But," Arcaena continued, twisting the knife in Rydara's spirits, "we cannot contest the High Wizards without doing violence to them and risking violence to ourselves and to the humans they control. Long ago, Nivalis gave his life for us, freeing us from slavery and deception, setting an example we strive ever to follow and imparting a legacy we swore never to forget. But if we were to do the same for humanity, what would be gained? They forgot Nivalis and rejected his legacy. They rejected us, and even now, they do not ask for our help or even believe they need it.

"During the Celestial Rebellion, every elf and mortal in the world forgot Nivalis and served the High Wizards. There was no one to remind us of the freedom we should have fought for and the god we should have served. No one but Nivalis himself. That is not the case now for humanity. They have the teachings of Dasyra, Aravae, Itylara, Nithenoel, Lyeneru, Thaciona, and

Myantha. They had your insight, Rydara, and your warning. They do not wish to be saved, and even if we did save them from the High Wizards, breaking our code in the process, they would not remain saved. Humanity ever invents new ways of doing evil.

"Better for us to remain here and keep our own hands clear of it. Here we can preserve Nivalis' legacy for ourselves and our children. Here we can even offer sanctuary to any who come to us. You and your brother are welcome to remain here as long as you wish, and if you bring your people as far as our border, Rydara, I give my decision now, as First, that we will lower the wards that conceal this place and accept anyone willing to honor our ways. Nivalis forgave us, and though once I swore to forsake humanity altogether, you have helped me see that I was wrong. We can let ourselves be found by those who seek us in need. We can show mercy, as Nivalis did.

"But I will not go out from here to seek out those who drove us away and did not ask us to return to try to save them from a threat they refuse to acknowledge. My answer to your petition is also no. Assembly dismissed." Arcaena nodded, and the crowd began to break apart, starting back toward the city.

Rydara could tell that Arcaena thought her offer of sanctuary generous, but it was an empty gesture. The tribes knew they were under threat from Alterra, but they had no idea how grave the danger was. None of them would abandon their lands and risk the perils of the Waste unless elves and dragons came to persuade them.

They certainly wouldn't do it based on a warning from Rydara. She had learned the limit of her influence with the tribes, and it wasn't enough to move even her own father.

"You're wrong." Rydara's words were quiet, whatever magic had been aiding them now gone. They reached only as far as Arcaena, and the First Elf turned to look at her. Rydara stood. "If you think you honor Nivalis best by staying here, you are wrong. You know you are."

"We honor Nivalis as best we can, each in her own way," Arcaena returned. "None of us attains perfection, but Nivalis is merciful." With that, Arcaena walked away, joining the exodus back toward the city.

Rydara stared after her, but there was nothing left to say. The First Elf had as much as admitted that she knew this decision was not the best expression of her code or her religion. Maybe they all knew it.

They were choosing it anyway.

If Rydara was honest with herself, it was hard to blame them. Rydara did not understand why they did not care more about the threat the High Wizards might one day pose to them, but she did understand why they would not want to risk themselves to save another race—especially considering their bitter history with humanity. Among the tribes, an argument like the one she had just made would have been regarded as nonsense, even if she could have changed it to feature the Six and the tribes' own religious principles.

One did not risk one's own people to save someone else's. It simply was not done.

Rydara had been a fool to think the elves might be different. When she had read about their honor for Nivalis and his sacrifice, the importance of the code they lived by, the beauty of the society they had built apart from humans and their endless infighting, she had dared to hope they might be different. In so many ways, they were better than the tribes.

Just not in this.

Rydara took a deep breath and sank back to her knees, not knowing what to do with herself or how to process her failure. Her mission was over. Her people were lost.

Rydara stayed kneeling there for a long time. She did not have the strength to compose herself and walk back to the city with the elves.

She did not have the heart to face Aander and tell him that she had failed.

She started when a hand touched her shoulder. Sundamar was looking down at her, his face drawn in sympathy. The last of the other elves had gone.

He withdrew his hand from her shoulder. "Your plea was beautiful and true," he said in Common. "I am sorry my kind decided against you."

Rydara wiped her eyes on her sleeve and blinked up at Sundamar, confused about how to feel. Part of her was angry with him for not flying with her and Chaenath to save the shards, despite Arcaena's orders. For not advocating for her before the assembly, even though she knew he was not eligible to vote. For not offering to fight for her people now, even if it would be just the two of them.

For caring about her in the way that he did. She could feel it now in her Knowing, as she often did in his presence. His admiration, his fascination, the depth of his compassion for her. It was magnetic—*he* was magnetic—and Rydara was not immune to his attention, even now.

He was still the most beautiful creature she had ever seen. He felt far too much for her, and Rydara could not begin to fathom why.

But it did not matter. What he felt was also not enough.

"Would you have voted yes?" Rydara asked in Elvish, turning her gaze out over the river. "If you were old enough to vote?"

The question discomfited him. Her Knowing suggested he had not considered the issue, and he had not thought he would have to.

The silence stretched, and Rydara could feel him weighing both sides of the argument. He wanted to be honest with her.

"Yes," he eventually said in Elvish, sitting down beside her. "I would have voted yes."

The rest hung unspoken between them, but they both sensed it. Rydara wanted him to offer more, to say that he was ready to act in accordance with the vote he would have cast even though the rest of Edriendor was unified against him. But he would not. He was loyal to his kind and to the First, and he would bind himself by their decision even though he did not see it the same way, just as he had before.

Rydara did not make him say it out loud. They sat in silence as the sun slowly lowered in the sky. Rydara had hardly had enough to eat during the seven days of Edriendor's fast, but she was not hungry now, and she and Sundamar remained on the bridge while the rest of the country took its afternoon meal. The shadows lengthened into evening, and Sundamar eventually stood.

Rydara could feel an obligation pulling him away, and she inferred he needed to see to Aander. He lingered for a moment, wondering if she might come with him, but he must have sensed that she was not ready. He left in silence.

Rydara did not understand how the elves discerned the timing of Aander's fits, but she was sure Sundamar had left her only because Aander was about to have one. There would be no point to her going along. Aander would not be aware of her visit or understand anything she might say until it was over.

Rydara's ankles had long since grown numb, and she resituated, wrapping her arms around her legs. She watched the sun set alone, and the colors blurred and ran with her tears.

Chapter 15

Lost Hopes

When Rydara let herself into the infirmary, hours later, Aander's screams echoed through the halls. She froze at the sound. His terrors had not been so loud in many days. Not since before she had left with Chaenath to chase Faedastan.

Rydara hurried toward his room, her breath sounding loud in her ears. *What is wrong with him?* She had thought he was past this.

She burst through the door to his room. Aander was lying on his bed, head tilted back and legs outstretched, screaming, but his arms remained at his sides and he was not turning over. Sundamar stood over him, humming a soothing tune with power that echoed loudly in Rydara's Knowing. Aander's muscles all looked taut, and every so often he twitched as if he were about to thrash, but Sundamar's tune settled over him like a heavy weight, holding him in place. If not for that, he would surely have been thrashing and dangerous.

Sundamar was keeping Aander safe for now. *But why did this happen?* Rydara's brow knitted in dismay, and she glanced at Sundamar as she crossed the room toward her brother, unsure if it was safe to approach.

Sundamar made no motion to stop her. Rydara's Knowing felt pity from him, but no fear, so she knelt by her brother's bedside and took one of his hands in both of hers as Sundamar continued to hum.

"It's all right, Aander, it's just a dream," she whispered to him, stroking his hand. "It's not real. Everything is all right."

The words caught in her throat as Rydara realized they were a lie. Everything was most certainly not all right. Their journey here had been in vain. Their people were doomed.

"It's going to be all right," Rydara lied again, unable to stop herself. "It's going to be all right." She rested her forehead against his hand, and her body trembled with emotion. She was so tired. "It's going to be all right."

***

Rydara startled awake to Sundamar's hand on her shoulder. The screaming had stopped, and Aander was tucked snugly beneath his blankets, his breaths coming slow and even. The room was dark.

Rydara stood and followed Sundamar into the hall, where little beacons of the aqua glow offered some light.

"What happened?" she asked in Elvish, wiping the sleep from her eyes. "Why is he worse again?"

"It is normal. He is gaining strength, and the fits grow less common. He will not have another like this for many, many days."

"I thought the fits were getting milder?"

"Most are. But not all." Sundamar's brow creased. "I am sorry. I thought Chaenath would have explained."

Chaenath had explained everything weeks ago, Rydara remembered. But with the language barrier, Rydara had not understood the subtleties.

"So fits this severe might keep happening to him, even after the forty days," Rydara said. Chaenath had been clear enough that Aander might never truly get better, but with Neremyn's optimism and the way Aander had been improving, Rydara had thought the worst was behind him. "This ... this will change his whole life." Even if he was well and normal for months at a time, Aander would need to be watched constantly if fits like this might still happen.

"No," Sundamar said, but his demeanor was not as reassuring as Rydara might have hoped. "Not his whole life. For a few years, fits this severe may recur, but with ever decreasing frequency. After that, only the nightmares."

"A few *years*," Rydara repeated. "How many?"

"Five to ten. Closer to five, I think, with the way he's been going."

Rydara blinked. Elves were immortal, so five or ten years must have seemed inconsequential to Sundamar.

To Rydara, it sounded like forever.

She sighed heavily and leaned against the wall behind her, wishing she had never come to this place. The repercussions to Aander would be difficult and long-lasting, and for what? He had claimed this quest was worth his life, but in the end, they had accomplished nothing.

Sundamar reached out and took Rydara's hand in the dim aqua glow of the light fixtures, surprising her. His touch sent shivers running up her arm.

"You could have a life here, Rydara."

The words were simple, but his gaze trapped hers with its intensity, and Rydara's imagination supplied the rest. It would be a good life. The land was beautiful and temperate, and the people were at peace. Rydara could learn all she wished from the many books left untouched in the library and the oral history of elves that had lived through the ages. She could fly with dragons and train with sorcerers.

She would be loved by this magnetic elf, son of grace and strength and beauty.

Rydara stared back into Sundamar's eyes, letting herself imagine the future he offered. The elves of Edriendor were not all filled with warmth toward Rydara, but they did not view her with hate and suspicion like so many in the tribes. She did not have to hide the color of her skin or keep silent in public and pretend her ideas were her father's or her brother's. No one resented her presence here, and she was not expected to earn her place day after day after day.

Rydara's chin trembled. She had had a place in the tribes, once, but they had banished her. She had come here thinking she could prove they had been wrong, thinking she might even earn their approval, but that had been a child's dream. If there had ever been any hope for it, it had died in the elves' assembly, along with her people's hope for deliverance.

If she went back to them, she would die as an outsider. An exile.

"Sundamar, why don't your people fear the High Wizards?" Rydara asked, searching his eyes. As long as the High Wizards threatened the world, surely the future she imagined here was as impossible as any with the tribes. "They enslaved the elves once before. Won't they try to again? You said you could escape to the Realm Between if it came to that, but couldn't the High Wizards follow you there? Wouldn't some of you die?"

"They might follow, but the Realm Between is closer to the Realm Beyond and we would have more protection from them there. It is true that if we wished to return to the physical realm and build another homeland here, we might not all have the strength to do so," Sundamar said. "It is a death, but it is not the same death. Those too weak to return to the physical realm would be strong enough to pass directly to the Realm Beyond. It is where all elves go when we have mastered the talent of Prophecy and are able to walk through the Realms, if we grow tired of our pilgrimage here."

Rydara was not sure that she understood, but it sounded as though this might explain why her appeal to the Council's self-interest had failed. Their books had used the word "death" to describe being stranded in the Realm Between, and Rydara had thought that meant it was just as bad as regular death and that it would be just as important to their code that every elf be protected from it. But apparently not.

She had been foolish to make assumptions about something she understood so poorly, let alone to rely on them in her plea before the Council.

"Well then, I could not go with you there," Rydara said, "even if I wanted to stay among your race. I am neither an elf nor a Prophet."

"The High Wizards may not come here in your lifetime. And if they do, two shards may be enough to protect the land. Not as much of it as was protected by all three, but our city may still stand."

It was probably true. The High Wizards would come to Edriendor, but conquering all the lands of humans would take them many years. There might be time for Rydara to live out her days in peace. And maybe the elves would be able to protect their city against the High Wizards when they came. What did Rydara know of their relative strength?

Sundamar reached out and touched her face. "And even if our city is not strong enough, I promise I would not escape to the Realm Between and leave you behind. We could find another way to flee. Together."

Rydara closed her eyes and leaned into his touch, wishing for a moment that she could say yes. A single tear ran down her cheek, and she did not know if it was for her failure at the assembly, her frustration with the elves, or her bitterness toward the father who had never loved her and the people who had sent her away. Sundamar brushed the tear away with his thumb.

She could stay with him and leave it all behind.

Rydara took a deep breath and remembered Tessex. She remembered how General Dameires had stabbed Kell through the heart. She imagined Kell's body being thrown into the mass grave she had seen. Then she imagined her father's body added, and her Uncle Sorovan's, and the rest of the people she knew.

Rydara leaned forward, letting Sundamar pull her into an embrace. She rested her forehead against his chest.

She had been wrong to think she could earn her people's acceptance. Wrong even to think she needed to prove to herself that she deserved it, as she had said to Neremyn. Her petition had failed. She had proven nothing, and going back alone would prove nothing to anyone.

But she still didn't want her people to die. She couldn't save them without the elves—not realistically—but she could still try.

Rydara's speech had not convinced a single elf that her people were worth trying to save, but somewhere along the way, Rydara had convinced herself. Trying to save them was the right thing to do, even if she gained nothing from the effort.

Even if it cost her everything.

"I can't stay here, Sundamar. I have to go back to my people and warn them. Even if I go alone. Even if no one listens."

Rydara's Knowing sensed deep disappointment and fear, but Sundamar did not argue with her. He just held her.

Rydara still did not understand the intensity of his emotions. There was no reason that disappointment should cut him so deeply, or for him to fear what might happen to her when she left. They hardly knew each other.

But somehow, this elf cared more about her than anyone she had ever met, apart from Aander. She had been too hard on Sundamar, maybe, expecting him to offer to save her entire race by himself. He had been kind to her, and Rydara believed she could have loved him. Despite her many resolutions never to be like her mother, Rydara imagined she could have left her people for his and been happy to do it.

If only it would not have meant her people would die.

She did not want the embrace to end, but she soon pulled away. She had made her decision. It would be cruel to let Sundamar hope for more between them.

"When will you go?" Sundamar asked. He seemed to understand that they could not be, but his eyes said he would not stop thinking of her soon.

"As soon as Aander is ready," she said.

***

Aander's room was empty when Rydara returned the next morning, and the glass door to the gardens was standing open. Rydara found him sitting outside with a blanket wrapped around his shoulders, awake and alert with a smile on his face. But for his sunken features and the newly-darkened circles under his eyes, Rydara might not have believed he had spent the night screaming in terror.

"Rydara!" His eyes lit up when he saw her, and Rydara's gut twisted. It had been a long time since his eyes had held so much light, and news of the final vote would suck it right out of them. "Look at this!"

Aander reached out one hand and held it open, studying it intently.

While Rydara watched, the air above his hand started to glow faintly yellow. Soon he was holding a glowing orb of light.

Rydara's jaw dropped.

Aander glanced at her and laughed, and the orb disintegrated. "I have the Showing magic," he announced. "I was waiting until your petition was over to surprise you with it. Sundamar taught me a little when you were away with Chaenath."

"A little?" Rydara exclaimed. "Aander, we don't have any Showers in the Noraani alliance who can make a light source. I've only heard of two, maybe three people who have ever done it."

"Really?" Aander's eyebrows rose in surprise. "Sundamar suggested it was pretty basic."

"For an elf, maybe. Can you do it again?"

Aander obliged, and Rydara sat next to him, leaning toward his hand to inspect the orb. She moved her hand over it, blocking the sun. She was stunned to see her hand cast no shadow.

"Aander, this is incredible," she breathed. Proximity to the elves' shards had strengthened her Knowing, and it must have been responsible for bringing out this magic in Aander.

She wondered how many in the tribes might have some hidden gift, and how strong they could grow if given the chance.

If it could somehow be enough to challenge the High Wizards.

The orb winked out. "I can't keep it up very long," Aander admitted. "Lousy concentration. But Sundamar says I'll get better with practice."

He was trying to be humble, but his eyes shone with pride.

"And time to heal," Rydara added, smiling. "Your concentration will improve as your body gets stronger."

"Yes, and time," Aander agreed. His gaze grew distant, and Rydara felt something of his frustration through her Knowing. His recovery was taking a long time. He was still so weak, and so vulnerable before the terrors.

But he pulled himself back from self-pity to meet her gaze. "Your petition. Tell me how the elves voted." Rydara's face fell, and Aander looked back at the garden. "They're not going to help us."

"Aander, I'm sorry. All they offered was sanctuary for any humans who come here. I … I don't know what I could have done differently."

"Don't be sorry. I couldn't follow half of what you said, but from what I did…" Aander reached out and grasped Rydara's hand. He didn't meet her gaze, and his eyes shone with moisture. He dashed a hand across them. "It was a beautiful speech. No one could have made our case any better. Including me." He pulled his blanket more tightly around himself. "Sometimes people just don't want to listen."

Rydara felt his pride in her as they sat together with Aander still holding her hand. It overwhelmed her. During her petition, she had felt, on some level, that she was doing well. She had wanted to believe her failure hadn't happened just because she was a sorry excuse for a diplomat who had had no business addressing the elves in the first place.

Hearing Aander say so meant more than she could say.

Aander turned to look at her, releasing her hand. "You said they offered sanctuary to any humans who come here? That's something, at least."

"It doesn't matter. Father would never come here. Who would? Who would risk the Waste based on nothing but our word?"

She expected him to contradict her, as he always did when she forecast gloom.

"You shouldn't come with me, Rydara," he said instead. His voice was heavy with regret. "I knew it was always different for you, growing up in the tribes, but I didn't know ... I never guessed how hard it was for you."

"I didn't want you to know," Rydara said, resting a hand on his knee.

"I didn't try hard enough to know," Aander returned. "As your brother, I should have. I let you down."

"Aander, you're the only one who never let me down." Rydara squeezed his knee, and Aander patted her hand. He did not quite agree.

"Still." He sniffed. "I don't want you to come with me to tell the tribes. You don't need to risk any more for them. You can stay here. Sundamar is a good man—well, elf—and he cares for you. I'll see you again when I bring Father and anyone else who's willing to listen."

"Don't be ridiculous. How do you expect to travel across the Hahiroth without any help?"

"I—" Aander frowned, and Rydara felt his deep frustration with his weakness. "I could—"

"No, you couldn't, but it doesn't matter. I wouldn't let you go without me anyway. You'll have to do the talking, since no one would listen to me—not that they'll listen to you either. But I'll be there to help you stand, at least."

Aander looked at her, his forehead wrinkled in concern.

"They might not love me as much as they love you, but I still don't want them to die," Rydara tried to explain. "I can't just stay here and do nothing. It wouldn't be right."

Aander nodded. "Together, then. We'll find a way to make them listen."

"We'll go together, whether anyone listens to us or not," Rydara said. "As soon as you're strong enough."

"We should go now."

Aander started to stand, and Rydara frowned as she moved to help him. Chaenath had suggested he would be bedridden for forty days, and it had been only twenty-two. "You're not going to get better any faster if you overdo it."

"You don't know that. No one's ever recovered from this before." Aander gained his feet and leaned against her, letting his blanket fall to the ground. He looked out across the garden and the stone path that led through it. "The tribes don't have a lot of time, and the petition is over now, so I can't afford to be lying around. When I can walk the path to the far side and back without your help, that's when we'll leave."

He pulled away from her and started walking, his steps halting and crooked. He made it as far as the fountain in the middle of the garden before a fit of coughing brought him to his knees. Rydara hurried to him.

"Can you find out if we can borrow a dragon?" Aander asked when he caught his breath. "I know the elves don't want to help, but maybe they could just drop us off back at home? They wouldn't even have to let any other humans see them if that's a concern."

"I think if Arcaena were going to allow that, she would have included it in her offer," Rydara murmured. She did know a dragon who had been comfortable breaking Arcaena's policy once before, though. "I'll talk to Lëanor—but even if she's willing to drop us off, you'll need to be strong enough to argue with Father. For now, let me help you back to bed. You can try again tomorrow."

"We'll go tomorrow," Aander said, his face set with determination.

Chapter 16

Leaving Edriendor

Lëanor, Rydara soon found out, had been dismissed from the Edren Guard, and it was not a simple matter to speak to her. She had returned to the northern cliffs, where the other dragons lived. Rydara had learned from her research that the other dragons were wilder creatures of narrower concerns than those who served in the Edren Guard. They were territorial, and anyone who ventured into the cliffs did so at their own peril.

Sundamar offered to arrange a meeting with Lëanor at the border. Apparently, the dragon was no longer welcome in Edriendor, and Rydara guessed that Arcaena would not approve of their meeting at the border either. Rydara regretted having to involve Sundamar. He had gone against Arcaena's wishes once already on her behalf, and asking him for more felt like abusing the affection he had for her.

But there was no one else she could ask.

It was a short flight. The three of them flew with Reluvethel and his dragon Mìsul, other members of the Edren Guard. The demarcation between forest and desert was just as abrupt as at Edriendor's southern border. Rydara could see the cliffs up ahead as they approached, but when Mìsul landed on the sandy gravel at the foot of the towering bluffs, Rydara glanced behind her, and the forest was gone. She saw only wasteland.

Sundamar whistled a long, low note as they climbed down Mìsul's wing, Aander with an arm around Sundamar's shoulders. The music was heavy with magic.

"Can they all hear that?" Rydara wondered aloud.

"Yes, but Lëanor will know it is meant for her," Sundamar answered, helping Aander sit on the desert floor.

Aander glanced at Mìsul and at the apparent Waste now behind them, equal parts awe and nervousness. "Are we in dragon territory, then?" He spoke in Common, and Rydara realized she had used Elvish without thinking about it.

Sundamar shook his head, raising a hand to shade his eyes as he searched the tops of the cliffs. "Their border is where the cliffs rise," he said to Aander in Common. "This ground is unclaimed. A march, as you say."

Kilethe and Lanimshar were sometimes called the "marches" between Alterra and Jeshimoth, but it was not a word often used in Common. Rydara wondered how Sundamar had learned it.

Sundamar turned to glance at Reluvethel, who was still sitting atop of Mìsul. "Thank you, brother," he said in Elvish. "You do not need to stay. Lëanor can take us where we need to go."

"We are happy to," Reluvethel assured him. "Lëanor is our sister, and we would see her again."

Sundamar nodded and spoke no more, but tension in his shoulders betrayed his unease.

This was an unauthorized excursion, and Rydara could tell he was unenthusiastic about involving other members of the Edren Guard. It might bring Arcaena's disfavor upon them, as he risked himself.

Eventually a flash of green appeared in the sky above the cliffs. The form was soon recognizable as a dragon, and Rydara breathed a sigh of relief. It was good to see Lëanor again.

The dragon's landing kicked up a cloud of sand and dust.

Lëanor's familiar touch brushed against Rydara's Knowing as the dragon fixed her attention on Sundamar. *What is the meaning of this?*

"I wanted to meet with you," Rydara said in Common. "Aander and I will be leaving soon. Sundamar told me you wouldn't be coming back to Edriendor, and I wanted to say goodbye."

Rydara sensed something like a chuckle in the dragon's exhale. *Is that really all you wanted to say to me? Goodbye?*

"No," Rydara admitted, glancing behind her at Mìsul and the two elves. She was still speaking Common, and she did not know if Lëanor's sending was specific to her or if the elves could hear it as well. She did know that the other things she wanted to discuss with Lëanor were the things that could get them into trouble. "I wanted to ask you for a favor."

"I wanted to see you, too, Lëanor of the dragons," Aander chimed in, climbing to his feet and taking a few steps to stand next to Rydara. He swayed a little, and Rydara took his arm to steady him. "Sundamar tells me that it was you who took pity on my sister and me in the Waste, and that you persuaded him to save my life before the end. I owe you a life debt, an obligation I can never fully repay." Aander sank to his knees in front of Lëanor and bowed his head, his right fist pressed against his heart and his left to the ground. "But my means, my sword, and my service are yours if you would have them. I offer you my oath."

Rydara's brow furrowed as she looked at her brother. He had not mentioned that he was planning to do this.

Does your brother believe this posture honors me? Lëanor's amusement tickled Rydara's Knowing.

Yes, Rydara thought back. *He waits for you to bind him to you or release him from his debt. It is our custom.* It was not a custom Rydara would have thought to keep, here among races who neither practiced nor knew of it.

Rydara glanced at Sundamar, and the elf nodded. "The human offered me this oath as well," Sundamar said to Lëanor in Elvish.

Lëanor shifted her head to the side and tilted it as she looked at Aander—an oddly human gesture. *Does he think I have any use for his service?*

He thinks you'll refuse it, Rydara thought back, looking at her brother. *But if you accept the oath, he means to keep it and serve you to the end of his days.*

Lëanor snorted. *Yes, I see that.* The dragon lowered her head, bringing it close to Aander's. *I have to think about this. Perhaps I could find a use for a human.*

"Lëanor," Sundamar's tone held a rebuke, and the dragon snorted again, withdrawing her head.

All right, fine. No oath. Dismissed.

"Lëanor declines your oath," Rydara said to Aander.

Aander nodded, rose to his feet, and bowed to the dragon. "My eternal thanks remain yours."

Yes, yes. Now what is this favor? Lëanor turned her head to Rydara. *It seems we're about to have company.*

"Company?" Rydara glanced at the elves and found they were looking behind them. There was nothing to see but empty Waste.

"Conall. What is he doing?" Sundamar muttered in Elvish.

A dragon abruptly appeared in the air above them, another elf perched on its shoulder. They landed next to Mìsul, kicking up another cloud of dust and gravel. The elf hopped to the ground, his gaze taking in Lëanor, Aander, and Rydara.

His forehead wrinkled, and Rydara felt his confusion. There was also a thread of urgency. "Sundamar. There is something I thought you should know." He glanced at Rydara.

The news had something to do with her. She was certain.

"What is it?" she asked in Elvish.

Conall glanced at Sundamar, uncertain if he should proceed. Sundamar nodded.

"The Alterran king has left his palace and gone to Byrn. I believe he discovered the grave there." Conall glanced at Rydara again, concern in his eyes, but the news did not surprise her. They had heard reports of people going missing from Byrn after the Alterrans moved in. It must have become another Tessex. "A corrupted shard left the Jeshim encampment and is moving north at the pace of a horse. Whoever carries it is on course to intercept the king. They may mean to kill him."

"You think the king found out what his general has been up to?" Rydara asked. "That he's now a threat to the High Wizards' plans?"

"There's not much the king could do to stop them," Conall answered, looking at Sundamar. "But if their hold on his mind has weakened, he could try."

Aander looked between them blankly, and Rydara offered a quick interpretation.

"We have to help him!" Aander said, growing excited. "If the king knows what the High Wizards are doing, he could order the Alterran army to stand down. To retreat, here to Edriendor, as our people must. With him on our side, Father would have to believe us."

Conall and Reluvethel were looking at Sundamar, and Rydara frowned, wondering why Conall had thought it important to bring Sundamar this news. Were they willing to take action to save the Alterran king, if Sundamar wished it?

Did they think that he might wish such a thing?

Rydara looked at Sundamar and realized he was more conflicted than she had guessed. It had been clear to her on the night of her petition that he had no intention of defying the decision of the elders. She had thought that meant he would do nothing to help her people, but maybe she had been wrong. He had brought her to see Lëanor without permission, after all.

But commanding an expedition to Byrn was another prospect entirely, and Rydara doubted his deference to Arcaena could bend so far.

She turned to Lëanor. "Lëanor, you have done so much for me and my brother already," she said in Common so Aander could understand. "I hate to ask for more. But the favor is this. Will you fly us to Byrn to rescue the Alterran king, and then to my father's encampment? Arcaena has offered sanctuary to any humans who come to Edriendor in search of it, but she will not send any aid. We must bring the news to our father and anyone else who will listen."

Lëanor's eyes turned to Sundamar, and her tail swished back and forth. Rydara sensed a challenge in the dragon's gaze, and she could almost feel a stream of communication between them, though the content was hidden from her.

Faedastan corrupted the fledgling of one of my roost-mates, Lëanor leaned her head closer to Rydara and snuffed hot air. *The High Wizards must answer for this. Yes. I will take you to snatch the Alterran king from them. In fact, you can count on my full support in your effort to help your people escape.*

It was the first good news Rydara had had in some time, and her face lit up with a smile. "Thank you, Lëanor! That is wonderful!"

"Aander cannot make this journey with you," Sundamar cautioned in Elvish. "He is too weak. He will regress."

"We have no choice," Rydara returned in the same language, glancing at Aander. The effort from standing this long was already wearing on him. His breathing was heavy, and though he glanced intently between her, Sundamar, and the dragon, waiting for someone to tell him what was going on, his eyelids drooped. Rydara figured it would not be long before he had to sleep.

Her gaze returned to Sundamar. "The Alterran king will not listen to a Rishara girl, even if she flies to him on a dragon. Neither will my father. I need Aander."

"You're not talking about leaving me behind, are you?" Aander demanded, suspicious. "I have to come. We don't have time for me to get stronger."

"I know," Rydara assured him.

"I will go with you," Sundamar announced abruptly, now in Common, and Rydara's lips parted in astonishment. "Only me," he said, glancing at Conall and Reluvethel before his gaze returned to Rydara. "I will care for Aander so you can bring your people the news."

"And save the Alterran king?" Aander pressed, hopeful. "He could help us enormously."

"And save the Alterran king, if he agrees to fly with us," Sundamar agreed.

"Thank you," Aander said, nodding deeply to the elf.

Sundamar's gaze met Rydara's, whose mouth was still open in surprise. She closed it and managed to nod to him. "Thank you," she said, feeling the words were wholly inadequate. With his help and Lëanor's, they might actually have a chance—not only to save the Alterran king, but to make their father understand the threat of the High Wizards. Perhaps they could lead all the tribes to take refuge in Edriendor.

Maybe the Alterrans would come as well.

The ghost of a smile touched Sundamar's lips as he nodded back at her, and she knew he understood.

***

It was night when they reached the Alterran king's encampment. Lëanor landed outside its perimeter, and Sundamar, Rydara, and Aander walked in alone. Rydara could tell from the faint distortion to the air that Sundamar had cast a Showing to hide them.

It was hard not to think of Kell and the price he had paid the last time Aander and Rydara had passed through an Alterran camp inside a Showing. But Sundamar's stride was quick and confident, as though rendering them invisible from every angle at once was second-nature to him. Even if his Showing failed, his voice could protect them.

The tent in the middle of the camp was twice as big as any other, a clear indication that the king was inside. There were two sentries guarding the entrance. As they drew near, Sundamar whistled a short note laden with magic and scuffed his foot against the ground. The sentries traded a few words in Alterran and moved closer to investigate, and Sundamar steered Aander and Rydara past them and into the tent. The flap of the entrance made no noise when he pulled it back or when it fell closed behind them.

The king's breathing was loud in the darkness, bordering on snores. Without the light from the moon and stars, Rydara could see nothing, but she sensed Sundamar's attention shift to her and her brother, as if to say his part was only to bring them here.

A small orb of light appeared in Aander's hand, pushing back the darkness. Rydara blinked, realizing Aander had produced it himself.

The Alterran king lay on what seemed a hundred blankets, making Rydara wonder how much time the Alterrans spent packing them and laying them out again each night of travel.

"Your Majesty," Aander spoke, and the king startled awake, blinking against the light. "We come in peace."

"What is this?" the king demanded. His voice was a powerful bass but his form was unimpressive as he sat and scooted away from them, clutching blankets around himself. He yelled in Alterran, summoning his men.

There was no answer.

"You have our apologies for this rude beginning," Aander said, inclining his head to the king. "But we needed an audience with you without delay. Your life is in danger."

"Are you here to kill me, boy?" the king demanded. "What have you done with my men?"

"Your men are well," Sundamar answered. "They cannot hear you. That is all. We come in peace."

Rydara felt a light touch of magic in Sundamar's last words, impressing their truth upon the king.

"What devilry is this?" The king rose to his feet, still clutching a blanket as he peered intently at Sundamar's features. The king was an old man, gray of hair and beard, and despite the strength of his voice, it was clear his best days were behind him. The elf stood nearly a foot taller. "You are no *ishra*."

"He is an elf, from the legends of old," Aander said. "One who comes from the Land Beyond the Waste. The ancient demons have also returned. They've taken control of your army, and now they want you dead. That is why we're here."

"*Ishra* stories," the king said, shaking his head. "Nonsense. I am in control of my armies."

"It is General Dameires and your queen, Lux Lucisa, who command your armies," Rydara countered. "They have killed many of the people of Kilethe without your orders. Did you see the graves?"

"Graves?" the king echoed, emphasizing the plural. He had found one, Conall had said. He must not have known about the others.

He shook his head again. "No, no. General Dameires, yes, is a bloodthirsty scoundrel, unworthy of his post. But Lux is innocent and fully loyal. She knows nothing of this."

"She, like your general, is a High Wizard, a Prophet who bonded a demon from hell and seeks to enslave our race," Aander said, sympathy in his gaze. "She has been using the Speaking magic to control you."

"No, no, no. No. I won't listen to this. You!" the king's eyes narrowed as they settled on Rydara. "You're that *ishra* girl who insulted Lux and our armies, aren't you? You were supposed to be banished."

"I was," Rydara returned.

"You're just spreading more lies. Guards!" the king yelled again, and Rydara winced.

She looked at Sundamar. "Can't you persuade him?"

Sundamar shook his head. He answered her in Elvish. "The human mind is delicate, and Lux's touch on this one runs deep. If I push against her directly, his mind may collapse. I can remove her work, but it will take time. It would help if the king were willing."

"What did he say?" the king demanded. "What tongue is that?"

"The tongue of the elves," Sundamar answered, and Rydara felt magic in his words.

"He told me he could free you from their magic if you will let him," Rydara said to the king. His eyes grew wide, and it was clear to Rydara he had no intention of allowing Sundamar to meddle with his mind.

"Would you like to see a dragon?" Aander asked suddenly.

"I would like you to leave," the king said, a menacing note in his voice. He eyed Sundamar warily.

"We will, and soon," Aander said. "But first hear us out. We have isolated you from your men with powerful sorcery. If we wanted to kill you, we could do it here and now without any trouble. I see you are an intelligent man and you have discerned this already.

"You can safely conclude, then, that we are not here to kill you." The orb of light in Aander's hand slowly lifted and moved to land atop his other hand—a feat of concentration that must have cost him dearly, but no effort showed on his face. "We come to you with a story that you do not believe, offering help you do not think you need. But you already knew something was wrong with your General Dameires, and now you see before you an elf. Have you heard of the flying creatures the elves ride?"

The king stared back at Aander. Then he surged forward, dropping his blanket. Aander moved to stop him, his light winking out in the process, but the king bowled past him and tore open the flap of the tent. He shouted "Intruders!" in Alterran as he stumbled into the sentries outside.

The sentries recovered quickly and charged inside, drawing weapons.

Rydara raised her hands and moved between them and her brother, who had fallen down and not gotten up. A sentry grabbed her hands roughly and twisted them behind her back, his knife at her neck. The other one hauled her brother to his feet.

Rydara's eyes darted toward Sundamar.

He was gone.

Chapter 17

Flight

The camp roused quickly. The king was in an uproar, yelling that there was an *ishra* sorcerer loose in the camp. The sentries marched Rydara and Aander to a tree near the camp's outskirts and frisked them for weapons while the rest of the soldiers organized themselves into units and combed through the area with torches, searching the darkness for Sundamar.

Rydara thought he would appear any moment to rescue them.

"Where is he?" one of the sentries demanded in broken Common. Sundamar had given Aander a dagger before they left Edriendor, and the sentries found and removed it. They tied Aander and Rydara to the tree on opposite sides.

Something was wrong—something besides Sundamar's absence. Rydara's Knowing was uneasy.

"You won't find him," Aander returned. Rydara could feel his confidence, but his voice was weak.

Another soldier approached, carrying a torch. His blue and white uniform was sharper and better-fitted than those of the sentries, and the single sword in his insignia indicated a low-ranking officer.

"Lieutenant." The sentries saluted as he approached, but the lieutenant's eyes stayed on Aander and Rydara.

Her Knowing registered some dissonance between the rank they had named and the man himself.

He asked his men a question in Alterran, and they nodded. Rydara caught the word for assassin.

"We're not assassins," she said, and the lieutenant narrowed his eyes at her. One of the sentries handed him Aander's dagger along with a brief explanation, and the lieutenant nodded. He waved a dismissal.

"What are you, then?" the lieutenant asked, gesturing to her with Aander's dagger. He eyed the weapon with interest, and Rydara could tell it impressed him.

"We're messengers," Aander said. He coughed. "We came here to warn your king of another threat. He doesn't have much time."

"Really." The lieutenant's tone was ironic. "What threat is that?"

"General Dameires wants him dead, and so does his queen, Lux Lucisa. The two of them are powerful sorcerers," Aander explained.

Rydara had not thought their story would find any more traction with this man than it had with the king, but the lieutenant's breathing paused. They had his attention.

He circled around the tree to regard her brother. "The queen and the general each must have had many opportunities to kill the king, if that was their desire. Why now?"

"Their control is slipping, isn't it?" Aander returned. "He found the grave. Doesn't he mean to strip General Dameires of his command?"

The lieutenant moved back into Rydara's line of sight, glancing between the two of them. Rydara's uneasiness grew, and she recognized the distant signature of a corrupted shard. It was getting closer.

"You knew, didn't you," Rydara challenged the lieutenant, speaking quickly. "You knew they were controlling him with magic you didn't understand. The Speaking magic, and more. You convinced the king to come here, to stop this. To stop them. You need our help."

"There was a third man with you," the lieutenant said, his tone grim. "Where is he?"

"An elf," Aander corrected.

"The elves made that dagger you're holding, and they have magic just as powerful as Lux and Dameires," Rydara told him. "We are your king's only hope against the assassins who *are* coming. They're coming now. I'm a Knower, you understand? I sense black magic coming closer."

The lieutenant eyed the dagger again. He flipped it once, caught it, and threw it into the tree.

It quivered in the trunk between Aander and Rydara's heads.

"If the sorcerer who came with you has such power, why are you tied up?" the lieutenant demanded. "Dameires could wipe out this entire camp with a word. Maybe Lucisa could, too."

It was a great question, and Rydara had nothing to say.

"We came here to offer our help to the king, and he hasn't accepted it yet," Aander answered. "What better use of our time than to answer his questions?"

"Except you're not answering the king's questions, are you? You're stuck with me—a lieutenant."

Rydara registered the lie more firmly this time. "You're no lieutenant," she said. "You're the king's Justicer, aren't you?" The king's Justicer was a high position in Alterra, and it was a secret one. His job included being the king's eyes and ears among the people, where he could investigate whatever matters the king wished to learn more about without anyone realizing they were dealing with the king's official representative. No one was closer to the king but the queen.

The dread in Rydara's Knowing had grown strong enough to localize, and it had nearly reached the camp. Rydara nodded toward it. "The assassins are here now."

A lantern came into view, held by a blonde woman riding side-saddle on horseback. A veiled woman rode close behind her, and so did a third woman and a pair of soldiers.

"That's the queen." The Justicer's breath sharpened as another rider rode into view at the rear of the party. He was at the edge of the light cast by the lantern, but it was enough for Rydara to recognize Faedastan. The Justicer glanced back at Rydara.

"Another elf, though not the one who came with us," Rydara said. "And not one who will fight on our side."

A pair of sentries moved to speak with the queen's party, and the blonde woman fielded the exchange. The queen turned to look in their direction.

It should have been too far for her to recognize Rydara in the dark. Somehow, it was not.

Lux Lucisa wheeled her mount and trotted toward them, and the rest of her party moved to follow. The sentries jogged to catch up.

Lux stopped her horse next to the Justicer and waved impatiently to her Voice. The blonde woman drew abreast.

"The queen wishes to know what the Noraani prince and his sister are doing here," said the Voice, glancing between her mistress and the Justicer.

"Noraani prince?" The Justicer raised his eyebrows. "They were caught sneaking into the king's tent." His demeanor gave nothing away, but Rydara could feel fear like a slick of hot oil beneath the coolness of his words for the queen.

"You may go," the Voice told him. "The queen wishes her questioner to speak with the prisoners alone. Tell the others not to disturb us."

"Take care we are not disturbed," Faedastan repeated, his words heavy with magic.

The Justicer bowed and retreated toward the camp, his eyes lingering on Faedastan's pointed ears.

His retreat intensified Rydara's terror. Only a fraction of it could be blamed on the shard concealed within Lux's royal blue cloak. The last man she had seen tied to a tree in front of the queen and her corrupted shard...

Where is Sundamar?

"Oh please, little *ishra*, surely it is not so bad as all that?" Lux's voice tinkled merrily. She removed her veil, and her green eyes fixed on Rydara. "You know, I'm still looking for a Knower to join my service. I have a Shower, a Hearer, a Perceiver, and a Foreteller, and Faedastan might agree to Speak for me, but that leaves me one short of a full circle. Tenebrus thinks I'm being too picky, but after meeting you, other Knowers just won't do. Will you reconsider joining me?"

Lux took off one glove and then the other. She reached into a pocket and withdrew the corrupted shard. There was a blackness in the shard darker than the night around them, but only a swirl of it. Not like the one Dameires had carried at their first encounter. More like...

"Yes," Lux laughed. "We took this one from Numbran, but it isn't finished yet. If you don't want to join me, I could add your magic to my collection in another way—but you remember how unsightly that is."

"Leave her alone!" Aander demanded.

Lux glanced at Faedastan, cross with the interruption. She pressed the corrupted shard into his hands. "Kill the boy first."

"Lucisa!"

Rydara, startled, glanced away from the shard and saw that the Alterran king was approaching, now dressed in a purple robe that looked more royal than his nightclothes. The Justicer was at his side.

"What happened to your veil?" the king demanded.

"Some Speaker you make," Lux snapped at Faedastan. She turned to the king. "Go wait for me in your tent, love. This won't take but a moment."

The king took a step back, but then he paused, and his eyes narrowed. "No. No, these are *my* prisoners. Who is this *ishra* with you? I was just accosted by one like him."

"Someone else is here," the Voice interrupted, her eyes searching the surroundings.

Lux snatched the shard back from Faedastan. "Change of plans. Kill the king now."

Faedastan leapt forward, but his dagger met the arm of the Justicer as the king turned to run.

"Stop," Lux Spoke.

Rydara felt herself pressed harder against the tree, and her ears filled with the sound of ringing. She blinked. The ringing was not in her ears. It was in her Knowing.

Sundamar stood before Lux, his hands held up in front of him.

Did her magic rebound off of him? Rydara did not understand what was going on. The king was running, but the Justicer was on the ground in front of Faedastan. The elf threw a bloody dagger at the retreating monarch.

It stopped abruptly mid-flight and fell to the ground.

Faedastan ran after the king, and Sundamar dove toward Rydara, disappearing again mid-dive. Heat seared the air. Faedastan cried out, staggering to a stop as his shoulder smoked, flesh and fabric charring.

Lux clutched the shard in her hand, muttering, and Lëanor appeared above them in a bloom of fire, stripped of whatever magic had concealed her. The dragon breathed more flames toward the High Wizard as the ones around Faedastan died out, but they whooshed harmlessly around Lux and her companions.

Branches above Rydara caught fire. She heard them crackle and pop, and her bonds suddenly went slack.

"Run!" Sundamar ordered, and Rydara sprinted after the king. She trusted Sundamar to save her brother, but she did not know if he would take any extra time for the Alterran king. The man had reached a group of his soldiers and was pointing at Lux — but whatever safety he thought he had found could not last.

"Kill the king!" Lux Lucisa's voice rang out behind her, and Rydara saw the words hit the soldiers and take hold. A pair of them grabbed their monarch and another drew his sword back, preparing to stab the king through the chest.

The group was heedless of Rydara as she bowled into them, aiming to tackle the king to the ground. But her weight was ineffectual, and when her shoulder connected with the king's chest, she merely knocked the wind out of herself and jostled the soldiers holding him. She closed her eyes, expecting the other soldier's thrust to skewer her when it landed.

"*Likrishest!*" The Elvish word for "stop" washed over the group, and Rydara looked up, toward the sound. A dragon was high over the trees, swooping toward them, but the voice had not been Sundamar's.

The soldiers, confused and now panicked at the sight of the dragon, scattered. The king yelled his displeasure after them, but Rydara grabbed the neck of his robe before he could follow and got as close to his face as she dared. "Her voice can control them, you understand? We need to get on that dragon."

She pointed upward, and the king's gaze followed, finally registering the dragon that was closing fast toward them through the night sky. An elf was hanging onto its shoulder, his figure limned by starlight. He was reaching out a hand toward Rydara.

Lux's voice cut through the air, heavy with magic, and an elf shouted back. Their words were lost in a sudden wind.

Rydara focused hard on her desire for the elf flying toward her to grab the king, hoping he could register her intent with his Knowing. She shoved the king toward him to reinforce the message, and he grabbed the king's arm as the dragon swooped past. She clung tightly to the king's other arm as they were yanked upward. Her arms nearly wrenched out of their sockets, but then the elf grabbed her and pulled her onto the dragon's back. They gained altitude as a clap of thunder split the air.

"Thank you," she gasped in Elvish. It was hard to make out the elf's features in the dark, but she thought she recognized

Conall. Beside them, the Alterran king clung tightly to one of the dragon's spikes, pale and trembling. Rydara strained to peer over the dragon's shoulder.

Storm clouds were starting to gather, blocking the moon and stars, but part of the forest was burning. By its light, Rydara could make out two other dragons ahead, near the queen's party where shadowy figures were tangled in combat. One dragon peeled away. Its wing was injured, and its flight lopsided. Rydara thought two figures crouched on its back.

She hoped one of them was Aander.

Rain started to fall. Wind whipped the drops against Rydara's skin like so many tiny needles.

They pulled up abruptly, hovering. Below them, Sundamar and another elf—Reluvethel?—stood back-to-back, fighting an apparent hoard of black-robed combatants. They sang as they fought, and Rydara could almost sense the spells forming and breaking around them. A wall of fire and charred bodies separated them from Alterran soldiers, who fired arrows at the dragon Mìsul. The arrows fell from the sky before they reached her. Rydara could feel a thrumming that originated from the dragon.

By the light of the fire, she could see Lux Lucisa sitting calmly on her horse in the steadily increasing rain, stroking the shard in her hands as the wind continued to blow, whipping her hair. Three of her people were still mounted beside her, all watching the confrontation between the elves and the hoard of attackers, all seemingly unbothered by the storm.

They were part of the attack, Rydara realized. All of them, using their magic in ways she could not perceive. Sundamar and his companion fought bravely, but it was only defense. They took no ground toward the riders.

Rydara's view was blocked by a stream of fire as the dragon she rode exhaled, but when it cleared, nothing had changed. The dragon could not pierce whatever shield the queen had erected.

Rydara sensed growing exaltation from Lux Lucisa as she worked her magic. She worried the High Wizard was ready to finish them.

Beside her, Conall ran up the dragon's shoulder and leapt off, falling toward Lux. The High Wizard looked up as they collided.

Lightning split the sky, and Rydara lost her view and her breath as the dragon beneath her dropped like a stone to the ground. The Alterran king screamed as they plummeted. Fire lit the air, and the dragon thrashed beneath them, lashing out with jaws and tail.

Then Sundamar was beside Rydara, pulling an unconscious elf onto the dragon's back.

"*Livarräeast!*" Reluvethel hopped onto the dragon's other shoulder as he bid them fly.

They took off, but Lux's voice thundered behind them, and it was as if the air became sludge, slowing their movement. It was so thick Rydara could hardly breathe. But Sundamar and Reluvethel sang out their response, and a heavy thrumming indicated the dragons had joined in with their own magic.

"Die, Demirjan!" Lux Spoke again, and lightning split the sky above them, striking the king who crouched next to Rydara. They broke into clean air at the same time. The dragon careened sideways as they sped away, nearly throwing them, but they leveled out as the second dragon drew alongside.

The king was slumped awkwardly next to Rydara. She reached out to touch his shoulder, and then she saw his eyes, open and unfocused.

No. Rydara moved closer to press two fingers against his neck, forgetting to breathe as she waited for his pulse to beat.

There was nothing.

Rydara withdrew her hand as Reluvethel moved toward the king. Now she was breathing too fast.

Reluvethel muttered an Elvish curse. Sundamar was a torrent of remorse and anger in Rydara's Knowing, louder than anything she had ever sensed from him. She glanced at him and realized the elf whose shoulders he was still holding was also dead.

Conall was dead, and they had not even saved the king.

Rydara pressed a hand to her mouth, dismay and guilt twisting her insides. She had asked for this mission, and the elves had finally listened. This was the cost.

The dragons flew for a few hours. The sky was lightening into pre-dawn when they came across Lëanor, who was waiting for them where prairie met the foot of the mountains to the south. They landed beside her.

Aander and the king's Justicer were standing in Lëanor's shadow, the Justicer with his left arm wrapped in what must have been Aander's sleeve, given his torn shirt. It surprised Rydara to see her brother on his feet. She threw her arms around him as soon as she dismounted, and he sighed in relief as he hugged her back.

"Aander! How are you so much better?" she asked quietly. "This is impossible."

"Sundamar helped with extra magic. It's temporary, though," he explained.

Rydara pulled back and studied him. There was something he wasn't saying.

"Don't do that Knowing thing this time, all right?" he said. "Just be happy for me."

Aander looked past her. Rydara was not satisfied with his answer, but she turned to see Reluvethel was carrying the Alterran king down the dragon's wing.

Whatever Aander wasn't telling her would have to wait.

"I am sorry," Rydara said, glancing at the Justicer. The man turned away, his face twisted in grief at the sight of his monarch's body.

Sundamar carried Conall down next, and the elves laid both bodies out on the ground. "Reluvethel will help you bury the

Alterran king here, according to whatever customs you wish," Sundamar told the Justicer in Common. "But time is short, and I must return Conall to Edriendor. Reluvethel will take you to the Noraani encampment, if you still wish to go." He turned and looked at the elf beside him, and then he frowned. "What is it?" he asked in Elvish.

Reluvethel's response was too quiet for Rydara to hear, but the darkening of Sundamar's expression was plain enough. His eyes met Rydara's when Reluvethel finished.

"I need to talk to you," he said, nodding to the open prairie. He walked in that direction, away from the group.

Aander inhaled beside Rydara as though he might say something, and she could feel his reluctance at being left out. But one of the dragons began digging a depression in the ground with its foreleg, and Reluvethel was gathering rocks from the mountainside to place on the grave. Aander moved to help him as Rydara followed Sundamar out into the rough golden grass of the prairie.

His pain was still raw and palpable to her Knowing, and now there was a current of something else in his anger — frustration or helplessness, maybe. She waited for him to speak.

"We are too late for your father's people," he said in Elvish, staring out at the prairie. "The Noraani have crossed into the mountains, and now Alterrans occupy the pass behind them. There is no route for them to escape back to the Waste. The Jeshim army lies before them, so there can be no escape in that direction either. It's only a matter of time before they will be crushed between the two."

As Sundamar spoke, Rydara felt each sentence settle an additional weight in her spirit, dragging her further toward despair.

Whatever hope her people had gained when Sundamar and Lëanor agreed to help carry the news was gone now. Rydara had gotten Conall killed for less than nothing.

"How do you know?" Rydara asked, wishing he could be mistaken.

"When you first told us about the High Wizards, we extended our patrols over Kilethe and Lanimshar. Reluvethel heard it from Sarya before he and Conall followed us.

"At best, we could save only a handful of your people. As many as the dragons could carry." Sundamar turned back to face her. "There might be time for more than one flight, but every time we go back there, we'd risk detection by the High Wizards. Tenebrus is already encamped within a day's march of that place, if he's with the main Jeshim camp. It holds at least two shards, maybe three."

Rydara nodded slowly, sensing his anguish. He wished he could help save her people. Perhaps almost as much as she did. She could feel that more strongly now than she had back in Edriendor.

"I understand," Rydara said, nodding. His effort had cost him so much already. She wouldn't ask for more. "Just one flight in will be enough."

"Rydara, don't ask me to leave you there." Sundamar grasped both her shoulders as if to shake sense into her. But his touch was gentle. "You will die."

"I will die fighting with my people, like my father will do." Her father was not a wise king or a great one—but he would do his duty as he saw it. He would not desert his people on the back of a dragon.

"It's not going to be a fight, Rydara," Sundamar said, tightening his grip on her shoulders. "When the High Wizards get there, it will be a slaughter. We lost, the three of us and our dragons, to one of them with a shard. There's nothing I could do to protect you from nine."

Rydara lifted her chin and stared back at him stubbornly. "Aander and I cannot stand by in the safety of Edriendor while our entire race is slaughtered. It would not be right."

Rydara did not want to die. But doing nothing while the High Wizards established their reign over all humanity would be worse. Now was as good a time to take a stand as any—now, while there were still people alive to defend that were kin to her and Aander.

It was the same calculation that had inspired her to return to her people before she had guessed that Lëanor and Sundamar might aid them. She had had as little hope then as what was left to them now, though the calculation had changed for Sundamar.

She laid a hand on the elf's arm. She wished things could be different, that she could undo his loss or offer him better comfort—but her duty still lay with her people. "I'm not asking you to come with us."

Sundamar stared into her eyes, searching for any hesitation, any opening, any hint of a possibility that he could change her mind. Rydara gazed back, letting him search. There was nothing to find. His jaw tightened and he trembled beneath her touch, his emotions a wash of desperation and agony.

Then he broke away from her, striding back toward the dragons. He became inscrutable to her Knowing.

The elves healed the Justicer and Lëanor, whose wing had been damaged in the fight, and Sundamar spoke alone with Reluvethel before leaving for Edriendor with Conall's body. Reluvethel helped them finish burying the Alterran king and inscribed a few words on a boulder the Justicer chose to mark the grave. When it was finished, the Justicer agreed to join their cause—doomed as it was—rather than flee to Edriendor. Reluvethel, to Rydara's surprise, announced that he and Mìsul would fight with them as well.

"Conall and I believed the elders made the wrong decision," he said in Elvish. "That is why we came to help you."

The younger elves have better wisdom. Lëanor snuffed. *I, too, will fight.*

Alone, Reluvethel and two dragons would not be enough to make a difference against the High Wizards. Their offer brought tears to Rydara's eyes.

She did not want them to die as Conall had, for no reward.

"You do not have to do this," Rydara said in Elvish, glancing between Reluvethel and the dragons. "We know we go to our deaths. We ask only for the means to arrive in time to stand with our people. But you should leave us with them. It is not your fight."

"The elders pretend it is not our fight, but they did not choose for Conall, and they will not choose for me," Reluvethel answered. "My help may not change the outcome, but you must let me give it all the same. It is how I honor Conall, and Chaenath, and the White."

Rydara looked back at him, mystified. Before the assembly, she had hoped her argument about Nivalis would sway enough elves to save her people. Now, it seemed impossible that even one elf agreed with it.

One elf, and it wasn't even Sundamar.

"Sundamar must honor Conall by returning his body for the *Tirisslythra*," Reluvethel said, seeming to discern her thought. "It is a captain's duty."

"Of course." Rydara blinked and shook her head. She did not understand Edriendor's customs enough to make sense of it, but she was glad Sundamar was gone. She wanted him to live, even if she could not convince Reluvethel to follow his example.

She looked at the dragons and felt in her Knowing that they would not be dissuaded from their offer either. She interpreted for the others.

Aander clasped Reluvethel's arm. "Thank you," he said. He nodded deeply to him and to each dragon.

Reluvethel gave his green cloak to the Justicer to hide his Alterran uniform, and then he mounted Lëanor with the rest of them. They took off toward the Noraani encampment with Mìsul flying behind.

Chapter 18

The Alliance

The Justicer's name was Eduare, and as they flew south over the mountains, Aander asked him what the king's death meant for Alterra. The young prince Gerard—the king's son by a previous marriage—was next to inherit, but at the queen's urging, the king had decreed that General Dameires would be Regent if anything happened to him before Gerard came of age. Finding the boy would not help their cause.

Aander turned to Rydara next and pressed her for all the details she remembered from the battle. She could not explain most of what he wanted to know. How had the Alterran king resisted Lux's command to return to the tent? What kind of barrier had protected the High Wizard from the dragon's fire? Had Lux been responsible for the sudden storm, and if so, how had she started it?

Rydara passed the first few questions to Lëanor, but it was not long before Reluvethel discerned what they were discussing and chimed in as well. Soon Rydara found herself interpreting his responses as both Aander and Eduare plied him with questions about the magic Lux and her Knights had used and what the elves had done to counter it.

They were both thinking about how to apply the knowledge to defeat the High Wizards, but Rydara knew of only a handful of magic users in the Noraani alliance. None had the Speaking magic. The Perceivers, Knowers, and Showers they had were paltry in talent compared to the weakest elf. Without shards, with only one elf to teach them, and without much time to train, the chances that the tribes' magic users could accomplish anything were pitiful.

But they had to try something.

Aander was the driving force of conversation throughout the flight, never seeming to run out of questions or ideas. His stamina encouraged Rydara, and she wondered why Sundamar hadn't been offering him this "temporary magic" all along.

It made her think there must be some catch, but Aander had asked her not to worry about it. She did her best.

They were nearly through the mountains when the dragons touched down in a narrow stretch of the western pass. It was a sharp descent ahead of them to where the mountains met the plain of Lanimshar. A walled city rose far in the distance.

They had landed on a large stretch of unbroken rock, but the terrain around them was interrupted by periodic boulders, and footing looked treacherous. The mountainside rose up on both sides of the pass, its face interspersed with curves, crannies, and caves, and though there was enough plant life to cover much of the gray rock with green and brown, nothing grew much taller than Rydara's knee.

"Why did we stop?" Aander asked Reluvethel, frowning.

"Litarìma," the elf answered, looking up toward the overhang on their left.

"We've arrived," Rydara interpreted, searching the rocks around them. She could see nothing, but she could feel eyes on them. Eyes that were dangerous and terrified.

Aander stood up on the dragon's back, turning slowly to face in each direction.

Rydara heard murmuring up in the rocks to their left.

"It *is* Prince Aander!" a boy's voice insisted, and then an archer came out from behind a boulder on the overhang, lowering his bow. It was Taada, the twelve-year-old son of her Uncle Sorovan. "Prince Aander?" the boy asked, staring at the dragons with eyes as wide as saucers.

"Yes, cousin, it's me," Aander assured him, smiling.

"What are those?" Taada asked, excitement growing in his voice. "Are they going to save us?" Taada asked. More archers came out from behind the rocks above them on either side as he spoke, most older and strangers to Rydara, but a few just as young, and a few more familiar faces among them. They gawked at Aander, the elf, and the dragons, murmuring exclamations of wonder and disbelief.

They did not all know her brother, but they knew they needed a miracle. By the looks on their faces, they thought one had just arrived.

Aander surveyed them grimly, setting his jaw. "We're going to try."

***

The bulk of the Noraani alliance had taken shelter in caves spread over and around the pass. The caves were not spacious or well-connected, and the people were many—far more than when Aander and Rydara had left. The Kerim had joined, and with them, the Jax and the Lancells. Jinn, the largest and most powerful of the northern tribes after Noraan, had also come to shelter in the caves of the pass, though their relationship was more an uneasy partnership with the alliance than a true belonging. They had been counting on Aander's marriage to their chieftain's daughter, Jemine, in exchange for accepting Cressidin as king. When Aander renounced his position, that plan had fallen apart, but Jinn and Noraan had been forced together anyway as both fled from the Alterrans.

Taada explained the situation as he led them to the cavern that housed the alliance's leaders. King Cressidin's accommodations were little more than a pair of blankets and a few chests of belongings near the back, not far separated from the families of his advisers and the lesser chieftains. He was standing in a small knot of other men as they approached, including Sorovan, the Rinton and Ferlore chiefs, and a few others Rydara did not recognize.

Heads turned and murmurs spread as Taada led them toward the king, and Cressidin looked up. His eyes fixed on Aander first, and the joy that brightened his features would have been unmistakable even had Rydara not felt it surge in her Knowing.

He took a quick step toward his son, but then his gaze fell on Rydara. He stopped, and his joy was choked out in a swirl of something else. His face smoothed to neutrality as they drew near.

"Sire," Aander greeted him coolly, briefly bowing his head. Rydara and Eduare repeated the gesture, showing more respect with it. Reluvethel, beside them, did not. "Chieftain Nelzed." Aander greeted the oldest of the strangers next, and Rydara realized he was Jemine's father. Aander had met the Jinn chieftain before, though she had not.

"My son." The king's voice caught, and though he made no move to embrace Aander, Rydara could sense his impulse.

"And daughter?" Aander challenged, glancing to Rydara and back at the king.

Her father looked at her, and his eyes clouded with hesitation. Rydara dropped her gaze. His reaction came as no surprise, but it stung to Know he wanted to hug Aander, but not her.

"I have no daughter," he said.

It had been less than two months since the last time he had said it, when those same words had brought Rydara's world crashing down around her and made her believe her life was ending. She had not thought she could survive rejection from the man she had always tried so hard to please. But life had gone on. She had managed to find purpose outside his approval, and even though she had eventually failed in that, too, she no longer accepted his opinion as the measure of her worth.

His words still hurt, but her pain was a smaller thing than she had once imagined.

Moreover, today Rydara Knew they were not the whole truth. She did not know if she had been too insecure to perceive it before, or if it was just because of how her magic had strengthened in Edriendor, but as Rydara raised her eyes to meet her father's, she could feel that he did love her, after all. It was not like his love for Aander, proud and uncomplicated, but it was there. It was just twisted up and overshadowed by guilt and grief. Both sharpened as he spoke the words, and Rydara sensed that they pained him even more than they did her, this time. She was his daughter, and he did not want to lose her — but he said them anyway.

He had disowned her already, and he could not find a way to reverse himself. He was too trapped in his own pride, even now.

"Then you have no son," Aander returned, steel in his voice. "We come to you only as messengers. General Dameires has entered the pass behind you. Alterrans will be upon your position in less than a week."

"I hope you have more news than that, Aander," Chieftain Nelzed returned. "We knew they would come. Who are these with you?" His gesture took in Eduare and Reluvethel, though his eyes were fixed on the elf.

"Reluvethel, of the elves of Edriendor." Aander presented him first.

"*Cith morgäelé,*" the elf greeted the king and chieftain in his own tongue.

"An elf," the Ferlore chief muttered, wonder in his gaze. "Are more of them coming?"

"No, but he has offered to fight with us, and we are beyond fortunate to have him. And this," Aander gestured to Eduare next. He hesitated.

"I am Eduare, a deserter from the Alterran army," the man introduced himself, throwing back the elf's green cloak to reveal his uniform. "But as recently as this morning I served as the king's Justicer. Then my king was murdered at the hands of his own queen. I owe no fealty to her or to Dameires, who now control my country, and I offer your cause my service, such as it is."

"The king's own Justicer?" the Rinton chief repeated, shocked. The men from Jinn shifted uneasily, glancing at their leader. Nelzed scratched his chin.

"I'll vouch for him," Aander said.

"Six know we could use all the help we can get." Nelzed shrugged, looking to Cressidin.

"I hope you know some secrets that can help us," the king said to the Justicer.

"We know that you cannot stay in these caves," Aander returned. "I don't know if you were hoping to hide here or if you thought you could hold the pass against an Alterran assault, but you can do neither. The Alterrans' sorcery will discover and overpower you in an instant. Our best chance is to put all our people behind the walls of that city out on the plain and defend them with magic users of our own. Perceivers. Knowers. Showers." Aander glanced at the Jinn chieftain. "If you have any Speakers among your people, they are dearly needed."

"Speakers?" the king shook his head, dismissing the idea. "It doesn't matter. We can't move the people to the city. The southern tribes control it, and they are preparing for a siege. Our only hope is to hide here in the mountains and harry the Alterrans if they stray from the pass to search for us. We know, now, that they have no compunctions about killing our people," the king glanced at Rydara, a hint of shame in his eyes, before looking back at her brother. "But the fight they really want is still with Jeshimoth. We are not far from the Jeshim lines here, and the terrain favors us. If we can make it expensive for the Alterrans to come after us, they will pour through the pass and channel their rage at the Jeshim instead of us."

"They'll take the time to slaughter you if you're here," Aander said grimly, staring back at his father. "It's not the Alterrans you need to fear, but the handful of elite sorcerers who command them. They do not care whether they kill Jeshim or the tribes or even their own soldiers. Every murder feeds their power, and their friends control the Jeshim army already. Once they've ruined both nations and sated their appetites for destruction, they'll forge an empire out of whatever is left."

The king looked back at Rydara, hearing an echo of the story that had gotten her banished. He did not want to believe it any more this time, even though it was Aander making the case while an elf and the Alterran king's Justicer stood beside him.

"Is this true?" Nelzed asked, looking to the elf and the Justicer and then back at Aander. "How do you know this?"

Reluvethel, sensing the import of the question, began to speak in Elvish, explaining the history of his people with the High Wizards and their compact with the lords of hell. He concluded with his account of facing Lux Lucisa and the power she wielded.

Rydara interpreted for him. The Jinn chieftain listened raptly, but her father grew ever more incredulous, and she could sense him hardening himself against the account as she spoke, looking between her and Reluvethel with growing suspicion.

"How do we know that the elf is the one saying all this, since we do not speak the same language?" the king demanded when she was finished. "When did Rydara learn this tongue?"

He may as well have spat in Rydara's face. Indignation surged in Aander beside her, but it was Reluvethel who spoke.

"*Rydara* … saying. True." The elf formed the Common words slowly and coolly, and Rydara could feel a firm disapprobation for the foolish human leader who stood before him.

His defense was a cold comfort in the face of her father's contempt.

"That clear enough for you, Sire?" Aander's words were acrid, and Rydara worried he might strike the king if the conversation went on much longer.

"What does this mean, then?" Nelzed asked, doing his best to ignore the personal tensions at play. Rydara could not tell what he made of her father, but it was clear he held her brother in high esteem. "Do we need to focus our attacks against these sorcerers?"

"Yes, but we need magic users of our own to contest them," Aander explained. "More immediately, it means that the southern tribes are our allies. Even the Jeshim and Alterran soldiers should have common cause with us against the High Wizards, though we are unlikely to persuade them of that." Aander glanced at Eduare, who nodded. He turned back to Cressidin. "But the southern tribes are like us, merely caught between forces that the wizards control. They can be made to see reason. They need our knowledge and magic, and our people need the protection of their walls. Our magic users cannot defend them when they are so spread out. They'll be hunted like sheep."

"The southern tribes spoke harshly with our emissaries," Nelzed said, his tone regretful.

"It is as I said," the king said. "They are preparing their city for a siege. They've made it clear they will accept no more mouths to feed. We are in this alone."

"I see you are determined to ignore all sound advice," Aander said to the king. "But as none of us are your subjects, we will waste no more time bandying words. You'll hear from us again when the city is ready to open to you—to all of you," he added, his gaze taking in the other leaders. "I hope one man's pride will not doom this entire alliance."

He turned to leave, and Rydara felt the king's heart fall. His eyes turned to Rydara, and then they fell to the floor. She sensed that he wanted to fix what was broken between them. He wanted to believe her and welcome her.

But he could not. He was too afraid of what he had done, too ashamed of how he had treated her. He needed her to be wrong so he could have some justification for having banished her.

"You don't have to be afraid," Rydara said softly as Aander walked away, Eduare and Reluvethel falling in behind him. For a moment, she thought the king did not hear her, but then he raised his eyes.

She had suffered so much because of him. She had always tried not to blame him, to follow her mother's example in showing respect. She had tried to understand how much trouble she caused him in the eyes of the tribes and to be grateful for the position he had let her have despite them. But she had always longed for affection she had never received, and then he had banished her.

She had deserved better. When she had struck out for the Waste, Rydara had thought that she could prove as much to him. She had wanted him to feel remorse, to reverse his decision and beg for her forgiveness.

But her time with the elves had changed her, and Rydara didn't need that anymore. She didn't want to be angry with her father. Instead, she wanted him to find that escape from his past and his pride that he was too lost to see. If she could forgive an elf who willingly hosted one of the lords of hell, who had enslaved the world and killed Nivalis—if she could do that, surely she could give a few words of kindness to the man who had raised her.

"I forgive you," she said, and she sensed the words break something in her father as she turned and hurried after Aander.

***

They flew toward the city walls in full view of the soldiers who manned them. A barrage of arrows assaulted them as they drew near, along with the war cries of the southern tribes.

Lëanor exhaled a bloom of fire, and the arrows melted out of the sky. War cries turned to shouts of dismay and panic as the two dragons flew over the walls into the city.

A small contingent of pikemen ran through the streets after them, ready to charge the strange reptiles when they landed.

Their yells drew more attention, and people soon flooded the streets, armed with swords and axes. The archers on the walls had managed to turn around, and they unleashed another hail of arrows as the dragons landed in the city's center.

Reluvethel spoke a word, and the arrows clattered against an invisible shield, falling to the ground in a circle around them. The display made the townspeople hesitate, but the pikemen kept running toward them.

"Taral ail llew." Reluvethel's voice cut over their shouts, heavy with magic. The pikemen faltered and stopped. They did not know the meaning—*We come in peace*—but the magic was enough to make them doubt their purpose.

"Men of Lanimshar, please," Aander addressed them, standing up on Lëanor's shoulder. "We have not come to fight, but to help you. Take us to your leader."

***

The southern tribes consisted of three factions: Entaren, Hatreth, and Rithadur. Each had their own prince. There was history of war between them, and the truce they had established in the city was fractious at best. The three princes each brought five armed retainers to their meeting with Aander and Rydara, and quarrels broke out between factions four times while Aander tried to bring them up to speed on the threat they all faced. The princes managed to keep their retainers from violence until the end, when the Rithadur prince insulted the Entaren prince personally and both factions drew steel.

"That's enough!" the Hatreth prince yelled, and the retainers hesitated. Rydara wondered if she sensed a hint of magic in his voice. "I'd like to hear the rest of this."

"I demand satisfaction," the Entaren prince growled, staring murder at the Rithadur prince.

"Will you recant, or will it be swords in the square?" The Hatreth prince seemed to consider them equally plausible options, though Rydara could not imagine why the insult would merit an actual duel.

The Rithadur prince considered for a longer moment than she expected. Then he sighed and said, "I recant. You have my apology." He bowed his head to the Entaren prince.

That seemed to settle the issue. "Enough about wizards and demons," the Rithadur prince said to Aander. "Let's cut to the chase. You have incredible war machines and we want them on our side. What is your price?"

"The dragons are not mine, and they are not for sale," Aander said patiently. "What you need to do is let us identify any magic users among you so we can train them to fight the High Wizards. We are willing to do this on the condition that you open your gates to the people of the northern tribes."

"Well, that's just ridiculous." The Entaren prince snorted. "We have limited grain here, and it could take months to break the Jeshim army."

"This contest will be over in hours if you are not prepared to withstand their magic," Aander returned. "Forget about months."

The southern princes did not agree on much, but they were united in laughing off Aander's claims until Reluvethel offered a demonstration. With Rydara interpreting for him, he asked for a volunteer, and the factions each supplied one. Reluvethel confirmed that each was willing to have magic used on him before commanding all three to throw down their weapons.

Their compliance stunned the room.

Magic users were regarded with suspicion by the southern tribes, but once the princes were convinced the battle's outcome would hinge on magic, they adapted. They sent word throughout the city that magic users would be instrumental to the city's defense and commanded all of them to report to Reluvethel, with promises that any who distinguished themselves in battle would be rewarded. When Reluvethel informed the Hatreth prince that he could Speak, he even seemed pleased.

Within the hour, Aander and Lëanor left to inform the Noraani that the city was ready to receive them. Rydara stayed with the southerners. Aander was strong enough to go alone, now, and her skills were better spent interpreting for Reluvethel. Not long ago, Rydara might have panicked at the task, considering how much attention focused on her whenever she repeated the elf's words. After her time in Edriendor, though, it was easy.

Only fourteen magic users came forward in response to the princes' call. Reluvethel started by teaching the Knowers—including Rydara and Eduare—how to identify magic in other people in case some were unaware of their talents, as the Hatreth prince had been. At the princes' command, everyone in the city presented themselves to be tested for an ability.

The Noraani moved into the city by evening, and the number of magic users ready to train swelled to perhaps fifty. Only three of them were Speakers.

Rydara was surprised—to say the least—to learn that Aander had exchanged marriage vows with Jemine and been named king of the Noraani-Jinn alliance. Cressidin had abdicated, though the extent to which he had been pressured to do so versus handing the kingship to Aander willingly was unclear. From her brother's demeanor as he relayed the news, Rydara gleaned it had been a bit of both. She did not have time to press him for as many details as she would have liked, but the upshot of it was that they did not have to waste time arguing with anyone from the northern tribes anymore. They obeyed Aander without question. No one voiced any objections when he reinstated Rydara as his adviser and declared she was restored to the Noraani family.

Typically, a tribal marriage would have been celebrated with seven days of feasting between the exchange of vows and consummation. They had neither enough time nor food to celebrate properly, though when the southern princes heard of Aander's marriage, they were generous with what they had. Aander spent little time at the evening meal and less in Jemine's presence, busy training with the new Showers and seeing to the city's other defenses. Rydara remembered how excited he had been to marry the Jinn girl and was sad to see the occasion inspire so little joy for him.

She barely had time to meet Jemine herself. Rydara worked with Reluvethel through the night, interpreting for him as he took turns instructing each group in the most efficient use of their talents. Both the northerners and southerners seemed reluctant, initially, to take all their instruction from a Rishara girl interpreting for a dark-skinned foreigner — even if he was an elf — but seeing Aander and the Hatreth prince throw themselves into the training without question eventually dispelled their concern.

The next day, Reluvethel suggested the entire city practice resisting the Speaking magic, and the princes arranged for everyone to do so in shifts of one hundred.

When they began, a single command from Reluvethel could halt a rush from the whole hundred. By noon, a handful of Knowers could resist his command to stop when they were expecting it, but only Rydara kept hold of her knife when he told them to drop their weapons. When one or both dragons joined their strength to Reluvethel's, the army became powerless.

The three new Speakers, by contrast, could force only one person to follow a command, and that only if they worked together.

Lëanor left for a few hours to scout, and when she returned, she estimated that they had two days before the Alterran army arrived. The Jeshim were camped less than a day's march from the city, but the southern princes said they had been there for two weeks, and they still showed no signs of breaking camp.

Rydara did not think it would make much difference if they had one day or one hundred. It was plain the city would never be ready to withstand the High Wizards, and she wondered at Reluvethel's patience as he drilled the people again and again. By the end of the afternoon, he was speaking mostly Common, freeing Rydara to train with the other Knowers.

Something changed in Reluvethel's manner as the sun began to set. Rydara sensed it in the dragons as well. Their attention oriented northward. Lëanor was eager, though the other dragon was harder to read.

From Reluvethel, she sensed something like hope.

Rydara left the other Knowers and jogged up the stairs to the battlements, where Reluvethel was standing among the Showers.

"What is it?" she demanded. "What's changed?"

"Look, Rydara," Aander said, pointing north toward the mountains.

Rydara looked and saw what appeared to be a dragon in the distance, flying toward them. She glanced behind her at Lëanor and Mìsul—they were both accounted for. She looked back at the horizon.

It was a dragon. Three dragons. Then—five dragons.

"What—" Rydara gasped. "How—?"

Reluvethel smiled. "Sundamar has come."

Chapter 19

Hope

Word spread through the city like wildfire. By the time the dragons landed in the city square—or as near to it as they could get, considering that the square was not big enough for all five—a crowd had gathered to meet them. The three southern princes were there with their retainers, and so was the Jinn chieftain. Rydara's father was notably absent.

Sundamar dismounted the lead dragon and strode toward the gathered leaders. Rydara was torn between the impulse to run and welcome him and confusion as to why he had come. He had told her he could not protect her here. Surely, with the whole of the Edren Guard behind him, they had a chance to save the city now.

But she sensed no joy from him.

Reluvethel, Aander, and Eduare moved to join the meeting of leaders. Rydara hurried to catch up.

"*Ciri taleäs golorìme nei for lisaelethavòn?*" Sundamar asked Reluvethel. *You have prepared the city for what they will face?*

Reluvethel moved his head slightly in neither a nod nor a shake, as if to signal, *As well as can be expected.*

"Princes, chieftain, this is Sundamar of the elves, Captain of the Edren Guard of Edriendor," Aander grinned, clasping Sundamar's arm. "I did not hope to see you again."

Sundamar clapped Aander's shoulder with his free hand. "I did not know if I would find help in Edriendor, but these came." He looked to the elves gathered behind him, and Rydara sensed his gratitude—but also sorrow. His eyes lingered on the one called Sarya, and both emotions intensified.

"*Inimsalorara yar icynfielara somnol Muirünikish,*" Sarya spoke, her eyes on the princes. She glanced at Rydara, and Rydara realized she was expected to interpret.

"The High Wizards are our foe and our responsibility," Rydara said. Sarya spoke again, and Rydara continued, "We will stand with humankind against this threat to our world."

"The city of Helos welcomes you to our defense," the Entaren prince returned, bowing slightly to the elves. The other princes repeated the gesture, though Rydara could tell each was irritated he had not spoken first himself.

"The Alterrans opened a second pass through the mountains and clashed with Jeshim forces in eastern Lanimshar early this morning," Sundamar told them. "Lux Lucisa and her shard are there, perhaps another High Wizard or even two, based on the levels of Speaking. But Dameires and another shard are with the company that is marching here, and they'll arrive by the end of tomorrow. We believe Tenebrus is with the main Jeshim camp just south of here, three shards with him and we don't know how many High Wizards. If they don't march at dawn to meet Dameires, they will come once they sense our magic. We don't have long to prepare."

The significance of this intelligence was largely lost on the princes, who greeted his words with silence.

"You are saying we may be able to fight them one or two at a time?" Aander asked.

"That is unlikely," Sundamar answered. "When Dameires realizes the strength of our resistance, he will leave the fight to his soldiers and bide his time until the others arrive. I am saying we do not have long before we must face them all."

"The walls are manned and the people have practiced resisting the Speaking magic," the Hatreth prince volunteered. "Albeit with very limited success. Reluvethel has begun training the magic users among us how to use our talents. What else do you recommend?"

"We must fortify the peoples' minds with Speaking of our own and have them try resisting it again," Sundamar said. "And your seers and imagers must practice supporting us in combat.

During flight." He glanced back at the dragons, and the Hatreth prince's eyes grew round as he realized he would be asked to fight from the sky. "But tonight, your people must sleep as well and as long as they can. Tomorrow's training will be more effective for the well-rested."

The leaders nodded and relayed the word to their people. Few had slept well or long the night before. Reluvethel had worked with rotating shifts of magic users throughout the previous night, not sleeping at all, and the rest of them had snatched brief, troubled naps when they could. The arrival of the Edren Guard brought the city new hope, and at their leaders' command, the people were given time to sleep. All training and preparation ceased after the evening meal. Every bed in the city was filled, but there were more people than beds. Many of the northerners slept on the southerners' floors or on the streets, huddled with their families with whatever blankets they had managed to carry in their flight from the Alterrans.

Each of the southern princes offered Aander and Rydara a place to stay, but they made their beds in the city square alongside most of the northern magic users. The night was not very cold, and a large fire in the middle of the square provided warmth for those who had no blankets. Lëanor and two other dragons also slept in the square. The tribespeople gave them a wide berth, but the dragons radiated additional warmth, and Rydara and Aander were comfortable lying close to them. Aander was asleep within seconds.

Rydara watched him sleep, remembering all the nights of his illness. He had been so much stronger the last two days, as if he had finally recovered.

But it was only temporary. He had said so, and when Rydara attuned her Knowing, she could sense the shadow of illness lingering over him. Sundamar's magic had pushed it back, but it was not gone.

"If he lives long enough, his sickness will return."

Rydara started at the quiet voice, sitting up and turning to see Sundamar. She would never get used to how quietly he moved.

He knelt beside Aander and laid a hand on her brother's head, furrowing his brow in concentration. If Rydara had had all six magics, she might have been able to perceive what he did, but she could sense only a subtle change within her brother. His breathing became a little deeper, his rest a little easier.

Perhaps the shadow pulled back a little further.

"Why can't you fully heal him?" Rydara asked, remembering how easily the gash in Eduare's arm had closed under Sundamar's touch.

"Diseases are not as simple as torn flesh," Sundamar explained, still concentrating on Aander. "And some are more complex than others. The hell plague is no longer in him, but its influence changed his body and mind. It is ... difficult to explain. He will heal in time, but I cannot make the process faster. What I can do is show his body how to cheat, stealing strength from the future so he has more available now."

"This will set back his recovery, then," Rydara said grimly.

"If he lives," Sundamar agreed. He took his hand from Aander's forehead and rose to his feet. His dark eyes met Rydara's, glinting in the light of the stars and the fire, and she was taken aback by the depths of the sorrow she read in them. "You should rest like these others," he said, gesturing to the other northerners. "It is important for your kind. The elves stand watch tonight."

He walked away, threading his way through the sleeping people as noiselessly as he had approached.

Rydara stood and hurried after him with considerably less grace. A few people stirred and turned in their sleep as she passed them, and Sundamar stopped at the edge of the square, looking back at her.

She took his arm when she reached him and led him farther down the street, away from the sleeping people.

"Why do you have no hope?" she asked in Elvish, letting go of his arm as she turned to face him. "Yesterday, I was sure we had all come here to die, but with six elves and seven dragons, surely we have a chance? Neremyn—Numbran—told me that he would convince others to defect with him. Perhaps we'll face no more than six or seven High Wizards?"

"Lux took his shards, Rydara," Sundamar answered in the same tongue. Neither wished to be overheard by any humans who chanced to wake. "I do not think we can hope for help from Numbran. He may not even keep his word to stay away himself."

"He will," Rydara insisted.

Sundamar just looked at her, and Rydara could feel his skepticism. She knew he could sense her own doubt, too.

"Even if he does," he said, "it is the shards that will destroy us. We have located five in varying stages of corruption. Five shards of Nivalis' raw power. That's more than Edriendor ever had, more than the Edren Guard can stand against."

Tears sprang to Rydara's eyes as she searched Sundamar's and found them utterly devoid of hope. He reached out and clasped her shoulder. "I told you, Rydara, there would be nothing I could do to save you if you came here. Did you not believe I spoke the truth?"

"Why did you come, then?" Rydara asked, but the answer was plain in her Knowing, as it had been ever since he had arrived.

He had come to die with them.

"It is my hope that our sacrifice will stir Edriendor to action," Sundamar said. "Arcaena could ignore Chaenath, and Conall, and me, but all the Edren Guard … together, we may become a symbol that will inspire the elders to act before it is too late. Before Tenebrus' reign spreads across the seas and all humanity is lost. Before the fight comes to Arcaena's doorstep."

Rydara's lower lip trembled as she took in his words. He had brought the whole Edren Guard here because of her. Perhaps they would inspire Edriendor as he hoped, but perhaps not. Either way, Rydara had dragged more young, immortal elves into her own people's struggle, and their deaths would be on her head.

Just like Conall's.

Sundamar cupped her chin with his hand, pressing her lip with his thumb to still its trembling. "I am here because of you, Rydara, but I did not come here *for* you, and the others did not come here for you either. We are here because it is right for us to be here. All you did was help us see the truth."

Sundamar let go of her, and Rydara stepped forward and hugged him. "I'm sorry," she whispered against his chest.

"Thank you," he whispered back, holding her tightly. "This is a decision we can be proud of."

It was what she had believed and argued for, and Rydara could not disagree or tell Sundamar to turn back now, just as she had not been able to dissuade Reluvethel. But she did feel sorry that because of what she had said to them, the best of the elves would die, and they would do so without bringing hope to her people.

Rydara stepped back. "What is Sarya to you?" she asked, remembering how Sundamar's gaze had lingered on her when he had announced that they had come to help.

"She is the future of our people," Sundamar said. "Or at least, she would have been. When Arcaena grows weary of her pilgrimage, she will make the crossing to the Realm Beyond, as is our custom. As her firstborn daughter, Sarya would have succeeded her as First and led our people."

Rydara had many questions about crossing to the Realm Beyond that she had not found answers to in the elves' library. She wondered if all elves eventually "grew weary of their pilgrimage," and how long they lived before this happened. If a mortal Prophet could pass physically through the Realm Between to get there, as the elves did. If it was possible to return and describe the Realm Beyond to other people.

But instead of asking, Rydara looked back at Sundamar and waited. She could tell there was something more between him and Sarya that he had not told her.

"She is also my sister," he said. The Elvish word he used included a familiar diminutive, which made "little" or "kid" sister a better interpretation. It still could have referred to a close younger friend or neighbor, as "sister" and "brother" often did, but Rydara sensed that in this case, Sarya was his actual blood sister.

"You are Arcaena's son?" Rydara furrowed her brow, taken aback. Sundamar merely nodded. That would seem to make him some kind of prince, and though the members of the Edren Guard looked up to him as their captain, Rydara had never perceived deference or any special regard from the rest of the elves toward Sundamar. She had certainly never sensed anything familial between him and the First.

Though, come to think of it, she had sensed something deeper in his grief for Chaenath than she had been able to explain.

"Chaenath was your aunt?" she asked next, and Sundamar nodded. A whisper of his grief clouded Rydara's Knowing. "Faedastan is your cousin."

"And Theodluin, who became Tenebrus, was my uncle," Sundamar agreed. "Though I was born long after that time."

After the startling revelations at Chaenath's funeral about her connections to Faedastan, the First, and the elf who had forged the High Wizards and killed Nivalis, Rydara was a little less surprised that Sundamar's connections to all of them had eluded her Knowing. But the information itself was still stunning, and she felt more than a little disoriented.

"Sarya is your sister," Rydara repeated. "Your little sister. And Arcaena's heir."

Sundamar nodded again, and Rydara sensed something of his pride for his sister. And his grief, guilt, and gratitude.

It all made sense now.

"She must have powerful magic, if she is Arcaena's daughter," Rydara guessed. Arcaena's talents were legendary, and strength of magic was largely hereditary among the elves, who all had access to excellent training. "As you do."

Sundamar made no answer, but Rydara Knew she had guessed right. They were among the strongest of their kind, though they had not trained long enough to be considered wizards.

Sundamar did not think it would be enough.

"Maybe she will not die here," Rydara found herself saying, wishing to mitigate Sundamar's pain. Wishing to give him hope. "Maybe we can win this battle."

It felt strange, to be the one suggesting the impossible might come true. Aander always did that, and she was the one who pointed to the obstacles. Even now, it seemed obvious to her that if three elves and dragons could not defeat one High Wizard with a shard, there was no chance that six elves and seven dragons could prevail against three High Wizards with two shards—let alone however many more they would face.

But maybe Aander was right to cling to hope, no matter the circumstance. Sundamar and the Edren Guard had come to aid them, and that was a miracle in itself.

Maybe it was right to imagine they could have another.

Sundamar did not agree, but he gave a half-hearted smile as Rydara struggled to offer him an optimism she could not quite justify herself. "It is all right, Rydara," he said. "I do not need hope for myself and Sarya to give this battle my all."

"I know," Rydara said. When she had first set out for the Waste, she had not expected to survive the journey. Then, when Aander had fallen sick, she had been sure he would die. She had not believed they would find the elves, and when they did, she had doubted she would be able to convince them of anything. But she had kept trying all the same.

Sundamar was like her, in that he did not need hope in order to try.

But standing there, confronted by someone with an outlook darker than her own—someone whose very presence was already more than she had dared to imagine even this morning—Rydara wondered if hope was worth having for its own sake. For reasons that she could not explain, she wanted Sundamar to have hope. Even just a tiny flicker of it.

"If we should live, there's so much I would like to do," Rydara said, daring, for once, to imagine a future where the High Wizards did not rule and they were still alive. "I've learned so much from your people and histories. I would like to share it with my race. To train them how to use the sights and imaging talents we've forgotten. As you and Reluvethel have begun to do, but with more time to explain the theory as well as the practice. A compact of High Wizards has already been formed twice, so if we defeat them this time, my people should learn to defend ourselves against them. We should not forget everything again and rely solely on Edriendor."

"If we could expose more of your kind to the shards, their magic would grow stronger," Sundamar said, indulging Rydara's fantasy. "If we win, perhaps we could take some from the High Wizards and give them to your people. Then they might get somewhere in their training."

Rydara smiled. There was still no hope in Sundamar, but she appreciated his willingness to play along. "Dragons could help."

Sundamar nodded. "They would definitely need dragons."

"We would train anyone with aptitude. Anyone who wouldn't abuse their gifts," Rydara decided. "We would need them to embrace some sort of code, such as the elves have. Only ours would need to be explicit. My people would not understand how to keep a code that doesn't consist of actual rules."

Sundamar nodded, a small smile breaking through. "I think the southern tribes would also struggle with a code that was only implied."

"Yes, anyone should be able to train with us. Northerner or southerner. Male or female," Rydara added, thinking of how many opportunities were denied women among the tribes. It was always the men who fought, the men who negotiated, the men who decided. Even had she been a real princess instead of her father's bastard, she would still have been relegated to the role of adviser—though the men would have resented her presence less.

"Rishara or fair-skinned," Sundamar added softly. Rydara nodded. "It is a pleasant fantasy," he said, taking her hand. "I should have liked to help you bring our knowledge to your people, for as many years as you might live."

Rydara was taken aback, and her lips parted. It was a completely different proposition than asking her to stay with him in Edriendor. Away from his land and its magic, he would lose his immortality. He would grow old and die, but first he would watch her do the same, for he would live many more years than she. It would be lonely, and he would be surrounded by ignorant, short-sighted humans instead of his own kind.

It could never happen, since they would both die tomorrow, but Rydara was touched all the same.

"But even if everything we hope for came true, you should know that it would take many years for Aander to recover his health," Sundamar continued, lowering his eyes. "And that I am to blame."

Rydara waited for him to explain, sensing that he meant something more than whatever spell he had woven to help Aander steal strength from his future. Whatever it was, it weighed on Sundamar as he stroked her hand, continuing to avoid her eyes.

"I knew when you entered the Waste," he confessed. "I knew when Aander fell sick. Had I intervened then, he would have recovered quickly, without the lingering threat of the terrors. Instead, Lëanor and I watched you for days. I knew each day that passed brought him closer to death, and still I stood by. If Lëanor hadn't called you up to that bluff ... if you hadn't come and discovered us..."

Rydara could sense that Sundamar had had to muster his courage to confess this to her. There had been a time, no doubt, when the revelation would have felt like a betrayal. Maybe when she had first started to think of Sundamar as a friend, or when she had found out what the illness would mean for her brother's future.

But now, Rydara realized, it was not even a surprise. She may not have taken the time to think through it, but she knew the Edren Guard routinely surveilled the Hahiroth. She had perceived right away that Sundamar had defied the elves' custom to save her brother and that he had done so only with great reluctance. And from the beginning, he had seemed more familiar with her than she was with him. As if he had had a bit longer to get to know her.

A bit longer to develop that inexplicable regard for her, which now had him fairly trembling as he awaited her response.

Rydara covered the hand that held hers with her free one. "You saved him. Aander doesn't hold the delay against you," she said, realizing her brother must have already known. Sundamar would have confessed to him first. "Neither do I."

Sundamar enfolded her in his arms and kissed her, then, and heat shot through Rydara's whole body. She was startled, but not so startled her lips did not move to kiss him back. He tasted like passion, and war, and tenderness, the sensations of his touch jumbling together with the intensity of his emotions in Rydara's Knowing so she could hardly tell where one ended and the other began. She reached up and clung to him as the kiss went on, holding him as tightly as he held her, dizzy with the promise of an impossible future.

Eventually Sundamar pushed her back, breathing heavily as he stared into her eyes. His hands still grasped her shoulders.

"Rydara. If Dameires doesn't know that we're here—if we can lead him to believe the magic he's been sensing from this city is the work of Tenebrus—he may seek to assault us before the others arrive. We might be able to overwhelm him, even take his shard. I do not think we could use it as it is, but if there is a way to reverse its corruption, that shard could be a great asset to us against the others. The Edren Guard will have its hands full during the battle—but if anyone else can discern its secret, it's you. You should take it and learn what you can from Dameires—if everything goes our way."

Rydara nodded mutely, and Sundamar turned and walked away into the night, gone to make whatever other preparations he had thought of. Rydara watched him go, her heart impossibly full.

For the first time that she could remember—the first time since, perhaps, her mother had died—it was filled with hope.

Chapter 20

The Battle for Helos

Rydara woke to the touch of a light rain on her skin. Dawn was stealing across the sky, and people around her were stirring.

Aander was on his feet. "This is it, Rydara," he said, extending a hand to help her rise. "The battle for mankind begins tonight. Can you feel it?"

"Feel what?" Rydara mumbled, wiping sleep from her eyes as she stood.

"The opening notes of the glorious refrain history will sing of this moment. The Rishara Knower who brought elves and dragons from the Land Beyond the Waste to rescue the tribes from annihilation at the hands of the nine High Wizards. With a little help from her sick brother, of course."

Aander smiled, but there were worry lines around his eyes. He did not have the same carefree audacity as when they had set out into the Waste, though his words were similar.

Rydara shook her head, but the truth was she did feel something. Something like anticipation, but with more ... power. She held out a hand and watched the raindrops pool on her skin.

There was magic in the rain. A smile slowly spread across her face, and she looked up at the rain clouds. What it meant or what it would do, she had no idea, but the rain was Sundamar's work. She was sure of it.

"What is it?" Aander asked, frowning.

Rydara shook her head again, marveling at the sky. "Maybe they really will sing about us, Aander. Maybe we have a real chance."

***

Three hours before sunset, Rydara stood on the city wall, watching the Alterran army approach through a steady rain. More and more soldiers came into view as they descended from the mountain pass, spreading slowly across the plain. There were thousands of them. Tens of thousands, maybe.

It was only a fraction of the enemies they would face.

A familiar dread grew in Rydara's Knowing, signaling the approach of a corrupted shard. She could not tell where it was at this distance, but it was out there somewhere, drawing closer until the Alterrans stopped moving forward. They left the city a wide berth, staying out of range of the archers on the walls, but they continued spreading to the sides, and within an hour, they had completely encircled the city.

A small party of horsemen broke from the lines and approached the city gate, flying a white flag. Rydara's nausea grew and localized, and she held her breath as Sundamar's party—including her brother, the Rithadur prince, and four other elves—rode out to meet the riders bearing the corrupted shard. All the elves wore hoods and scarves, disguising their features as they rode behind the human leaders.

"Foryar somno Dameires," Sarya muttered. *Dameires is with them.*

Sarya stood next to Rydara and Eduare on the wall, the only elf not riding out with Sundamar to counter the first High Wizard. Rydara could feel her frustration. They needed an elf on the wall for the next phase of the plan—but Sundamar had given the task to Sarya to protect her, and the elf did not like it.

"Do you think he's suspicious?" Rydara asked. The elves had intercepted a messenger from Dameires earlier in the day, seeking to learn the meaning of the magic rainfall. Sundamar had pretended to be Tenebrus and terrified the messenger, sending him back to Dameires with the message that he had not taken the city fast enough and Tenebrus was considering taking it himself if there was any more delay. The rain was his device and would make everyone in the city more biddable.

Rydara had been surprised to hear that Sundamar had lied so directly, considering the elves' code. But Dameires' messenger had been one of the High Wizard's Knights, who had traded away his soul in the deal Lux had once offered to Rydara. Sundamar explained that the mind of such a person was no longer their own, and his code did not require him to respect its autonomy.

"*Lipsydavàn aurmi,*" Sarya said, her expression grim. *We will know soon.*

A typical elven answer, Rydara noted. She herself was optimistic. If Dameires was showing himself now, he must have fallen for their ruse.

Or he knows everything and still thinks he can beat us. Rydara worried her lower lip.

The two parties met in the middle of the plain, too far from the walls for Rydara to make out the general's features. The lead rider had to be him, though. He carried himself with the arrogance of one who held the power of a god, and the spot of black in his hand was surely the corrupted shard, devouring all light and goodness around it. When he Spoke, Rydara could not hear the words, but she felt an echo of their haughtiness in her Knowing.

His power broke against a wall of elven magic, and Rydara felt haughtiness turn to shock before Dameires' touch disappeared from her Knowing. The elves on the plain sprang at Dameires, and the battle was fierce and fast, aided by the rain and a surge of power from the dragons who hid inside the city walls.

"Men of Alterra!" Eduare cried beside Rydara, his voice rolling across the entire plain with Sarya's assistance. The elf cast a Showing of him in the sky like the ones Lux and Dameires had used, showing the Alterran army his face and the blue and white uniform he wore. "Your king is dead, slain by his queen and your general, Dameires! Stand down, and let us bring him to justice!"

The elves on the plain had grabbed Dameires, separating him from his shard, and the whole party rode like mad for the city gates with some of Dameires' Knights tearing after them. A salvo of arrows from the city supported the retreat. Most were deflected by unseen waves of power, but a few found their marks.

The Alterrans on the front line surged forward when they saw the elves attack, unaware that their general had broken the truce of the white flag first with his Speaking. But their fellows behind them had not seen the general's abduction, and they were distracted by the image of Eduare in the sky. Eduare went on to speak of his former position as the king's Justicer and what he had learned of the High Wizards and their efforts to subdue humankind. The rain kept falling, washing every soldier with its subtle magic, designed to weaken any Speaking the High Wizards might have placed to control them and make minds more receptive to Eduare's words.

It was not enough to sway everyone. The army rippled in a haphazard charge, perhaps half of them closing toward the city. The archers on the walls sent waves of arrows into their ranks where the charge had the most momentum, breaking some of it.

Then the dragons took to the sky. Their fire ended the charge as Sundamar's party reached the gates, dragging Dameires with them. Rydara ran down the nearest stairs to meet them as they were let inside, relieved to count all seven had made it back.

Dameires was conscious and screaming, thrashing against invisible bonds that held him fast against Sundamar's horse. His screams were muffled and quiet, but they rent the air and Rydara's Knowing with their power, pulling at her to come closer and free him. Everyone in range must have felt the same urge, but the tribespeople had been warned this might happen, and they left a wide berth around Sundamar's party. Their practice and the rain had given them enough strength to resist coming closer.

Sundamar's eyes met Rydara's briefly as they rode in, and he reached down to pass her the corrupted shard. Rydara nearly dropped it as the elves continued past her. Being close to it was sickening. Touching it was worse.

But the elves had done it. They had captured not only the first High Wizard, but also his shard. It was one less for their enemies to use against them.

The struggle with Dameires was not over yet. Two of the dragons were flying back now to meet Sundamar and the other elves in the square. With their combined talents, they would drag Dameires' spirit into the Realm Between and separate him from his demon. From there, they could banish the thing back where it came from.

Rydara was not clear on exactly how it would work, but she had been made to understand that if they could separate Dameires from his shard, the elves and dragons would be able to banish his demon eventually. Dameires could not stop them on his own.

But they would not be on their own for much longer. Rydara almost fancied she could feel other shards stirring far away. Coming closer.

Maybe with the corrupted shard in her hands, she really could.

Rydara gnawed her lower lip, staring at the corrupted shard. It made sense for the task to fix it to fall to her. The elves and dragons were too important to the struggle with the High Wizards, and Rydara was the strongest Knower in the tribes.

Figuring out the shard was infinitely more important than whatever support one more Knower might have been able to offer the elves during battle. The shards were the reason Sundamar did not believe this battle could be won. The enemy had had five of them. Now they had four, but four was still too many for their forces to overcome without any shards of their own. If they had one they could use, though...

Rydara furrowed her brow at the shard, as if staring at it could make it give up its secrets. She could feel power radiating from it, and she also felt the slick stain of its corruption. *How many of my people were murdered to feed this power?*

Before giving it to Rydara, Sundamar would have confirmed that the elves could not touch its magic. He had not known what might happen if a human tried to use it, but now that she was holding it, Rydara could guess. The dread in her Knowing was still hard to bear, but through it she could sense a thread she might draw on, a thread that promised immeasurable knowledge even as it repulsed her with the threat of absolute doom. Rydara could use the shard, she believed. It might even give her the secret of how to restore it.

But she Knew that if she did, if she pulled on that thread, she would let all that darkness inside her, and even if she did learn how to restore the shard, she would no longer want to.

I will not stain my soul with the blood of my people, Rydara promised herself. It was an easy promise to make, considering how the thought of using the shard made her want to vomit, and especially considering how clear it was to her Knowing that trying to use it for good would simply not work.

The longer she held it, the surer she became that the shard was enhancing her Knowing even without her pulling on the thread—as if to entreat her to seek more of what it offered. She *could* feel the other shards. One in the east, three in the south, all coming closer with the promise of doom and immeasurable power.

She set the shard down on the street and stepped back from it, checking her Knowing. She could not sense them at all on her own—they were still too far away. When she picked the shard up, though, she could feel them again. Rydara looked down the street toward the square, anxious that Sundamar and the others would run out of time.

The southern princes had suggested simply killing Dameires when Sundamar had briefed them on the plan. Sundamar had explained that Dameires' demon granted him supernatural regenerative powers that made him nearly indestructible. The princes had wanted to try tearing him limb from limb and setting the pieces on fire—but in the end, it did not really matter whether killing Dameires outright was theoretically possible or if it could have saved them any time. The elves' code forbade killing, and though it seemed strange to Rydara that there was no exception for High Wizards considering the special carve-out for lying to their Knights, she did know that Sundamar would sooner die himself than break this part of his code.

It was just as well. There was no one alive who knew more about corrupted shards than the High Wizards, and Rydara would not have been able to interrogate Dameires if he were dead.

The minutes ticked by, and Rydara's worry grew as she perceived other shards coming closer. They were moving faster than horses could run, and she guessed they would arrive within the hour. The dread of all five of them soon became unbearable, and Rydara set the one she carried down on the street, eyeing it warily. Eduare's speech had finished. Through the pouring rain, she heard the shouts of officers and the stamping of feet, but it did not sound as though the city were under a full-fledged assault.

She could sense the shards without holding the one in front of her now.

Rydara staggered backward as rage hit her Knowing like a shockwave. Something had ... broken. *Is that anger from the shard?*

Rydara blinked rapidly, wiping rain from her face. It must have been Dameires' bond with his demon. Taada had been assigned to bring her the message once the struggle was won, but she guessed she didn't need to wait for him.

Rydara snatched up the shard, steeling herself against the shock to her Knowing. It was worse, now, but she could not just leave the thing in the street.

She ran toward the square. The sight of a dragon overhead confirmed that she had been right. The elves had finished with the High Wizard and were flying out, ready to defend the city.

She nearly collided with Taada as she turned a corner. "This way!" he said, grabbing her hand and leading her toward the square at a run.

He pulled her to a stop outside one of the shops that bordered it. There was an entrance to an underground cellar, and two southerners were standing guard.

"He's inside?" Rydara asked.

"He's tied up," one of them answered, nodding. "Call if you need us."

Rydara nodded and went down the steps, suddenly nervous. Sundamar had advised that no one but Rydara should speak to Dameires, even after his demon was banished. A Knower would have more defense against any attempts to manipulate her, and given her task, Rydara was the only one who had reason to speak to him anyway.

But if no one else should be speaking to him, is it really safe for me? Rydara wondered, wetting her lips. This man had been one of the nine High Wizards. He had murdered Kell right in front of her. Her whole body tensed as she reached the cellar floor.

The light was poor, but there was enough for her to see Dameires lying awkwardly between two barrels in front of a wine rack, his hands and feet both tied together. His face was bruised and his upper lip cracked and swollen. His breathing was slow and even.

He looked like he had aged twenty years. He had been a man in his prime the last time she had seen him, when he had broadcast his image across the sky during the fight with

Chaenath and Neremyn. Now, his hunched shoulders did not look so broad or well-muscled, and besides the bruises, there were wrinkles in his face that had not been there before. Rydara could make out gray in his hair.

Some of the tension left her shoulders. This was not the General Dameires that had terrorized her people and murdered Kell. This was just a man who had once hosted a demon—a demon that was now gone.

He was like Neremyn, as he had been when she had met him.

He stirred. "What now?" he demanded, squinting up at her in the poor light from the entrance. "Did they send a girl to interrogate me?" Even his voice was different. Hollow, compared to what it had been.

"An *ishra* girl," Rydara agreed.

"Oh, it's you," Dameires wheezed and spat on the cellar floor. There might have been blood in it. "What do you want?"

"I need to know how to fix your shard," Rydara said simply, studying him.

He laughed. The sound was jarring, coming as it did from someone so beaten and bound. He looked half-dead, lying there on the cellar floor, and Rydara's Knowing registered a profound state of defeat—a defeat that went far beyond his physical condition. This man had been destroyed and then unmade, and there was no fight left in him. No mirth. No glee.

But he laughed anyway. A sense of doomed irony echoed in Rydara's Knowing.

"What makes you think it can be fixed?" Dameires managed when his chuckles died down. His eyes glinted as he stared up at her in the partial darkness, and Rydara furrowed her brow. It was harder for Knowers to glean an attitude behind a question than a statement of fact, but there was something more complex behind Dameires' words than the mockery he intended.

"Can it be?" she asked.

The follow-up disturbed Dameires, and Rydara sensed anger.

"You don't have the Speaking magic anymore," she remembered. "Or even Knowing." She had the advantage of him in this conversation, with her Knowing able to interpret more than he spoke. He could not have enjoyed the reversal. "You must feel blind and dumb."

A flare of bitterness told her she had hit the mark.

"But what does it matter?" she asked. "My motives are transparent here. There are no games left to play."

His anger dissipated at that, fading back into a grim sense of doom. It felt … final.

"It won't matter to you if the other High Wizards defeat my people, will it?" Rydara guessed. "They won't welcome you back." His sense of doom deepened, and Rydara supposed she had understated his situation. "So, you don't need your magic, then. It doesn't matter what you say to me."

"Are you trying to make me feel better?" Dameires chuckled — faintly, this time. "You have a strange way of interrogating your prisoners."

"If I struck you, would you answer my question?" Rydara said. "You are not my enemy."

Dameires scoffed. "I must have killed thousands of your people. You've seen my work."

Rydara tightened her lips, remembering how he had stabbed Kell through the heart. The mass grave in Tessex. Byrn. Dameires was no longer a High Wizard, but he was still the man who had chosen to become one. The man who had chosen to partner with a demon to seek godhood, not caring how many of her people he slaughtered on his way.

No different than Neremyn, she reminded herself. Except, in Neremyn, she had sensed an earnest desire to be her friend. A desire to escape from the person he had been. A wish to somehow find a way to be good again, though he had not been able to see or act upon it.

She sensed none of that in this man who had been the High Wizard Dameires. He was broken now—broken almost beyond recognition—but he had no wish or even conception of becoming anything other than what he was: her enemy.

"How many High Wizards are coming against us?" Rydara asked. "There are eight others. Will they all come?" Dameires did not answer aloud, but Rydara could read his reaction. There would be fewer than eight. "Seven? Six? Five?" A twinge of confirmation in her Knowing suggested she had struck the right number. "Five, then. Neremyn kept his promise to me. He left and convinced two others to leave with him."

Rydara smiled. It was more than she had hoped for—certainly more than Sundamar had.

"The new Numbran isn't interested in helping Tenebrus attain godhood," Dameires returned, "and he, Auror, and Ei Desidi may not be a threat to your tribes today. But they will cause misery to your kind elsewhere. It's what we do."

"It's what High Wizards do," Rydara said. "You may be right about Numbran, now, but when I met him, he was only Neremyn, and there is some of Neremyn in him still, despite the demon. You have no demon. You are not my enemy."

Dameires did not answer for a moment, and Rydara could sense irritation. He was defeated, and he had nothing left to fight for—nothing even to hope for. When the High Wizards took the city, Rydara sensed that his fate would be worse than death, and he had resigned himself to that.

But it still irritated him that he did not understand her, and he had no Knowing to help make sense of her words. "Why do you keep saying that?" he demanded.

"You think there's no way out for you. No escape. No redemption. But you're wrong," Rydara said, her conviction growing. If she could believe it for Neremyn, the same could be true for Dameires. "Help me. Tell me how to fix the shard. If the elves can use it, we'll stand a chance against the High Wizards. If we defeat them, I can't promise you won't be executed, but you'll be spared whatever fate they have in store for you."

Her words were met by silence, and Rydara sensed that she had miscalculated. Defeating the High Wizards would not spare him the fate he anticipated.

"No. It's what will happen after death that concerns you," Rydara corrected herself. "The Realm Beyond is closed to one such as you. You'll cross to the place your demon came from instead, is that it? He's the one that will punish you?"

More silence. Nothing changed in Dameires' expression or his breathing as he lay tied up on the floor, but Rydara Knew this guess was right. There was a thread of irritation in Dameires as she struck upon the truth, demonstrating her advantage over him again, but it soon faded. There was little room for other emotions in the hollow defeat that enveloped him.

"What if there's still time?" Rydara asked, urgent. The darkness in the shard secured in her pocket was growing and so was the sick sense of doom in her Knowing. The other shards were still growing closer, perhaps only minutes away from joining the battle. Rydara could feel the haughty sadism of the High Wizards who carried them—or perhaps their demons. They were angry at the rebellion that had happened in this city, at the blow to one of their own.

They were ready to slaughter.

"What if there's still time for you to choose a better path?" Rydara repeated. "For you to escape the demons and gain entrance to the Realm Beyond? You must have heard of the All-Color's mercy. Help me fix the shard, and Nivalis will take notice. He must. It is your best hope."

"Nivalis can't see us. His presence here was destroyed." Dameires' gaze drifted up to meet hers, his eyes glinting in the darkness, and Rydara was taken aback by his conviction. He believed what he said. "I should know—I helped kill him. Didn't the elves tell you that?"

He can't be right, Rydara told herself, searching him for any doubt. Any glimmer of an acknowledgment that he could not really know for sure.

But there was none. Dameires believed that the god who had allegedly created elves and humans, who had allegedly loved them enough to sacrifice himself for them, who had allegedly still existed in the Realm Beyond and had allegedly designed the criteria for entrance—Dameires believed that this god was irrevocably blind to their world and oblivious to their concerns because of what the High Wizards had done to him. He believed he knew for sure.

It was not what the elves taught about the White. They believed Nivalis still watched and cared intimately, though his power was limited and he could no longer take physical form as he once had. Rydara did not know how or when she herself had come to believe this about Nivalis, or when she had started to hope that he had heard her desperate prayer in the Waste and been responsible for sending Lëanor and Sundamar.

But somewhere, somehow, she must have developed this hope, because Dameires' conviction that they were alone and unobserved by any benevolent power shook her to the core. He believed redemption was not possible, and there was no doubt in him at all.

"You're wrong," Rydara breathed, but her words evoked no change in him—and why should they? *Shouldn't he know better than me?* She certainly hadn't been there. She could not begin to understand what the High Wizards had done to their god to break his power and remove him from the physical realm. This Dameires had not been there either, but the demon he had been bonded to had, and that demon would have understood what happened better than she did, better than any human or elf. This man had the knowledge of that demon. She should be learning from him, this man with more knowledge of other realms than anyone she would ever meet. *And I tried to tell him he was wrong? Me, an ignorant mortal?*

What had she been thinking? If this former High Wizard knew Nivalis was dead to this realm, then it must be Rydara who was wrong. She, and the elves, and their wishful clinging to a way of life that had never made sense after their god was killed. Why had she ever thought there could be anything more to it? Hadn't it been Lëanor who had convinced Sundamar to take pity on her and Aander after watching him waste away for days, and not any miraculous intervention? She had been alone out there in the desert, aside from them. No one had heard her pray.

Just like she was alone now. She was going to die here, and the entire city with her—along with the six elves and seven dragons who had come to fight for them. They would all die in this lost cause. Just like Conall and Chaenath.

Panic and despair clutched at Rydara, and she tried to breathe, aware of Dameires' gaze, watching her with indifference as the weight of his knowledge choked out her newfound hope. *Calm, flowing, glowing water,* Rydara summoned the meditation, not knowing what else to do. *Calm, flowing, glowing water.* Her hope may have been a deception, but she would not lose her mind to fear. She had to try to figure out the shard, even if she was doomed to failure.

The meditation did not silence her panic or her despair, but it did push them back a little. Just enough so she could breathe. In that little pocket of stillness, Rydara realized the doom threatening to overwhelm her was not coming from her mind, but from her Knowing.

The shard in her pocket was its source.

Rydara ripped it out of her pocket and threw it across the cellar, angry with it and angry with herself for nearly succumbing to its deception. Throwing it did not alleviate her sickness much, but it did help, and her anger sharpened her focus.

"You're wrong!" she repeated, panting as she glared at the shard. She shifted her gaze to Dameires and found he was unimpressed. Of course, he was not going to take her word for it. He thought he knew for sure.

"What if you're wrong?" she tried again. "What if Nivalis *can* still see us? What if he still *could* offer you mercy? You weren't there. You only know what your demon told you about his so-called death, isn't that right? What if it lied?"

This, finally, inspired a glimmer of doubt in Dameires.

"Wouldn't it prefer you to believe you could never make it to the Realm Beyond?" Rydara pressed. "I'm told they are creatures of darkness and hate. Wouldn't it like you to join it wherever it goes, rather than search for a way of escape?"

She pointed at the shard she had hurled across the cellar. "Tell me how to fix it. Please. It's your best hope."

Dameires weighed her words, and Rydara strained to make sense of his feelings through her Knowing. It was becoming harder to sense much beyond her nausea. The other corrupted shards were too close.

She did not think her words had much of an impact. Dameires had already accepted his doom. He was too far gone to hope that she was right. He could not even imagine it. But ... there was a glimmer of *something*. Maybe a wish?

"I don't know how to fix it," Dameires said. "I don't even know if it can be fixed."

It was the truth. Rydara fought a renewed crush of despair. There was just the faintest flicker of something else in her Knowing.

She clung to it like her last piece of driftwood from a shipwreck. *Maybe it's not the whole truth?* "Please. Is there anything you suspect?"

Dameires wet his lips, and then he spat again. He was thinking about it. Rydara held her breath, daring to hope.

"Tell you what, *ishra*," he said. "Your god is dead, whether you believe it or not, and what you think you just offered me is impossible. We'll all be dead soon no matter what happens. But in the meantime, my wrists are chafing and I've a terrible thirst. So, untie me, get me something to drink, and I'll tell you what I do know. Though I can't imagine how it would help you from in here."

It sounded like the type of bargain Sundamar had been worried Dameires might try to make, and Rydara knew her brother and the southern princes would never have allowed it. But they were not here, and she was.

"Deal," she said. She approached cautiously but without hesitation, stepping around Dameires to reach the wine rack behind him. The other corrupted shards had stopped moving closer, and Rydara guessed they had already reached the Alterran lines outside the city. The High Wizards had joined the fight.

Rydara needed an answer.

She took one of the glass wine bottles and struck it against the edge of the barrel beside her, breaking the top off and splashing herself with wine. She used the glass to saw through the rope binding Dameires' hands, fully aware that with his hands free, he could probably overpower her and kill her with the broken glass.

He had no magic left, though, and no means to deceive her Knowing. He had no intention of killing her.

When she freed his hands, he winced and pushed himself up to a seated position, leaning against the barrel. There were angry welts on his wrists. He rubbed them and grimaced.

He looked at Rydara, and for a fleeting moment, she Knew he had the same thought she did: he could take the broken glass and slit her throat.

Rydara held his gaze, reaching out to offer him the broken bottle. Her hands were steady, but she held her breath, realizing she may have miscalculated. Dameires may not have intended to kill her when she agreed to his deal, but he could change his mind.

His gaze drifted away from hers. Rydara breathed again when he took the bottle.

He sipped from it and cleared his throat. "Before we killed Nivalis, he gave us his scepter of power. You've heard of it? We used it to kill him."

Rydara nodded. "But you weren't there, were you? That was the Dameires before you."

He shrugged. "Me, Meridies, whatever. I've seen the memories."

"Meridies—your demon?"

"He preferred 'lord of hell,' but sure. The scepter was transparent, with a kind of white glow. Like the shards used to be. And we couldn't use it."

"Are you saying..." Rydara trailed off, frowning. The elves' histories had never mentioned anything about the scepter's having been corrupted. Then again, they said nothing about corrupted shards, either.

"Tenebrus anticipated it," Dameires went on. "He killed a thousand mortals before we brokered the deal with Nivalis, and he kept a drop of blood from each one in a glass bottle. When we got the staff, he poured the blood over it, and then the darkness started to bloom inside of it, until the whole thing was black, like that." Dameires nodded at the corrupted shard, still lying against the wall where Rydara had thrown it. "Then we killed Nivalis with it."

"And the scepter shattered into the shards," Rydara concluded.

"White shards. Like it had never been stained to begin with," Dameires added. He took another sip from the bottle.

"The backlash from the god's death broke the High Wizards' power and wounded them for a time," Rydara remembered. "You're saying it also cleansed the scepter? But how could that help with the shards?"

Dameires shrugged again. "Maybe it doesn't." He cleared his throat, and Rydara waited. Her Knowing was consumed by the dread that had come with the other shards, and she could hardly sense Dameires anymore at all, but there had to be more to his story. However much of a longshot it was, Rydara needed to hear it.

"When I could remember that moment—the moment we killed our creator," Dameires continued, "the most salient part of it was the love that resounded in my Knowing. Or, Meridies' Knowing, I suppose. It repelled him, filled him with terror. He hated the memory. Never wanted me to look at it. But I did, once or twice. Enough to know that the love that filled Nivalis' heart at the moment we killed him with his own scepter wasn't just for the elves and humans he had made the deal to save. It was for us, the High Wizards who murdered him." Dameires took another drink of wine. "I never cared for the memory, either, but to Meridies, it was … toxic. Antithetical. When I remembered that love, it was almost as if he … shrank." Dameires' eyes met Rydara's. Her Knowing was next to worthless at the moment, but she could see a challenge in his eyes.

"You think … the love of a god…" Rydara stared back at him, puzzled. He was challenging her, but to what?

"Pure love, at the moment of sacrifice." Dameires' voice was almost a whisper. He shook his head and smiled—an odd, ironic smile, with his eyes never leaving Rydara's. "I told you, I didn't think it would help you. That's all I know."

Rydara's breath quickened as her mind raced through the implications. He was right. His story didn't help her at all. *What am I supposed to do, ask one of the southerners to kill me and hope it helps?*

"I think you would have to have a High Wizard do it, though," Dameires said, as if reading her thoughts. His Knowing might have been gone, but spending all those years with it must have made him astute. "There's a lot of magic involved, getting the shards to take essence from the blood. And their intentions in killing you might be as relevant as your own in letting them do it."

"So—to be clear. You're saying that if I *let* a High Wizard murder me, and if I have love in my heart while they chant my blood into the crystal, that *might* reverse the corruption so we can use the shard again and they can't. *That's* your best guess? Your only guess?"

"Not just any love. Pure love. *For* the wizard who kills you."

"But ... *why*? Why would you think that might work?" Rydara demanded.

Dameires laughed. He shrugged his shoulders and took another drink from the bottle. "I don't know, *ishra*. I used to share my essence with a demon, and I had Knowing magic at the time. Call it an informed intuition.

"But it makes sense, if you think about it. Nivalis was goodness and love. The shards were his power. They were meant to be used for good. Murder is just the opposite. When Tenebrus killed, he found a way to capture the evil of the act, the fear and the despair that it caused, and to transfer that essence into the shard through the victim's blood. If the victim had power, he captured that, too, and it made the shard even stronger. I don't know exactly why it worked, but I know that it *did* work, and so do you. The shards' corruption is evidence enough.

"And I also know that when we killed Nivalis, Tenebrus tried to transfer the god's power into the scepter in just the same way. But instead of an act of murder that generated fear and despair, Nivalis' death was a sacrifice made in love. I think Tenebrus channeled that love into the scepter inadvertently, and it clashed with the evil that was already inside and dispelled it."

Rydara tightened her jaw and crossed the room to the corrupted shard. She didn't know if Dameires was making any sense. He seemed sincere, but her Knowing was not giving her a very clear signal through the doom of the shards. Her Knowing would not have been able to tell whether his speculations had any basis in fact, anyway. Only whether he believed them.

Rydara did not want to die to test a theory. Besides, even if she assumed Dameires was right, how was she supposed to approach a High Wizard in the middle of a battle? She would have to pass through the enemy army to get to one, and even if that was possible, a High Wizard would surely Know everything she was up to as soon as she asked to be murdered.

No. It couldn't work.

Rydara eyed the corrupted shard. It would do no one any good on the floor of the cellar. As much as Rydara hated to hold it, she needed to take it with her in case there was any way to fix it. If Dameires' theory was absurd and impossible, she would just have to find another.

When she picked it up this time, the panic and dread didn't assault her as fiercely as before. Perhaps because the other shards were so close, now, and their presence so oppressive already, the change in intensity was milder.

Rydara glanced back at Dameires. As much as she hated what he had said, she did believe he had told her all he knew or guessed.

He could have killed her instead. "Thank you," she said.

He lifted the bottle toward her in acknowledgment, and she hurried outside.

Night had fallen, and the rain was pouring down in sheets. The two guards were gone from the cellar's entrance. A look down the street told her why. A section of the city wall had collapsed, and Alterran soldiers were fighting hand to hand with tribespeople in the gap, trying to force their way inside. Stray fires burned, inside the city and out, only partly contained by the rain. A dragon swooped over Rydara's head, closing fast toward the gap in the wall.

Lightning split the sky, striking the dragon mid-flight. It was followed hard by an earth-shattering clap of thunder. Rydara stumbled, slipped on the wet cobblestones at the cellar's entrance, and fell to her knees.

To her horror, the dragon tumbled from the sky. It landed with a crash where the armies were fighting, crushing friend and foe alike.

Someone was screaming. Maybe everyone.

Rydara ran toward the crash. *Was Aander on that dragon? Was Sundamar?*

The rain slashed down relentlessly, and Rydara dimly noted that its magic had changed. It was a fainter echo of the shard, now, promising failure and death.

The High Wizards had seized control of it.

The dragon up ahead was thrashing, wounded but not dead, meting out fire and wrath to the Alterrans in front of it. The tribespeople had pulled back, giving the dragon room and engaging only the Alterrans stupid or brave enough to try to get around it. Lightning flickered again, lighting up the scene.

The elf draped over the dragon's shoulder was dead. Rydara recognized Ildylintra.

Thunder resounded. One of the tribespeople tried to stop Rydara as she kept running toward the fallen dragon, but she gave him no heed, pushing forward. Neither Sundamar nor Aander had been flying with Ildylintra, but other magic users were on that dragon, and some of them had survived the fall. They were disentangling themselves now, limping back to the tribal line.

Rydara helped one who was half-dragging a companion. The man being dragged, she saw as lightning flashed again, was Praxtus, the Hatreth prince. His left leg was torn and bleeding heavily, but she thought he might recover.

They regained the safety of their lines as thunder shook the city, and Rydara left them, running up the nearest stairs to the city wall. She wasn't sure what she was looking for, but she needed a broader sense of the battle. Despite the crashed dragon and the turn of the rain, the tribes were still holding the walls.

Can Sundamar still win if I fail my mission? She Knew it was a foolish thought, but Rydara did not really trust her Knowing with the rain and the corrupted shard still broadcasting doom. There had to be a way for them to win. There had to be. *Where are the rest of the dragons?*

Rydara gained the top of the wall. The battlements were slick with rain and crowded with soldiers. Officers yelled orders, and Rydara tried to stay back and out of everyone's way.

She saw the dragons first. They were much higher in the air than she would have expected, and farther from the city. The occasional flash of lightning lit their struggle.

Their struggle? Rydara stared, confused. Two of them were locked together, rolling and striking each other by turns. They were fighting *each other*. It seemed to be two against four.

Dread that had nothing to do with the rain or the shard she was carrying seeped into Rydara's heart. She attuned her Knowing, fighting the sick sense of terror that grew louder as she tried to locate the other shards.

Two of them were in the sky. Their positions corresponded to the rebel dragons.

No. Rydara gaped, not understanding how it was possible. If the dragons could not resist the High Wizards' magic, what hope did the rest of them have?

The other two shards were on the ground. One of them was ahead, out of range of the archers on the wall. The other was on the other side of the city.

There were *more* soldiers surrounding the city than there had been when the battle began. Rydara did not understand it at first, but another flash of lightning revealed that aside from the contingent of Alterrans charging the wall, most of them wore red and black. Jeshim colors. They seemed to be supporting the Alterran charge, though they were avowed enemies.

The Alterrans held shields up against the steady rain of arrows from the defenders as they assaulted the broken wall. They took heavy losses, but their formation pressed forward anyway, spurred by the will of the shard-bearing High Wizard behind them.

A flash of lightning illuminated a group of riders on horseback a safe distance from the city wall. The one in the center rode side-saddle in a violet dress. There was a veil atop her hair, but it was thrown back, leaving her face exposed.

Lux Lucisa.

Rydara's breath caught. Suddenly, she knew what she had to do.

Chapter 21

Sacrifice

Rydara stumbled down the stairs to the street and ran toward the closest building. The tribespeople were taking their wounded there, though there were not many healers to tend them. Rydara ran inside, searching the rows of the maimed and bleeding who lay on the floor. Most of them would die.

All of them will die, Rydara corrected herself, *if nothing changes.*

There. Two healers were seeing to the gash in the leg of the Hatreth prince, but it looked as if they had already sewn it up. One helped him stand as the other fussed with his bandages.

"Praxtus!" The prince looked up at the sound of his name, and Rydara bowed her head. "Your highness. Can you walk?"

He waved the healers away. "I think so," he said, testing his left leg. He winced. "Not that it will matter much longer. We're losing."

"I need you to come with me," Rydara said.

He looked down at her. He was twice her age, male, fair-skinned, and a prince besides. Two months ago, Rydara would not have dreamed of speaking to this man, let alone telling him what to do.

But he looked at her and nodded, his expression grim. He started limping toward the exit, and Rydara hurried alongside. He tried walking on his own for a few paces, but then he put a hand on Rydara's shoulder. He leaned on her only a little.

"Where are we going?" he asked.

Rydara explained what she wanted him to do. He gave her a skeptical look, but when they got outside, they found the tribal line had broken. The dragon in the gap was no longer moving, and Alterrans poured into the city and up the stairs to the battlements, engaging the tribespeople there.

"Just one soldier," Rydara reminded the prince. "That's all we need."

He must surely have thought her insane, but he just nodded again. They kept walking toward the gap in the wall and the incoming flood of soldiers until a group of Alterrans noticed them and charged, swords drawn.

Praxtus picked the one in the lead. "Wait!" he shouted, holding up a hand. The word carried all the magic he had, and Rydara was surprised by how much stronger he was now than when they had met. "We have a message for your queen!"

The soldier slowed, gesturing to his fellows. "Who are you?" he demanded.

"This is Rydara, the Noraani *ishra*. She wants to take up the queen on her offer. You were informed about her, yes?"

It had been a long time since Lux had left a note on Rydara's horse promising that her soldiers had been given orders to take Rydara directly to the queen, should she change her mind about wanting to become a Knight. Rydara did not think Praxtus' talent for Speaking was enough to get them safely through the Alterrans on its own, but if this soldier should happen to remember such an order, even distantly...

"Now?" Confusion was palpable in the Alterran's voice.

"We don't have much longer to think about it, do we?" Praxtus gestured to the city's crumbling defenses. "Take us to the queen. Quickly."

It had been her plan, but it still amazed Rydara when the soldiers sheathed their weapons. They formed a tight knot around the two of them and marched out through the press of their own invading army, exchanging a few shouted words with officers as they passed.

Once they were clear of the wall, one of them ran ahead to inform the queen. Rydara's pulse quickened when a flash of lightning illuminated his hurried conversation with Lux Lucisa, some thirty paces ahead of them.

The queen was staring directly at Rydara, and the clap of thunder that followed shook her to the core. She was a High Wizard. Surely, she would see through this ruse. She would see right into Rydara's soul and laugh at her ridiculous plan.

But the soldiers took them all the way to her, and Lux waved a hand, dismissing them. She stared at Rydara and the wounded Hatreth prince as their escort left them in the pouring rain.

Suddenly, the rain stopped, and the sounds of the battle behind them were gone. The riders next to the queen vanished, and all Rydara could hear was the magic in Praxtus' nearly inaudible hum.

Rydara looked over her shoulder, startled. She couldn't see the city anymore. No starlight, no fires. No soldiers or dragons. Only black.

"You're ready to become my Knight, Rydara?" Lux asked, her voice as musical and winsome as always. An orb of light appeared above her hand, illuminating her face. "Who is this that you've brought along?"

"I'm not here to become a Knight," Rydara said, hoping Praxtus was doing enough to distract the High Wizard. With her Knowing consumed by the proximity of the shards, she had no idea what Lux was thinking. "I want to take you up on your other offer."

The queen's face wrinkled in a pretty frown. "You'll have to refresh my memory, *ishra*. I don't remember leaving any other offers on the table."

"The last time I saw you, you said, if I would not become a Knight, you could add my magic to your collection in another way," Rydara said, glancing behind her again.

It was still dark and quiet. Lux Lucisa must have created this bubble of privacy for the three of them.

"Yes, I meant I could kill you, and add your magic to my shard through your lifeblood," Lux sneered, and Rydara felt a pulse of contempt break through the pervasive doom that clouded her Knowing. "If you wanted to die, you could have just waited in the city. My army is taking it now."

"One of the other High Wizards might have found me and taken me instead," Rydara countered, taking a deep breath. "I wanted to give you the opportunity."

Lux stared, her brow furrowing in suspicion. "Why?"

"I want to make a deal," Rydara said, swallowing as she tried to clear her mind. *Calm, flowing, glowing water.* This was the part where she needed to lie to a Knower whose power dwarfed her own. "The city is falling. Whoever survives today will fall under your power, and I know what you do to the people from my tribes. I want you to spare my brother."

"You're not that stupid, *ishra*. I can't make you a Knight against your will, but I can take your life and your power. Why would I offer you anything?" Lux's gaze flicked toward the Hatreth prince, who was still quietly humming. "Stop that." The strength in her command was an ocean to the few pitiful drops in the prince's voice. He fell silent. "You'll explain yourself next."

Rydara's meditation broke, and her eyes filled with tears as the sick nausea of doom promised by the shards washed through her. The prince couldn't help her. The queen could see through her. She should never have come.

You were going to die tonight, anyway, Rydara, she told herself. *No matter how this ends, you'll be dead soon.* Her tears fell, their heat mixing with the cold rainwater that wet her cheeks, and Rydara shivered as she looked up, her gaze meeting the High Wizard's. "I can't watch them all die," she said, and it was true. She did not want to watch the city fall, the dragons turn, the elves fail. She did not want to see their deaths added to the tally of immortals slain in her cause.

She did not want to see life and hope leave Aander's eyes. "Please. Just kill me first."

"And you?" Lux turned her gaze to the Hatreth prince. "Speak."

"Any fool can see that this battle is lost, but I don't want to die tonight." Praxtus looked at Rydara, regret in his gaze, and then turned back to Lux. "Once she's dead, I'll be your Knight, if you want me."

"I could still use a Speaker," Lux mused, frowning as she scrutinized the prince.

He's willing to become a Knight? Rydara felt deaf and blind in the blanket of despair that enveloped her, but the High Wizard would have known if the prince were lying. Rydara had given him only the briefest account of what a Knight was, but he understood enough. The betrayal stung.

Why did I ever bother trying to save these people? They were all just as selfish and evil as the elves had said, weren't they?

Calm, flowing ... The rest of the meditation escaped Rydara as Lux drew a dagger from the belt at her waist. The High Wizard still held a corrupted shard in her left hand, its signature only slightly fainter than the one in Rydara's pocket. They pulsed with power, and the image of the fountain Rydara searched for was replaced by Aander's face, pale and beaded in sweat as he screamed and thrashed on the ground of the Waste.

My brother is ruined, and for what?

The Hatreth prince volunteered to sell his soul. Elf after elf voted no in the full assembly. Neremyn became a High Wizard. Chaenath killed herself to spite him. Lightning seared the Alterran king, and Conall, and Ildylintra, leaving their bodies charred and empty.

"Very well." Lux stared into Rydara's eyes, and Rydara closed hers against the rage and despair that clawed at her soul. *I need to love this person,* she reminded herself. Love seemed an impossible emotion to find in the storm within her, but Rydara searched for a memory of Aander's smile, and she managed to summon a flicker.

"Come closer," the High Wizard bid her.

Rydara opened her eyes and stared into Lux's, clinging desperately to her little flicker of love. Somehow, she needed to direct it toward this High Wizard. "What is your name?" she asked.

"Hmm?" Lux Lucisa drew her dagger across the shard, producing a sick ringing noise as she sharpened it. There was a slight smile on her lips. She was enjoying this.

Her reaction sickened Rydara, and her memory of Aander's smile turned into one of his screams.

"Before you became a High Wizard and took the name Lux Lucisa," Rydara said, shoving the image aside. "You had your own name. What was it?"

Lux paused her sharpening, and her eyes narrowed, becoming distant. "It was ... Fayna."

It was an Alterran name, derived from *faine,* their word for "faith" and "faithfulness." "What broke your faith in humankind, Fayna?" Rydara asked, determined to see something in the creature before her besides the demon who lusted for Rydara's blood and that of the rest of her people.

"Are we going to do this or not?" The High Wizard's voice was heavy with disdain. She dismounted her horse, and Rydara's pulse raced.

She tried to reach for her memory of Aander's smile, but instead, she found herself thinking of the broken city wall. Falling rocks and dragons crushed men's bodies. Weapons hacked them apart. Blood and fire ran through the streets. Rain turned allies into enemies—and this creature walking toward her was responsible.

Lux Lucisa had ripped a hole in Chaenath's abdomen, and Rydara thought she could *love* her?

Calm, flowing...

How could Rydara love anyone, when no one had ever loved her? Her people had rejected her. Her father disowned her. Her mother abandoned her.

Anguish choked out Rydara's meditation, choked out even her flicker of love for Aander. Somewhere in the back of her mind she knew she wasn't seeing the whole truth, that the shards and their power were to blame, but she was too weak to fight it, too weak to meditate.

Far too weak to love.

Nivalis, Rydara thought silently, not knowing if that counted as prayer, not knowing if Nivalis could have heard even her loudest shout. But Lux was coming closer with a dagger in her hand, and Rydara was out of time. *If you can hear me—if you can help—please…*

Lux paused, looking at her. She must have sensed that something was off, but Rydara did not think about that. She did not think about how, if Nivalis had indeed heard and answered her last prayer to him, she had utterly failed to follow up on her end of the deal and did not deserve his help now.

Instead, she looked back at Lux Lucisa and tried to love her, fighting the sick despair that clawed at her from the shards, fighting memories of rejection, shame, and bloodshed that she hadn't been strong enough to stop—and then something changed.

The effect of the shards vanished, and love flooded into Rydara like a wave, showing her something different. She saw the southern prince standing beside her, supporting her as best he knew how in her desperate gamble to save them. She saw Arcaena and all the elves bewildered by humanity's treachery after the Celestial Rebellion, trying to do the right thing by escaping and founding Edriendor. She saw Chaenath, giving her life to confront evil, and Conall and Ildylintra, laying theirs down to defend the weak.

She saw a Rishara woman on her deathbed in the house of a pale-skinned king, using the last of her strength to make his little boy vow to protect her daughter.

More tears flowed down Rydara's cheeks as she realized her mother had never left her alone. She had given her Aander.

Rydara felt such love for them, and for Sundamar, and for the elves of the Edren Guard, but not only for them. She loved the people of the tribes who had rejected her, and she loved the elves who had refused to take pity on her people.

The love that enveloped her extended even to Lux Lucisa. What was Fayna but a human, lost and broken like any other? Like Neremyn, like Dameires—like Rydara's father? They chose evil because they did not know how to choose good. Somewhere, somehow, they had taken a wrong turn—whether out of fear, ambition, disillusionment; it hardly mattered. They kept going because they did not believe they could find their way back. They had forgotten how to hope for it.

Rydara looked back into the eyes of the High Wizard Lux Lucisa, and for one fleeting moment, she loved her. It was a stronger, purer, deeper love than she had ever felt before—even for Aander. She Knew she could never have produced it on her own.

A shadow crossed the High Wizard's face, and then she scowled. She plunged her dagger into Rydara's heart.

Rydara felt more shock than pain. Lux started chanting as her wound bled, holding her corrupted shard against Rydara's chest, but Rydara felt neither horror nor fear. She did feel sorrow, sorrow that she would never have that future with Sundamar after all, but she was still full of the new, strange love—love that seemed to run through her and around her and to hold her with its warmth. A light started to grow in her mind's eye, brilliant and white, and Lux's image began to fade.

She had one more thing to say to the High Wizard before she left. She was moving toward the light, and it was hard to pause, hard to breathe, but Rydara wanted Fayna to know that this evil did not have to define her. She wanted Fayna to know that Rydara did not hold it against her, that there could be hope yet, even for her. With her last breath, Rydara summoned the strength to whimper, "I forgive you."

The shards erupted with light.

Epilogue

Songs were sung about Rydara that very night. They were the first of many.

The songs of the southern tribes drew on the Hatreth prince's account. In the wake of Rydara's death, Lux Lucisa and all her Knights had screamed her demon's agony, and Praxtus had taken up the two cleansed shards. His shout, amplified by their power, had caused Alterrans in the city to throw down their weapons and Jeshim in the field to flee. Everyone had heard his shout and seen the tide of battle turn, and the southerners celebrated Praxtus as the hero of the day.

But their songs also honored Rydara. To them, she was strategy, the one who figured out how to turn their enemies' weapons against them, and courage, for she had marched with their prince deep into enemy lines.

The songs the elves would sing in Edriendor spoke more of Sarya. She and her dragon had been the first allies to reach the Hatreth prince after his shout, and he had thrown the shards to her. They spoke of how the shards had shone like stars in her hands as she turned them against Atra and Tenebrus, the two High Wizards in the sky, and of how the dragons they rode had gained the strength to resist their control and throw them to the ground. They spoke of how Sarya had single-handedly ripped Tenebrus' demon into the Realm Between just as Conall's dragon broke through the High Wizard's defenses and mauled his falling body. They remembered Theodluin, the elf the High Wizard had been—the elf who died that day in talons, teeth, and fire. The elves remembered Theodluin, but his death was not regretted, for if his shard had not fallen into the hands of Sarya's magic users, the High Wizards might still have won the day.

As it was, the High Wizards were left with only two shards among the four of them, and only one was brought to bear.

Atra, her Knights, and her shard were surrounded by the Edren Guard, and only Os Noxcint came to aid her. The Edren Guard subdued each of their Knights with nonlethal blows until only the High Wizards were left. These, they dragged into the Realm Between and separated from their demons, as they had done with Dameires. Dameires wandered from his cellar during the battle and was killed by a stray arrow, but the elf who had been Atra and the man who had been Os Noxcint were taken as prisoners to Edriendor, where Arcaena determined to receive them with a better mercy than had been shown to Neremyn.

To Arcaena and the other elders of Edriendor, Rydara was *nimkeïass*. She had come back to them to remind them of the choice their seven lost daughters had made and to call them higher in the way of Nivalis. Arcaena never did admit she had been wrong to deny Rydara's petition, and she removed Sundamar from his position as leader of the Edren Guard because of his defiance. However, she could not condemn how Sarya and the others had acquitted themselves in the battle for humankind. When Arcaena's songs spoke of Rydara, they did so with respect.

The songs that Sarya sang with the Edren Guard held more depth of feeling. They chronicled the lives and loss of Conall and Ildylintra, and they spoke of their brother Sundamar's love for a mortal. They told how he had come to love the beautiful Rishara girl while he watched her care for her brother in the Waste, despite his understanding of Arcaena's code and his efforts to inure himself to the humans' plight. They spoke of how Rydara had taught him to see the true meaning of his own code and to choose the best good despite its cost.

To the Edren Guard, and especially to Sundamar, Rydara was beauty and inspiration. Her death strengthened their resolve to serve her people. They founded the order of magic users she dreamed of, and though the others returned to Edriendor after a few years, Sundamar stayed behind. The songs of the Edren

Guard remembered him and how he trained four generations of humans before crossing through the Realm Between to be reunited with the mortal girl he loved.

The songs of the northern tribes told more of Rydara's story and of Aander's. They told of Rydara's banishment and of how Prince Aander had renounced his heritage to journey with her through the Waste. They told of Aander's falling sick with the White Plague, and of how the illness receded while he fought with the elves that day in Helos. It returned when the battle was over, as soon as he saw his sister lying dead in the arms of the Hatreth prince. He had his first of many convulsions, and when the fit passed, he was too weak to stand. But Sundamar was at his side, pulling Aander's arm around his shoulders to hold him up. The elf remained by his side through many years.

So did Aander's wife, Jemine, who would hear nothing of his offer to annul their marriage on account of his condition. She wrote many of the songs herself during the years that she cared for him. They spoke of the hard-won unification Aander and Sundamar brought about between the northern and southern tribes. They spoke of how Aander gave up his kingship to take the title of High Prince alongside the southern princes and two others Aander chose from the north so that their new country would have balance. Aander named the country *Ellyrian*, which meant "memory of the elven way" in the Elvish tongue, and Jemine's songs told of its purpose to hold strong against the assault of evil and to promote the way of peace. Her songs also recounted how Aander and Sundamar founded a university to train their new order of seers and imagers, and of how applicants were welcomed from north and south, male and female, Rishara and fair-skinned, as part of Rydara's legacy.

To Jemine, Rydara was the sister she had never had the chance to know. Her songs, and the songs of others from the north, immortalized Rydara for her loyalty and self-sacrifice.

One song told Cressidin's story. It began with his failure to marry Landri and legitimize their daughter, and it told of the pride and fear that led him to banish Rydara and refuse to welcome her back. It told of how he had refused to lead the northerners to take refuge in the city where Rydara was staying, and of how Aander had negotiated with the Jinn chieftain and other leading men from the alliance to have himself named king in his father's place.

And then it spoke of how after the battle, the deposed and prideful king had fallen to his knees at the sight of his daughter's body. He had cradled her head and wept, begging her lifeless form to forgive him while the men who had recognized Rydara's value in life looked on with little pity.

Rydara had given him her forgiveness already, but it took Cressidin many years to forgive himself. After her death, he left the Noraani alliance and the priests he had been so loathe to disappoint and sought out a Rishara tribe, where he converted to their religion. After a few years, Jemine prevailed upon Aander to follow Rydara's example in offering the old king forgiveness, and he was welcomed into their home, where he taught his grandchildren stories about the All-Color and the song of his own repentance.

Through his song, Rydara became forgiveness and a second chance he did not deserve.

But the songs of the Rishara were the best. Precious few of them had sought refuge in Helos or taken part in the battle that day, and none had known Rydara—but they learned her story afterward, when Sundamar and Aander invited them to the new university.

To them, Rydara was the rydar flower, born of two worlds, who brought love and light to dark places. They sang of her mother, her struggle, and her triumph, and they sang of her blooming forever in the brilliant light of Beyond.

Over the years, the Rishara came to be regarded with less suspicion by the people of the tribes. Intermarriages grew more common, and mothers of Rishara descent taught a new song to their daughters:

Go, my rydar, sing
Despite what you may see
Stand, my girl, and roar
For love will set us free

Acknowledgments

Thanks are due to so many people for helping me make this book as good as it is! First, to my two sisters, Christina Sekutowski and Anne Angel, for your excitement to read each new chapter with me in its very roughest form and for being my first line of encouragement and feedback. A special shout-out to Anne for her vision for the epilogue; the closing poem was written entirely by her. (Any poetry fans may want to check out the collection she and I wrote together with our brother Matthew Flaherty, *In Sunshine or in Shadow: Poems for Every Season*.)

Next, to my Inklings writer's group: Sarah Binger, Abigail Morrison, Kimmy Schwarzenbart, Pat Daily, and Jaime McCall. It means so much to have monthly accountability with other writers pushing me to produce the best work I can. A special additional thanks to Kimmy for making the map at the beginning. I'm so happy to have one, and it looks fantastic! (And let me put in a plug for Abigail Morrison's *The Yochni's Eye* and Pat Daily's *Spark* for anyone looking for their next read!)

To other readers of early drafts who offered instrumental feedback and/or encouragement: Patrick Fessenbecker, Matthew Flaherty, John Sekutowski, David McHugh, Kimberly Belmarez, Erin Viale, Jaemyn Sorenson, Sandy Kruse, Tom and Alice Flaherty, and Eleanor Teasdale. This project couldn't have become what it is without you.

To Kelsea Reeves, the sensitivity reader I hired through Fiverr. There were industry professionals who told me I shouldn't write a book with races that looked Black and white or feature a Black POV character on account of my own whiteness and the heightened tensions of today's political moment. Your enthusiasm for this project and appreciation of its themes played a big role in my decision to leave the races as they are. I hope others find it a story as worthy of telling as you believed it to be.

To Krystina Kellingley, who provided the first of my reader reports from Collective Ink. After many, many months of deafening silence from the agenting community, I had all but given up on becoming traditionally published when I saw your glowing endorsement of *The Land Beyond the Waste*. To you, G.E. Davies, and Vicky Hartley, for offering me a traditional contract despite how completely unknown I am, and for putting me in touch with your sister company, Angry Robot Books, for consideration of future projects. However it all turns out, your belief in me means more than I can say. To you all and to the rest of the team at Collective Ink, I am so grateful for your production of a book I can finally hold in my hands, after so many years of labor, rejection, and failure. Here's to hoping we now go on to turn a profit together.

To Stephanie Jones, my boss at the Wisconsin Institute for Sleep and Consciousness, for hiring me and accommodating a work-from-home lifestyle. I could never have invested so much time and energy into this project if I was still stuck in a traditional 9 to 5. To be able to write this while working for someone so supportive has been a great blessing.

To fantasynamegenerators.com for providing all the elf-y names that I used to name the elf characters in this book. It really helped streamline my process.

And finally, to you, dear readers, for making it all the way through not only the book but also the acknowledgments! Thank you for letting me share this story with you. I hope it entertained and inspired you. An extra special thanks to those of you who go on to share it with your friends and family, post about it on social media, and/or leave a review. Selling enough books to make a career out of writing is a herculean task, and if I ever get there, I'll be blissfully indebted to all of you. Keep an eye out for *The Ellyrian Code*, my next project and the first in a series I hope to dedicate the next ten years of my life to. You're helping it happen.

About the Author

B.F. Peterson is a poet, philosopher, and fantasy novelist with a BA in Psychology from Johns Hopkins University and a day job in sleep research at the University of Wisconsin-Madison. She lives in Madison with her beloved husband and dedicated spikeball partner, Junior Peterson, and their two adorable half-pugs, Landon and Cici. You can find her on X (formerly Twitter) @bflahertypeter1, on Instagram @sfcpoets, or at bethlflaherty.wordpress.com.

Recent bestsellers from Roundfire are:

The Bookseller's Sonnets
Andi Rosenthal
The Bookseller's Sonnets intertwines three love stories
with a tale of religious identity and mystery spanning
five hundred years and three countries.
Paperback: 978-1-84694-342-3 ebook: 978-184694-626-4

Birds of the Nile
An Egyptian Adventure
N.E. David
Ex-diplomat Michael Blake wanted a quiet birding trip
up the Nile – he wasn't expecting a revolution.
Paperback: 978-1-78279-158-4 ebook: 978-1-78279-157-7

Blood Profit$
The Lithium Conspiracy
J. Victor Tomaszek, James N. Patrick, Sr.
The blood of the many for the profits of the few... *Blood Profit$*
will take you into the cigar-smoke-filled room where American
policy and laws are really made.
Paperback: 978-1-78279-483-7 ebook: 978-1-78279-277-2

The Burden
A Family Saga
N.E. David
Frank will do anything to keep his mother and father
apart. But he's carrying baggage – and it might
just weigh him down ...
Paperback: 978-1-78279-936-8 ebook: 978-1-78279-937-5

The Cause
Roderick Vincent
The second American Revolution will be a
fire lit from an internal spark.
Paperback: 978-1-78279-763-0 ebook: 978-1-78279-762-3

Don't Drink and Fly
The Story of Bernice O'Hanlon: Part One
Cathie Devitt
Bernice is a witch living in Glasgow. She loses her way
in her life and wanders off the beaten track looking for the
garden of enlightenment.
Paperback: 978-1-78279-016-7 ebook: 978-1-78279-015-0

Gag
Melissa Unger
One rainy afternoon in a Brooklyn diner, Peter Howland
punctures an egg with his fork. Repulsed, Peter pushes
the plate away and never eats again.
Paperback: 978-1-78279-564-3 ebook: 978-1-78279-563-6

The Master Yeshua
The Undiscovered Gospel of Joseph
Joyce Luck
Jesus is not who you think he is. The year is 75 CE. Joseph
ben Jude is frail and ailing, but he has a prophecy to fulfil …
Paperback: 978-1-78279-974-0 ebook: 978-1-78279-975-7

On the Far Side, There's a Boy
Paula Coston

Martine Haslett, a thirty-something 1980s woman, plays hard on the fringes of the London drag club scene until one night which prompts her to sign up to a charity. She writes to a young Sri Lankan boy, with consequences far and long.
Paperback: 978-1-78279-574-2 ebook: 978-1-78279-573-5

Tuareg
Alberto Vazquez-Figueroa

With over 5 million copies sold worldwide, *Tuareg* is a classic adventure story from best-selling author Alberto Vazquez-Figueroa, about honour, revenge and a clash of cultures.
Paperback: 978-1-84694-192-4

Readers of ebooks can buy or view any of these bestsellers by clicking on the live link in the title. Most titles are published in paperback and as an ebook. Paperbacks are available in traditional bookshops. Both print and ebook formats are available online.

Find more titles and sign up to our readers' newsletter at www.collectiveinkbooks.com/fiction